GODFALLEN

TIM MEYER

GODFALLEN

A novel by Tim Meyer

For all the Jesters.

CONTENTS

THE BOY WITH STARS FOR EYES

"After all the gods had up and left the lands, the world ran amok with prophecies and legends, each claiming a special child would rise above the chosen rest and claim dominion over Endlia. To date, this has not occurred, nor have the signs of such revelations been drawn in the sky, but that did not stop prophets from heralding their own arrivals and singing their songs, calling for a new epoch. The *Godfallen* remain a myth."

— MENYARD MINOTOA, *THE GOD SYSTEM*

———

Twilight birthed innumerable stars, and somewhere beyond—perhaps too far beyond—a god sneezed, and their thunder crashed all around the small fishing village of New Hope, rattling the windows of every shanty on the east side of the bay. Bolts of bright light dissected the night sky, drowning themselves on the blackwater horizon. Fish and salt laced the wind, no different from other nights, but from somewhere deep in the village, a scream echoed, a tortured soul screeching for the gods to relieve them of their agony. The kind of scream that carved a bloody, ragged path down the ear canals of all who heard it.

A woman's scream, the call of a new mother-to-be. And once the villagers heard her voice shatter, they knew not only the source of the woman's pain, but also her identity.

Merrygo Pierce, like most women in New Hope, was married to a fisherman. And like most fishermen, her husband had wed the sea.

Jerrin Pierce watched his wife squirm on the blood-soaked mattress, the sheets sticking to her flanks, her feet sliding through the red filth as she grunted through several contractions. She lay, legs spread, pushing in even intervals at the insistence of her midwives, Brielle and Vivia, the two women the church had sent who were blocking Jerrin's view.

"It's fine, Jerrin," the Highbeard priest said, putting a hand on his wrist, an act meant to comfort, to soothe. All it did was jack Jerrin's heart rate up another ten beats per second. "She's under the eye of the Highbeard now. He will watch over her, pass her through this pain, and deliver the child safe and sound."

This reassured Jerrin not a speck. He gripped the wooden knob of the bedpost and prayed—not to the Highbeard specifically, but to any of the Seven Gods who would listen. Listen and grant safety to both mother and child.

But Jerrin never had any luck through prayer. Worshipping certain gods was forbidden in the country of Glane, a territory still under the controlling eye of the Rovans to the east. Some were approved—like Highbeard, obviously, and Ciminen—but most were frowned upon, and a few were outright forbidden. Praying to the Witchmaster, Arkos himself, would earn anyone a trip to the Silver City's expansive gallows.

Jerrin shed his dark thoughts with a shake of his head. He had to focus on the safety of his family. His *new* family. And whatever god could guarantee that...well, he was a free-agent follower, ready to sign on the dotted line for their well-being.

Father Bowen, the Highbeard priest, chanted ancient scripture in the high tongue, words and phrases Jerrin Pierce did not know the meaning of; it had been an age since his indoctrination into the Highbeard religion, and the little belief he had, he let lapse. The bounty of the sea and the love of fishing had replaced any religion he once had—worshipping gods that could not be seen by mortal men.

To give the priest no inkling of his heresies, Jerrin had posed as a casual Highbeard worshipper; doing so simply made his life easier. Giving the church or the Silver Towers a reason to investigate his religious allegiances did not benefit his wishes for a long, happy life. There were plenty of horror stories about the church's secret hunt for nonbelievers, marking them as Arkos-worshipping scumsuckers; they used their power to eliminate innocent non-practicing folks with the assistance of the Silver City.

No, it was much easier to pretend Highbeard was his one and only god, demanding his nightly attention. Jerrin attended church just enough to keep suspicions at bay.

The priest's chanting became more fervent, the high tongue growing louder with each intonation, competing with Merrygo's troubling labor cries. Merrygo was winning, no question about it. The midwives crouched by her knees, stationed in their delivery posts as if readying to catch dirty sheets from the castle laundry chute.

Dread closed its jaws around Jerrin's chest, the imminent disaster puncturing his heart like the tiny teeth of a lamprey. Tears burned his eyes at the realization that one—or maybe both—of his loves might not survive this ordeal. The bleak hypothetical question—*who would you rather keep?*—snaked through his mind before he buried it guiltily. He did not wish for a stillborn, but for him, Merrygo's survival was paramount.

An impossible choice, because he loved his wife with every fiber of his being, and if forced to hang in the gallows beneath the Silver Towers of the Rovan King or choose a survivor, then he would choose his wife every time.

"*Merrygo,*" he whispered beneath his breath, "*stay with me.*" No one else heard the message over the priest's prayers and chants, but Merrygo's eyes sharpened on him with sudden intensity. She leaned forward, keeping eye contact with Jerrin, who flashed her a hopeful smile. Despite her agony, she forced a distressed smile in return. Then her eyes rolled back and she let out a throat-ripping scream that made Jerrin's ears ring.

"The babe is cresting," one of the midwives crowed, breaking the priest's concentration, stopping him mid-prayer. "I can see its crown."

The midwives huddled closer, their reaching arms ready to deliver the child. The priest did the same, as if getting a closer look would help somehow. The only one who remained distant was Jerrin; he backed his spine against the wall, not wishing to interfere with the duties of the professionals. He froze, realizing he knew the outcome of the day before the world could play it out in real time. Call it instinct, a hunch—but the truth was revealed to him in his wife's attempt to flash him that one last smile; she knew it, the future, and now he did too—she would die today.

The infant's fate had yet to be decided.

Merrygo pushed and panted, grimacing through the agony as she tried to relieve her body of the life inside her. The midwives encouraged her, corrected her breathing, rubbed her belly in the hopes of soothing the little one as it made its exit. Finally, through the bodies in front of him, Jerrin saw the crown of his baby's head slide from between his wife's legs, and the rest of the infant tumbled out in a wet, bloody discharge. Merrygo cried a final time before her head snapped back, and her body went limp as she succumbed to her fate.

"No!" Jerrin rushed to her side and grabbed her hand, wishing her life wouldn't end that way. "Merrygo! Stay with me!"

Brielle grabbed him and pulled him aside. She was a stout woman with broad shoulders, who looked like she could lift a yak. Jerrin fought against her, but she was set on removing him, depriving him the sight of the tumultuous birth.

But Jerrin would not go easily.

The priest blocked the view of his wife's corpse, holding up his palms, begging for Jerrin to mourn in a calmer, repentant manner. Jerrin would have punched him, but striking a member of Highbeard's clergy was a death sentence. Not that he cared for his own life in that moment.

It was for the sake of the child.

The child that might not live.

And then what would he have? His fishing boat, his fishing poles, the nets that captured hundreds of fish each week, all of which provided a decent living, more than most could have said about living in Endlia. Yet now he felt like he had nothing, without Merrygo, that she made life itself worth living. Without her he only felt darkness, as if life was a big black tide crashing into him. Like the hand of the cowl-headed god, Arkos, sweeping across the heavenly plains of Highbeard's golden domain.

He did not know how to live without her, and he did not know how to live under that kind of darkness. It was like losing an arm or a leg. And like a phantom limb haunting his every step, Merrygo would never let him forget. She would ghost his every step.

Knees buckling, Jerrin wept in the pale, flickering light the candles provided. Brielle of Narthgoth and the priest exchanged worried glances. The other midwife cradled the bloodied newborn in her arms, trying to soothe it. Jerrin couldn't control himself, and it wasn't until the second midwife ceased pacifying his crying son and stood rigid, like the god-hand of Arkos had reached into her chest and stolen her beating heart, that he rose from the grief that had broken him. The newborn still wailed, which was a good sign. *Wailing* meant alive. And alive was good. But...the look on the midwife's face...

Something was monumentally wrong.

The priest turned to her, concern flickering across his eyes. "What is it, Vivia?"

Vivia glanced up from the swaddled newborn like she was holding a ghost instead of a precious child. "Its...eyes."

"What of them?"

Jerrin did not wait for the woman to reply. "Is the child..."

"He…" Vivia choked on her response, then cleared her throat to try again. "He's alive. Very alive. But…his eyes."

The priest did not give her another opportunity to explain. He marched over to her side, then glanced down. As soon as he set eyes on the child, he shrank back, revolted. "Lord," he said, slapping a hand over his chest, like maybe his heart was at risk of exploding. "That's…not possible."

"What is it?" Jerrin asked, tears streaming down his face. He could not blink them away fast enough. More rose with each passing second. "What is wrong with my son?"

Vivia hesitated, then rotated to show him.

And then he saw them.

His eyes, the star-shaped pupils that seemed to expand and contract, were brighter than the lowest moon.

———

In the hours that followed, the priest and the midwives debated what should become of the child in the other room. Their hushed conversation told Jerrin everything he wanted to know, everything they weren't saying to his face.

They wish to bring the child east to the Rovan Territories and hand him over to their northern king. I know it.

Jerrin despised that idea and wasn't shy in saying so when it was his turn to speak, but he had trouble articulating his exact concerns. Chief among them, however, was that the king would take the child from him, and the only connection that bound him to his now-dead wife would be stripped away. Raising a child in New Hope by himself would be a difficult life, but he wasn't unwilling to carry that burden. He could keep the boy safe, free from those who would misinterpret the fabled prophecy and use him for nefarious gains.

Like the king in his Silver Tower.

Jerrin would not allow it. Not his son. Not his blood.

Once the baby had stopped crying and was stable, sleeping on his father's lap, the Highbeard priest approached him, biting his lip, his eyes flicking up at him like a snake, only to dart away again. Regret glimmered in the light of his eyes. "A decision needs to be made, Jerrin. It is my strong belief that you should not shoulder this burden alone. Let us take the child to the Rovan King, and allow him to rule on this matter."

"No," Jerrin said solemnly. He had been through too much that night. A decision so big could not be made in such a moment.

"A decision has to be made," the priest repeated.

"A decision…" Jerrin eyed the priest warily. "One you have made already, priest? And I'm simply to go along with whatever you say?"

The priest did not speak, but his face revealed everything.

Jerrin was to surrender the boy. The prophecy was too much to risk, the fate of the Endlands hanging in the balance, and the boy could not live unsupervised, far from the eyes of the king.

He finally understood. This was why Highbeard priests were to be present during each and every birth. The old tradition that never died had finally proved its worth.

"Do not make what comes next hard on us both," the priest whispered.

"You will take him from me? My son. On the night of my wife's death."

Movement at the front of the house, outside the door, beckoned Jerrin's attention. Heavy boots, stomping on the deck boards. The clinking of metal armor. Swords slipping their sheaths.

"I will do no such thing," the priest said, tears welling in his eyes, regret and hopelessness and exhaustion laid bare on his face. His duty to the king outweighed his own feelings. "But the king… you know what kind of man he is. If he were to discover that we hid this from him…it would mean all our executions."

Jerrin watched the king's troop crowd the doorway to his home. They bore the Rovan mark on their armor, the giant lizard from old lore—*The Salamandian.* The ancient beast was etched into each guard's chest plate.

Jerrin laughed bitterly. "You were supposed to help me, priest. Not betray me and my family."

"I am only doing what's in the best interest of the people of Endlia, and above all else—I serve the Highbeard, for I *am* his people."

Jerrin's mouth filled with the tart taste of betrayal. He spat on the floor near the priest's feet. "Fuck your Highbeard cunt."

The blasphemous retort caused the priest to snarl. What little regret that lay hidden in the depths of his eyes was quickly extinguished and replaced by anger.

"Then you have made your choice," the priest said, venom on the tip of his tongue. He turned his back on Jerrin and the newborn, the boy with the stars for eyes.

The guards rushed the room, immobilizing Jerrin by removing the clubs that dangled from their belts and smashing his kneecaps. Another whisked away his child, stealing him into the night. Before Jerrin could plead, the other swordsmen joined the cause, beating him unconscious. The last thing he saw before darkness flooded his eyes was the hand of his wife hanging limp from the bed, slowly dripping red onto the cold stone floor.

A WITCH DIES TODAY

"Highbeard remains the most popular of the seven gods in Endlia, favored in all five countries (Glane, The Rovan Territories, The Crosslands, Owlton, and Springgaarden), though popularity for the goddess Ciminen has seen an increase in recent years, specifically in and around Springgaarden. Highbeard continues to be celebrated as the one true god in the two largest regions—Owlton and the Rovan Territories. The capitals in both countries have continued to praise his name, hold weekly masses, and erect statues to honor and give thanks for his benevolent ways."

— MENYARD MINOTOA, *THE GOD SYSTEM*

———

Twelve years later...

In the southernmost reaches of Endlia, south of the Rovan Territories and the expanse known as The Crosslands, lies the country of Owlton. Although never officially surveyed for acreage, it's widely considered the second largest country in Endlia, and is chiefly known for its vast plains, and the beautiful ancient Endlian architecture of its cities. But what often goes unnoticed, what escapes most minds, are the regions in the south-west corner, the farms placed—seemingly—in some faraway nowhere, where people seldom travel, mostly due to there being no good reason to. It's a quiet land, spaced out and sparsely populated, home to generations of farmers who settled, living off the land and providing for their families. Where the cities of Braag and Stapleton and Hornrake (the capital) all get their meat, dairy and vegetables from, with or without their knowledge. These faraway regions, hidden from the sight of even the most seasoned wanderer, are known only as Peaceview.

And they are untroubled lands.

Which is precisely why Ket Norlath likes it.

He treats the sunrise like any other; makes his cup of coffee on the stove, wanders outside, treks across his property and approaches the bluff overlooking the Arcadian Sea, and watches the molten heat rise over the cerulean horizon, its citrus light sparkling the tips of the waves to make the grass shimmer, erasing what darkness lingered over his land. He watches until the orange light coalesces and becomes the burning ball of fire that gives life to all things, until he can feel the warmth of its touch on his cheeks. Then he heads back inside to prepare for the day; waking up his two sons to help with the various chores on the schedule—milking the cows, culling the chicken eggs, jarring the jellies. But not before he strolls back into the bedroom and presses his lips upon his wife's forehead. He lets Jennah sleep as long as she needs, though she's usually up in time to feed the boys breakfast and get them prepared for their daily studies.

He heads down the long hallway and knocks on the boys' door, pokes his head in, and sees the two lazy lumps under the covers, not twitching a muscle in response to his intrusion. Ket smiles; the boys take after their mother. The more he thinks about it, the more they're like her in every way. They've got little-to-no *Norlath* in them.

Maybe that's for the best.

"Boys," he says in that deep, *up and at 'em* voice, the one that's served as their wake-up call since they've become old enough to assist with the morning routines. "The cows will not milk themselves."

Clive, the oldest—ten years now—is the first to awake with a drawn groan. "Daaaaa…five more minutes?" he begs, groggily.

"No, Clive. Rise now and rouse your brother. We have much to do, and your mom has new studies for you after lunch."

Clive rises like a ghoul from a crypt, slowly and seemingly disturbed, his longish hair sticking up in messy tufts. He'll make a mighty fine curmudgeon in his elder years, but for now, his grumpiness is reserved only for the early morn. "I hate studies. What do we need studies for?"

Ket leans against the door frame, the one he'd cut, clam-cased and finished himself. "Well, son of mine—studies will help broaden your knowledge of the world. And help so you don't end up a poor, dumb farmer like your old man."

"You're not poor. Or dumb. And besides—I like farming."

"Ah, I'm sure you do," he says, ignoring the part about him not being poor and dumb, because they're both semi-accurate in some respects, and because it's way too early to explain. "But… there's a whole world out there. And it might do you some good to learn about it."

"What for? I want to stay here. Forever."

Their talk rouses the little one, eight years old, from his deep slumber. "What are you two sods talking about this early in the morn?" Bentley asks, yawning and stretching his limbs, a soft crackle and pop accompanying each twist and turn.

Ket raises his brow and tightens his lips, holding in a hearty laugh. "Young man, what have I told you about cussing before breakfast?"

Bentley throws off his covers and sits up. "Cussing before breakfast is not permitted, especially on days of work."

"That's right."

"But every day is a day of work, Da," Bentley says, sorely disappointed with this realization.

"Right again, pup."

"And," Bentley adds, "it might anger the Highbeard. And if the Highbeard is angry, he might rain piss on our crops, ruining the season."

" 'Rain piss?' " his father repeats, granting him the opportunity to rephrase.

Bentley rolls his eyes, so hard it must've hurt. "Urinate?"

"Better. Still coarse before breakfast." He gives them each a nod. "Five minutes. We start milking and collecting eggs."

"Da?" Clive shifts around in his collection of blankets.

"Son?" A wave of concern breezes through Ket's body, prickling his fatherly instincts. "How goes it?"

"Is Highbeard real?"

The question shocks him. Not that it has come, but that it has come—of all the times the question could have—*now*. This early in the morn. Before breakfast. Before finishing a cup of coffee.

He's not prepared to answer without Jennah by his side. "Of course," he says.

"You don't seem sure," his son quips back.

"I'm sure."

"You hesitated."

"Only because I wasn't expecting such a silly question at this unholy hour. Highbeard is real. And in this house, we worship him."

"Brick Hill from down the Row says he doesn't believe in Highbeard. Or any of the gods. That his family does not worship."

"Really?" The news hits, Ket's shocked response automatic, and it takes everything in his bones to play the part correctly. "Is that right?"

"Yes, he says gods are folly."

"Well, I'm sure Brick is just having a bit of fun with you. The Hills worship—I've had many conversations with Ernesto, Brick's father, on the subject, inside the church itself, in fact."

"Have you?" Clive squints. The boy's stare drills into him. It's hard to shake.

"Yes. Now get up. Both of you. We can talk gods and worship over dinner, if we must. After all the chores are complete and you've become learned for the day."

"I would like that. Very much actually."

"Good," he says, shutting the door. "Looking forward to it." And of all the lies he's ever told, this one comes out possibly the smoothest.

———

There comes a time when every child has questions— uncomfortable, thought-provoking, and in some cases, downright life-altering inquiries, regarding philosophical thought trains which require guidance from knowledgeable adults, in order to flourish or flounder.

Ket has dreaded this day. The topics surrounding the gods of Endlia, their histories, their existence, their powers, the tales of their adventures in the days long past, when they walked the earth alongside mortal men—these were not comfortable conversations for Ket to hold even with adults, let alone his own children. Not easy because of one simple reason.

He has his doubts.

The Seven Gods, in his formative opinion, were stretched truths, passed down from generation to generation, and the tales of their adventures and the teachings of their religions and the guidelines of their worship were nothing more than instruments used to keep society normal, to prevent chaos and anarchy from reigning over the Endlands. Ket had seen his fair share of the unnatural, so he knew there were things present in the world that could not simply be explained with a quick observation and a sprinkle of logic. But gods? Supreme beings that ruled the Other-worlds, bestowing gifts upon those who worship them, and placing hideous curses on those who don't? Ket can't exactly say with confidence he's seen any proof of such things.

And he's a man who's seen a lot.

Ket could never express these feelings aloud, of course, unlike the Hill boy, if Clive is to be believed. Publicly speaking ill of certain gods—such as Highbeard, the most worshipped figure throughout Endlia's history—could earn you a trip to the gallows, depending on whose ears those misgivings fell upon. Yet ever since Ket read the *God System* by Menyard Minotoa in grade school, he had an inkling that the whole *System* was fabricated, to some extent—that Highbeard's *Good Book* was pure fiction, instead of being written by some unnamed author claiming to channel the voice of the god himself.

He has never told this secret to anyone, not even his own wife. Jennah knows nothing of his semi-agnostic nature. It's certainly not the only secret he's kept from her; the many lies he's uttered over their ten blissful years of marriage were for her own protection. Heresy of any kind against the Highbeard is punishable in Owlton cities. In some cases *by death*. Ket has no intention of leaving the true love of his life (in a life previously devoid of love) a widow.

But the day has come. The day he must further complicate his own lies, his sacred untruth, all for the sake of protecting his children. He hates the lies he will tell over dinner. He hates corrupting their young, impressionable minds to uphold centuries and centuries of established fallacies. He wishes it wasn't like this, that he could choose to not believe, freely, in the safety of his own home, free from guilt, from expectation. But he can't. The lie must live on.

His workday is marred by this knowledge. Every time he sees Clive, he wishes today's tasks would last longer, that dinner would never come.

But the day flashes by, and before he feels even partially ready, Jennah calls them in for lunch.

The two boys sprint to the front door, running past their mother without slowing. She barely avoids being trampled by the two hungry youths. Ket isn't far behind them, though he doesn't run.

"Hello, Farmer Norlath," she says, squinting at him like he's an acquaintance and not the man who shares her bed. "Fancy meeting you here."

He leans in and kisses her as if the world will stop turning tomorrow. He's so damn happy to have her, to feel something other than how he's been feeling all day, and he can feel her grinning around their kiss, not pulling away, her tongue like a flame heating his own, and there's only her and the moment and her breathing, her hands on his neck pulling him closer, and he wants the moment to last forever, even though he knows it can't.

Nothing lasts forever in this world.

"Hungry?" she asks, one eyebrow raised, her grin open, and he's not so sure she's referring to the sandwiches.

"Always," he says.

She leans closer to his ear. "You can send the boys off on an errand. We can enjoy dessert *alone.*"

"Come to think of it, we could use more tools from the blacksmith off Pike Road."

"That sounds very fine."

The idea tickles him. But his thoughts are too scattered to concentrate on anything else other than the impending conversation he owes his sons.

"It sounds very fine, indeed," he repeats, unable to strip the disappointment from his voice. "But perhaps bedtime is better for such activities."

She frowns. "Prude."

"Clive was asking…troubling questions this morning. It's thrown me."

"Oh?"

He explains the situation, quietly so the boys do not overhear. Ket hears the two eating at the table, gobbling down their sandwiches and discussing some book they've read recently—a fictional storybook Jennah brought back from Braag during last week's excursion.

"Well," she says, folding her arms, "the time was coming sooner or later."

"I was hoping for later."

"I'll handle it." She taps his chest. "I can see how much it stresses you, talking religion. I know your father was rough on you about it. He left scars." She traces her finger across his pecs. "Many of which I cannot see."

"My faith is complicated," he says, lying again. *Just the King of Lies this morning, aren't we?* he thinks, feeling ashamed, wishing things could be different. But he's worked so hard to build his life —this near-perfect homestead—and cracking now, uttering one truth could bring down the whole structure.

"It'll be fine," she says. "I'll explain how it is, how the world works, and they will have no choice but to believe it. Such is the way of the gods."

"Yes, but…" He peeks into the kitchen, where Clive acts out a scene from the book, spreading his hands and making an explosive noise with his mouth, pushing air out with his cheeks. Perhaps he's imitating a great and fearsome dragon. "Clive's different. He's headstrong, that boy. I don't know if we can convince him. I sense all this…doubt in him."

"What makes you say that?"

Because he's my son, he almost tells her. *And though he's like his mother in most ways, I fear he's inherited my heresy.*

"Ket?" Jennah asks, snapping her fingers before his eyes. "You with me?"

"Yes."

"You faded."

"Sorry." He collects his thoughts. "I see the doubt in him." Ket grits his teeth, blowing a feeble breath from his nostrils, his shoulders sagging almost in defeat. "He asks too many questions, looking for proof, not comfort. A road mortared in search of proof leads to heresy."

She swats his arm, not hard, but not lightly either. "Ket! Our son is not a heretic. Do not even bring up such an idea!" Her faux anger bleeds away in no time at all, making Ket certain she was never truly mad to begin with. She squeezes his fingers, the way lovers do. "Just leave him to me. Have I ever let you down before?"

He forces a smile because he knows the answer. "No, you never have."

And that's the truth.

———

After lunch, the boys head to the barn to clean the horses, polish the saddles, and pour slop into the pig troughs. Ket gives his wife's suggestion a second thought—it has been almost a week since their last rendezvous. But no; chores needed doing and he doesn't want to risk the boys walking in on them in broad daylight. *One* serious conversation over dinner is more than enough.

Late afternoon creeps in like a purpling bruise, and a few chores short of quitting time, hooves pound in the distance. Riders. Not far away, a whole company. This far southwest it's almost background noise along with the squeal of the pigs, but as the hooves stamping the earth grow louder, closer, uneasiness slithers into his gut, a sensation he hasn't felt since he left his previous life all those years ago.

The galloping of a dozen or more steeds ushers back harsh memories. His days of violence and bloodshed, the days of swords plunging through flesh and organs; sharpened metal separating limbs from bodies, heads from shoulders, the victims' only crimes that they served a different king.

Old times.

Bad times.

He's never forgotten, but has done well to bury the memories beneath the happiness of his ranch, family, and what this fresh release of new life has awarded him.

Ket eyes the hills, chewing his inner lip, waiting for the troop to pass over the green mounds near the edges of his property. The nervous pang in his gut and the twitch in his left eye says everything he doesn't want to suspect. Eleven years out here, and not one single courtier from King Edwill Ragland III's company has visited. There's no reason. He's too far south and west.

No good reason at all.

They know, he thinks. Then he shakes his head.

Stop it, the calm part of him insists, that remnant of his old life that's kept him alive all these years. *You don't know anything yet. Don't fret about things that have not yet transpired.*

But then he sees them.

A dozen-plus horses with armored riders spilling over the rolling green hills, like ants fleeing their underground lairs after a flood. Fast—not quite charging, but nearly. Not a *let's-take-a-stroll-out-to-the-farmlands.*

They mean business.

Ket spikes his shovel into the dirt and releases the breath he's been holding, realizing it's better to meet them. Two of the riders in the middle of the pack raise Ragland's banners—the fierce, owl-sky-diving-for-prey emblem, centered atop a patchwork of black and purple. Closer, the rankings stamped into their chest plates begin to take shape. A lieutenant leads the pack, and Ket's palms go sweaty with the knowledge.

What the hell is a lieutenant doing all the way down here?

The troop pulls up to the farm's gate, and Ket is halfway across the property, hustling now, not wishing to keep the men waiting. Whatever business they have here, it's best not to delay them. He figures it's probably something stupid, like he forgot to pay his quarterly taxes awhile back, maybe when Jennah was sick with weasel bumps, but then again—there's no way they'd send a small army out here, a lieutenant, to collect some shortchanged payment. No, whatever this is, it's serious.

"Good morn," Ket nods to the gentlemen on horseback, the second he's close enough for them to hear. "To what do I owe the pleasure of this unexpected visit?"

The lieutenant takes off his helm and hands it to the rider next to him. He has a short but sturdy frame and a dark devil's goatee with a single verticle stripe of silver. His eyes glimmer with keen intelligence, and after one quick glance, Ket doesn't trust the man. "Are you Keten Norlath? Of Bankston?"

"Aye, I am."

"The name of your father and mother, please?"

He shakes his head, not understanding. "What does this have to do—"

"Their names, please."

"Edward and Moirwan."

The lieutenant checks the paperwork on his lap. Then nods. "My name is Sir Henry Tenner, First Lieutenant of King Edwill Ragland III's Golden Company. I am requesting a conference with you and your wife, Miss Jennah Norlath. Would you be so kind and grant my request?"

Ket's heart pumps good and steady. "Yes, of course. You and your men are welcome here." He goes to the gate, unlatches it from the inside, and swings open the barricade, allowing the men access to the plain that connects to the farmhouse, resting near the bluff's edge, overlooking the Arcadian Sea.

Ket follows their dust. When he reaches the house, most of the men have dismounted. Clive and Bentley hover, their curiosity insatiable, clothes dirtier than at midday. They must have had a scuffle in the horse stalls. *Rascals.* Wouldn't have been the first time, nor the last. Ket almost opens his mouth to ask what happened, but given the situation, it's a story that can wait.

Jennah has wandered out the back door, casting a suspicious gaze, her forehead wrinkled. She opens her mouth to ask the question on every Norlath's mind, but then decides against it.

Even to her, these must look like men who do the asking, not the answering.

"Perhaps," Sir Henry says, leaving his horse's side and undoing the wrist straps of his black riding gloves, "it's best if the children were not present."

The boys perk up, hearing themselves named. Jennah's face relaxes, but not in a good way—it's like she knows why they are here. An *Ah-it's-finally-time-to-face-the-music* calmness resets her expression. Something monumental shifts inside Ket, his composure like an ancient statue finally toppling, its base completely eroded, surrendering to gravity, hitting the cobblestones and splintering apart. Panic floods his veins. He doesn't know why his wife acts so fatalistic, so comfortable with their presence, yet as if this was inevitable; it's like he doesn't know her at all.

"With all due respect, Lieutenant, I would very much like to know—"

"If you do not wish to send the children away, that is up to you. But know: it brings me no pleasure to do this in their presence."

Do what? he can't bring himself to ask.

With that thought, Ket understands the dynamic of their perfect family is about to change. Forever.

"Boys," he announces, his voice catching in his throat. "Go to your rooms."

"But, Da—"

"Now," he spits, cutting off Clive, shooting him a look that screams, and Clive shuts his mouth like a clamshell.

The boys do as their father says, and Bentley groans on his way toward the house. Jennah ushers them inside, then stands in the center of the brick pathway that runs to the back of the house, out near the barn.

Waiting.

"Very good," Sir Henry says, and cracks his knuckles, each one sounding like a whip smacking a naked back. The whites of his teeth show between the neatly trimmed hair of his goatee. His smile burrows under Ket's skin and nestles there. "Now, to our business. Can you provide me with your papers?"

"My papers?"

"Yes. Your identification papers. For the whole family. I should very much like to see them."

Ket turns to his wife, nods for her to run inside and grab the family documents. She disappears inside the house.

"How long have you known your wife?" Ket swings his head back to the Lieutenant at the sound of his voice, and notices the guardsmen straying from their horses. How they've migrated around to the other side of the house, circling the premises like a band of blood hawks, waiting for their injured prey to expire.

Anticipating an escape.

This is madness.

"Eleven years, thereabouts," he answers, his voice lacking confidence. Concentration. Everything is slipping from him. He's losing control. Of himself. His emotions.

My future.

Come clean, a voice begs him. *Come clean and maybe they will go easy on your kin.*

"And, I suppose, you know everything about your wife—her history. And she's aware of yours?"

Ket gulps. *Shit.*

Not ready to admit the truth, Ket does what he's done best for the last decade and a half, or longer now that he thinks of it. He attempts to sell his lies.

"We share pasts like any husband and wife. What the hell is this about?" He's lost his patience, dispensing with the niceties and hospitable tone. Acting like an innocent man would.

"Do you know what your wife was up to during her last visit to Braag?" His pencil-thin eyebrows dance, entertained by Ket's squirming.

"She went to drop off some vegetables and eggs at the market for sale. Then I believe she purchased the boys some books. Fictional stories. I forget the names of them but—"

"What else?"

Ket shakes his head, unable to think of the answer he's clearly fishing for. "I don't know. Nothing else, I believe."

Jennah reappears on the brick path, the family paperwork in hand. As she hustles over to the lieutenant, Ket can't help but notice the dark clouds gathering on the horizon behind her, a sea storm suddenly forming off the coast. The wind has picked up, blowing her auburn hair in all directions, leaving it frizzy and wild. Just the way he likes it.

Sir Henry plucks the paperwork from her fingers, and mouths a *thank you* before perusing them, scanning each line, each word, carefully. As if he's looking for something specific, something hidden in the text.

He holds them closer to his eyes, focusing on them with librarian-like concentration. A smaller, bespectacled man sidles his horse up next to him, waiting for his turn to browse the documents.

Ket's patience has worn thinner than the papers in the lieutenant's hands. "If there is something amiss with our paperwork, I'd be happy to resolve the issue without protest."

Sir Henry ignores his remark and continues to examine the information in front of him. After a moment, he hands one of the papers to the man next to him. The man pulls the paper closer to his eye and takes all of ten seconds to announce, "Ah-ha! See? A forgery."

"Forgery," Ket bristles. "I assure you, there must be some mistake. Those documents were signed off by the royal ch—"

"Silence," Sir Henry says calmly. Then, to his assistant: "The children?"

"The seal is official," the man says, squinting at Clive and Bentley's papers.

"Both parents'?"

The assistant gives his final glance over the two documents. "Fakes. Both."

"I can explain," Ket says, raising his hands, begging for them to give him a chance to correct these wrongs. He doesn't need to look at the guardsmen to know they're crowding him from all sides.

No escape.

There's no escape from this.

From your lies.

Your awful past.

"I would love to hear it," Sir Henry says, his sword hand dropping to his hip, his fingers gripping the hilt of his blade.

"It's me. Mine's the fake. My wife's...she's innocent."

The assistant opens his mouth to protest the claim, but Sir Henry silences him by putting his arm across his chest. "Let him explain."

"I...before I came to live in Owlton...I'm from the Rovan Territories...specifically...from the Silver Towers...I lived under the eye of the *Salamandian* himself."

Sir Henry closes one eye while the other one remains half-shut. "Served King Salah Rovan, did you?" He licks his lips.

"Yes. I was..." He glances back at his wife, sees her expression crumbling with each half-truth he utters, "...a mercenary for the king."

"You were in his service as an assassin?"

Ket doesn't confirm this, just says, "I've done many terrible things for his cause."

"Killed many Owlton warriors, I suppose. Spilled our blood?" Sir Henry paces now, perhaps trying to walk off the hate mounting the walls of his chest. "Many of my own friends, no doubt."

"I have done many things and have many regrets."

"And so you left our adversary's company, defected from the north and snuck past our borders, procured fake documents, and expected to live out the rest of your life in the countryside, happily ever after. Is that it?"

Ket nods.

"Well, that is an interesting story." There's a 'but' coming, Ket can sense it. There is more to the tale than the lieutenant has disclosed. "But that's not why we're here."

Ket follows Sir Henry's line of sight past his shoulder. He spins once again and finds his wife standing there, the subject of the company's collective gaze.

How long have you known your wife?

That question has bothered him since the lieutenant spoke it to life, but now it bothers Ket for a different reason. The Lieutenant's examination into her trip to Braag suddenly has darker overtones.

"Jennah Elizabeth Norlath," Sir Henry says, reading the documents. "Maiden name Houzoo. Daughter of Nolan and Joan. *Lies,* we suspect."

Jennah doesn't outright refute the allegations, and Ket's heart sinks a foot. He doesn't know why. It's not like he should be angry with her deception, not when he's guilty of exactly the same thing, lived their entire marriage underneath the guise of a fictional character he invented for himself. Ket Norlath is no more real to him than the Legend of Baskin Poppa, the legendary swordsman who axed the head off a dragon a full century before the last god walked the earth. No more real than a dragon itself, a species said to be extinct for at least six centuries. But her…Jennah…his wife…

It feels different on this side of a lie.

"Not all lies," she says, wearing a coy smile. "My father's true name really was Nolan."

"Ah." Sir Henry shreds the document in half, lets the two pieces scatter among the grass. Lets the wind carry them beyond. "A truth hidden within a lie. I respect the effort. Now, let's start with your real name."

"My true name cannot be spoken in common Endlian," Jennah says, her tone changing, becoming darker. Heavier. Sinister almost. It's a tone Ket's never heard.

Sir Henry hardly reacts. *He knew.* "Can you tell us why that is?"

Behind them all, off the coast, thunder grumbles. The collection of dark clouds builds a tower in the sky, a maelstrom of lightning unleashing upon the shore.

Ket stares at his wife. Everything he's known about their family, the life he's chosen to lead out here, this safe and idyllic living, is crumbling, falling apart before his eyes. He almost wishes the guardsmen would end his days by blade point, to spare him the pain that must follow. The heartbreak. His family's love torn apart, like the documents halved by the lieutenant. Torn and blown away.

But follow it must. His jaw firms. His knuckles turn white as his hands form fists.

That whole morning and afternoon, he had fretted over the dinner table discussion with his sons, but now, he would long for it. Would trade the entire world, every kingdom in Endlia, just to have that talk instead of what is sure to follow.

"You know why," Jennah speaks. She takes a step to the left, which is enough movement to activate the company's defenses. The guardsmen unsheathe their swords. Twelve iron blades lift into the air, triggering Ket's most unpleasant memories. Flashes of blood in the soil pass through his mind's eye, bodies sans limbs lying in the dirt, piled on top of each other like ordinary waste, waiting for the kingdom's trash collectors.

"Tell us," Sir Henry prods. "Go on. For your husband. He deserves to know the truth…*witch.*"

A winter frost touches Ket's heart. *Witch.* "You do not know what you accuse me of," Jennah says, her tongue as sharp as an assassin's dagger.

"Oh, I know very well." Sir Henry points his sword at her. Instinctively, Ket shifts in front of the threat. Automatically protecting her, should the lieutenant strike. "You were seen entering what has now been uncovered as a secret coven-hole in Braag. Just two days ago, my men entered the hole and found a congregation of the most despicable vermin this world has to offer. I will spare you the sordid details of the ceremony we stumbled upon, but it included naked bodies and animal blood, filthy acts."

"Liar," Jennah snaps.

"I wish that were so, witch. But I do not lie, unlike yourself and your husband here, who apparently have seasoned tongues in that regard." The Lieutenant's fingers snap, signaling one of his guardsmen, who sheaths his sword, then turns to the horse closest to him, and removes a black package hanging from his saddle. The guard brings it over to the gathering and presents it like a gift, holding the object out in his open palms. Sir Henry grips the top of the package and dramatically yanks its cover away to reveal what's beneath the black material.

A decapitated head stares soullessly at Ket. Streaks of dark blood fissure the man's face. Teeth are absent, others bent sideways, gaps of black between the crooked arrangement. The flesh has bruised to black in patches. Maggots claim the pockets of missing skin and muscle where the man's cheeks once were.

Ket almost retches. From the smell more than the visual. That familiar malodor tickles the back of his throat. Jennah gasps.

Sir Henry delights in her reaction. "His name was Barlow Mak, and he was the orchestrator of the underground coven and the blood orgy my men swear witness to. Do you deny this truth?"

Jennah doesn't respond, her body hitching from the lack of oxygen in her lungs. Instead, she swallows her reply, along with whatever she had wanted to say. "Seize her," commands the lieutenant, his finger trembling in her direction. "Seize the witch."

The men move. Silently. Ket steps into their path, raising his arms to protest, like that will quell the afternoon's craziness and set everything right again.

"Stop," he shouts. "Let us discuss these matters like rational, civilized human beings. Let us—"

"You lost any and all opportunity of a *civilized* discussion when you chose to defy the king's order and rebel against the state." Sir Henry almost laughs through his teeth.

The men advance, pushing past Ket, who does nothing to impede their order.

"Mom! Da!"

Ket spins on his heels, sees his children inside the house, looking out through an open window. "Stay inside, boys. I will handle this."

But he won't handle this because there's nothing to handle—the situation is so far from his grasp that it might as well be taking place on the other end of Endlia, maybe in the farthest reaches of The Black Isle. He stands there, helpless, watching it unfurl as the last of the men shoulder past him. Panic splits his chest like an axe, and his world becomes a fuzzy, soundless void. His memories flash in his mind, dashing through days past; meeting his future bride, how he bumped into her at the market, how it was love at first sight, just like the mushy-gushy fairy tales for children; the birth of their kin; how he helped usher them into a world he'd grown to hate but had refound, to love again—all because of her.

"*Morgust anta vellum,*" Jennah hisses from somewhere behind him, and the memories of the good old days break. Her hands rise, fingers outstretched, like she…is…

Casting a spell?

Her face is different, her complexion changing, becoming darker, *grayer*, if such a thing is possible. *Am I imagining this?*

One of the guardsmen screams. The rest of the men shrink back, raising their swords as if expecting bolts of lightning to spring from Jennah's fingertips. The screamer rips off his helm and tosses it aside, then claws at his own face, digging thick red gouges into his cheeks with his fingernails. Within seconds, the flesh around his mouth is peeled back like a fruit, reducing it to bloody flaps of skin. Frantic, the man digs his bloodied fingers into his eye sockets, fishing out his eyeballs. He tears them out with a wet snap, his throat continuing to project the most unnerving and agonizing sounds, his body trembling in horror.

Terror hits Ket's body like the frigid shock of an ice bath.

Jennah focuses on her next target.

"She's hexed him!" shouts one of the guards. Whatever he wishes to say next is abruptly cut short when his body goes rigid, and his hands tighten around his throat. He gags, chokes on some unseen object. His companions hustle toward him to assist with removing his helm. But by that time, it's too late—Ket watches something punch through the bottom of the man's throat, as if escaping its own prison, a long, ribbon-like object, bloody and pink.

The man's tongue...

The muscle has hammered through the soft flesh at the base of his gullet and fallen against his chest, and hangs like a limp flag in the windless aftermath of its country's defeat. The man collapses, his mouth opening and closing like a beached fish as some pink froth erupts from the jagged wound in his throat.

Ket's stomach turns. He faces his wife, whose face is transfixed on the task at hand—dispatching every single one of their enemies in the most gruesome ways imaginable.

"Jennah!" he calls to her, and to his surprise, she faces him. Her gray, dead-like complexion fades suddenly, and her normal pallor returns. With her regular blue eyes, soft and wet and innocent, she returns his desperate, pleading gaze.

"Ket..." she says softly.

"Don't do this." He's trembling but trying not to, trying to slow the fear that's running through his veins like deadly venom. The old Ket Norlath, the man he was before this new life, before he met *her*, would not have been afraid. Old Ket would have risen to the violent occasion.

Jennah remains still in that pose, unable to speak as if her brain and mouth have gone to war with each other. The battle lasts about ten seconds, and when it's over, it's clear which side has won; her skin darkens once again, hardens with an almost reptilian film, goes gray, and her eyes light up with an intense orange glow, as if ignited in the hateful fires of Arkos's nightmare realm.

"I love you." Her voice does not sound like hers. Too deep, too hateful. Too menacing to have come from the woman who holds his heart.

Something hisses past his ear, and before Ket can blink, he sees an arrow plunge into Jennah's throat, just below her chin. She goes pale again, the gray flesh fading. Her mouth drops in surprise, her jaw trying to work, but a spell of silence captures her tongue. Blood bubbles between her lips, gouts of crimson hiccupping out behind them. Weak, trembling hands reach for the arrow, attempting to pull it free, remove the kill shot, but to no avail. The arrow has found a new home and won't budge. Her hands slip and slide in the slick flow of red pouring from the arrow's entry point.

Ket follows the arrow's trajectory, finds Sir Henry at the beginning of its flight. He's still clutching the bow in his post-kill salute, eye looking down the notch, the string thrumming its death-rattle vibration.

"Another witch dies today," states Sir Henry, his lips stretching with instant satisfaction.

The remaining guardsmen rush Jennah's standing corpse, swords engaged and ready to strike down the sorceress.

Ket can't react fast enough. By the time he does, the first sword enters Jennah's stomach, slicing through her with ease, and emerges out her back. The sickening sucking sound of the blade withdrawing reminds him of his mace being pulled from pig heads during the culling season, wet and final. She doesn't scream.

Their children do the screaming for her.

Her eyes find her husband's as the next blade enters her shoulder, shattering her collarbone. One guard swipes his blade across her knee, cleaving her at the kneecap, severing her lower leg.

Ket screams, grabs the first guard he can get his hands on, and twists his neck in a furious rage, his shout rivaling the booms of thunder overhead. The man's neck snaps with a loud *crack*, and his corpse drops to the earth like a sack of pumpkin seeds. The murder seizes the attention of the remaining guards, and a few of them spin on him, blades out. If armed, he would still be no match for them. Though, it doesn't matter anymore. Nothing does. He's prepared to give them a fight, and if he can take out one or two before they can run their blades clean through him, then so be it.

He's ready to die today.

No, a disembodied voice floats through his mind. Jennah's. He locates her stare once more. The life has gone out of her eyes, although something there remains, some last spark of consciousness. *No, you will not. Think of our children.*

He sinks to his knees before the men. They keep their swords pointed at him like they expect him to bounce up and resume his killing spree, but there is nothing left in him. Other guards stab his wife several more times, plunging their blades in and out, working her corpse like a seamstress's pin cushion. After her body shows more blood than unmarked flesh, they drag her across the property, over to the edge of the bluff. Almost routinely, they heave her body over the edge, delivering her to the gigantic crags below. The men stare down until satisfied, until they have visual confirmation of the woman's demise. Then they shrug and return to Ket—his eyes wide, pulled open in grief—and the children who have not stopped wailing since the first sword was bloodied.

Through his tears, Ket can barely see them being pulled towards him. He lowers his head, submitting to the torturous, frantic cries coming from his sons and his own despair. He wants to call to them, tell them everything will be fine, that this is just a nightmare they will all soon wake from—but he can't.

For the first time in a long time, a lie dies on his tongue.

The men close in around him.

Something heavy crashes into the back of his head, and a dark veil is drawn over the world he had grown to love.

PART ONE
EVERYTHING OLD

ABOUT TWO YEARS
LATER...

SUMMON THE PRISONER

CHAPTER ONE

"After the gods ended their wars with each other and left this mortal plane, it became strictly forbidden to worship a specific god of the pantheon in the bigger cities, and his followers were sentenced to death in the most horrific ways, without trial. Arkos, forever dubbed *The Blackstone Angel*, sometimes labeled *The Witchmaster*, is the only god considered a threat to civilization. Prophesied to bring plagues and chaos, and plunge the countryside into eternal darkness, remain vigilant and wary of those who display the symbol of the black billygoat, as their allegiance to the dark lord is lawless and morally repugnant."

– PHILIP GROTTON, *DISCUSSING THE DARK GODS*

———

LIKE EVERY MORNING in this shithole, his mouth is as dry as a desert in hell. A water bowl sitting just out of his desperate reach contains a few worthless drops. Not enough to quench his thirst, and if his internal clock is tuned correctly, it'll be at least another hour before the guards fetch him more.

Ket works his fingernails into his beard, scratching the irritated skin beneath. What he would give for a crude razor, or better yet—a trip to the barber.

His cell is dank and dark, and on most days the sun eludes him. The only light down here comes from a few torches stationed along the dungeon's long hall, though occasionally the guards draw back the shutters in the empty cells, allowing squares of sunshine to dazzle. Seldom does the warmth of the sun reach his skin. But gods, he longs for it. Sunlight *and* clean air. Being able to walk upright, without one of the guards threatening his guts with a knife blade.

Maybe today is the day he'll find the courage to kill himself, using the metal fork given to him at mealtimes. Shoving it into his eyeball, popping out his eye and skewering his brain in the process. But the worry gnaws at him. The possibility or *probability* that he wouldn't complete the job, and he'd be forced to live out the rest of his imprisoned days brain-dead. He could get lucky; King Ragland's men might have mercy on a vegetable and put him down like a terminally sick animal.

If they had given him bedsheets to sleep with, he'd have hung himself at the first opportunity.

Every time those suicidal tendencies creep in, another voice whispers insidiously into his brain. He knows it's himself, his own voice, but it comes to him in Jennah's soft, soothing tone. *Stay alive for them. They will need you.*

His sons are likely dead or enslaved, and if they are the latter, then he hopes they die soon.

I'm dead to them, if they are alive, he tells that other voice.

The voice doesn't respond, and it is almost more than he can bear. He is alone again, in his cell, with no one to talk to, no one to argue with. He is struck with the sudden notion that life never existed before this prison. Not his sons, not his beloved wife. It was all just a cruel mirage he dreamt while waiting for meals that never satisfied his hunger, and the pittance of water that never quenched his thirst.

Metal sliding against metal interrupts his ideations of self-harm. The slide bolt holding the entrance shut has been released, and a parade of the king's men stroll through the gate and into the dungeon's long hall. There aren't too many other prisoners down here with him; this section of the castle's dungeon is reserved for those who deserve to no longer view the outside world; for murderers and blasphemers. Those waiting on death sentences, harsh punishments, or the most creative, pain-inducing tortures. Common criminals—thieves and disorderly drunks—are held in the holding cells in the main keep.

Ket counts five guards, all escorting one prisoner. The new addition has a rice sack over his head, blood so dark it's black, staining the fabric. Ket shifts in his seated position, watching the men bring the prisoner to the cell across from him. They remove the sack from his head, shove him inside, and then key the lock. The prisoner stumbles to the ground on worn, weary knees.

"You're all going to regret your actions here today," the prisoner says, his voice calm and measured, with a surprising hint of joy, like he might have relished the violence to some marginal degree. "Mark my words."

"Consider them marked, jester," says the head guard, whom Ket doesn't immediately recognize. He and the rest of the men laugh, barking with malicious glee. Whatever the joke is, Ket doesn't catch it. But it's at *the Jester's* expense.

After the guards leave, Ket stares into the shadows across from him. The man sits enshrouded in dusky light, and Ket can't catch a clear glimpse of his neighbor.

"See anything you like, friend?" a voice comes out of the gloom, and although he can't see him, Ket pictures the prisoner smiling.

Ket doesn't bother answering him. He's barely spoken all of ten words since his imprisonment, and he sees no need to break his vow of silence now, not for this man who might be hanging from the gallows pole come morning. Prisoners come and go. No one lasts forever down here.

Except me, he thinks, considering the duration of his imprisonment. Two years, yes, but it feels like an eternity. Most prisoners are booked, sentenced, and either moved out or put to death in (at most) a couple of weeks. He's always wondered why he's been treated differently, why in all his time here he hasn't sat before a judge or King Ragland's jury. Why he hasn't had to answer for his crimes against the crown. They certainly haven't forgotten about him.

"Cat got your tongue, friend?" the prisoner asks.

Ket goes back to picking at the skin around his fingernails, the only entertainment his cell provides. He's scraped them raw, his fingernails outlined in red.

"Nasty habit you got there, friend," says the man. Ket curses himself for even looking in the man's direction; he's clearly the blathering type, and if Ket had known, he would have kept his eyes on his own lap. *Ignore him,* he decides, hoping he'll clam up, eventually.

Minutes pass, but then…inevitably…

"What's on the menu in this place? I could go for a nice slab of deer steak and apple-berry pie, myself. What say you, fellow convict?" The man leans forward, emerging from the shadows of his cramped surroundings. Ket's heart skips a beat when he sees what's become of him, the…*the damage? Damage* is the best word for it. The guards called him *Jester,* and now Ket can see why. Someone—one of the guards, he assumes—has sewn a jester's hat to the man's scalp. Not just *to* the scalp, no—it appears the man *was* scalped, and the three-pronged hat has replaced the flesh and the hair that once sat atop his head. Thick black stitches conjoin the green fabric of his hat and the bunched crown of skin of his upper forehead. In addition to that cruelty, someone has cut and then stitched the corners of his mouth to meet the skin under his ear lobes. The disfigurement makes the man permanently smile, and would explain why his voice seemed like it came through a mouth that wasn't working properly. "If you could have any meal in the world right now," he continues without skipping a beat, "what would it be?"

Ket feels compelled to answer, if for no other reason than he feels sorry for the man, for suffering through that involuntary facial reconstruction. He opens his mouth, and for a second, it's like he's forgotten how to speak. How speech is formed.

"Yes?" Jester impatiently awaits his answer.

"Uh," Ket says, and that single syllable burns his throat, like inhaling a frosty gust of wind. He clears his throat and tries again. "I…" He sounds so hoarse, so unlike the voice he remembers. "I would take a…a burger."

"A burger!" Amused, Jester claps his hands together. "Now we're talking! What would you like topped on your burger meat, fellow inmate, whose name I do not know but would very much like to learn?"

Ket narrows his eyes. There's madness in Jester's shrinking pupils, a glint of it. The dangerous kind. The kind that affects innocent bystanders, influencing the stories of their lives. And not in a good way. Ket doesn't know what to make of him yet, friend or foe, but his eyes scream a warning.

"Ket," he says, continuing to adopt his pseudonym. He's been Ket so long that it just rolls off his tongue, naturally. He doesn't care to ever hear or utter his birth name again. "And I would very much like…like pickles on my burger."

"Pickles! How delightful. I am a pickle man myself. With lettuce, tomato, and a brush of mustard, no doubt."

Ket hates tomatoes, but the mere mention of other toppings makes his mouth water. He nods, opting for silence. Speaking hurts his throat too much. And it only makes him thirstier.

Jester must have taken the hint because he retreats into the shadows and stays there, a pregnant silence descending over the cellblock that lingers and lingers and lingers…

THE DAYS PASSED. Long days. Tired days. Days filled with boredom and hunger and aching from sitting in the same place, the same position. Muscles cramped. Bones stiffened. The isolation of the underground quarters sank him deeper into the hole of his depression. A prisoner six cells down contracted a terrible illness, and started coughing and hacking up globs of creamy-green phlegm. Soon after the coughing fits ceased, his skin broke out in gruesome red bumps that oozed small rivers of pus. Prisoners in the surrounding units cried plague, but Ket knew it was no such thing. Just a bad case of bed fever, something his body would fight off with some high-quality rest and the herbal benefits from a conficus plant root. He hoped the infirmary was educated enough to see the man through—but in the end, Ket didn't care. A dead inmate he had never once traded words with, was of no consequence to him.

As the days passed, however, he grew fond of Jester. As fond as one could be of a criminal. Though—technically—he was a criminal himself, even if he didn't think of himself as such. Of all the other criminals that occupied the cages over the years, Jester was the only one he spoke with more than a few times. And those conversations with others had always been brief, never more than a few words back and forth. Ket's lips had been like the impassable gates protecting the legendary Hero's Gold of Nashandy, when it came to questions from strangers.

He enjoys those small talks with Jester. He finds the man interesting—his way with words, his razor-sharp intelligence, his smug wit. Throughout their chats, Ket wonders what led the man to his incarceration. What had he done to deserve that unusual treatment? Why had the king's company decided it was fitting to scalp him, sew that cloth atop his head, and stitch his lips in that creative, always-smiling manner?

One afternoon, after the guards finish their scheduled patrol through the dungeon, Jester asks him the very same question that's nagged him since the poor fool was dragged in here: "So, now that we are well-acquainted, what brought you to this pit of despair, Ket Nortlath?"

Ket leans his head against the wall that has cradled it for the last eight seasons, as he sits on his stone bench-bed. "That's a long story."

"We have nothing but time. Unless you want to try your hand at guess-what-number-I've-scratched-into-the-wall again?"

Ket kicks around the idea of telling him everything. The truth, the way he sees it. But what if he's a plant? The words he was about to speak die in his throat.

He's often wondered how many prisoners passing through here were nothing more than ears for Ragland. How many men have incriminated themselves by sharing secrets with their cell-mates? Can he really trust a man he only just met? There's a nagging suspicion that Jester could be a valuable ally. But he's been very wrong about people before.

He decides on the hybrid option of truths and omissions of truths, which, he gathers, is a form of lying. He tells Jester about that day the king's company rode out to his farm in the southwest corner of Owlton, how they stampeded his property, accused his wife of dark witchcraft and conspiring with the fabled deity, Arkos, assassinated her without fair trial, before the eyes of his children and himself, and the abduction that followed.

What he omits are the details of his past, far away from the farm he hunkered down on, in some nowhere corner of Endlia, where his former allegiances to a foreign king withered away; how the woman he loved transformed into some hideous witch-queen moments before her murder; and how he still hasn't ratio-nalized it all. How he still doubts what he saw was real.

"That's an awful tale," Jester says, almost pressing his face against the iron bars that contain him. He frowns, tilting his head to the side, his head half-cast in shadows. "They left you alive?"

Ket presses his fingers to his neck, mimicking a pulse check. "Unless I'm dead and don't know it. Which, I must confess, it feels some days."

Jester snorts. "Curious. Seems like a waste to keep a simple farmer, guilty of dark allegiances, alive for two whole years. Waste of good cell space and food. Are you sure there's nothing more to the story?" His eyes glimmer. There's humor dancing there. An eyebrow rises. Hopeful, perhaps.

Bastard's fishing. He denies the jester a satisfying conclusion, his jaw firming around his decision. "I told you all of it."

Jester smiles with his eyes since his real smile is always present and hard to read. "There's more to you than meets the eye, Ket Norlath. I'm sure of it."

"What about you?" Ket asks, finally gaining the courage to pry. "Why have these savages disfigured you and thrown you in here with us lawless citizens?"

Jester barks a single laugh. "Ha! Well, my story is much simpler and far less tragic. I tried to assassinate the king, and I did it for money." Ket sucks in a breath, a chill cooling his marrow. "I posed as a court jester to get close to my target, Ragland the third himself, and tried to finish him with a concealed knife. A slash across his neck. I botched the attempt before I could open the bastard's throat, though." His lips thin, his jaw grating underneath the fixed smile, breathing hard through his nostrils. He stays that way, his gaze distant, and just as Ket thinks he's finished, his voice cuts through the silence, his words almost spat. "Captured in the act. And the King saw it fitting to have one of his surgeons remove my scalp and sew on my disguise as one of many punishments." He flicks one of the hat's floppy ears, and the bell jingles. "Then they fixed my face like this." His finger traces the red, irritated scar tissue that hasn't fully healed yet. "Still hurts to talk, but I like talking, so I will never shut up. Just to spite them. Can't let them win, can I?"

"You only tried to kill the king for money?"

"Well, certainly. Didn't do it for the fun of it. I'm an assassin, man. That's what I do. *Assassinate.* For coins."

"You've killed many men before?"

"Oh yes. Before this, I was a very proficient killer. Was once part of the Circle of Slayers, if you can believe it. During my prime years."

The Circle of Slayers. An underground outfit dedicated to the craft of assassination—a band of traveling contract killers, very skilled at what they did. Ket had never heard of them murdering kings, though—or any party close to the five crowns. There was some kind of truce in place—the Circle was left alone, allowed to operate in the shadows of the world, as long as no royalty was attacked. Ket doubted the Circle would allow Jester's attempt.

So, gone rogue, perhaps? That might fit. If he was caught, then it's true—he'd lost his touch. The Circle was always rumored to have few members, efficient executioners who left behind little evidence of their misdeeds, or in some cases, left deaths that almost looked natural. Rumors. Myths. Sometimes the Circle was talked about lightly, the punchlines of bad jokes. Something that could not exist. Yet Ket knew otherwise. In his previous life, Ket knew one of them.

One like Jester, who also broke the code of killing kings. Or tried to.

Ket's not sure he believes Jester is telling the truth when it comes to his prior membership with the Circle. The ring of his tale feels more like credible boasting. "Impressive," Ket concedes.

"You've heard of the Circle?"

"Who hasn't?"

"Simple farmers, I would suspect. Unless you're something more than a man who plants seeds and tugs on cow titties each and every monotonous day?"

That damned smile. "You don't believe me? My story? You think there is more than what I've told you?"

"Oooo." The bastard grins, his hands up in mock alarm. "Defensive. And I don't *think*—now I'm entirely convinced. I'm like the cat in all those old wives' tales, don't you know. Who are you, Ket Norlath? Who are you really?"

Ket breathes in the musty odor, hates the stink that fills his lungs. "A farmer. That's all I am."

"Sure you are. You hold onto your secrets, lot of good they'll do you down here."

The slide bolt to the dungeon door creaks open, then stops

with a metallic, groaning pop. Three guards step inside, and the pandemonium begins immediately. Prisoners nearer the door scream, begging for their release. One pounds his fists against the iron bars, shouting over and over, wanting to change cells, to be separated from the supposed plague victim. Another captive bangs their head against the wall in what Ket believes is an attempt to gain the guards' attention. But they ignore him and continue until they're standing outside Ket's cell; they stare down at him like he's street vermin.

Ket recognizes the leader of the three. His veins flood with fire. His heart quickens its pace. Dizziness fights his vision. It takes everything he has not to jump up and reach through the bars for the man's throat. The man's goatee is gone, replaced by a full beard, bushy but well-groomed, and that streak of white remains. His eyes look endlessly tired, have lost their youthful brightness. It is the face of a man who's seen terrible things over the last two years, but has not had the time to process what he has seen.

Ket understands.

"King Edwill Ragland III demands your presence," Sir Henry says through his teeth, like this is frustrating news. The man's displeasure is not nearly satisfying enough.

"Fuck you," Ket says, not moving an inch. "And fuck the King."

"You will think differently when you hear what he has to say, *farmer.*" Sir Henry snaps his fingers, and a guard steps forward, key in hand, ready to pop the lock. Ready to *free* Ket.

There's no such thing as freedom, Ket reminds himself. *Not anymore. That ship has sailed over the horizon, has been swallowed by the raging sea.*

"I'm not interested," Ket says.

The cell lock pops anyway. The door shudders open, vibrating as it swings out into the corridor, almost too heavy for its hinges. The vibration is smothered by the guard's fist clenching around one of the bars, his knuckles white. Perhaps he's ready for a fight.

If Ket had the energy, he'd give him one.

"Your sons' lives depend on it, so I imagine you will be very interested." Sir Henry steps aside, allowing an unobstructed exit. He waves Ket on like a theatre usher. "Hurry. Time is tick-tick-ticking away, and the King is not known for his patience."

Tears fill Ket's eyes. He jumps to his feet, the mention of his sons and receiving confirmation of their health renewing his energy, reinstating his life's purpose. "Do not lie to me. Not about this."

"I promise your sons are alive and well. Now, my suggestion is to not leave the King waiting."

Ket stumbles forward in a daze. He's still not sure how to feel, how his sons could be *alive* and *well*. Seems impossible. He's spent the last two years believing they've been murdered, snuffed out for simply being the spawn of an Arkos witch.

It seems he was wrong.

They tell me lies.

Even if they are lies, it's worth investigating.

He raises his wrists so the guards can put the chains on him. As they march to the exit, Sir Henry shouts to the guard in the corridor, "Bring the jester. The King wants a word with him, too."

———

THE THRONE ROOM isn't far off from what Ket has imagined, on the way up through the palace—a purple roll of carpet stretches across a smooth square of obsidian stone, leading from the towering entry doors to the dais, where the king and his queen sit on golden thrones. Fine and intricate scrollwork has been carved into the thrones' side panels: a detailed engraving of Highbeard's image. The god's face is shown on both sides of the thrones through a network of intricate, careful shavings, the artist clearly possessing a talent for such sculptures. The walls stare down upon Ket in disapproval, covered in stone reliefs of the prior Owlton kings, the Ragland lineage, including everyone who's ever sat on the throne. From the last few Edwill Raglands, all the way to the first king of the first age—Desmond Ragland, the fierce bastard ruler with narrow eyes, wild bushy eyebrows to match his bushy beard, and a heart full of pure hate and rage, which is not explicitly captured in the artwork, save for his stony eyes. Ket knows enough tales of the world's history to know the intentions behind those eyes—murder, conquer and enslave. What the first king of Owlton was best known for.

Ket quickly scans the rest of the statues before facing the dais, where the newest king sits on his throne in front of his expected company.

Ragland himself is a portly lump of a man who sports a kingly beard, which aims to rival that of the Highbeard's and falls epically short. His powdery white facial hair is peppered with streaks of gray, and his eyes glow a cold blue, same as a sun-kissed sky. As his audience crosses the threshold and makes their way down the carpet, the king remains still. Not even a smile. No nod, no expression of any kind. Just eyes that stare down his narrow nose, targeting his approaching subjects. Ket can't help but notice the bandage on his throat, covering a wound a little worse than your typical shaving accident.

His queen remains just as still. Her raven-black hair shoots straight down from her crown and falls below her shoulders. Her Owltonion dress fits snugly against her slim frame, and the royal purple trim that outlines the entire garment captures Ket's gaze for more seconds than he wishes to acknowledge.

Standing before the two royals, no more than twenty feet away, Ket shifts his gaze back to the king who has summoned him. Ragland gives the prisoner a once over, a head-to-toe examination that sets Ket on edge. He doesn't believe the king has brought him all the way here just to sentence him to execution—if he wanted Ket dead, then he wouldn't have kept him in that dungeon for almost three summers. Jester was right about that. Ragland has kept him alive for something. A once priceless token he now wishes to cash in, upon it reaching peak value.

"Prisoner," the King bellows, projecting his voice with the

gusto of a theatre actor. "They tell me your name is Ket Norlath, but there is reason to believe you have lived under a different name, once upon a time ago."

Ket feels the heat of Jester's smile on the back of his neck. He swears he hears the bastard make an *I knew it!* gasp.

"I have, my king," he says, figuring any lie told today will not benefit him. "I once went by the name of another and lived a very different life from when your men came to my farm that day… when they executed my wife and stole my children."

The king passes a look from him to his smiling wife, then back to Ket again. "I appreciate your honesty," the king tells him, no enthusiasm in his voice. This is all mundane conversation for him, or so it seems. "My men have a working theory on who you were before defecting from King Salah's army. The name men in the north gave you as you carried out your dark deeds in the war against us."

Ket hangs his head in shame. "I have done terrible things in my past, my king. And I've regretted them all."

"I know it."

Ket raises his head, a glimmer of hope rising to the surface of his feelings. His heart swells with the prospect of a benevolent king's full pardon. Or maybe even a partial. "How can I serve you, Lord Ragland?"

The king pauses, his frosty blue eyes drilling deep into Ket's, as if judging his soul, determining if Ket is worth the trouble.

Ket flashes glassy, doughy eyes at Ragland, bowing his head reverently, hoping to coax the king's charitable side. If he has one.

"Have you heard of the prophecy of the *Boy with Stars for Eyes*? An old tale, from old texts."

Ket looks up at the king, confusion settling in, a shiver running the length of his spine. *The Boy with Stars for Eyes?* Ket has never been one for prophetic tales, but he's certainly heard that one—a standard myth, taught in classrooms all across Endlia, and has been for centuries. It predicts that a child will be born with star-shaped eyes, who would bear the power of the gods, rise up and put an end to war, famine, plagues, the supernatural beasts and spirits that roam the free territories. And that they would unite the Five Realms.

Ket shakes his head.

"I've heard that one!" shouts a voice from behind him, a familiar and somewhat grating voice, considering the situation. Everyone in the king's court turns to the Jester, as he holds his shackled wrists in the air like he's celebrating a victorious war effort. "It's a lovely little tale of love, death, hope, and—"

The guard closest to him drives the flat side of his sword into Jester's kneecap. A quick *snap!* and Jester drops to the ground, hollering like a siren in a ferocious sea gale. *"Yoweeee!"*

"Speak again, clown," Sir Henry warns, "and I'll have Petr cleave you off at the knee."

The Jester regains his footing, rising to a standing position, scowling at the man who hit him.

"Want another, ya cunt bastard?" Petr says, spinning the blade so the sharp side is aligned with his knee.

"There will be no mutilations or acts of savage violence in the presence of my queen," Ragland says evenly. "She hasn't the stomach for it, and we just had tea."

"Yes, my king," Sir Henry says.

Petr puts his sword back in its scabbard, then pays his respects to his overlord with a curt bow.

"As I was saying," King Ragland continues, "The Boy with Stars for Eyes is a prophecy from the olden times, back when the gods first left our realm. It was told that one day a boy would be born in the north, that he would have star-shaped eyes, and his birth would mean the second coming of the gods. Once again, the deities would come back to Endlia, rule over us, and bestow upon us a paradisiacal realm of eternal harmony."

Ket narrows his eyes with suspicion, playing the part of a skeptic.

Ragland's eyebrows arch, letting Ket know he should become a true believer. And fast.

"Fancy tale," Ket says, "but what does it have to do with me? I am no longer a soldier of the northern army, no longer serve King Salah Rovan, and no longer believe in the teachings of the all-powerful Highbeard. If he is real, then he's condemned me and my family to eternal suffering."

Ragland's eyes slim, but he seems to ignore the blasphemous outburst. "I believe it was your wife who condemned your family. When she shackled up with the Blackstone Angel, decided to worship the Witchmaster, Arkos. That devil be damned."

Ket feels a fiery rage coursing through him. "My wife did not worship any devils, and she did not serve Arkos. Of that I am certain."

"I would think twice before selling me untruths. My men swore an oath on Highbeard's Good Book, on grounds punishable by death if their testimonies are proven false, that your wife broke a man's neck from where I stand to you. Made a man scratch out his own eyeballs by planting the idea in his head. Are you going to tell me that's not what happened that day? And don't lie to me! Your sons' lives depend on your next words."

Ket lowers his head, shame and grief and confusion piling down on him. "I don't know what I saw that day. I cannot explain it. The woman in that pasture...she was not the same woman I married."

"You were deceived," the king states, his tone suggesting there is no other plausible explanation. "And for that my heart breaks for you." Ket can't tell if this last statement is sarcasm or not. If Ragland knows who he is, who he *truly* is, then it just might be. Because no heart would break for the man Ket was.

"I've summoned you here today," the king continues, his expression remaining as still as hard clay, "because my spies in the north have reported information that I cannot ignore. Because the entire world depends on it. Whispers and rumors from the Silver Towers suggest that twelve years ago, the Boy with Stars for Eyes was born in a sleepy seaside town in western Braag. And that the Rovan King is keeping the boy in the Silver Towers, locked away, with the hopes and aspirations of using the boy's powers to conjure up some dark, ancient magic. Not using it to unite the Endlands, but instead intending to destroy it by launching a new war effort against his oldest enemy—us."

"War," Ket says, shaking his head like one ear is waterlogged. "I thought the last war ended over a decade ago and brought times of peace."

"You've been isolated for the last two years, Ket Norlath. Times are dark. And they darken quickly. We attribute the sprawling darkness to the birth of the boy and his coming of age. As he grows, so do his powers. His…*witchery*." The king spits that last word like poisoned soup. "Creatures, thought to have been extinct for hundreds of years have again reappeared, populating our forests, tunnels and caverns, hiding under well-traveled bridges. Our companies and tradesmen are attacked on open roads, left slaughtered, disemboweled and in pieces. Witchcraft and sorcery are rearing their ugly heads. Monsters. Ghouls. Beasts born of legend have all risen from the depths of Endlia's imagination, and pose new threats to all the Endlands. And that boy…that boy is the key to ending this madness. He just needs to be brought to the right mentor."

"*If* the boy exists," Jester intrudes, then braces for another blow. Sir Henry seems to let his comment slide. The king's lieutenant side-eyes the poor excuse for an assassin. "A big *if…*"

"Indeed, assassin," Ragland says. "Indeed."

"I've enjoyed your tale, my king," Ket says. "But again—I'm not sure what any of this has to do with me."

"You are my prisoner and you wish to be freed. Correct?"

"Well…yes, of course. But my sons—"

"Are alive and living splendid days. We've paired them with a family who's aware of their…*situation*."

Ket shudders with the confirmation that his boys are fine. The news knocks the breath from his lungs, his entire chest stiff and aching. It is as if he is suffering a heart attack. "Oh gods," he swears right after he's regained control of his lungs once more.

"Their situation being, of course, that their mother was an Arkos witch and their father is a traitor to the crown. Them being born of witchblood—"

"Witchblood?" Ket grows angry, feels every cord in his neck tighten. Heat burns his forehead. "Witchblood?"

"Will you stand there and deny your wife was a witch, an Arkos-worshipping cunt?" The King speaks the insult all too calmly, knowing there are no repercussions for his words. In a pub, if someone spoke to Ket like this, they'd be swallowing their teeth.

Ket doesn't answer. Doesn't need to. He was there that day, saw what happened. In her final hour, she possessed a power that was beyond his knowledge. Long ago he had done unspeakable things, things that defied the common laws of reality, and had witnessed his fair share of what most considered *magic*. Whatever *magic* he once possessed was long gone. Recalling those long days and nights spent in the Silver Towers, under the eye of the Raven and the eye of the *Salamandian*, is like recalling a distant dream; the details are fuzzy, and it's hard to pinpoint what was grounded in reality and what his imagination added.

"In my ten years of marriage, I never witnessed any signs of witchery. Not until that day. That is the honest truth."

Ragland's eyes thin to slits. "And I believe you, new son of Owlton. You were simply bewitched by an agent of Arkos. There's no shame in admitting you were tricked into loving something inherently evil."

In his bones, he does not feel that's the truth. He had not been tricked into loving Jennah—his love for her was of his own doing, and that love still runs through his veins, pumping through each of the four chambers of his heart, even long after her departure.

Still, it's the part the king wants him to play; an innocent man tricked into loving an evil witch. If it saves him, his sons, then it's a part he'll play, and play well.

"Yes, it must have been that," he says, betraying his true feelings. Hating it. "I was deceived. A love spell was cast upon me."

King Edwill Ragland III closes his eyes, and for the first time, a faint smile plays with his lips. "I'm happy to hear it. Your sons, alive and well, are flourishing in their new household, and are being monitored to ensure they do not exhibit any of their mothers' abilities—her dark desires to conspire with the Blackstone Angel." He snaps his fingers. Two guards advance and undo the shackles around Ket's wrists. "They will be returned to you, *but*—there is the matter of your crimes against my crown, and your allegiance—although unknowingly—to the ways of witches. That must be dealt with."

"I am ready to cleanse my soul with your permission, my lord."

King Ragland lifts a wary brow.

"I bet you are. I am asking you to return to the Silver Towers, where that pathetic self-proclaiming emperor Salah Rovan sits on his silver throne—undoubtedly stuffing his face with pork pies and creamed ice every hour—and locate the Boy. If you find that he exists and the prophecy is true, then you will bring him to me. If he does not exist, then your mission is to slay the king and return with his head.

"The king's head or the Boy with Stars for Eyes, in exchange for your two sons and a full pardon of your crimes. Does this sound like a fair exchange?"

Ket can't focus. The trade in question has left him with no voice.

My sons live. He'd risk everything just to see his sons again, let alone the chance to be forgiven for his transgressions. For the opportunity to rebuild what was stolen from him.

"My offer will not stand forever. I dislike waiting..."

"Yes," Ket blurts out. "But, my king—riding into the Rovan Territories and gaining access to the Silver Towers will be no simple task. Those lands are heavily patrolled, and the northern king faces assassination attempts daily from all kinds of independent factions. And if the boy does exist—I am but one man. How do you expect me to achieve this, successfully?"

"I believe your prior allegiance to the northern king makes you a suitable candidate to solve those problems."

"I am but one man," he repeats.

"That's the deal. Or, I can order your sons' executions this evening. Along with yours. But they will die first, and we will cut off your eyelids so you can watch them hang."

Ket swallows any doubts he has about the journey. "If I will die on this quest—what will become of them? Will you kill them anyway?"

"If you do not return within the year, I promise to keep them safe. As long as they do not exhibit symptoms of their mother's disease."

Ket bows to his new king. *I am one man,* he thinks. *One man against an entire city—one that would love to see me dead.*

"Very well," Ket agrees, holding his head high. Proud. A faux confidence that makes his skin crawl.

"Excellent. Sir Henry will take you to the armory, where you can equip yourself with the necessary weapons. A good horse will be provided for you, as well as some food to get you started."

"*Ahem,*" a small, quiet voice says, and Ket knows to whom it belongs almost at once. "My king," Jester starts, his weaselly voice sounding more weaselly than ever. "If I may be so bold as to inquire about my presence through this little…uh…enlightening palaver."

Sir Henry snaps his fingers, and the guard who shelled out the punishment to Jester's knee happily positions himself for another strike.

"Wait," Ragland says to the guards, who freeze. "Jester, do you know how many assassination attempts my men have thwarted during my reign?"

"At least one."

"I've lost count myself, although I'm sure if we search the records, we will find a staggering tally. Of all the attempts, only three got close. So close, my life was in peril. Once at a tourney, I took an arrow to the shoulder. Once, someone tried slipping poison into my wine and was caught in the act. And you—the closest attempt. You got so close to slitting my throat that night, I thought surely I was destined to die by your hand." His fingers flick subconsciously to run across the bandage over his neck wound.

"If only my fingers were seconds quicker and my escape route was not blocked by your staff." Jester sighs in an *oh well* sort of way. "Damn the gods on your side, kind sir."

"You are a funny man," Ragland tells him, which is surprising to everyone in the room. A king calling his attempted killer anything but the devil is somewhat curious.

Ket watches Sir Henry's face redden as the comment is uttered.

"Surely we will put this man to death, my lord," Sir Henry says, clapping Jester on the neck. Squeezing. Until his fingertips blanch. "And we should do it soon, before the sun downs."

Ragland breathes in a deep sigh of relief, as if the worst part of their conversation is past them. "No, I feel a man of his talents should not be wasted. Certainly he is a worthy adversary of kings. To attempt to kill a king in his own throne room certainly takes balls that not even the most valiant knight in my army can display. Would you agree, Sir Henry?"

Sir Henry looks like he's sucked a bitter coffee bean. "Aye, it takes balls. Brass ones, my king. Yet, I cannot completely agree that letting a man this dangerous—your enemy—live beyond sundown, is a conscionable decision."

King Ragland glowers at his lieutenant.

"But..." Sir Henry says, glancing up at the ceiling as if High-beard might come down and help him cover his gaff. "Whatever you believe is best, I will see it done."

"I think it best," King Ragland says, leaning forward as if he needs a closer look at the jester and his recent disfigurements, "we send this man to accompany Ket Norlath—as long as Ket is agreeable."

Ket faces the Jester; the man does not plead with his eyes. He seems to favor neither decision. "And if I refuse his company?"

The king shrugs like nothing about Ket's decision matters. "In that case, the assassin has no further use to me. Where he may excel as an assassin, he leaves much to be desired as a fool. If you refuse his company, then I will leave his fate in Sir Henry's capable hands."

So be it. "He may ride to the Silver Towers with me."

"Very well. It's settled." The king claps his hands together, twice, then grabs the goblet off the table next to him. The queen raises her own and clinks the golden cups together, as if this is a moment worthy of celebration. "To your good health. May Highbeard's eyes watch over you, and his heart guide you along your righteous path."

———

IN THE ARMORY, Ket's equipment has been chosen for him, except for a blade. Sir Henry walks him over to a long wall where swords are kept in racks, some of them loose and lying on the floor, some of them leaning properly upright. Swords taken from those slain in battle, no doubt, both friendly and foe. Sir Henry presents the options with a sweeping wave of his arm, offering Ket his pick of the collection.

Running his eyes over the weapons, Ket walks the corridor. Most of his options are dirty and worn, some of them still stained dark with splotches of dried blood. Some show rust and neglect near the edges, chipped and bent. None look in peak condition, all requiring a good sharpening stone. Picking up a sword, Ket tests its heft by raising it above his head. He slashes through the air, the wind of his assault slicing the air before him. *Whip! Whoop!*

"If you're getting any ideas about slaying me down here," Sir Henry says, eyeing him from across the room like a shopkeeper would stare down a potential thief, "then know you will never make it up the stairs alive."

Slowly turning to him, Ket points the sword's tip in the man's direction. "I have considered that. It's a pleasant idea."

Sir Henry's hand slips to his sword's hilt. He hesitates to draw it, but he has plenty of time to draw and parry any attack, should Ket choose to strike.

Ket doesn't. He knows Sir Henry isn't lying; there are enough guards above them to dispatch Ket with relative ease. All it would take is a quick whistle from Sir Henry's lips, and Ket would be outnumbered by two dozen at least.

"But I've decided to let the past lie," Ket says, flipping his sword in his hand and examining both sides of the blade. It's the cleanest he's seen so far, but still needs some love from a sharpening stone. "For now."

"I'm afraid this moment is the only opportunity you will have for revenge. For the orders I carried out on your wife. For that arrow through her throat."

He's baiting me. Wants me to attack. He reads the invitation in Sir Henry's eyes, that desire for violence.

Ket flashes him a smile, hoping the flames behind his cheeks will extinguish themselves. "She was a witch," he says, a pang of betrayal stabbing his heart. "You did what you had to, otherwise, who knows…maybe we would all be dead. I suppose—in a funny way—I should be thanking you. For saving my life. And those of my sons."

Sir Henry studies him for a beat. Finally, he nods.

"Thank you, Lieutenant," Ket says, doing his best to sound genuine.

"It's Commander now," he says, removing his hand from his hilt.

"Ah. Congratulations."

"Is that the blade you're choosing?"

Ket gives it another glance. "It will do, I suppose." He points to another blade that's caught his attention. The sword is all black, the blade included. The length of the sword is stunted in comparison to the others and what he's accustomed to, but it's longer than any knife he's ever seen. "What is that one? I don't believe I've ever seen a blade cut from obsidian before."

Sir Henry shrugs. "Not sure where it comes from. Most of these blades are taken off dead men, remnants from old wars. That one looks cut from some desert rock, if I had to guess. Won't do you much good in a real fight—the blade is dull."

"I will take it. Its dark nature appeals to me."

Sir Henry grinds his teeth as Ket goes over and picks up the black blade, and holds both swords next to each other as if he's ready to duel. "So be it, heathen."

Following Sir Henry to the exit, Ket clenches his jaw, imagining how good it would feel to slip his newfound sword right between the bastard's shoulder blades, impaling his rotten heart.

TO ONCE AGAIN BREATHE FRESH AIR

CHAPTER TWO

"The roads through Owlton are generally safe to travel, but beware of thieves and bandits, for many who travel those paths are not always who they seem."

– UNCREDITED ADVICE RECORDED BY THE
OWLTON TRADE COMMISSION

———

"HOW COME you got to choose your sword, whilst I was left with this?" Jester holds out a small knife with one hand; his other hand grips the saddle horn like he's in danger of sliding off.

Ket glances over his shoulder and chuckles upon seeing the brandished blade. "Still has Ragland's blood on it."

"Well, not nearly enough. You have no idea how close I was to emptying his throat."

"I still don't understand how you got that close and didn't finish the job."

"The guards pounced on me like a pack of mouse-cats. In my prime, I would have slit his throat and killed all three guards in the time it would have taken most men to unsheathe their sword."

"I somehow don't believe you."

The two slow their horses to a walk, having run them hard for almost four hours. The Long Green Road—given its name due to the grassy nature of its path, and the lengthy distance it covers—has taken them around Braag, right on up through the heart of Owlton. Stapleton is the last major city they must skirt before they leave the territory and enter the Crosslands, safely passing to the north. Their path avoids most of the major traffic, Ket's own personal route planned, despite the paperwork provided by King Ragland's scribes, which would allow unhindered passage past heavily patrolled roads and checkpoints. The breeze delivers cool relief from the sun, merciless on his skin after his years spent in the dark. As he thinks about passing crowds of fellow travelers along the usual routes, he shivers. Solitude had grown on him, and he's lost his appreciation for crowds.

Been too long since I toured these lands, he thinks, trying to recall the last instance when he rode somewhere other than the farm's neighboring towns and cities. He estimates it was a year before his incarceration, when Jennah was sick with the flu and required medicine they didn't have readily available.

Jennah.

All thoughts lead back to her, and now that he's on this journey back north, his thoughts drift to the day she died. The last moment he saw her. How easily she was tossed over the bluff. How he imagines her bones splintered on the rocks below. His eyes mist, his head turning away from Jester.

"Quiet all of a sudden," Jester says, kicking his heels into his horse's ribs and accelerating to Ket's side. "What's plaguing you?"

"Nothing," Ket blurts. The last thing he wants is Jester prying into his past again. He's certain the discussion with the king has stoked his companion's already burning curiosity. More questions are inevitable, but he's not ready for them.

"You lie and lie," Jester says, hissing like a serpent. "Ket Norlath, keeper of juicy secrets. You know, if we are to travel the Five Realms together, I feel we need to know more about each other. I'd like to know more about the man who will be watching my back as I lie asleep. I wonder greatly about his past."

"Well, keep wondering. My past is my own, and when I wish to divulge any information regarding my time spent under the northern king, then I will do so."

Cocking his brow, Jester snorts. "All right then, hold on to your past as you see fit. It's just...if I may be so bold as to say, I see pain in your eyes."

"My wife was murdered. My children are prisoners. And I have been tasked with a long journey toward certain death. Do you expect me to happy-dance around a party fire?"

"Maybe not a happy-dance, but surely being alive is worthy of a thank-you to whichever god you credit your survival." Jester's prying eyes latch on to him. "Which god is that by the way? I think I deserve to know if I'm traveling with an agent of Arkos or one of those X-er lunatics—have you seen those people? Maddened barbarians they are."

"I don't know what I believe in," Ket says firmly. "I haven't given the gods much thought of late."

"Finally. Some truth." Jester shrugs, snorts under his breath. "I guess that fits with your tough-boy attitude. Too cool to worship the gods. I get it. Fits perfectly with your—" He wiggles his fingers at Ket, like he's trying to grasp something he cannot see, "—swagger, as it were."

Ket shakes his head. "What about you? What god does the man who only reveals himself as *Jester* believe in?"

"I'll tell you mine if you tell me yours?"

Ket holds his tongue, ignoring the offer.

"Very well," Jester continues, speaking through his sly smile. "I don't know which god I believe in. Like you. But unlike you, I do think about them. Quite often. They are curious, aren't they?"

"They seem like fairy tales to me. Tales based on some truth, but mostly I think gods are the invention of men, made up to control people and fan the flames of war."

"Interesting theory. So, I guess it doesn't comfort you that some supreme wizard or being is looking out for your safety in exchange for a few prayers and daily worship? That possibility doesn't intrigue you?"

"No one is looking out for us." Ket turns his horse and walks him up ahead, putting distance between them. "If the gods are real, they're looking down at us and laughing. We are their entertainment."

"Interesting and interesting." Jester catches up to Ket in a few gallops. "I pass no harsh judgments, friend. I assure you, during our journey, I will see to it well that whatever lie you tell when asked about the deity you serve, I will back you one hundred percent."

"I expect you will." Ket narrows his eyes at him. "Because don't forget—your freedom hinges on our king's crusade. And pardon me if I'm mistaken, but you appear to be a man who relishes his freedom."

Something in Jester's eyes tells him he's right, though the fool doesn't speak a word.

———

AT DUSK, a small village with a stone statue of an archer outside their wooden gates comes steadily into view. The statue is weatherworn, the details of the archer's face and clothing washed away by storms and time. Ket dismounts his horse, strolls over to the gate's wooden window and knocks three times. The window slides open and a bearded face appears, sporting two squinting eyes.

Jester stays on his horse, allowing Ket to do the talking, as was agreed upon before their journey began. His scalp wound itches something fierce, and he picks at the headscarf he's wrapped around it, which also conceals his funny new accessory—his colorful jester hat, bells and all. As he scratches, the bells jingle softly against the fabric, not loud enough for Ket or the gatekeeper to hear.

"What business brings you to the humble village of Toutin?" the gatekeeper asks. This type of questioning is common among private villages throughout the Five Realms—places like this vet strangers before welcoming them past their gates. Helps keep ruffians and swindlers from preying on their simple ways of life.

Ket seems to have forgotten this because his tongue is having trouble coming up with a viable answer. "We...uh...have come to..."

The gatekeeper squints harder, and Jester wonders how many more stuttering seconds Ket has before the man disappears behind the sliding window and calls the village's cavalry. Jester was looking forward to not spending the night on the road. It's hard to sleep when some man or beast could sneak up on you in the dark, murder you while you wade deeper into pleasant dreams.

Nah, Jester is not into that at all.

"We are scribes," Jester announces from his position on the horse.

"What?" the gatekeeper asks. "I cannot hear you!"

Jester pulls down the cloth bandage masking his face wounds, just enough to project his voice but not enough to reveal his disfigurement. "We are scribes, writers of the Five Realms. We are traveling from town to town, documenting our journeys for the annals of history."

The gatekeeper seems impressed. "Really? Celebrity writers? In Toutin? What a surprise!"

Jester rolls his eyes. "We are not celebrities—not yet anyway. Maybe once we're published authors, we'll see. But we do not write for fame or fortune, my friend. We write because there are stories that need to be told, and there are people who enjoy hearing them."

The man barks with excitement. "Ha! May I see your documents?"

Ket, eyeing Jester over his shoulder like he can't believe Jester had the skill to improvise like that, hands over his papers. The man checks them, finds no faults, and then hands them back to Ket without even requesting to see Jester's.

This man is a total shove-over, Jester thinks, *honest-to-Highbeard, the worst gatekeeper I've ever come across.*

The man opens the gate and lets them in. Jester dismounts, and the two travelers walk their horses to the nearest tavern.

Once inside, the warmth from the active hearth and boisterous crowd falls upon their skin at once. Ket loosens the buttons on his jacket as he heads toward the nearest free table. Jester follows him, eyeing the patrons as they kick back ales in towering mugs and stuff their faces full of greasy meats, smashed potatoes, and crisp vegetables. His stomach growls at the prospect of a decent meal.

A waitress dances over to their table a few minutes later. She puts her quill to her parchment, and asks, "What will it be to drink for you gents?"

"An ale," Ket says without skipping a beat. "Tall one."

"Aye, and for you?"

Jester squints. "Water for me."

"Anything else?"

"Bread and butter to start, love." She jots this down too. Jester clears his throat. "Are you familiar with the area?"

The waitress squints, then smiles curiously. "Yes. Lived in Toutin my whole life. Why do you ask, stranger?"

"Looking for a medic," Jester says, ignoring Ket's stare. "Any medic will do. Although I prefer someone proficient in surgeries."

The girl closes one eye, puts a hand on her hip. "I think…nope. No one in Toutin comes to mind. You'll want to travel up to River-spell for that. Good doctors there. And everyone will be in town tomorrow for the big festival there, so you'll have your pick."

"Festival?" Jester grins behind his cloth covering. "Oh, I do love a fancy occasion."

"Then you should be in attendance. Food, games, dancing— it's quite the annual festivity. King Ragland himself attended no less than a few years back."

"Really? The king?"

"Swear it on my father's grave," the girl says, raising one hand in the air and folding the other across her heart.

"Well, if it's enough to get that old fart off his stool and traveling that far north, then I suspect it's good enough for me." He winks at the waitress, who giggles at the mention of "king" and "fart" being used in proximity to one another. "Thank you, love."

"My pleasure. I'll be back with your drinks and bread in two shakes of a whore's tit."

After she's gone, Jester rotates to Ket, feeling his smile reach his eyes. "I think I'm in love."

"Calm yourself."

"I'm serious. If I was a bit younger and less scary-looking, I'd bend my knee and ask her hand in marriage this evening."

"A medic?" Ket says, ignoring Jester's antics. "What do you need a medic for?"

"In case you've forgotten," he replies, peeling back the fabric that's sticking to the stitched flesh, "I have fresh wounds that need attention. Those sons of bitches Ragland sicked on me were hardly professional surgeons, and they didn't provide me with any healing potions. Unless you have a magic wand hiding up that tight ass of yours, then I'd say I need a medic. A doctor of some sort. Just to prevent infection."

"You'll need some worm root and clean water," Ket says, then looks over his shoulder like there's something more important happening.

"Ah, you continue to impress me with your wisdom, man of mystery. Were you a medic in the northern army, is that it?"

"Not a medic," Ket says.

"Hmm. Just seen your fair share of injuries then?"

"I don't wish to discuss my past, if it pleases you."

"It doesn't please me one bit, but I have decency and will respect your wishes. Besides…a godlike tingle tells me I'll come to know all about Ket Norlath before our adventure ends."

Ket keeps silent and scans the room like he's waiting for something to go wrong. Or someone to attack them. The man hasn't let down his guard since they left Ragland's castle.

"You look disquieted," Jester says, pretending to sound like a concerned friend. "We're safe here."

"Are we?"

Something in his voice sounds off. Jester can't touch on what it is. "What do you see?"

"Three men. On the other side of the bar. Came in after us. Haven't taken their eyes off us."

Jester moves his head to—

"Don't look," Ket grumbles. "Not directly."

Jester freezes. Tenses. Takes a deep breath and fiddles with the napkin in front of him. The waitress comes back and plants their drinks on the table. She's back three seconds later with the bread.

Jester doesn't hesitate and digs in first.

"See them?" Ket asks, waiting until Jester is done filling his plate with a portion of bread before sinking his fingers into the wicker basket. "Three goons. Dark clothing. Looks like they aren't here solely for food and drink."

"No one else on the Long Green Road," Jester says confidently. "I would have noticed."

"They are definitely watching us."

"Rangers in Ragland's employ? To protect his investment? Making sure we don't run off at the first breath of fresh air?"

Ket shakes his head. "I don't think so. I can't put my finger on what they might want, but I don't much like it."

"Perhaps they are ordinary bandits looking for a mark."

"Do we look like easy marks?" Ket cocks his brow. "I may have half the strength I once possessed, but I assure you I have not lost my height. And you—though bony and weird-looking—"

"Weird-looking?"

"—you don't exactly spell out an easy target."

"I'm offended, sir."

"You don't look offended."

"Fine, I'm *not* offended per se. I guess I do look weird to some, even before those maniacs scalped me, but that's not the point."

"What is the point?"

"Point is, no one likes being told they look weird. Have some decency, man."

Ket leans across the table, agitated. "I don't have time for decency. My sons are—"

"Yes, yes," Jester says, then yawns rather loudly. "We're aware of your predicament—no need to preach to me. You will see your sons again, but only—and I do mean *only*—if you listen and do exactly what I say when the situation calls for it."

Ket's sour face doesn't twitch.

"You've been gone from this world a long time, Mr. Norlath—two years in prison, and trapped on some farm for a decade more before your incarceration. You will need me to see you through it. To guide you."

Ket digests Jester's words, then picks up the bread. He bites off a chunk and then starts chewing like a grazing cow. "I don't like anything about those men."

"Those men are fine, I can handle them."

Ket stops chewing. "Handle them?"

"Yes—I know who they are and what they are doing here."

Ket slowly swallows his mouthful. "You do?"

"Uh-huh. They're here for me. They want to kill me."

KET ISN'T SHOCKED by the news. If he had been forced to wager, he would have put good coin down on the three men being there for the jester. Jester seems like the kind to have a great number of enemies, his personality likely to attract an unrelenting manhunt.

Ket and Jester order their food when the waitress comes back. It takes fifteen minutes for the cook to prepare their meals, and fifteen minutes later the men have plates of roasted duck and carrots and fresh asparagus sitting before them.

Ket's mouth waters. It's been so long since he's eaten real food that he has almost forgotten what it tastes like. The duck is juicy, and the sweet meaty flavor sits in his mouth for several moments before he decides it's time to swallow.

"Nothing like a fine meal to kick off an adventure," Jester says, eating half his plate before Ket takes his first few bites. He opts to only pull down his face covering to put food in his mouth, and hikes the cloth back up over his ugly smile while chewing.

"What are you planning to do with those men?" Ket asks eagerly. The three bastards cloaked in black have not let up their icy staring.

"Oh, them?" Jester asks as if he's forgotten them. "I will lure them outside into some dark alley and have my way with them."

Ket cocks a brow.

"Kill them, you fool," Jester clarifies. "Not fuck them. You are a dirty bird of the highest order."

"I didn't suggest anything of the sort." Ket shoves another strip of duck meat into his mouth. He's eating faster now, the anxiety of having three men gaze upon their table really settling in. "How will you kill them?"

Jester sets down his knife and fork gently on the edge of the plate. "My dear friend—please understand, even though I was captured trying to kill a king and you witnessed me at my worst professional moment, I am quite good at what I do. I will dispatch those men quicker than a whore disrobes her gown for top coin."

"You seem to have an affinity for whore metaphors. Are you sure you are not the dirty bird who soars?"

Jester's eyes shine with delight. "Well, call me guilty. Now…" Jester shovels the remaining food into his mouth, swallows, then pushes himself up from the table. "Allow me to take my leave."

"If you don't come back, should I come look for you?"

With a cunning look in his eyes, Jester replies, "I will come back."

"But if you don't?"

"You have a hearing problem, Ket Norlath? I said I will come back."

With that, Jester turns for the front door, but not before slipping the waitress a personal tip of two coins in the front pocket of her apron.

Ket smirks. Then watches the three men get up one by one, fall in a single line, and head to the door. After his new friend.

TOUTIN

CHAPTER THREE

"It is forbidden to attempt an assassination of any royal party without the express written agreement from the Grandmaster. To break this sacred oath is to invite death."

– CODE OF THE CIRCLE OF SLAYERS

JESTER MOVES INTO THE NIGHT, slinking through the small town of Toutin like a mouse through a maze in search of a treat, only Jester does not follow the scent of cheese. Here, no pleasant aromas exist; only horse stink, shit, piss, and vomit from idiots who couldn't handle their wines or ales. Laughter echoes down the streets. Passing drunks stumble across his path, missing contact with Jester by mere inches. Behind his mask his face sours, unable to comprehend how someone could leave themselves so vulnerable to pickpockets. Drunken minds are the easiest prey, and there are countless predators in this part of the world, near the edges of Owlton, closer to the Crosslands' border.

He glances over his shoulder, sees the three shadows continuing to follow him. He figures they will trail him all the way to the Silver Towers if he'd let them. But it's probably best to end this song and dance before it hits the first chorus.

Jester dashes down the closest alleyway, dark enough for dark deeds.

The men hustle forth and enter the mouth of the alley, from which there is no escape. The tallest pursuer wheezes, a sure sign of chronic blacklung, pinpointing his exact location. The thickest man staggers on a wobbly right leg, waddling like some extinct ice bird. The third member might have some skill. But his brisk movements show no concern for the environment. The back wall of the alley, layered in shadows, is much too smooth to climb. The soft earth absorbs his footsteps. No one will hear them here. And that will make them confident.

Oh yes, let them come.

Laughter from one of the men reaches the alley, finds Jester's ears. Smiling beneath his covering, Jester turns to them. The trio forms a line, blocking any potential escape. One of them holds a lantern, shooing away some of the darkness the alley provides.

"Well, well," the laughing man says, and Jester wonders how long the bastard's good mood will last—not long if he has his way. "If it isn't our old pal."

"Gentlemen," Jester says, and he can't tell if they can see him yet, if the lantern's glow is in range to pick up his appearance, but he bows to them anyway. "How may I be of service?"

"Been waiting a long time for this, you yellow bastard."

Yellow? Coward? These are names, he thinks, that do not suit him. He's many things, but a coward isn't one of them—if it were true, he'd have tried plunging that knife into Ragland's back, not tried slitting his throat from the front while he looked the king in the eyes.

"You went ahead and pissed off the baron, good and plenty," another one of the men adds. "Trying to kickstart a war on his behalf, huh? Tsk, tsk, Tent. You should know better."

"Honestly," the third man says, sleepily, almost as if he's bored of this rigmarole, "we're surprised Ragland let you free. We were sure he was gonna kill you. Would have spared us the trouble of hunting you down."

"Well, you know how it is," Jester says, walking toward the tangerine glow of the lantern, peeling back his cowl and tugging on the bandages of his face mask, revealing his fresh new look. "I have a filthy habit of staying alive."

He can see the men's faces now, and he can see in their eyes that they see his. The horror and shock as they gaze upon his seamed flesh flashes like a ripple across their faces. Their expressions surprise him. Surely the men have looked upon faces in worse condition, the victims of their own handiwork. But Jester's face has gotten to the core of them. Something about the stitching must sicken them because the confidence they strolled in here with has all but evaporated.

Jester revels in their disgust. It gives him a distraction, precious seconds he uses to free the blade strapped to his hip, angling it in a perfect position.

"Highbeard's ghost," curses one of the men. "What have they done to yer face?"

"Are we sure we even have the right man?" another says, chortling. "I mean, he doesn't look like—"

"It's him," the wheezy one confirms, swallowing his revulsion and drawing his long blade. "Come now. Let's not dally, and finish what Ragland's incompetent mercenaries should have done weeks ago."

They rush Jester just like he anticipated: swords out and all angled for the center of his heart. Jester's ready for them. He takes the first sword strike and knocks the blade aside, then plunges the arched metal of his knife into the chest of the lead attacker. The man's eyes go wide as he spits a gout of blood. Jester maneuvers the dying body in front of him, using the fresh corpse as a shield against the other attackers.

"Get him!" shouts the thickest one as he lunges at Jester, ignoring the presence of the human shield, striking as if there is no barrier there at all.

Jester flings the stabbed man aside, sending him tumbling through the darkness, where the lantern light cannot reach. Both swordsmen charge forth, and Jester has no choice but to retreat—only a few steps. Once the men are fully engaged and their balance committed to their forward rush, Jester hops to the side of the bandit on his right. Quickly, he stabs the man in the gut, spilling dark red down his trousers. Blood leaks like an uncorked wine barrel. The man staggers, spinning in tight circles, his free hand clenching his stomach, desperately holding himself together, his teeth bared, eyes glassy, as he swings his sword in desperate retaliation, a weak attempt, and Jester easily sidesteps out of danger.

He won't try that again, I wager, Jester thinks, winking as the dead man mindlessly tramples through some alley trash.

The other man has rounded him, gaining free access to his back. Jester senses his movement the way an elderly deer might an unseasoned bow hunter, the sole of his attacker's boot sticking to the muddy alleyway. Jester turns in time to block the sword from cleaving through his spine.

"Die, you bastard!" the man shouts angrily. Jester holds the blade against his own, pushing against the man's strength, then drops to his knees, releasing his own dagger, which falls to his other hand. The man's downward swing has lost almost all its momentum; it bites into Jester's leather tunic near his shoulder but doesn't penetrate the mail beneath. Jester shrugs off the blow and thrusts his blade into the assailant's groin. The howl that erupts from the man's lips reminds him of a mother wolf pining over a lost cub. His blade falling to the alley's muddy terrain cannot be heard over his hysterical shrieking. Jester ends his loud outburst with a quick slash across his throat, opening a shallow trench that vomits a healthy stream of bloodfall into Jester's face. He doesn't mind and casually cleans the mess with his sleeve. Turns and—

The pain registers before he realizes where it's come from, before he can assess what has happened. He looks down and sees the sword. Not just *in* him, but *through* him. The third attacker—the one he'd temporarily ignored—has buried the sword in his abdomen all the way to the hilt.

Jester tries to raise his arm, hoping to get the knife to the man's throat before he can withdraw the blade and run it through him again, but he can't even get the blade above his waist before his strength ebbs, leaving him numb, shaking, and utterly powerless. The knife slips from his fingertips, disappearing into the darkness below. His whole existence loses its corporeal feel. The world grows weightless, everything liquid, loose, the twilight sky fading into darker territories.

Light from the lantern fades. Jester tries to speak, but his thoughts form no words, and moving his lips becomes a riddle his body is incapable of solving.

"You will die, oathbreaker, like the filthy, mangy dog you are," the assassin whispers in his ear as he finally withdraws his weapon from Jester's body. He feels *that*: every inch of metal sliding out of him.

Footfalls, the sucking of mud. Behind him. Coming fast.

His killer's eyes widen. "What the—"

Jester falls on his back, losing his grip on the conscious world, but fighting to stay alive long enough to see what has spooked his murderer.

A tall man with dark skin emerges from the shadows, and Jester recognizes the man, even if his eyes and the alleyway's dusk will not allow a clearer view. Ket Norlath. Come to save him.

Can't save me, he thinks.

I'm already dead.

Before Jester closes his eyes and succumbs to that long sleep, Ket runs a blade up and through the man whose hands are saturated with Jester's blood. Ket's sword pokes through the murderer's back, and the bastard makes a short, shrill scream that seems final—like that's the last sound he'll ever make.

Then the lights go out.

For a good long time.

———

WHEN HE WAKES HOURS LATER, dizzy and nauseous, Jester believes death has crept inside him and sought refuge in his bones. If it weren't for the glow of at least thirteen candles, he would have assumed himself dead, sentenced to dwell in some dark cavernous afterlife for the rest of eternity.

But I am dead. I watched myself die.

That clearly isn't the case. Because here he sits in the material world, staring up at Ket Norlath, his own personal knight in shining armor—minus the knightly status and the effects associated with such a prestigious title.

"You're awake," Ket says. "And alive." He sounds surprised. But not entirely.

Jester opens his mouth to speak, but Ket wags his finger. Not quite scolding him; more like a recommendation to keep silent.

"Rest. I borrowed thread and a needle from a woman down the hall. I'm not the best seamstress, but I managed to patch it up well enough to get through the night. Tomorrow we will need to find medicine and a proper doctor. When the first cock crows, we head into Riverspell."

Jester nods, remembering what the waitress said about Riverspell, the festival taking place tomorrow. That there will be doctors present.

"Was able to scavenge some mintbush to help ease the pain. It will wear off, but it should help you sleep."

Jester winks at him—it's practically the only movement his body will allow. He feels like a stiff piece of wood, not a single flexible muscle in his body. But a wink will do. It lets him know he's grateful for Ket saving his life. Though, tomorrow he may wish differently. And that gets him thinking about death and how much he wouldn't care even if he died. He's lived a full life. Checked all the boxes he's wanted to since sixteen years old. Since he was old enough to care about life. He's drunk good ales, smoked the finest and purest starleaf in Endlia. Hiked the great mountain ranges in Elmoria. Bathed under the majestic high waterfalls of Springgaarden. Made love to beautiful women and handsome men. Killed evil lords and slavemasters, plenty of them. Philosophized with Endlia's brightest scholars about the nature of the gods, the worlds, and all the places humans hold dear in the chasm called life.

A full life lived indeed.

"Sleep now," Ket says, and then gets up to blow out the candles. The room quickly falls under the spell of night. "Sleep."

The next thing Jester knows he's slipped into a dream, swimming through the depths of the ethereal springs of lands unknown.

———

KET SLIPS out of the room and back into the tavern, where the leftover drunks and townsfolk—who are in no hurry to head back home to their partners—still dance, and laugh, and gluttonously shove more food and ale down their gullets.

He heads out the tavern door, back into town, in search of the dark alley where Jester claimed two lives, and Ket himself ended one. Or…*almost* ended one. When he returns, the bastard is still in the same spot—hogtied, a sock strategically stuffed in his mouth, muffling any cries for help. Luckily, the sword Ket ran through his chest didn't kill him. Only left him bleeding, badly, a fatal wound, eventually. But the eternal black tide has not swept him under just yet.

Ket sits the man up and props him against the side of some barn wall. Carefully, he removes the cotton from the man's mouth. When the man's eyes flutter and his gaze falters, Ket slaps his cheeks, twice. When the man doesn't react, Ket cracks him harder. The strike sobers the man quickly. Angers him. His eyes become red like the blood leaking from his chest.

"Wake up, filth," Ket says.

The man grunts.

"I need answers, and you will provide them to me."

The man doesn't seem inclined to answer a damn thing. Ket sticks his finger in the hole where the sword tunneled through his body. The man howls, and Ket places his hand over the sock to help contain the sound.

"I will get my answers," Ket says, barking with confidence. "Because there isn't a bone in your body I can't break, and holding your tongue will start the snapping."

"What...do you want?" the man rasps. Blood fills his mouth; each word sounds wet. "You're nothing...a traitor...to your true king."

The comment hits Ket deeper in his heart than he would care to acknowledge. "Do you know who I am?"

The man hesitates, studies Ket, reading his eyes like a promise. But after he's done assessing, the man shakes his head. "No. Jail rat. If you're traveling with Tent, you're the worst kind of...scum. The dregs of the trough."

"Tent?" Ket tilts his head to the side. "Is that his name?"

The man throws his head back and laughs. His pain cuts his humorous outburst short. Wincing, the man shifts back into a more comfortable position. " You didn't know? What did he bribe you with? The Thousand Riches of the Decode?"

"I know of no such riches. What do you mean *bribe?*" Ket grips the man by his throat, hating the way the man seems to be enjoying this exchange—Ket's lack of knowledge. He's toying with him, intentionally letting this conversation drag. Ket squeezes his throat, hard enough to close his airway. "What do you know of our mission? And who sent you to kill us?"

The man wheezes the second Ket lets go. After a spell, he regains his breath, but it takes longer than it should. "Mission? I know of no mission." He holds his chest like he's securing a newborn baby close to his heart. "We were sent by the Warden of Iradon."

"Who?"

"Warden...of Iradon."

"I heard you the first time. I don't know who that is."

The man offers a weak smile. His eyelids flutter, the heaviness of his eyes weighing him down. "Lucky for you."

"Why does he want us dead?"

"Not you. Him."

"Why does he want…Tent, you called him? Why does he want Tent dead?"

"Lots of reasons. Money. Love."

"Love?" Ket shakes his head, unable to comprehend. "What does love have to do with any of this?"

"Tent fucked…Warden's wife…Often."

Ket bites his lip. "An adulterer."

"Trying to kill…King…didn't help, either."

Ket nods.

"If what you…what you say is true," the man says, taking deep breaths and trying to absorb every available puff of air, wheezing while doing so, "and you don't know Tent, understand him…then…keep far, far away. Or let him die. His wound…worse than mine."

Ket glances down at the blood leaking from the wound; the red has run black. Something vital was pierced. "Not quite as serious, I'm afraid. I've gone and skewered your liver. Your organs are shutting down. You'll be dead in less than five minutes."

"You are…mysterious. I cannot…see…future in your eyes, but…your past…your past is very dark."

"You're a clairvoyant now, that it?"

"Maybe once…but like you…my past is…dead…buried…a long time ago." The man suddenly stiffens, his teeth clenched, his eyes squinted, his legs tremoring as he slumps forward. Ket remains squatted, holding his features as still as stone. The man's last breaths are short and desperate. His rheumy eyes snap up to stare at his killer. As one last shudder rides through him, Ket grips his hand until he passes.

Once gone, Ket closes the man's eyes, unable to stand the sight of the corpse looking up at him. When children come frolicking down this alleyway tomorrow, they won't have to witness his death stare.

He stands, walks back to the main road, and debates taking the man's advice, leaving Jester behind, for dead.

Something makes him turn back to the inn. Fate maybe. Though, Ket hardly believes in such things.

Ket believes in choices and consequences, and he's living proof that the gods control nothing; that humans are the only ones who influence their own destiny.

He'd bet every coin on that philosophy. He'd bet his life.

FESTIVAL
CHAPTER FOUR

"There's nothing better than a festival to praise the gods; it's good family fun, and promotes healthy worship. In Highbeard's *Good Book*, the god demands at least one festival per calendar year."

- MENYARD MINOTOA, *THE GOD SYSTEM*

———

AS THE SUN rises over the horizon and scatters gold over Endlia, Ket Norlath finishes re-saddling his and Jester's horses. The injured assassin still hasn't roused from his near-death slumber, and Ket hesitates waking him. But the time has come to move on from Toutin and head for Riverspell.

Re-entering the room, Ket inches toward the dying man, his chest rising and falling like wee waves breaking against the sandy shores of the End Lakes. He places a hand on Jester's shoulder and shoves, hoping to wake him. Alas, the man continues to snooze.

Ket peels back the bedsheets to inspect the bandaged wound. It looks no worse than the previous night, but it doesn't look better either, nor infected, and only time will tell the whole story.

Ket fears medical intervention is needed, and soon. He's seen men die from shallower stab wounds.

"Wake up," Ket says, shoving him again.

Nothing. But Jester's body is warm, and his wrist has a pulse.

Another push, Ket fully extending his arms now, moving Jester's body considerably. The man's eyes flutter. Twitch. But he remains somnolent.

"Goddammit," Ket swears, then grabs a cup of water from the dresser and splashes it across Jester's face. The water hits like a smack, and Jester splutters in a state of shock and fury.

"What-the-fuck?!" Jester bounces to a seated position. The mintbush must have worn off, because Jester grunts, grimaces, and holds a hand over the bandage. "Highbeard's weathered cunt, what the fuck happened last night?"

"You were stabbed by three men in an alley."

"Yes, I vaguely remember that, before the night terrors began." Jester's cheeks suddenly swell, and he tilts his head to the side as a stream of vomit shoots forth, dousing the bedsheets in a sticky, tan-colored puddle. The smell of acid—pure bile—floods Ket's senses.

"Lovely," Ket says, making his way across the room, where Jester's clothes are stashed on the dresser. "Can you dress yourself?"

Jester shakingly nods.

"Good. I'll meet you downstairs in five minutes. We ride to Riverspell, to see a doctor about your wounds. You need treatment I cannot give you."

Jester looks displeased with this news—either that, or he's thinking about puking again.

"I'll leave you to it," Ket says, and then exits the room.

———

THEY TAKE the Long Green Road all the way to Riverspell. Once close to the small town—bigger than Toutin, but only by a rabbit's hair—Ket smells the festival on the blowing southwest winds: baked dough, sour cakes, buttered corn, and the collective stench of sweaty, shitting horses. The roar of the crowd grows louder, and the sound of a lance connecting with a shield rings out, as the spectators go wild for the sport.

"Oh goody," Jester says weakly. "A tournament. My favorite." Ket can't tell if the man is being a sarcastic bastard or not—he's looking much too sick to display a tell.

"You should keep quiet here. Let me do the talking."

"Because you were so good last time," Jester quips, remarkably sharp considering his situation.

"Try not to puke on the guards."

"Yes, *father*."

They round the path's next corner, the gates of Riverspell looming before them. Two guards stand stationed in front of the gates, each gripping long swords, their ends speared into the ground. The guards are dressed in knightly armor from helm to boot. Shiny metal, too. Expensive. Not the kind of armor typically worn in battle, Ket would bet his last two coins on it. This exterior wear is for show only.

When he approaches, the men raise their swords and form a line across the gate's opening.

"Morning, fellows," Ket says jubilantly, summoning the strength to sound like a chipper young adventurer, looking for a good festival to attend. "We were told by a young woman in Toutin that today's festival is not to be missed."

The guards opt for silence, keeping their hands steady on their swords' pommels, offering no welcome or challenge. Ket's attention flicks upwards. Above them, standing in the center of the cross-bridge that runs behind the gate's doors, a man dressed in a fancy robe, purple and white swirling patterns running throughout the fabric, crosses his arms. Clean-shaven, with long graying hair and a nose reminiscent of the trolls in popular fairy tales, Ket wonders if he'll shout down riddles for them to solve.

"State your name, your business," the man says, his voice not unwelcoming, but not exactly warm either. Ket wonders if the other attendees endured this line of questioning upon their arrival.

"My name is Ket Norlath, and my business is the festival taking place beyond your gates." Ket swallows, hoping that's enough to satisfy them, but knowing deep down, things can't go that smoothly. Not for him.

"And your friend?"

Ket glances over at Jester, who can barely keep himself upright in his saddle.

"My friend is…is…his name is Tent."

Jester perks up as if someone broke open a strong salt pellet under his nose. His eyes shoot wide, his complexion white, draining of color. A part of Ket realizes he picked the wrong damn time to divulge that knowledge, and for a second, he believes Jester will turn his horse around and gallop off in the opposite direction, take his chances in the wild rather than seek the medicine available in town.

"Tent?" the gatekeeper says, licking his lips, tasting the name on his tongue, unsure of the flavor it represents. "Strange name. But then again. You look like strange folk."

"We're not so strange. We come from Hornrake. We are guests of the king. We have paperwork to prove our status. If it pleases you, of course."

Just the very mention of Hornrake, the king, and official documents changes the man's outward perception. The gatekeeper's lips morph into a thin smile.

"Royal folk! How magnificent! Just, um…" His expression sours for a beat. "Why is Tent there concealing his face? He's not sick with weasel bumps, is he? We cannot afford any type of outbreak in Riverspell, god freak ya."

"Not sick," Ket answers for him. "He was disfigured in the Last War and prefers not to scare anyone by his appearance. Children sometimes get spooked by his look, though they shouldn't be. A scar is not a disfigurement—a scar is a story waiting to be told."

The gatekeeper seems appeased by this nugget of wisdom, his apprehension abating. "A scar is a story, yes. Yes, I like that very much. Fine then! Guards!" The men remove their hands from their sword hilts. "Open!"

The gears on the gateway begin to turn and grind on rusty wheels, screeching and groaning. The gate opens and the entranceway of the town is revealed, fully stocked with townsfolk ready to enjoy an afternoon of jousting and carnival foods and games to win prizes.

Ket bows to the man for allowing them passage, then clicks his heels against his horse's ribs. He senses Jester's hesitance to follow, but after Ket passes through unharmed, Jester speeds ahead and catches up.

"Full of surprises you are, Ket Norlath," Jester whispers.

The gatekeeper climbs down the ladder on the east end of the cross-bridge, and waddles over to Ket's horse. He gives the gelding a loving pat on the nose, then requests the aforementioned paperwork. Ket provides the materials without any comment, and the gatekeeper inspects them with a close eye.

When he hands the papers back, he says, "Apologies for the tight security—we've had many threats lately, and this festival is a big event for our town. We want to ensure everything goes as planned."

Ket puts up a hand as if to say, *It's no problem at all.* "Seems like all of Endlia is on edge lately."

"Can't be too cautious with rumors of Arkos's witchmen on the loose. Witchwomen too! Heard whispers of a secret coven in the woods not more than three miles west of here. Witches! In our time! Can you believe it?"

"Aye," Ket says, as if he's caught wind of the same rumors himself. "Can't be too certain of anything in these dark times."

"Amen to that, brother of Highbeard."

Ket gives a respectful half-bow once again, then asks, "Where can one find a doctor in Riverspell?"

"A doctor? What for? You two look healthier than the horses you're planted on. Unless—I dare not to accuse a man of such a thing twice, but—is he sick?"

"I assure you, again, that my friend here is fine in that regard. No, it's me—I've come down with a splitting headache. Long rides get to me sometimes. Looking for something to ease this small suffering."

"Ah! I get the head splits too! Doctors tell me it's the tobacco, but shush! What do they know, right?"

"I say 'smoke if you have them'."

"Fucking right-o." The gatekeeper squints, points down the path that winds around some trees, bending toward the center of town. "Doctor Mellick is just down the row, a few establishments that way, just past the Rusty Hook Inn. You should find him there, unless he's taken the day off to be with his family during the festival. In that case, good luck finding him in that crowd!"

Ket nods ahead. "Are there alternative options? Doctors, I mean. Should we be unable to locate him."

Gatekeeper shrugs, indifferent to the idea. "Maybe! But Doctor Mellick is the only one I'd trust, even for a simple lousy headache."

The gatekeeper half-bends a knee, bows his head, then jogs off back to his post.

"How are you feeling?" Ket says, rotating to Jester once the man and his guards have wandered out of earshot.

"Feel like a bucket of gold coins."

"Liar."

"You called me *Tent*. Why?"

Ket sighs, realizing now what a mistake it was mentioning the man's real name—for more than one reason. "Perhaps we will discuss that later. After we get you well."

Tabling the discussion for now, Ket rides down the path

leading to the town's center, where the cries and jeers from the festival reach their ears.

The festival sounds like it's in full swing.

And it sounds like a party not to be missed.

———

IT'S BOTHERING HIM. Like a toothache, a nagging distraction that won't go away. *Ket must have interrogated one of the assassins whilst I was passed out.*

Damn him.

He follows Ket into the center of town, where a large fountain statue rests, three Highbeard angels made of mortar stone, stacked atop each other, each one spitting a stream of water in a different direction. A place for children to toss low-value silver coins and make silly wishes. Jester fleetingly considers how many silver coins he could scavenge from the bottom before someone notices. He refrains, due to the waves of nausea crashing through him—all he wants to do is sit, close his eyes, and wait for the sick sensation to pass.

Ket weaves them through the pedestrian traffic, searching for a hitching post.

Shortly after they pass the fountain, they detour through a sparse patch of woods that divides the town in half and pull the horses up to some empty posts outside a small inn. It's off the main road, with far fewer pedestrians.

After the horses are settled, Ket extends his hand to Jester. "Think you can walk?"

"I don't know. Don't feel all that great." It's the truth—mostly. The pain ebbs and flows, its intensity varying, but the most concerning aspect is how far the pain has reached, hitting nerves nowhere near the source. Of course, the more he moves, the more everything hurts.

"You can wait here then. I'll acquire the medicine from the doctor and bring it back."

Jester nods, agreeing with the plan, and watches Ket slink off back toward the center of town. Once he's gone, Jester slumps in the saddle.

Why did Ket care enough to double back and interrogate the baron's henchman? What difference did it make?

Ket's sudden interest in Jester's past, his identity, has him wondering if he should skedaddle, make off into the woods and take his chances as a lonesome survivor—a part he's played for the better part of his life and, hey, it's worked out well so far. The Patient Mountains are not far. He could make a living there, carve out a home in the tunnel systems, if they don't already belong to carnivorous creatures or Wilders. A harsh living, but it would keep him safe from the bastard sons of Iradon who have already caught the scent of his trail.

They were watching me. This whole time, while I was imprisoned, they were watching me…

Jester hates himself for getting into this mess, his carelessness, for picking the wrong time to act upon his murderous tendencies —although, there really is never a *good* time to start a new war in the Five Realms.

Sleep calls to him, his eyelids dragging, the lure of dreams too strong to ignore. He shuts his eyes for a second, just to sample the lightless realm that beckons him, then finds himself unable to look away from that welcoming twilight.

———

KET WALKS through the streets of Riverspell, weaving between the merry folk who act as though they've never attended a festival before, everyone shouting and cheering and clapping along with the rhythm of performed music—the angelic tunes of simultaneous lutes and the beat of the tom-toms, their sounds rising above chipper conversations and drunken celebrations. Some flat-footed drunkard spills half an ale into Ket's chest as he stumbles past, and Ket resists the urge to make him eat the pint glass. The man apologizes after he catches Ket's menacing gaze, then disappears back through the crowd in search of the wagon that sells refills. Ket has a taste for the ale after last night's sampling, but now is not the time for a drink. It's time to find the doctor, start Jester's healing, and then get themselves back on the road, heading north.

My sons are waiting for me.

He hasn't ruled out the idea he's being double-crossed by the king. If he returns to the king's court with the star-eyed boy in hand or Salah's head in a basket, and then discovers his boys have been dead the whole time, he'll bring Highbeard's wrath down upon Ragland's kingdom. He vows it.

Once he's back near the town's center and makes his way around its fountain, he asks for directions to Doctor Mellick's. Some of the townsfolk look at him stupidly, surprised he's even asking such a thing. Drunken responses, mostly. Some sober individuals point in some nonspecific direction. One woman who seems like she's the helpful sort doesn't verbalize, but holds her finger in the air, pointing east. He tries to follow the woman's finger through the crowd, sees a few structures that look like several houses strung together. He thanks her, then squeezes his way through the massive throng.

One house has a door marked with a red bird wing, the Endlian symbol for renewed health. He strolls up to the door and grabs the handle.

"No one's home," a small voice alerts him.

Ket tries the door anyway but finds it locked. He spins in the direction of the voice. A girl, no more than sixteen years of age, stands at the end of the housing row, her straw-blond hair tucked beneath her hand-knitted cowl. A wagon and two horses take up the space behind her; an older man—maybe the girl's grandfather—sits at the end of the wagon's gate. Boxes of supplies lie open near the landing, and Ket can see prices scrawled on tags attached to each of the items.

Traveling peddlers.

Probably selling crap. Highbeard merchandise and cheap prayer books.

Yet they don't look like Highbeard faithfuls. Their garments are clean and colorful, not the pure white and gold colors typically worn by official members of the Church of Highbeard, and their loyal fanatics. The man's beard is clipped to a respectable length. The girl wears a red shirt beneath her peacock-colored shawl. A vine necklace and silver pendant hangs loosely from her neck. Both look like they have money to spare, which makes them prime targets for road bandits. Ket wonders if they're not travelers after all.

"Left about an hour ago, with his wife and child," the girl explains, walking toward him, her hands clasped together, almost like she's praying. But as she creeps closer, Ket can see she's cracking her knuckles. "Are you in need of a doctor? Of medicine?"

Ket doesn't have time for this. Tracking Mellick in this crowd is damn near impossible and getting anyone's full attention in this environment feels like a useless endeavor as well. As he scans the crowd for help, he realizes Jester is going to die.

So be it, he thinks, finding himself not at all upset about the prospect of making the journey to Rovan alone.

"I asked you a question, sir," the girl says, and even though it sounds like she's perturbed, she's smiling. "I would very much like to help you. You seem distraught. And there's kindness in your eyes."

He rotates toward her once again, returning a half-moon smile. "Perhaps you can find me a doctor then."

"Not likely in this ruckus. Most businesses of that sort are closed today."

"Of course." Ket throws up his hands, surrendering. "I bid you good day then, milady." He dips his head with respect.

"Wait," she says, reaching out with her hand and taking his. He almost recoils from her touch, but there's something…*nice* about it. Gentle. Amiable. "I can help you. Maybe. At least, I can try."

"Why?" It's a rude question, though honest. Usually, when peddlers are eager to help, it's not because they have anyone else's best interests in mind. The obvious strikes him—it's all about the gold coins in his pocket. Which he's not unwilling to part with if he can find professional help—not from some teenager possibly hocking Highbeard wares.

"Because...your soul is clean. And I enjoy helping good people."

What kind of bullshit is this girl shoveling? he thinks. Ket's soul is about as clean as a pig stall after a slop meal. He can't help but think this spiel has been rehearsed and performed a thousand times before.

"Respectfully, I don't have time for this. I need to find a doctor. My friend doesn't have much time, and you don't have anything you can sell me to—"

"I won't charge you a single silver piece," she says, and this line seems more genuine. "What ailment is your friend suffering from?"

He gazes at her, wishing he could see past her *I'm-an-innocent-girl* façade and see her for what she truly is, the angle she's playing. "Took a sword to his gut, pierced all the way through. The blade missed vital organs and his spine was not touched, but his wounds might be infected."

"Sounds like lady luck has touched him." She squints. "Just an infection then? Something to close the wounds?"

He nods.

She holds up a single finger. "Give me one minute."

The girl scampers back over to the wagon. She digs through the back of the cart, tossing items aside. To which the older man in the wagon whispers something to her. He doesn't look satisfied with her decision to help Ket, and Ket catches the man's eyes darting back and forth between whatever items the girl is messing with and Ket himself. Ket counts down the seconds, and the girl's minute has almost expired. Just when he's about to abandon her in favor of seeking a different solution, she pulls something out of the wagon, holds it up to the brilliant beams of daylight, and grins at what appears to be a phial of some powdery gray substance. She jogs back to him.

"What's this?" he asks, taking the phial from her fingers.

"A blend of a few different things, but mostly crushed phrivian leaves to help fight off the infection. Works immediately."

"Phrivian leaves?" The name is unfamiliar to him and sounds almost like a made-up word. "Never heard of them."

"Rare plants, found on the western edges of the Crosslands. They grow in bogs mostly."

"You're a greenlove then, is that it?"

Her eyes slim to slits. "Something like that."

"If this works, I shall return and pay you for your troubles in gold coin."

"There's no need. I wasn't lying when I said you have gentle eyes and your soul is clean. Even if you don't believe it yourself— it's the truth."

The words hit him somewhere deep in his chest. "My name is Ket, and thank you for the help."

"My name is Ralyanna. That's Borgadine," she says, directing her thumb back at the wagon, the man inside studying Ket as if he's a wild animal bearing his teeth. Ket flashes the old man a smile, hoping to put his concerns at ease.

It doesn't work.

"Peace be with you, Ralyanna," Ket says, and then turns toward the direction of his dying friend.

———

WHEN HE GETS BACK to the hitching posts, he finds Jester on the ground, passed out. Luckily the fall didn't break his body, nor did the horses accidentally step on him while he lay there. Ket runs over, scoops the man into his arms, and throws him over the saddle. He slaps Jester's cheeks three times, hard enough to wake him from his slumber. Slowly, he regains consciousness.

"Whaaa…" Jester murmurs, fighting waking. *"Where…am I?"*

"We're still in Riverspell, you mope. Can you stand?"

Jester winces, nods. Then tries to stand. His knees wobble, buckle, and Ket catches him before he falls to the ground.

"Infection is working your blood faster than I anticipated," Ket says. "Makes me wonder what those bounty hunters oiled their swords with."

Ket lifts Jester over his shoulder, carries him over to the side of the inn, and plants him in the grass, sitting him against the log siding. He rips open the man's shirt and tears off the old bandages. The smell from the exposed wound releases into the air, causing Ket to turn his head. He's smelled worse, but not in a long, long time. Sour, deathlike; the odor reaches the depths of his stomach and stirs up a throat-clenching wave of nausea.

"This may or may not burn," Ket warns him, then uncorks the phial. He sprinkles the gray dust over the wound that has grown to the size of an avocado pit. The dust melts on the injury with a sharp hiss. Smoke wafts up from the ruined, punctured flesh.

Jester recoils. Then flails. His eyes widen, and from behind his mask of filthy bandages, he cries out a long anguished mewl that reminds Ket of a cat getting its tail accidentally stepped on.

"Hold still," Ket says, sprinkling a second helping across the badly mutated flesh. "They definitely rubbed their swords against something sinister before attacking you."

The reaction isn't any better the second time around. Jester clenches and squirms, but Ket holds him rigorously still.

"Now —we have to attend to the hole in your back."

Jester shoots him an evil glare, one of hateful design. But knowing what must be done, he concedes.

He flips over, exposing the wound on his back. Ket repeats the process, watches the infected cavity absorb the dust, the gray powder working its way into the pink flesh beneath the black, ruined skin and muscle. After it's over and the remedy has been applied, Ket helps Jester back to his feet. He examines the puncture in his stomach and can't believe what he's seeing.

The wound has already begun to heal. The pus and yellow fluids that had seeped to the surface are almost gone. Though far from normal, at this rate, the wound should close and scab over by sundown. Ket applies new bandages.

Ket returns his curious eyes to the now empty phial. *What in Arkos's Darkhell was that?*

Jester's face scrunches with discomfort. "What kind of doctor did you procure this magic medicine from?"

"A girl…"

"A girl? Little girls can become full-fledged doctors now, aye? What a world."

"She had a man with her—her grandfather, I think. Not sure."

"Witches."

It's not an inquiry or a suggestion. Jester shrugs as if there is no other explanation. Witchcraft is often the best rationale when something unexplainable occurs. "Hold your tongue on the topic of witches," Ket whispers sharply, unable to ignore the twinge near his heart.

"Sore subject, I know. But still…for medication to work this fast…the ingredients can't be natural."

"She said they came from phrivian weeds or something. Some leaf I've never heard of."

"Hmm. Sounds like Witchspeak to me."

"Are you serious?"

Jester grimaces as he shifts into a new position, on his knees. "I have never heard of those leaves, and I consider myself something of a greenlove. But continue to deny the existence of witches, if it helps you sleep."

Ket doesn't know what he believes in, these days. "Can you ride on your own?"

"Yes," Jester hisses, climbing to his feet. He puts one weak foot in front of the other, walking like he's padding across a mud-stuck field, but continues his awkward pace until he reaches his horse. "Yes, I believe I can."

"Good, because I don't think—"

Ket is cut off by a shrill scream that slices through noise from the center of town, that reaches the inn. It's just one scream at first, but it multiplies quickly, drowning out the sounds of the celebration. Children's laughter, drunken adults yelling happily, and the music that makes one want to jump up and dance—all die off in an instant, replaced by madness, fear, and shrieking.

Ket looks over at Jester, and Jester returns the same look, his eyebrows raising.

"I was going to ask if you could introduce me to this witch-girl so I can request more magic powder—for old wounds and new— but I'm getting the notion we should leave Riverspell for good."

Metal strikes metal, and hooves beat upon hard soil. The cries of a town that has suddenly become a bloody battlefield, familiar and grim.

"I'll be right back," he says, drawing his sword.

"Oh, please don't—" Jester pleads, but Ket barely hears him.

He's already running full speed into the woods, back toward the center of Riverspell, when Jester curses his name and demands he return at once.

It's too late. The smell of blood has summoned him.

WHEN KET CRASHES through the brush and arrives on the dirt path leading back into town, he spots the outskirts of the ensuing pandemonium. Sprawling clouds of dust kick up from the hooves of desperate horses. Women flee, pulling their children into any nearby building, and a flood of people attempt to escape through the gates of the village. Some have completely abandoned their retreat and have thrown themselves on their knees, clasping their hands together, begging for the mercy of whatever villains have stormed their peaceful event. Ket stalks down the path, stepping over the dead. A woman runs into him at full speed, tears streaming down her eyes, sobbing without control. She bounces off him, eyes wide in shock, and then sprints off, screaming to her God to save her.

The gods won't interfere. Never do.

But Ket will.

As he moves closer to the center of town, the riders come into view. Twenty or thirty of them. Galloping through the madness. Well-armored and unarmored alike, dented breastplates and torn tunics. Mad horses, slicked with blood. Crooked swords and stone axes. Bared teeth underneath misshapen helms. Feral riders on stolen saddles, some bareback, screaming through the chaos, charging the innocent, running them down, bathing in the blood of the fallen.

Wilder People.

Scarcely seen in populated towns like Riverspell, the Wilder People are marauders and bandit communities that stick to the mountains and underground tunnel systems in lesser traveled parts of the world. Living off the land, and only occasionally attacking travelers, raiding when desperate enough, their survival depending on it. To Ket's knowledge, Wilder People have never flat-out pillaged a community and slaughtered innocent people. Wilders were hit-and-run combatants. Dangerous to travelers. Small groups. Not towns.

The rider closest to him holds a bloody sword in the air, roaring with victory after severing the head of an old, defenseless man. Clad in dented armor, obviously stolen, the visor of his helm is left open, so Ket can stare deep into his sun-starved eyes and the pale flesh around them. Ket runs up to the man, hops on the back of his horse, surprising the proud warrior, and rips his helm off by pulling it back over his head. With the man's neck exposed, Ket runs the obsidian blade across his throat, slitting him open before he can scream. Not that Ket expected one. As the gush of red spurts from the enormous and life-ending gash, Ket heaves him from the horse, allowing his near-limp body to land bone-lessly on the dirt below.

The horse bucks and Ket jumps off, landing on his feet and crouching so his legs absorb the impact. With his permission, the horse gallops off to safety.

A few of the town's guards have come rushing out of their quarters to enter the fray. Armed with swords, they engage with the Wilder People, but the men on horseback have the advantage and most of the guards on foot are cut down with ease. Ket watches one of them take a sword to the neck and is surprised at the distance the severed head travels through the air, before hitting the dirt, rolling another six or seven feet, a scarlet trail left in its wake.

The people of Riverspell flee through the open town gate, beneath the swinging gatekeeper, who the Wilder People have left to hang. His face has turned purple, his death stare gazing out beyond his perimeter, forever.

Ket moves quickly through the dust clouds, pushing frantic survivors out of his way, yelling for them to flee to their homes, but his advice is quickly obsolete: near the edges of town, the Wilder People set torches to the straw roofs. Igniting the houses and watching with glee as the structures catch instantly, they throw back their heads and howl like wolves, sick with bloodlust.

A Wilder, with a leopard-skinned cloak swirling behind him, dismounts, a thick chain around his neck jangling as he lands, his fist closed around a wicked, bloodied knife, grinning at his target near an overturned wagon. A young girl.

Ralyanna.

Surrounded by the ruins of her crates, their contents spilled over puddles of blood, she freezes, facing down the new threat.

Where's her guardian? Ket wonders. *Borgadine. The grandfather.*

Ket eyes him a second later, lying on the ground, hand over his heart, his scalp bloodied from a gash across his forehead. Ket sprints. He smacks into a woman cradling a baby in her arms, spinning her aside. The woman stumbles for balance as Ket scrambles to the girl who saved Jester. *Too late, I'm too late.*

The Wilder closes in for his next kill. "HEY!" Ket screams.

The Wilder stops, spins, his blade held out before him. His awkward posture suggests he's untrained in proper combat techniques.

Good. That will make what comes next so much easier.

The Wilder lets out a feral hissing scream, teeth blackened with rot. Then he charges at Ket, hoping to catch him off guard, but Ket's already reacting, positioning himself perfectly. Ket thrusts his blade forward, skewering the mountain man through his guts. The Wilder's eyes widen with alarm, his mouth a perfect O, before Ket shoves the blade deeper inside him, twisting and turning the hilt, rotating the sword to make sure everything inside is shredded. He yanks his blade out, now slicked with red. The Wilder's eyes roll before he collapses to the dirt, dead before his head smacks the ground like a child's inflated kickball.

Ket spins toward Ralyanna and her grandfather. "Run. Now. Past those woods and toward the inn. That way. You'll see two horses and the man I rode in with. Stay there until I come back."

Ralyanna's eyes grow distant. Her flesh pales. She doesn't speak.

"*Now,*" he commands. Ket glances at the old man. "Take your granddaughter and run."

"He can't," Ralyanna says, tears welling in her eyes. "His leg..."

She points. The man's ankle lies twisted at an odd angle, the kind of broken bone that defies human anatomy.

"Damn it." Grimacing, Ket kneels beside him. "Can you walk? At all?"

The man shakes his head. Ket can't carry him, not unless he wants to chance a sword in his back. He grips the man by the back of his jerkin, hoists him up to one leg. The girl's grandfather whimpers all the way up.

"You can hop on one foot then, yes?"

The man nods.

Before they can move, Ralyanna releases a shrill scream that splits Ket's brain in half. He turns in time to see a sword swinging at his head, and ducks, seconds before the blade can bite into his throat. The old man behind him isn't so lucky. A rider wearing a dented helm and rusted mail thrusts his long sword, skewering the girl's grandfather in the throat. His head mostly comes off. It hangs on like a stubborn tree trunk after a few good whacks of an ax. A red geyser shoots from the stump of his neck, petering out after a few volcanic spurts. His good leg gives out, his body toppling to the earth like a house of cards having the basement card flicked out from underneath.

Ralyanna screams. Louder. Shriller. The sound brings Ket back to the Owlton bluffs, two years in his past, and he can hear the lost echo of his sons screaming their mother's name, as the death arrow struck her in the throat. His eyelashes moisten.

The rider gallops off, no remorse in his gait. *Damn the 'Beard,* Ket thinks. *Save the girl, or slaughter the savages?*

He chooses the girl.

Sheathing his sword, he marches over to her on weak, unsteady knees. The killing has come back to him easily, but consoling a heartbroken human is a fine skill that's always eluded him.

"Ralyanna..." he says, reaching out and touching her shoulder.

She dodges his fingertips and pushes past him.

"Where are you going?" he asks, but it doesn't stop her; if the look in her eye is any indication, nothing will. She scrunches her forehead, puckers her lips tight against her teeth. Her jaw flexes with a smoldering rage.

A rider mounted atop a wild black stallion stampedes toward her, swinging a battle ax in great wide arcs, howling like a mountain wolf in heat.

"Ra—!"

He can't call her back quickly enough. She must see the rider speeding at her, must know his violent intent. But still—she walks languidly in a straight line. Like she's dreamwalking, tripping on some wild mushroom, unknowingly headed toward a fatal collision.

Then, she raises her hand, palm out, facing the rider. Stops walking. Narrows her eyes and concentrates harder than anyone Ket's ever seen putting their mind into something. Time stagnates. The air around them cools like walking into a damp cellar to retrieve fresh ales. The wind all but stops, and the dust clouds clear if only for a single moment. Ket watches everything unfold in slow motion, like a nightmare that bends time to its own advantage.

The rider sticks out his tongue, pinching the pink muscle between his teeth, concentrating on the kill to come, angling the ax at the girl's soft neck. Then his eyes pop wide like he's just witnessed a mountain troll emerging from the black mouth of its lair. Like he's seen Arkos's under-realm, the horrors of that hellish pit fire. And then—then the unbelievable happens.

The man's head snaps sideways with a giant *crack!* His eyeballs pop like air bubbles on the surface of a calm lake, liquifying in their sockets. Lifelessly, the rider slowly falls from the saddle and goes under his horse, getting caught in the stallion's powerful gallop, chewed up by the massive legs' incredible force. When the violent instant is over, the rider lies in the middle of the town's square, trampled and bleeding and convulsing.

Did she…

Ket can't even think the words, let alone speak them out loud. He's instantly taken back to the day his renewed life was stolen from him, when Ragland's men seized his property and murdered his wife. *Witch.* Jennah had fought back that day, killing a few of Sir Henry's men, and they had died similarly to this Wilder.

The girl takes two steps forward, then sinks to her knees like someone imbedded a few arrows into her chest.

But there are no arrows. Her eyes roll back, and she hits the ground with a soft thud, falling prey to the stress her actions have placed on her mind.

Mindful of the invasion, Ket runs to her, though most of the Wilder Men have moved away from the town's center and have started raiding the other sections, the small districts near the outskirts, where Riverspell spills out to embrace the forest and the mountainous terrain. Rivers of blood channel through the center of town. The fountain centerpiece is stocked with bodies of the slain, the water cherry red and overflowing. The smell of smoke and fire dominates the air, thinning it, making it difficult to suck down a full breath without gagging. Most of Riverspell is in flames, the huts and well-built structures, comprised of solid redwood oak, caught in the firestorm these mountain maniacs have brought with them.

Ket reaches Ralyanna without further interruption. A few survivors lie on the ground near them, whimpering and praying to whatever god will come for them, pick them up from this nightmare, and take them to paradise.

Ket ignores them, especially when they turn to him for help— help he cannot give.

Near the girl, he spots a silver pendant sticking out under some debris, fragments of a smashed-up wash barrel. He kneels, snatches the silver charm looped around some wiry dead vine, and shoves it in his pocket. Then he collects Ralyanna in his arms and heads back for the horses, hoping Jester is still there and that the chaos hasn't reached him.

———

KET SETS the unconscious girl down in the grass, then surveys the area where he last placed Jester. The horses lie where he left them, their heads separated from their bodies by a few bloody yards. The blood hasn't congealed yet, so the slaughter was recent. A wilder with a slashed throat lies dead in the grass, soaking in a pool of his own red demise. Ket eyes a trail of bloody footprints that head toward the nearby woods, but fade closer to the treeline, impossible to pick up. *Jester? Did the bastard make it out alive?* It's unlikely the Wilder killed their own, and he bets the mountain man did not do that to himself.

Ket takes a few paces in each direction to scope either side of the inn, which itself looks vacant.

"Damn it," he murmurs before attending to Ralyanna. He checks the girl's pulse. Still there, still strong. "Ralyanna?"

No reaction. Whatever happened, whatever invisible arrow she fired into the Wilder's face, has zapped every last drop of her energy.

Feeling it's safe to leave her lying in the tall grass, mostly hidden from anyone who happens to ride past, Ket makes his way over to the slain horses, expecting to see Jester's savaged body among them. Surprisingly, the man's corpse is not amongst the carnage. A trail of blood leads from the horses to inside the inn. He follows the scarlet path through the doors, into the main bar area.

Dead patrons lie scattered around the pub's floor, most of them dissected into several pieces. It's hard to tell which limb belongs to which body. He examines the bloodbath, surprised by how quickly his mind has adjusted back to survival mode. Keeping an eye out for that familiar diamond-patterned jester hat, Ket moves about the room, stepping over the bodies of the less fortunate. He heads upstairs and checks the rooms; most of them vacant save for a few bodies that have been hacked open, their blood used to scrawl unintelligible messages on the walls. Ket can't make out their meaning, but they are clearly the work of a mind gone completely mad.

Ket quickly moves on from the inn, hoping Jester escaped.

He doubts he'll ever see the man again.

Leaving the inn, he strides past the headless horses and kneels beside Ralyanna, combing away loose strands of hair from the sleeping orphan's face.

What to do with you, girl, what to do.

He scoops her up, tosses her over his shoulder, and begins to trek in the opposite direction of the mountain range, where the raiders came from and where he assumes they will return, once they've had their bloody fill.

He hopes there's an orphanage on the way north, because the girl is much heavier than she should be.

THE BOY
CHAPTER FIVE

"Certain Highbeard sects have scoured the Five Realms for signs of validity for the most well-known prophecy, the Boy with the Stars for Eyes. In the north, it is mandatory that a Highbeard priest must oversee every birth. In the South, they document eye color and shape during the child's baptism. The hunt for the Boy who is said to signal the second coming of the Gods, is a fight for supremacy, and reigning kingdoms will go to great lengths to secure the powers bestowed upon this special individual."

- MENYARD MINOTOA, *THE GOD SYSTEM*

———

THE BOY WAKES the same every morning—with a parade of attendants beating down his door, scurrying into his room, and dragging him out of bed, prying the sheets from his tightly curled fingers. It isn't the best way to exit a pleasant dream, but the boy doesn't know any different.

This is just the way things are.

Once risen and dressed, in the same pure white garments they've always provided him, the boy is marched down the hall, down a long spiral staircase, and into a private chamber, where they feed him his daily breakfast—scrambled goose eggs and hickory-smoked bacon, with a side of sliced red apples. He eats this morning meal under the watchful eyes of two Rovanian guards, who regularly take up the post inside his secluded chamber.

"Where's Harry this morning?" the boy asks, voicing the missing party's name. Normally the guards do not speak much, nor have they divulged personal information like names. But the boy has his ways of obtaining secrets. There isn't much to do around the Silver Towers except spy on people, and eavesdrop on their private conversations.

The two guards stick to their posts, refusing to engage, not even twitching a single muscle. Their eyes do not stray from the wall across from them.

"Asked you a question. It's rude not to answer," the boy explains, but this still does not elicit a response. "I'm just worried about him. I like him. He's a good guard."

One of the guards breaks his stone-statue façade, shifting his eyes toward his partner. In a blink, he returns his gaze to the wall.

What kind of consequence would he face, should he respond? the boy thinks. *What level of punishment would speaking to me merit? A trip to the whipping post, or getting hung in the gallows?* The latter seems too harsh to consider, but King Salah isn't known for his benevolence. He's a stickler for laws and rules, and above all else —loyalty.

"Did Harry do something wrong?" he prods again. "Has he been beheaded for speaking with me? It was just once. Very brief."

Still no answers from the two men, their vow of silence holding throughout the entire meal, despite the rapid-fire questioning that never relents. The boy can see his persistent inquiries make the men uncomfortable, and a part of him likes that. It's sometimes fun to mess with the king's men, or members of Ravenborn's knighted squad. Men who live and visit the Silver Towers behave differently around him. They don't speak, make eye contact, or acknowledge him in any fashion; they treat him like a well-known spirit wandering the halls —a ghost left to haunt. An eerie presence that can't hurt them, if left completely ignored. Some of them are afraid, fearful he might curse their souls, perform Highbeard magic on their minds, drive them insane with just one thought—all hocus pocus, of course. The greatest secret in the Five Realms is the one that everyone in the Silver Towers is too afraid to admit—that he, the star-eyed child, is powerless—has not an ounce of magic in him. Just a condition that makes his pupils appear star-like, and a prophecy that supports some looney theories, making grown men—*feared* men if placed on the battlefield—tremble in his presence.

Even though his powers haven't amounted to anything over the last thirteen years, his presence alone is paramount. The king still needs him.

For what?

The answer to that is something the boy has been waiting on, his whole thirteen-year existence. Perhaps one day all will be revealed, but for now, it's business as usual. Stolen away in the dark. Well, not the *dark*. The dark is somewhere sinners and betrayers of Rovan are sent to. The boy is kept in the light, high in the sky, in one of the kingdom's renowned Silver Towers. *Closest to the sun,* the Rovan King once told him. *Closer to God.*

God. *Gods.* A topic the boy is tired of learning about. No matter how many lessons he's been taught about the days when gods roamed the earth, no matter how many parables of their adventures have been explained and examined, no matter how palatable the scholars of Rovan try to make this dense information, the boy can't swallow any of it.

He finds *belief* a funny thing—hard to accept, even though the evidence of their existence stares at him in the mirror every morning—*those eyes.* Yes, belief in the gods is tricky, hard to grasp, and he wonders how many other people out there struggle with the same doubts but can never voice their opinion, because believing in nothing is somehow worse than believing in the Witchmaster himself—Arkos, the Blackstone Angel.

He keeps this all to himself; can't speak a word of it to anyone who is permitted to speak with him. And, certainly, he can't bring up these feelings to Ravenborn. The king's right hand will hear none of it—will only punish the boy for having those thoughts troubling his skull.

There is only one person to whom he can admit such truths, and that person is Fenir, *Fen* for short, and he is the son of one of his personal servants, a nice woman named Margot—who slips him extra candies after dinnertime. Occasionally Margot brings Fen to work with her, and, with permission from Ravenborn, the boy gets to pal around the castle with him, sometimes unsupervised, but most often *not.*

So, there is only so much trouble and so much secrecy that can exist. Still, it's enough to ease the pain of missing out on so many *normal* kid things, the common activities he's been excluded from —playing tag with friends in the common district, fishing in Rovan's vast and fruitful rivers, kicking a ball around, or throwing rocks at prisoners being carted to the gallows.

You know, *normal* things all Rovanian youths get to experience.

The boy will never get to do any of that because…because… he's…

I'm a freak, he thinks. Their words, not his, but he's beginning to believe *they* are right. *They,* of course, being the boys and girls he tried to befriend when Ravenborn approved the integration program, where the boy would sit in normal classes and lectures and participate in all the usual activities the other children have had since the dawn of the Rovan Territories. But it proved Ravenborn's (and the rest of the king's most trustworthy advisors) concerns true—he was too much of a distraction to be treated like a normal child coming upon the delicate age of thirteen.

Because I'm a freak.

The boy sets his fork on the edge of his plate, the eggs and bacon only half-eaten, his red apple slices only nibbled, his appetite already abating. Just in time too. Ravenborn steps into the room, the hollow sounds of his boots striking the floor, the jangling of silver pendants around his neck dominating the unwelcome silence. The boy's guards turn and face Ravenborn, saluting the king's most trusted advisor with proper posture, and utter a brief, throaty vocalization, an old Rovan greeting that the boy doesn't quite understand, but his best guess at pronouncing it is *Hyutt!* All the military men and hands of the king greet each other like this, especially when addressing a higher rank. Ravenborn practically ignores them and hustles into the room.

"Boy," he says, his dry, cracked lips parting as he puts his hands on his hips. "Are you ready for your training?"

Ravenborn is a big man, built like a giant but not as tall as a real one, not that the boy has seen a real giant before. He has raven-black hair and a neatly trimmed beard that match in color, though wisps of silver run throughout both. His green eyes seem to glow, depending on the ambient sunlight angle and how it hits them, reminding the boy of the alley cats he's seen begging for scraps in the common district. Ravenborn is always dressed in the same attire—the boy has never seen him don anything other than his all-black leather jacket and pants, the jacket sporting a frill of raven feathers around his chest and neck. He moves like a man half his age. Not a creak in his bones, Fen's mother might say.

The boy has heard it said, that Ravenborn has killed over a thousand men in the old wars, the last of them ending around the same time the boy was born. He's wise enough to know that number is likely inflated, but also knows it's maybe not that far off, and the fact the man has taken any lives at all is exciting, and intimidating, all at once.

"Yes, sir," the boy says, getting to his feet.

"You look tired."

"Didn't sleep well last night."

"The dreams again?"

The boy nods. His dreams have been worse lately. More

frequent and intense than usual. More bizarre too, if he's being honest. He can't trust his tutor with the whole truth. Ravenborn seems to believe too much in the nature of dreams.

"No matter," Ravenborn says, walking over to the boy and putting an arm around him like a proud father would an obedient son. In a sick, sad way, Ravenborn is the closest thing the boy has to a father. "Come. We have much to learn today, much to set your star-shaped eyes upon."

The boy walks with Ravenborn out of the antechamber, then down the hall, his mentor leading him to another full day of training and work. Later, Ravenborn will fill his head with tales of prophecies and gods, religious splendor.

None of which the boy truly believes.

Maybe that's why it's not working, why my powers aren't showing.

Maybe today might be a day of change.

Because today will be different.

Because the woman in his dreams told him so.

PART TWO
SECRETS OF THE SILVER TOWERS

RALYANNA

CHAPTER SIX

"The gods were said to have many spawn; though it is impossible to tell how far their bloodlines reach, it's important to know their lineage is never gone, only forgotten."

– MENYARD MINOTOA, *THE GOD SYSTEM*

———

UPON OPENING her eyes and discovering an unfamiliar setting, she fights to remember the minutes leading to her blackout. She sits up and rotates. Endless rows of green-topped trees surround her, bursting with lush leaves, crisp enough to eat. Of course, she knows most of the leaves here are toxic—not enough to kill a person, but enough to make them spend the afternoon squatting against a sturdy trunk. Still, they're lovely to wake to, their greeting invigorating. Though still evening, the night creeps closer, edging closer to the fringes of the visible sky.

Her mental fog refuses to break, slowing her waking mind. She registers the crackling of a hungry fire. Spinning, she sees a man sitting on a fallen, rotted timber, his hands hovering over the fiery tongues that lick at his fingertips. He looks familiar, and when her eyes find his she starts to remember.

Riverspell. The festival. The…attack.

Borgadine…decapitated.

The flashes of the past strike like lightning bolts crashing into the plains of her memory, her synapses sizzling with their hot burning force. Touching gingerly at her throbbing temples, she winces, and then manages to flip over, kneeling on the soft earth.

"How are you feeling?" the man says. She tries to recall his name, or if he told her.

She massages her scalp, crying out from the pain needling beneath the surface. Gritting her teeth, she fights through it.

"Not well I take it."

"Where are we?" She hates the groggy sound of her voice, the biting pain radiating down her jaw.

"In the forest. Not sure where, exactly. Or if these parts even have a name. But we've been here a few hours and it's been—miraculously—quiet."

"The man I was with…" she says, sadness burning up her eyes. Warm tears spill down her cheeks.

The man—Ket, she suddenly remembers—observes her with a curious gaze, squinting like she's a difficult riddle he's been asked to solve. "Borgadine. Was he not your grandfather?"

Grandfather, she thinks. Yes, she supposes that's the role he's played in her life—among others. *Grandfather. Father. Friend.*

Guide.

"I guess you could say that."

"Come," he says, scooting to the edge of the timber. "Caught us a few rabbits for dinner."

He presents her with a skewer, fresh from the spit, crackling with savory meat. There isn't much. But the slivers of juicy, shredded rabbit will satisfy her grumbling stomach enough. She wavers to the log, takes a seat, and accepts the tray from the man. She picks at the meat, popping small strands into her mouth, chewing the tender strips, cooked to perfection. It's the best thing she's eaten in some time, much better than most food served at random inns.

"Secured some supplies from the inn back in Riverspell," Ket says, running his fingers through his hair, pushing the long strands away from his face, a few crusted with dried blood. "But we couldn't stay. Those Wilders will likely come back and scavenge the dead."

The dead. She stills. Her eyes settle on the flickering flames and stay there a beat, her mind replaying the moment the Wilder severed Borgadine's head clean off his shoulders; the way the old man's neck separated, astonishment on his face as his head tumbled to the side. The shock. The horror he experienced in those last few fatal seconds.

"I'm sorry," Ket says, bowing his head out of respect for the fallen. A soldier's courtesy.

"It's fine." She tries to sound unbothered but knows she's failed. And miserably.

"He wasn't your grandfather?"

"It's complicated."

"Fair enough. I know when to mind my business."

"You saved me," she says, turning to him, putting down the rabbit bits. The memory of blood and death and her newfound grief have driven away her appetite. "Why?"

"I saved *you?*" The man chuckles, then shakes his head. "No, no. You saved me. With that magic trick you pulled."

"Magic trick?"

An eyebrow rises. "You don't remember?"

She remembers seeing Borgadine's fall, but everything after is shrouded in a fog she cannot lift. She vaguely recalls the cloaked rider—Borgadine's murderer—galloping off in search of more violence, but from there her memory remains hazy.

"No."

"Curious," he says, biting his lip. "You don't remember removing the Wilder from the horse with only your mind?"

She tries to call the memories back. But once again she draws a blank. "No, I think I would certainly remember something like that."

"I would think so too. Maybe it will come back to you. I'll spare you the gruesome details."

"Gruesome?"

He smiles around his words. "I'm sparing you, remember?"

A chill spirals down her spine, running the entire length of her back.

"You seem unnerved by the news," Ket says. "Has anything like this happened before?"

She chews her lip. He's probing for secrets, her secrets, secrets she doesn't want to tell him. After all, he's a stranger. Even if he saved her life, stole her away from the violence, from the Wilders, and didn't disturb her while she slept...

There's a chance he might discover my truth, she thinks. *The thing that makes me bad...*

And then he might just change his mind about not hurting her. Or worse.

"No," she lies. "No, not at all. I will keep this mystery at the forefront of my thoughts and try to learn more about it."

"Hmm," he replies, a noise that lets her know he's not buying any of it. "Very well. I should also thank you for saving my friend —though, his whereabouts are currently unknown."

"Your friend?"

"Yes, you gave me phrivian weeds for his wounds."

"Phrivian *leaves*," she corrects. "And yes—I remember now. It worked?"

"Like a spell. Which I don't doubt you cast while bottling the leaves."

"Are you accusing me of witchcraft?" She stands up and retreats, three steps toward the trees at their backs. She's prepared to run and flee in the first clear direction she comes across, if he so much as takes one aggressive step toward her. Her feet have been put to the test before, and they haven't failed her yet.

"No, no," he says, putting down his plate. He holds up a hand that hopes to keep her from running. "I meant nothing like that. I just...if you saw what happened...what you did to that man...his face…I've seen something like that before and…" He shakes his head, wiping away the memory of whatever it was he'd seen. It's clearly something that haunts him. "Never mind."

She stands there, not sure why she isn't halfway to the Crosslands by now. She knows not to trust strangers—it's never worked out for her in the past, save for meeting Borgadine. But he was a one-in-a-million chance. A sewing needle at the bottom of a hayfield. He took her in. Cared for her. Didn't harm her. Kept her out of the dirty orphanages and the unpleasant living conditions of those places, irreparably broken homesteads, not suitable for the life of any child. And not just the homesteads, but the people who owned them. She was tired of being taken into these random huts and having to escape several months later when she realized she would be better off living under a castle bridge with troll folk rather than those "guardians."

Some of them were monsters.

"Please," Ket says, motioning to the log. "Sit."

"I'd rather stand."

"Fine. Suit yourself."

Defiantly, she stands, keeping the campfire between them.

"It will be full-dark soon," he finally says. "The cold will infest your bones. I stole blankets from the inn, but they might not be enough."

"I'm not cuddling up next to you, if—"

"That's not where I was going with this," he interrupts, hanging his head and sighing, either out of embarrassment or just plain frustration with her assessment of the situation. "One of us should stay awake and keep watch, keep the fire going through the night so we have some heat."

"Uh-huh…"

"I volunteer for the first shift," he notes. "You can sleep as long as you need. You still look like you could use more rest."

She shakes her head. "No, I'm rested. I can't fall back to sleep now anyway. I have…" She lowers her head like she's ashamed to admit it. "I have many things on my mind, the kind of things that steal sleep."

Ket nods. "Very well. I'll grab a few winks. I would hate to assume you don't know how, but can you—"

"I can keep the fire going," she says, jaw firming, trying to sound more like a confident adult than a scared child. "I'm sixteen years of age—you don't have to baby me. I've lived on the road almost my entire life."

He raises his hands, letting her know she'll receive no further argument. "Didn't mean anything by it."

She collects a few sticks from the pile Ket assembled, then feeds them to the fire. Appeased, the fire busies with more flames. The heat intensifies, and she removes her fingerless leather gloves, places her hands over the warmth and keeps them there as she basks in the blaze's tangerine glow.

"Goodnight," Ket says, grabbing the small blanket he got from the inn. "If you see or hear anything unordinary, wake me. Anything at all. No disturbance too small."

"Got it." She waves him away, ignoring his final glance.

Her mind is already elsewhere. The past, Riverspell, Borgadine's death, what that means for her future—which seems every bit as hopeless as the dark days before it.

She waits until Ket is sound asleep before crying her eyes out.

———

RALYANNA'S NEARLY NODDING OFF, not keeping her end of the bargain, not keeping up with the fire, when a noise disturbs her.

The noise is close, but she can't locate the source or any evidence of its maker. She considers waking Ket but ignores the notion as fast as it comes. Instead, she stiffens, turns from the diminishing flames, and scans the treeline, swallowed by the late hour's darkness.

Nothing.

No one.

Just the stillness and the dark.

She waits to the count of fifty before giving up and returning to the flames. Tossing another bundle of sticks into the fire, she doesn't give the noise a second thought, chalks it up to some passing harmless critter or just her weary mind conjuring up false disruptions.

Until it happens again.

A rapid crackle in the woods, as if a bigger fire is burning back there, eating away at the lumber, feasting on the leafy branches. She spins, her eyes spearing the spot it came from. She scans the dark, her concentration sharp as she fixates on the swollen shadows.

Nothing emerges.

Again, she passes on waking Ket. She may regret it later, but in this moment, he's not even a split-second notion to consider. Relying on strangers to bail her out of bad situations has never worked out well for her.

She moves away from the log and the fire to the fringes of the darkness, where the campfire light and the moon above cannot cut through the unremitting nighttime.

This is stupid, she thinks, and at least she has the good sense to know what she's doing is dangerous. Self-awareness of the situation might just save her, should some giant hairy winged beast pop out of the shadows, flashing blood-speckled incisors, ready to pierce the succulent flesh of her neck. Having no fixed idea of where she is, makes it hard to judge whether these woods are safe, or if this domain is incredibly treacherous.

"Hello?" she says timidly, keeping her voice soft and inviting. "If someone is there, please show yourself, or I will—"

Will what?

Use your abilities again? Kill someone else?

The voice inside her head laughs at her. A gurgling, throaty laughter, unhealthy, plagued by terminal illness.

That isn't me, she berates the voice. *I do not do those things. I am no murderer.* It sounds like a bluff, even to herself; even if part of it is true. What she means to say is, *I do not want to do those things. Murder. Hurt people.*

You have done those things, though, the voice croaks back.

It's not my fault. I didn't want to…

Ket stirs in his dreams. The voice leaves her with those words, those thoughts. She blesses the stars for making the invisible speaker disappear, granting her a reprieve from its goading, and she refocuses on the unmoving dark before her. The night swallows her doubts, noiseless save for the faint screeching of nocturnal creatures in the faraway distance, and the hooting of owls, perched in the branches above.

"That's what I thought," she says aloud, and then turns her shoulder to head back to the campfire, where it's warmer, safer.

"Girl," whispers the dark, and she feels her chest collapsing into her stomach like the top of an eroding bluff free-falling into the turbulent waves of the Sea of Echoes. She spins, her breath catching in her throat, and sees a pale face emerge from the swollen shadows, the sagging mutilated flesh around its mouth bleeding and dripping bile, its wrinkled skin gray like a thunder-cast sky.

The lips of the monster fix into a smiling snarl.

She shrieks, loud enough for the Wilders back in Riverspell to hear her, and the figure steps out from behind the leafy brush, moving toward her, his gnarled fingers reaching for her throat.

JESTER'S ESCAPE
CHAPTER SEVEN

"Northern Wilders are radically different from their southern counterparts. Though Central Wilders are considered the deadliest, they typically leave populations near their settlements alone. They're like bees; mess with their honey, and they will mess with you."

– TIMTOO CROUCH, MOVING THROUGH ENDLIA: A BEGINNER'S GUIDE TO TRAVELING

Several Hours Ago

WITH KET LEAVING to chase after the commotion, Jester looks for safety inside the inn. Several Riverspellians cluster around the bar, hunched, listening as the roar from the center of town reaches their ears. As Jester stumbles in, the nearest patron, in a pinecone-brown tunic, raises his brow, lifting his hands in a silent question, lips pursed, as if frightened to question the uproar. Jester shrugs, unwilling to comment, and slinks past them towards the back of the bar where everyone else is standing.

"What do ye want?" the female bartender asks in her thick, northern Owlton accent.

"Nothing," he says, raising empty hands, showing them he means no harm and doesn't have any weapons on him. "I'm friendly."

"What's going on out there? Heard screamin'," another fellow inquires, crouching behind the bartop as if he's waiting for a glass to fly at his head.

Jester shrugs, says, "Wish I knew. But with that much screaming, I'm inclined to believe that nothing good is taking place inside your beloved town."

The rest fall silent, one gulping. A married couple hustles out the back door, leaving the safety of the inn, taking their chances on the open field behind the establishment. Others hide under tables, waiting it out.

"Dark times," mutters a man wearing a straw hat, chugging ale from a glass mug. "Signs of the End, I'd say."

"Shut your yapper, eh?" barks another man. He scratches his big red beard, but Jester has the sneaking suspicion the man has another itch to scratch—a violent one, one that can only be resolved by engaging in fisticuffs. The man stands up and puffs out his chest, the universal signal for *Let's brawl*. He has six inches on his potential opponent—the pessimist—and twice the muscle. "No one needs to hear about your prophecies and apocalyptic god storms—heard it all before, and nothing's ever changed. Now scram, before I put your arse in the chopper and dice you to bits."

For all of three seconds, Straw Hat looks ready and willing; but then he sits back on his stool, common sense intervening.

Jester thinks it's a shame—he was looking forward to the entertainment.

But entertainment will come soon enough. While the patrons argue over what could be causing the distant screams and disconcerting commotion from outside the inn, Jester creeps to the window.

There's nothing, no one, no sign of Ket or anyone else. Alone in the corner of the inn, he lifts his shirt to peek at his wound. The skin has fused almost completely, and no longer oozes with early signs of infection. He marvels over his repaired flesh, then wonders about the substance that was used to achieve the miracle. Maybe it was magic, but maybe it was something else—something he's never heard of, come across, or seen with his own eyes. As far as he knows, no medicine in Endlia can do this.

The front door booms open; the wood frame holding it cracking from the force of the aggressive entrance. Two men stand in the broken ingress, taller than most and oddly shaped at that, wearing battle armor several sizes too small for their hulking frames, and dented helms that have clearly taken swords in battle. Their sea-foam white flesh suggests these are mountain men, cave-dwelling Wilders. Blood stains the silver of their chest plates, still dripping. The swords they wield are fresh with clotting clumps of gleaming scarlet, fresh from the slaughter. The Wilders roar in unison and storm into the inn, striking at anything in their paths. The first man's blade slices clean through a man's midriff, spilling his intestines. The second's blade thrusts through the neck of a woman pleading for her life. As the Wilder removes his blade, she stumbles to her knees, vomiting gouts of dark blood, whimpering in agony. Jester's attention is lured by the sudden slash of two swords—both have cut down a boy just old enough to enjoy his first mead, his arms held up in surrender. The blades come down on his shoulders with brute force, severing his arms.

I guess they haven't come for mead and tea, Jester thinks.

One of the Wilders glances up at him as the screams from the other patrons fill the stunned silence. *Best not linger.* Everything explodes with motion. Customers and inn-workers alike scream their way towards the exits—the back door, the stairs, the available windows, anything that removes them from the carnage. Some have luck and make it out unscathed, while others are not so fortunate. Their bodies are hacked, cut apart like raw meat slapped down in front of an eager butcher.

While the mountain men continue to engage in their slaughter, Jester sneaks his way to the back of the inn, and up the long flight of stairs to the second story. People have gathered at the top to gaze down at him with wonder and fear in their eyes, and he simply tells them to scatter, that trouble is nipping at his heels and headed their way. When the people do not part, he barks, "Get out of the way, you imbeciles!" and then tries to shoulder his way past them. They don't provide any resistance, although a few shout obscenities at him. Once he passes them, he calls back over his shoulder, "You should have run, fools!"

Jester ducks into the first available room and goes for the window, kicking his foot through the glass. The shattering noise is hidden by the hysteria below. From his height, some of what is taking place near the center of town is visible through the limited view—the trees from the small patch of woods separate the road from town, and thankfully hide the full brutality. Chaos rages, and people sprint into the streets from burning cottages and huts and storefronts, towers of flames gobbling the structures, jumping from the straw roofs to the trees of the neighboring forests, insatiable. Some of the townsfolk have made their way to the main road and are screaming, running in any direction, heedless of the inherent dangers of entering the trees and concealment. Their clothes are torn, full of soot, and stained with dark splotches of blood.

The jingle of chainmail grabs his attention from below. A pair of armed mountain men approach his mare, along with Ket's gelding, with swords drawn, their eyes swollen from bloodlust. In mere seconds, they take down the horses, silencing the mares' panicked neighs with wide arching swings at the animals' jugulars. Enormous gouts of blood shoot from the horses' gashed throats, before the men continue to work the metal through the horses' sinew, until the gentle creatures are beheaded.

Jester goes queasy at the sight of the senseless carnage, even though it's far from the worst he's seen, and certainly not as bad as the things he's done to his own victims.

Must be the medicine making me...feel...

He hears that the two Wilders from downstairs have brought their death party upstairs, and the people he warned are now receiving the same violence he notified them about.

A man's head tumbles into the room, his eyes stuck wide open, flesh awash with blood.

Jester moves out the window, onto the roof, which is shingled with a thick and tarlike black paper, which sticks to the bottom of his boots as he creeps across it. He makes his way to the end of the roof, glances down, determines the coast is clear enough, and drops himself onto the grassy ground below. Luckily, he lands just right—no snapped ankles, not even a stinging sprain in the knees.

Free now, with the two Wilders that brutalized the horses back inside the inn with the other members of their tribe, the tightness in his chest is gone; the prospect of actually escaping this madness energizes his step.

I made it!

He almost smiles beneath his cloth, then realizes he already is. Always. But in this moment he feels it on the inside, and that's enough.

Jester turns his back on Riverspell, away from the people sprinting down the main road and the bareback riders that chase them down, wielding axes and swords and makeshift skull-breakers.

Someone coughs behind him.

One of the mountain folk who butchered the horses stands in his way. The only thing separating him and the open field that leads back to the Long Green Road. A tall blockade of fishbelly-white flesh and secondhand armor. The skin on Jester's neck begins to crawl like a bug pit.

So close...

Jester is weaponless. The Wilder, sadly, is not. He holds his ax sideward with both hands, the head of it still dripping with the mare's gore.

"Now, you look like a reasonable fella," Jester says, holding up a finger and blinking cutely. Neither reaction seems to work. Jester doubts the feral man can even understand the common tongue.

"I'm going to break you apart!" the Wilder screams, almost unintelligibly.

"So, you do speak the common tongue. Well, I applaud you. You're much more sophisticated than the Wilders of the northern Crosslands, I assure you. Much uglier though."

"Silence! DIE!"

The Wilder lunges, swinging his ax at Jester's neck. Jester ducks under the handle, still nimble despite his wound, and while he dodges the attack, he slams his knuckles flush into the Wilder's ribs, a blow that would have knocked the breath out of an amateur brawler. But this Wilder appears to be of sturdier stock, built like a bear, and Jester believes he's done more damage to his own hand than to the Wilder's midsection.

The Wilder recovers in seconds, turning on him, seemingly more annoyed than in pain. The way a knight might look after being tasked with ridding a castle of elusive wall mice. He comes at Jester again, but Jester is quicker; not only does he feel fully recovered from last night's near-fatal stabbing, but he feels an energy he hasn't felt since maybe his teenage years, long before the incident in Iradon.

What was in that wonderful potion?

Whatever it was, it's enhanced his senses. He can smell better, move quicker, and react to the Wilder's movements almost as if he can sniff out the hulking man's moves before he makes them.

The ax comes for his head once more, so Jester gets low to the ground. While ducking, he spots a knife tucked in the Wilder's leather boot sleeve, and before he can process his own thoughts, acting purely on instinct, Jester snatches the knife. The mountain man attempts to stomp on his hand, but Jester predicts the move instinctively, and adjusts, the man's foot hitting nothing but air as it splashes into the mud.

In a blink, Jester works the knife into an opening between two plates of armor that cover the Wilder's midsection, stabbing him in the ribs and twisting the blade as far as it will go, until he hits some resistance. The Wilder growls and swats Jester's hand away. With the knife still stuck inside him, the Wilder moves on Jester, swinging his ax in the air with incensed fury. It's all Jester can manage to backpedal, dipping and ducking under each wild swing. After several attempts to decapitate him have failed, the Wilder takes shots at Jester's knees. Jester jumps over each one, and as he does so, he thinks back to the days when he was a child living in the town of Grimold, located in the southeast corner of Glane, when he and the other children would play in the streets, a game called hop-swing. The rules of hop-swing were simple—two children would hold opposite ends of a long bedsheet and swing it in wide loops, while other children would stand between them and hop over the cloth, continuing to do so until they ran out of energy and tripped. Jester won, often.

After about three swings, as soon as Jester's feet touch grass, he lurches ahead, grabs the knife stuck in the Wilder's ribs, and yanks it out, all within a blink. The move takes the Wilder by surprise. He tries to readjust his swing; however, the game of hop-swing has clearly taken its toll on the mountain man's stamina; he's slow to react, and Jester beats him to the mark just before he can maneuver the ax and deliver a victorious blow to Jester's skull. Jester pokes the blade into the Wilder's throat, opening a sizable gash and spilling freshets of blood.

The Wilder's eyes freeze open in a state of unbridled shock, and the ax falls from the large man's fingers, landing in the muddy grass with a solid thud. Jester doesn't allow the bastard to recover a single breath and sticks him again, this time underneath the ribcage, deflating his left lung. The Wilder crumbles to his knees, grabbing at his throat, trying to contain the continuous flood of crimson as it pours through the cracks of his fingers.

As the Wilder chokes, he sinks to his knees, and Jester, gloating, mimics the fall himself, taking to one knee. Inching close to the man's ear, Jester pauses and sighs deeply, as if thankful for the workout. "I bid you farewell, dear sir. You were a worthy adversary but not worthy enough. If I shall fatefully stumble upon your corpse in future travels, I'll be sure to piss on it."

And then he laughs as the man falls on his face, dying in the muddy green spread of grass beneath him.

Jester runs away from Riverspell, cackling madly at the setting sun.

JESTER MEETS THE PORTNOYS

CHAPTER EIGHT

"When the gods walked the Five Realms, mythic beasts roamed free. After The Departure, most species fast-tracked toward extinction. Rumors suggest some have survived, hiding themselves, perhaps to be rediscovered. But who really knows? Did they ever exist? Or are we seeking something from our own imaginations, perhaps in an effort to prove the existence of the gods themselves? I believe Endlia still has monsters. You just have to know where to look."

– JOHNWILL CRANYARD, *MYTHIC BEASTS OF ENDLIA*

———

HOURS LATER, Jester stumbles, almost blind, lost in the woods after dark; not the time one wishes to be lost in the woods, not that anyone wishes to be lost there *any* time. But if given your pick, nightfall would not be the obvious choice. And especially not alone. With creatures howling in the near distance, announcing their hunger to the moon. You would not want this at all.

Jester gropes his way through the sturdy shadows, nothing on him to light the way, only the Pale Sister hanging overhead, her crescent light providing some ambient visibility. Jester picks his way through the undergrowth, the thorny branches constantly threatening to scratch and tear. They could blind a less wary traveler, guarding the path to…

Well, he doesn't know where. He was wondering aimlessly in a direction that wasn't Riverspell—that was all he knew, and it had been good enough until now.

Until the dark.

If I can find the Long Green Road, he thinks, *I will have come out of this alive.*

Alive, but to where? He has nowhere to go. No guild's haven to return to. No kingdom in the Five Realms will open its arms to him. Before his incarceration, he spent the last five months on the road—and that was hard work, simply surviving. Before that, he had burned every bridge, drowned every relationship. He was a betrayer, a backstabber and a warmonger, with whom no respectable party would dare associate themselves. Even less-reputable assassins guilds want nothing to do with him, and that says something.

No, he's alone in this world, and the only person in his corner was Ket Norlath, real name unknown, although Jester has his suspicions about who he was, back when the war between the Rovan Territories and Owlton was peaking. Maybe not his exact name. But he knows the genes that flow through Ket's veins. He's a Rovan, maybe a cousin or distant cousin of King Salah himself. If Jester had a few gold coins to spare, he'd wager on it.

Hours of feeling his way through the dark have led him to a path carved out in the forest. He follows the path for another thousand paces, taking the winding trail with no hesitation. Crickets continue their chirping and frogs repeatedly belch their nightly sonnets. Occasionally a concerning howl or growl reaches his ears, but they sound too far for him to worry. Still, he keeps his eyes on the shadows, on the lookout for any sudden movements, and always marks a tree in his periphery, should he need to climb one in a hurry.

His feet begin to ache after several miles on the beaten path, the harder ground easier to travel yet taking its toll on him. A faint glow appears in the distance, something man-made, and at first, he believes it's a passing carriage, a traveler on the road at night—dangerous, but some prefer the anonymity of traveling in the waxing or waning hours of the day, hoping to avoid conflict with other travelers and potential bandits. Yet when Jester nears, he notices the bright spot does not move.

A stationary light in the forest. Likely a structure: a house.

In ordinary conditions, he might have passed by without giving the house a second look, fearing that no normal person would choose to live out here, this far from civilization. But he is hungry. And tired. And although his wounds have miraculously healed (not just where the blade pierced him, but the open wounds of his stitched scalp and face have also fused nicely), his body suffers from bone-deep exhaustion. There's no way he could last a full night of walking without passing out somewhere. Those last few miles have beaten his feet into submission; he's also had trouble keeping his eyes open.

As he approaches, the lantern glow coming from the hut's porch eave reveals more of the home; a quaint three-room structure with a sturdy front door comprised of oaken boards. A sizable garden sits out front. A scarecrow—that gives Jester's veins a rush of ice—watches over the lettuce heads, the zucchini growths and tomato vines, along with a spread of corn sprouts and green beans—a vegetable lover's dream. He slinks past the scarecrow and its black watchful gaze, toward the oaken front door of the hut. He considers knocking, then thinks better of it. The dwellers of this house are likely sleeping, and maybe he doesn't need to wake them up. So, instead, he saunters into the garden and begins to pluck the vegetables from the soil. He bites into a tomato and relishes the acidic burst that runs down his throat. The tomato is consumed in less than sixty seconds, and then he searches for other food, such as a watermelon the size of a fabled dragon egg. He uses the knife he stabbed the mountain man with, and slices open the belly of the fruit, not bothering to clean off the blade before sinking the metal into the fruit's green shell. Once open, he stuffs his face with the sweet juicy snack, chewing and not bothering to spit out the seeds. He just gulps them down. Halfway through, he hears something snap behind him.

A footstep?

He's too late to turn around. A blade is already at his throat.

"Who are you?" a deep voice asks, and the person applies enough pressure to draw a dribble of blood.

"Just a hungry nobody," Jester replies hoarsely, his tone careful. "Looking for food. And board. If you have it. I can pay in coin." He taps his pocket so the land's defender can hear the jingle of his small riches.

This promise placates the man; the knife is retracted at once.

"Well," the man with a gruff voice says, "why didn't you just knock?"

Jester turns to the silhouette of a tall, lanky figure. He can't see his face, his view obscured by the dark and the long, wild, untamed mess of hair that looks like it's never been combed or cut, ever. "Didn't want to wake you, good sir."

The man waves off this remark like it's pure nonsense. "Don't sleep much these nights, not living out here. Woods are dangerous. Full of dark, lurking things, here."

"Well, by the power of Highbeard's Beard, I count my blessings I've made it this far." He nods to the hut. "Live alone?"

The man's head falls sideways, his nostrils inflating. "Why?"

"Curious—I mean you no harm, honest. I was injured in a massacre and—"

"Massacre?"

Jester turns his head in the direction of Riverspell—or where he thinks Riverspell should be. "There was a festival in Riverspell."

"Aye, heard of it."

"Mountain folk raided the grounds in broad daylight. Left few survivors. It was quite ugly. I barely escaped."

The silhouette doesn't move. Then he points at Jester, his face. Jester figures he should get used to this kind of questioning finger. "Why's you got a cloth covering your face? You look bandit-ish."

"I'm no bandit, sir. Just..." He pulls down the black cloth, allowing the light from the house to shine on his new scars. "Had an accident, and I'm not proud of my appearance."

If the man is fazed he surely doesn't express it. "Looks like more than just an accident, aye? Someone had some fun with you?"

"Too much fun, I bet."

"Well, it's just me and my wife in there. Small place. Peaceful. We live alone. No one bothers us out here. We're not big on meeting new people. But you're welcome to spend a few hours and get some rest. After that—you'll be on your way."

"I appreciate your hospitality. May the light of Highbeard's Golden Crown shine down upon your soul."

"Very well then." He extends his hand. Jester takes it, and the man pulls him to his feet. His hand is maybe the hairiest Jester's ever shaken, tufts of black straw poking out his sleeve, collections of long whiskers on his knuckles. "Come inside," the tall man says. "We've just made breakfast."

JESTER DEVOURS HIS SCRAMBLED EGGS. When he's finished, he attacks the sausages, ignoring the needling pain from his facial scars that surge every other bite. The meal is so good he licks his fingers clean before shoving the plate into the center of the table. He sits back in his chair, grabs his belly—now full, almost too full—and lets out a long, measured sigh.

The two owners of the quaint hut simply stare at him.

"You weren't shittin'," the lady says, impressed by this gluttonous display. "You were hungrier than a Bagwell Mountain wolf."

Jester licks his lips, lapping up every last layer of grease. "Are the wolves of Bagwell Mountain known to be hungrier than wolves from elsewhere? I've never come across one."

"Oh yes," the lady says. "Hungry creatures indeed."

"We didn't get your name, friend," the husband says. "I'm Sandy, by the way. My wife here is Marlta. We're the Portnoys."

"Sandy, Marlta. Lovely names. The Portnoys. Pleasure to meet you both. I'm…" He stops himself, thinking twice about revealing his true name. There's likely no risk of Iradon's infamous warden or his nefarious associates finding him out here. But still—the Warden was tricky and employed many. And Jester has been in the eye of his vicious manhunt for longer than he cares to remember.

"They call me Jester," he finally says, pointing to the corners of his permanent smile. Next, he shoves back his hood to reveal the clown hat that has replaced his once-long mane of hair. He toys with the bells, letting them jingle, to maximize the full effect of his appearance.

"Interesting choice," Sandy says, rubbing his chin.

"Wasn't mine to make, but yes—interesting is one word for it."

"You piss off a gang of bandits, that it?" The man bites into a humongous turkey leg, ripping off a whole strip of juicy meat.

"Yes, you could definitely say that. They didn't like what I almost did to their leader. They were offended. So, they scarred me."

Marlta leans over the table as if she's ready to hear a secret that would rival her husband's dinner's succulent nature. "And what did you almost do to their leader?"

"That, milady, is personal. Deeply so. As deep as the knife that cut me. But for what it's worth, it was a very bad thing I'd tried, and they had every good reason to scar me."

"You mean, you were trying to kill him," Sandy says, his eyes knowing.

"Perhaps. Like I said—personal. Deeply."

"We don't consort with killers," he says, leering now. The turkey leg is back on the plate, and the man folds his arms across his chest.

"Well, lucky for me, the man is still alive. And no one was harmed in the making of these scars—except me."

"Hmm," Sandy grumbles, as if he's not buying Jester's story—mostly about the fact he didn't hurt anyone. Jester wonders if he looks as transparent as Sandy is making him feel, or if Sandy's just that good at reading people.

"Thank you both for your hospitality," Jester says, changing the subject. "I would like to make you an offer..." He digs into his pocket and produces a small pouch, which jangles when he sets it down on the table in front of him. From the pouch he pinches three gold coins, just a small fraction of the peridium provided by the king's private bank back in Hornrake; three times the rate any small inn would charge for a night's worth of undisturbed rest. The Portnoys' eyes bulge when they see gold slapped down on the table in front of them. "Three golds for a day of rest. It's late—or early, depending on how you go about your days and evenings—but I wish to stay through tomorrow and get some much-needed shut-eye. My bones ache and need to heal. I've been on the road a long time. Do we have an agreement?"

The husband and wife exchange looks, but Jester sees they seem wary, as if there is a secret price to pay, one that costs more than what's shining up at them from the table.

Sandy's jaw firms, his mouth a thin slit, his eyes heavier. "Who's after you?"

This takes Jester by surprise. Even if they suspect men are after him, three gold coins that still smell like an Owlton bank vault should have eased the minds of the most cautious sorts. Especially those keeping to themselves and who live in the woods far, far away from any town or city. Unless...

Unless people are after them too, Jester thinks, and soon after he thinks it, the thought totally consumes him. Then another thought sweeps him away: he might be safer in the forest.

"No one is after me," Jester lies, then giggles like the idea is so preposterous that one can only laugh at the idea. "No, the people I offended are a long way from here, I'm afraid. Long in the past."

The man points to Jester's cosmetic misfortunes. "Those wounds don't look all the way healed. Not fresh, but probably not more than a week old, I'd wager. That right?"

Jester winks. "You know your wounds. Were you a doctor in your past life?"

"No," the man says, smiling wickedly. "Not a doctor—just a man who has seen many wounds."

Not comforting in the least, Jester thinks, flashing the widest grin he can muster, testing the fused skin. Slowly, he returns the gold coins back to the pouch. "You know, on second thought, I think I ought to—"

The man lashes out, stretches across the table and grips Jester's wrist, preventing him from placing the pouch back in his pocket. Jester feels the man's strength, the brutish potential. He may have presented himself as a gentle giant, but Jester is certain—this man could wrench his head off his shoulders with a few wicked twists, if correctly motivated. There's something…*feral* about him.

A smell hits his nose just then, something sour and familiar. It smells like the dog pens back in Iradon, home of hundreds of mangy mutts that no one wanted to take in, but nobody wanted to slaughter needlessly either. So they lived in cages and the townsfolk took turns feeding them and giving them water. Yes, the unique pungent scent from those cages comes back to him, tickling the depths of his nostrils. Wet, smelly fur.

With each passing second, the man grips his wrist harder and the smell grows bolder.

"Sir," Jester says calmly, afraid to show any outward anger or fear. "I recommend letting go of my wrist. I'm not sure if either of us will benefit from any type of nasty confrontation."

The man is baring his teeth now. It isn't until Marlta

touches him, rubbing her husband's shoulder, that he stops. His eyes have gone dark, turning black and beady, and the second she places that hand on him, that fades—his normal eyes reappear. He retracts his hand, letting go of Jester's wrist, leaving behind marks that might bruise. Sandy takes a deep, gasping breath, as if the act has zapped the air from his lungs.

"You're quite strong," Jester tells him.

"I-I'm sorry," he says, still catching his breath. "I don't know what came over me."

"No need to apologize. I'm a stranger who told you a worrisome tale. I meant nothing by it. However, I do think—in light of recent events—it's probably best to move on. I would have stayed and paid you well for it, but—"

"No," Sandy says, pushing himself up from the table. His grease-slicked bib falls to the floor. "No, no."

Jester arches his brow. "Sir, I must say—my offer is no longer available. I don't mind taking back to the road, although…"

Sandy shushes him with a wave of his arm, then says, "No, he can't."

Marlta stands now, clinging to her husband's arm. "Now, Sandy, think about this—think about what you're saying."

"No, no. He can't. He can't leave. He has silver in his pouch. SILVER. I can taste it."

Since Jester is the only one still sitting, he stands. "I'm sorry if I was a bother, but—"

The scent cuts him off again, the overpowering stink of a hundred dogs seeking shelter from a rainy afternoon.

"What in the world is that stench?" he says, on the verge of sneezing.

Marlta freezes, pinches her eyes shut as if she's just received terrible news. "Oh dear…"

"He knows," Sandy says, his suspicions now confirmed. "He fucking knows."

"Maybe not. Maybe he doesn't know anything."

"Look at him." Sandy sniffs the air, as if he can smell Jester's thoughts, his intentions. "He's not an imbecile. He knows."

Then it clicks.

Sort of.

He knows this, this one thing: he should fucking run.

————

"BOTH OF YOU?" Jester asks, wishing he could frown.

Marlta shakes her head. "Not both—just Sandy." She pulls up the sleeves of her lacy gown to reveal a network of scars running up her arm. Hundreds of slashes—claw marks—that have healed over. Scars on top of scars. Now that he sees it, he can see some of the white lines on her neck as well. "Apparently I'm immune to the infection. He's got at me a few times."

"How are you still alive?" Jester asks, perplexed by the dynamic of this relationship.

She reaches down the front of her gown and yanks on the chain around her neck, a pure silver pendant of a star-shaped Highbeard insignia. Sandy looks away, unable to stand the sight of it. "It repels him. Just a touch of silver—"

"Burns his flesh," Jester finishes for her. "Yes, I am familiar with the lore, however, I'm embarrassed to admit, I've never seen one before—I was led to believe your kind went extinct centuries ago."

Sandy seems to take offense to this. "Not extinct. *Driven* from society. Those that remain live in caves, isolated areas, hiding in fear. Fear that men will discover us, hunt us down, ensure our extinction."

"Well, I suppose this place keeps you safe enough. Not too many travelers out this way."

"Rare, a soul wanders this far from Riverspell. Occasionally stag hunters find us, but they usually pass without incident, not looking for food or lodge—certainly not stealing from our gardens."

"I do apolo—"

"We can't let you leave," Sandy interrupts. "You know too much and we don't know you—we can't risk you running back to Riverspell and crying werewolf. They will send hunters of a different sort our way."

"Well, that's the thing—Riverspell is no more. So you needn't worry—"

"Riverspell isn't the only town around here," Sandy says, hatred gleaming in his eyes, and Jester can tell there have been other incidents. The fact that Sandy is still here, living, breathing, means those incidents were handled.

Just like he will handle me.

"I won't tell a goddamn soul," Jester says, unable to strip the fear from his voice this time. "Because I have no friends, and no one will listen to a fool. Even if they did," he says, looking around the room as if searching for something he's unable to locate, "I don't know where I am! I'm lost. Utterly. Isn't that a hoot?"

"I believe him," Marlta says, and Jester can tell she's not one for violence or confrontation, and will do anything to avoid both if she can help it. Jester gives her a subtle nod in solidarity.

"Now, dear," Sandy says, not letting this go. "You know what will happen—you remember what happened last winter."

Marlta's eyes go soft in the orange haze of the cabin's candle glow. She drops her gaze to the floorboards. "I remember."

"Then you know what I must do." His jaw flexes with agitation. He starts unbuttoning the top of his shirt, revealing a thick blanket of wolf hair covering his chest, teeming out from beneath the fabric. He's already starting to shift. Jester doesn't have much time, not that he knows how long it takes for a man to become a beast. Seconds? Minutes? It doesn't matter. He needs to get himself gone. And fast. "I'm sorry," Sandy says, and Jester truly believes it, believes the man doesn't want to turn into a monster and tear him to shreds. "I'm sure you're a really good person just looking for a place to rest, that you mean us no harm, but—I have a family to protect." His eyes fall on his wife's belly.

Jester notices—for the first time—the small roundness of the woman's stomach. She cradles the bump with both hands and smiles. "Congratulations," he wishes her; them. "And to answer your statement—no, I'm not a good person. Quite terrible in fact. I've killed many people. Probably more than you have with your wolf hands." Jester stops unburdening these secrets just long enough to hear Marlta gasp. "Many, many persons. So many I've lost count. But they were mostly people who deserved to die. Mostly. And yet—I have no desire to kill either of you, nor seek out those who wish to harm you. That is the truth, plain as I can tell it."

The werewolf reflects on this. Then he finishes removing his shirt, and Jester watches the hair covering his flesh thicken and lengthen and curl, erasing the human skin beneath the coat. "Thank you for your honesty," the werewolf says, its voice deepening, becoming less human and more bestial. "But honesty will not save you. Not here. Not today."

"Very well then," Jester says, and moves quickly toward the sharp knife Sandy has left next to the turkey legs. It may not be made of silver, but it's his first best option. Jester has learned from his mistake inside Ragland's throne room. This time, there is no hesitation. He's far quicker than Sandy, as he rams the knife deep into the werewolf's gullet before it can react.

When it does, it swipes at Jester's face with a hand that's half-transformed into a meaty claw. Jester ducks out of the way, then summons the strength to flip over the dinner table. The table smacks into the werewolf, pushing him back against the wall. As he's forced backward, he strikes his pregnant wife, knocking her to the floor. Upon hitting the ground, she exhales a wheezy breath, her wind stolen from her. Jester hopes the collision with the ground hasn't complicated her pregnancy, but then again— she's done nothing to prevent her shape-shifting husband from trying to remove Jester's head. "Sorry," he shouts, adding "Good luck with all of that," before he turns and dives through the closest window, breaking the glass and landing in the bushes outside. In a three count, he's springing toward the woods, running for his life.

Behind him, the most intense howl he's ever heard echoes through the dark. Follows him. Weaving through the night.

The smell of wet, blood-soaked fur draws near.

SIGNAL FROM THE STARS

CHAPTER NINE

"Any magic that still exists in our world is a treasure from the gods; however, we will always keep a vigilant watch for practitioners of witchcraft, because witchcraft is the most dangerous sort of magic, and it must be snuffed out like a nighttime candle. We will slay and banish all blackhearted magic, the same way Highbeard slayed Arkos and banished him from the Outlands."

– KING EDWILL RAGLAND I, KING OF OWLTON

———

FOUR ROVANIAN SUBJECTS escort the boy, their jaws locked, their eyes flitting every time the boy attempts to catch them staring. The boy tries talking to them like he does with every guard, squire, knight, and soldier he's met through the years, who's been tasked to watch him, escort him, keep him safe. But like those others, these four young subjects ignore him as if he doesn't exist. It makes him sad, but that's the life he's been born into, and as his best buddy Fen sometimes says, *At least you have godlike powers! Think of all the miracles you will get to perform! People will love you!*

He does think about it—quite often. Maybe too much.

He wishes Fen were here this morning, accompanying him during his training exercises. Fen is not permitted at these types of sessions, private school lectures, or anywhere near the boy when Ravenborn is present, a man who regards most of the people behind the castle walls like venomous snakes waiting to strike at the most opportune moment.

He treats Fen maybe worse than all of them.

The boy doesn't know why exactly, other than Ravenborn has major trust issues, even amongst his closest confidants, born from a rumor that traced back to the Last War, around the time the boy was born. The boy suspects Ravenborn doesn't even trust *him*, the boy whose "powers" will one day emerge, be harnessed, used to restore balance to the Five Realms, to usher in the second coming of the gods.

Powers.

Gods.

Psssh.

The boy has spent years training with Ravenborn, ever since he turned eight, and yet, proof of his abilities has never once shown. The countless hours spent in the courtyards, the afternoons wasted in the botanical gardens, and the nights out beyond the Silver Towers' walls, charging through the wilds of Rovan, have not brought a single spell out of him, not a drop of magic. He is already convinced that the foretold prophecy he's supposed to fulfill is "pure horseshit" (Fen's phrase, his colorful way of describing rules and regulations he sometimes disagrees with, or flat-out does not believe to be true) and has resigned himself to believing he's just an average teenage boy with no special mark. He suspects Ravenborn believes the same thing, and that only King Salah still believes in the old fable—the boy with the star-shaped eyes; the ender of wars; the usher of old gods; Highbeard's prized descendant. It stinks of rotten, desperate persistence.

The boy loses more faith with each passing day.

Ravenborn waits for him in the courtyard. He dismisses the four guards with a simple nod, and they scatter, hurrying to their next chore. Once out of sight, the boy stands across from his elder, forced to stare at his intimidating scowl. The courtyard has been set up like an obstacle course, with various posts and activities to hone his "skills." Dummies made of burlap and straw stand strapped to the fence posts, primarily used for striking with wooden swords. Targets are tilted in positions to be penetrated by arrows. Hoops, comprised of recycled metals, hang from long ropes, tied to sturdy beams, wait to instruct the boy's strength and conditioning. And, of course, Ravenborn's favorite—the crystal whipping post, where he ties his students and whips them furiously until he has no more strength. The lesson? The boy has always suspected it's in case a soldier is taken hostage: a lesson in torture tactics from an enemy.

But a part of him thinks it's also for Ravenborn's amusement. The man has a mean streak, on display too often.

"Welcome," Ravenborn says through tight lips. "Did you rest well?"

The boy nods. Part of him knows to tread carefully around the man. Ravenborn is wildly unpredictable, and the boy often fears at some point the man will lose so much faith in the prophecy that he'll put the boy out of his misery just for wasting years of his life. Ravenborn's best years are behind him—lost in the wars—but he's entered his silver age, and the boy can tell that the man is living out those glory years inside his own head. The old warrior wants to get back to his former self, that fighter who claimed the lives of well over a thousand men.

"Good. Let's get to work then."

Work begins with some swordplay. The boy swings the stick at scarecrow-like dummies, practicing moves he's already been taught while Ravenborn introduces new ones.

"Stick him here," Ravenborn instructs, pointing to a vulnerable spot under the ribcage. "Owlton armor always has a weak spot, and it's usually just under the lower rib. Unless they've adjusted things over the last decade or so." He says this with a delicious smile, relishing those old battles. "But knowing King Ragland and his penchant for cheap wars, I'm certain nothing has changed at all."

"Why do you hate Owlton?" the boy asks, a question he believes he knows the answer to, but has never heard it confirmed from Ravenborn's mouth. He knows only what his teachers have told him in private.

"What kind of question is that, boy?" Ravenborn studies him up and down, as if he's caught the little punk stealing lumps of gold from under his mattress. "Have your teachers taught you nothing about our realm's history?"

"They teach me fine," he says back, his voice growing smaller with each word, more dubious. "But I want to know why *you* hate them."

Ravenborn seems shocked by the inquiry. He scans the court-yard as if maybe giggling knights are hiding behind the stone pillars, watching a practical joke unfold in their favor. Like someone put the boy up to this. Then he combs back his black hair, chews his lower lip, and answers, "Because...they are our enemy."

"But why? Have you tried talking peace with them?"

"Dammit, boy!" he snaps, red rushing into his cheeks, burning beneath his beard.

The boy flinches as if Ravenborn is about to backhand him. It wouldn't have been the first time.

"I'm just curious," the boy says, persisting, keeping a hand raised in self-defense. "Why do you want another war with them?"

Ravenborn sighs, collecting his composure. The red in his cheeks has faded to a baby-girl pink. "War is good for the state. The Five Realms. We need them to progress as one nation."

"But we aren't one nation."

"Precisely the point. There should be one king to rule over the Five, as it was during the time of the gods. Now...Five Realms.

Four legit kings. The Crosslands—our biggest land—is bereft of true leadership, populated by barons who act like kings, wishing themselves successful conquerors. They are slime, glorified criminals, and they will be dealt with once our score is settled with our enemies in the south." He shakes his head, disgusted by the state of things. "It's chaos. The world needs order, direction, and unity—all things one true king can bring us. Our Emperor Salah."

"But if you lose again?"

The boy's question sparks a flash of anger in Ravenborn's eyes. The man wants to lash out, strike him, and hard. But he refrains, keeping his hands resting on the pommel of his iron sword. Perhaps he's feeling benevolent this morning, or perhaps he's afraid of abusing the boy too much. If Emperor Salah comes down for a visit and sees his prized possession with a bloody lip or nose, what would he think? Surely he'd have no choice but to believe that Ravenborn probably shouldn't be the one who nurtures the boy's talent.

"We never lost the first time," Ravenborn says, practically spitting through his teeth. "Which is why you're not wearing Owlton purple right now." He taps the boy's green vest to punctuate the point. Just because they didn't win doesn't mean they lost.

"We're still separate realms, though. Yes?"

Ravenborn's eyes twitch, like he's calculating some complex equation. "Yes."

"What makes you think the next one will be different?"

Ravenborn reaches out and grabs the meaty part of the boy's shoulder, between his shoulder and neck, squeezing him harder than a father would a son, before imparting wisdom. A squeeze laced with hatred. More than he can measure. "Because now we have you." With that, Ravenborn releases him, but not before patting the boy on the back three times, hard. "Now. Onward. We have lessons. Stand behind that line there."

Ravenborn points to a white line in the dirt, salt, that one of the subjects poured out before their appointment. The boy does as he's instructed, goes and stands behind the salt line, and faces the dummies.

"Lay down your sword," says Ravenborn.

He places the wooden stick at his feet. Then looks dead ahead at the dummies. He knows what's about to be asked of him.

"Now, boy. The time is now. Reach out with your dominant hand."

The boy stretches his right hand toward the dummies, feeling the air with his fingertips. He can feel the energy, like touching a metal door lever and receiving a static shock, only this sensation is constant, yet weaker.

This is how it always begins, with a promise of power.

How it always ends is with bitter disappointment and a torrent of cussing from Ravenborn's mouth.

Maybe not this time, the boy thinks, and yes, today does feel different. The air feels different, the way one can sense a change in the winds or weather.

"Good. Do you feel it? The power coursing through you, flooding your veins?" When the boy doesn't answer straight away, Ravenborn clears his throat and says, "Yes?"

"Yes," the boy replies, but it's hard to speak *and* draw energy from the courtyard's air. There isn't much of it here, and what he can harness isn't powerful enough to make an impression on his tutor. The boy finds it funny—a man who has no magic in him, not in the least, is providing *him* lessons on how to activate his abilities. The boy always thought the lessons would come from a Highbeard priest, rather than Emperor Salah's most celebrated military leader. But…it's possible the emperor trusts Ravenborn more than his religious fanatics. That's probably smart; even at this young age, he's aware of the danger of religious fanaticism.

"Now push outward," Ravenborn demands.

The boy does as he's told, tries pushing the mounting power through his fingertips. The wind moves, but that's it. A calm zephyr shoots past them, kicking up spirals of wayward leaves that had fallen across the courtyard's grass.

"Concentrate," Ravenborn coaches, his voice stern.

"I am."

"Again."

The boy pushes. Sees and pushes. Concentrates and pushes. Pictures the dummies falling over, knocked down from his own hand, his mind, and he pushes out once again. But nothing stirs. The wind dies as it reaches its desired target, the straw sticking out of the dummy's ragged attire barely moving an inch. He engages again, repeats the doomed process, filling the palm of his hand with energy from the arena, then pushes with such force that he cries out, his shoulder feeling like it's been separated from the socket. Gentle winds move on the dummy's rags, but no forceful blow lands.

"That's it?" Ravenborn asks, his voice thick with disappointment.

Same as ever.

The boy drops to his knees, begins to sob into his palms, weakened from the moment, not from the summoning of energy.

It's all so useless. *He's* useless. He might as well lay his head on the chopping block so Ravenborn can end his misery.

Ravenborn sighs, places his hands on his hips and looks away.

The boy continues to sob, oblivious to the shadow of the emperor pacing the keep above. Completely unaware of his watchful gaze.

ON THE ROAD AGAIN
CHAPTER TEN

"The Crosslands have always named a king, but have split into so many kingdoms and territories, it's hard to keep count. It's a mess of a region that always faces pressures to join the north and the south, the Rovan Territories and Owlton respectively. Partnerships have been built with neighboring realms, but those partnerships are fragile and only come into play in times of war."

– BENJI HUBBARD, A CLOSER LOOK AT THE CROSSLANDS

THE JINGLING of bells is the first thing that registers. Next comes the man's twisted smile, the stitching that's fixed his mouth that way, and the worry in his eyes that doesn't match the lower half of his face. He launches himself from the dark and into the clearing, scurrying past Ralyanna and heading toward the center of camp.

She can't help it. Not knowing why this man is here, or what his intentions are, she screams.

The man wearing a jester hat puts a finger over his lips and shushes her. She doesn't listen, turns and retreats back to the fire. "Ket! Ket! KET!"

Ket springs forth from the dreamworld. Alert, he scrambles to his feet and focuses on Ra. "Wha—what?"

She turns and points to the approaching figure, who's now hustling over to them at an alarming speed. "A man came out of the woods, he's—"

"Jester? Is that you?"

"Gods among us, Ket?" Jester places a hand over his heart, his eyelids fluttering as if he's blinking back tears of joy. "Am I happy to see *you*."

"What's going on?"

Before he can respond, Ralyanna grabs fistfuls of her hair and says, "Wait? You two know each other?"

"This is the friend I was telling you about," Ket says.

"Friend?" Jester says, his mood changing at the mention of the word. He clutches his heart like a swooning princess. "You really do like me..." A second later his features darken, his eyes narrowing as if he's about to divulge the spooky part of a ghost story. "But no time to hug and make up for lost time—we need to skedaddle. Come now. Chop-chop. Not a single second to waste." He snaps his fingers at them, like that's going to motivate them to move faster.

"What's going on?"

"What's going on, Ket, is that I have one very large man after me. Actually, he's a wolf. A wolf-man. A fucking werewolf, all right? So, tip-tip, let's *goooooo*."

Ket doesn't budge. Neither does Ralyanna. The two stand there facing Jester as if he's putting them on.

"This is not a joke," he assures them.

"Jester, there's no such thing as—"

Before Ket can finish that thought, the force of a tremendous howl echoes through the trees, bristling the leaves on their branches.

"I wish there wasn't," Jester admits, "but the world you knew, sir—the world I knew—no longer exists. Werewolves, apparently, are very real and there is one hot on my trail, and I can't shake him. So, it's run or—"

It's too late. Emerging from the darkness, a shadowy figure steps between the thick tree trunks, a bipedal hulk at least ten feet tall. Ralyanna is so surprised by the monstrous presence that she nearly backs into the flames. She can't take her eyes off the tremendous beast.

"Ralyanna," Ket says, and when she doesn't respond, he grabs her arm and forces her to stand behind him. "Stay back. If I say run, you run."

She understands, tries to tell him she understands, but her voice doesn't work.

Ket draws his blade.

"I hope that thing is silver," Jester mutters. Then he nods to Ket's secondary weapon, the obsidian short sword. "May I borrow that? I lost my effects during the massacre."

Without removing his eyes from the towering creature, Ket tosses Jester the shiny black blade.

"Hmm," Jester says, tossing the handle between his hands. "So heavy for such a short blade..."

"Shut up," Ket scolds. "Keep the enemy in front of you."

"Watch out for his claws. If you get infected by its disease, you will become one of them."

"Noted."

The werewolf bellows, then charges.

Ralyanna screams again, much louder this time.

———

THE BEAST DARTS toward him with an alacrity he's never seen from any living creature. *A werewolf.* The concept would be laughable to Ket if those fanged teeth and the dog-haired body weren't streaking toward him. He notices the wound near his neck, the bib of blood staining its brown coat.

As the werewolf charges, Ket thrusts out his blade, daring the beast to skewer itself. It stops, hurling a massive claw at Ket's head. Ket steps back, easily dodging the attack while Jester moves behind the monster, the two silently coordinating an attack from opposite sides.

Ket responds aggressively, slicing toward the werewolf's left shoulder. The beast shrugs backward, but as it retreats, Jester stabs the creature from behind with his black blade. It grunts with obvious pain, then turns and backhands Jester across the face with enough force to send him reeling back. Unbalanced, he stumbles, his knees falling to the soft earth. While the werewolf fixates on Jester, Ket plunges his blade through where the beast's kidney might sit. This time, the werewolf howls in agony, throwing back its head, protesting his pain to the Pale Sister, her luminous half-smile. Ket pulls back on his sword, blood spurting onto his own face. Then he levels his sword horizontally in front of his eyes, ready for the beast's reaction, prepared to block any straightforward attack.

A hot blur the size of a fist whizzes past him, the heat from it flaring, making him wince and cower from its blazing tail. The ball of fire smacks into the werewolf's chest, sending sparks and embers—like a gathering of hell pixies—airborne. Ket turns, sees Ralyanna standing by the fire, lowering a small chunk of firewood over the flames until it catches. Once the wood becomes the fiery projectile she desires, she heaves the makeshift missile at the beast again, though this time the werewolf sees it coming, and sidesteps the attempt.

"Ralyanna," Ket grumbles, his tone almost that of a worried father. "Run into the woods. Now."

"But—"

"Hear me, girl! Now!"

Ket faces the werewolf once more, knowing that in the next few minutes one of them will be dead—himself or the wolf-man. Jester gets to his feet and shakes off his disorientation.

The wolf-beast tracks Ralyanna, its entire body tensing to

pounce after her for what she did with her fireballs. It springs after her, and Ket cries, "NO!" hoping to attract the monster's attention, but it doesn't work—Ralyanna sprints for cover as the beast bears down on her.

Ket chases after them, Jester not far behind. Ralyanna dips into the darkness and positions herself behind a thick oak trunk, shielding herself from the oncoming attack. The werewolf swipes at the tree, raking huge claw marks into the bark. Splinters of aged wood sail through the air.

Ket and Jester reach them before the monster can orbit the oak and get his sharp claws on her body.

"Beast!" Ket shouts, pounding his chest like some primitive warrior. "Over here! It's us you want to fight, our flesh you seek!"

Jester separates from Ket, trying once again to round the creature.

The werewolf tunes its gaze to Ket's call and shows him the potential of its ferocious bite. Drool as thick as a creamy stout drips from those sharp ivory fangs. The man-wolf seems intrigued by the prospect of a more difficult prey. Ket waves his sword in the air, inviting the beast over, luring it to a swift death.

"You're a coward to attack an unarmed girl," Ket snarls, unsure if the human hidden beneath the fur can hear him, or if all that remains is a senseless beast, driven by bloodlust. "Come, fight me."

Whatever the case, his invitation is accepted, and the beast crouches down on all fours and breaks into a charging gallop. Ket waits. Before the werewolf can close half the distance, Jester comes at him like a lightning strike, fast and deadly. He leaps onto the werewolf's back and jabs the black blade into its throat. The wolf roars, probably alerting everything and everyone within a ten-mile radius, and then rears back, throwing Jester from his mount. The clown goes sailing in an impressive arc, into the darkened shadows where the moonlight doesn't reach.

Ket pays no attention to Jester's flight, using the precious seconds of the werewolf's recovery to close the gap between them, charging forth with his sword aiming at the creature's throat. The werewolf can't recover in time and Ket jabs the blade into its fur-covered gullet, ramming through the tough hide with relative ease.

The werewolf turns, howling and screaming, a discordant but even blend of human and wolf-like wailing that grates Ket's ears. The man-wolf's paws go for its throat, covering up the bloody leak, and then it backs away from Ket, moving past the campfire toward the opposite end of the clearing. A wet howl escapes its snout, and then it spins—clearly wounded, mortally so—and limps off into the black yawn between the trees.

Ket considers following and finishing the job, but tracking the blood trail with only the moonlight to guide him will be difficult. Besides, he has to make sure the girl is unscathed (and Jester too, he supposes) before leaving, and doing so will almost guarantee the beast a clean escape.

Ket sheaths his sword, then turns for the woods. "Ralyanna?"

The girl cautiously removes herself from behind the oak, peeking out with blinking, scared eyes, hands at her side, breathing as if she's just completed a whole hard day in the mines for some slave master baron.

"You hurt?"

The girl shakes her head sheepishly, wipes her nose with the back of her hand.

"Good," Ket says. "Jester? You alive?"

Stumbling from behind some brush, Jester appears, holding a limp arm. "Alive? Yes. Broken? Also yes."

Ket inspects the arm, cocking a dubious brow. "Minor dislocation."

"Are you sur—*Aaaarghhh fuck!*" Before he can spit out the question, Ket takes the liberty of popping the bone back in place. The audible crack echoes through the trees. Through his teeth, Jester tells him, "Next time fucking warn me."

"Too much anticipation and you would have fidgeted too much. Trust me."

Jester spits a wad of frothy saliva on the ground. " 'Trust me' he says. How can I trust someone who won't even reveal his true name?"

Ket rolls his eyes. "We're not having this conversation right now. What happened back in Riverspell?"

"What do you mean what happened? You were there."

"How'd you escape?"

Jester shakes his head. "T'wasn't easy. That's for sure." He quickly recounts his tales of escaping the inn and stumbling upon the Portnoys in the forest.

"You watched that man transform into that…wolf-thing."

"He's a werewolf," Jester says. "That's what they do—turn from man to beast."

Ket glares at him, unconvinced. "Werewolves are stories. Fables."

"Yes, I thought so too. But alas, my eyes do not deceive me."

Ket's don't either, though he grapples with the concept—the scary truth that this is not the same world he once knew. There are things emerging in the dark, no longer content with staying secret.

"Listen," Jester says, clapping him on the shoulder the way a good friend might. "The world has gotten really spooky this last decade, since the Battle of End-La. You're familiar with that one, I'm certain."

"I've heard of it."

"Highbeard's Golden Testicles, you really were on an island in south Owlton."

"Everything I've heard regarding the conclusion of the Last War is whispers and hearsay. News didn't exactly travel to where I was. I picked up what I could during my trips to Braag, from the mouths of drunkards at dives. Not exactly reliable news sources."

"Well, you have a lot of history to catch up on. I shall do my best to inform you on our journey north. We'll have time. Just know this—the battle may have been the last of that war, but the war is far from over. It's only just begun. And I'm afraid taking this journey, agreeing to be Ragland's loyal hound in the biggest game of fetch ever played, has made you an integral part of it." He pauses, scanning Ket from head to toe. "*Again.*"

Ket hates the way he breathes life into that word. *He doesn't know anything about me. How can he?*

"I just want my sons returned to me. I have no interest in wars."

"But the wars have interest in you. And you can *want* all you want—the world doesn't give two chicken shits what *you* want. Neither does destiny, Ket Norlath."

Ket's mouth fills with a sour taste, forcing him to spit on the smoldering fire. "I make my own destiny."

"I can't wait to see it." Jester nods to Ralyanna, who's come out of the shadows and is now basking in what's left of the campfire. "What are you doing with this girl? She's a little young for—"

"She's the one you should thank for your miraculous recovery," he says, gritting his teeth. "I suggest you show her a little respect."

"Reeeeally?" Jester's brow bounces up and down, several times. "A witchling, perhaps?"

"Don't use that word," Ket scolds.

"Touchy, touchy, Ket Norlath." Jester pats Ket's chest, a friendly tap-tap. "Don't worry, I'll behave myself."

"See that you do. She's an innocent girl."

"What will we do with her? Obviously she can't come with us. To Rovan." When Ket doesn't answer, he adds another, "Obviously."

"We'll have to find an orphanage along the way. Her grandfather—guardian—was killed at Riverspell."

"Sad circumstances. Finding an orphanage that will take her might not be easy, especially since we're so close to the Crosslands, which you no doubt remember from your traveling days?"

Ket eyes him closely. "Of course."

"Nasty territory, filled with bandits and barons, bandits that wish to be barons and barons that desire to be bandits. I'm not confident we will make it all the way to the Silver Towers with our heads still attached. With this girl in our company…well, that will just make the trip ten times more difficult."

"There has to be somewhere we can place her. A family willing to accept her, take her in—provide food and shelter."

"Aren't you a hopeful bastard." Jester groans. "We can't take her back to Riverspell, that's for certain."

"I want to go back," she says, overhearing their conversation. "To Riverspell. For Borgadine."

"Borga-what-now?" Jester rudely asks.

"Borgadine," she repeats, sounding irritated by Jester's flippant remark.

"Her guardian," Ket clarifies.

"Ah, yes—well, that's a no-can-do," Jester says sharply. "Place is a fiery ruin by now, nothing but ash and smoke. And if it's not, then those Wilders have made camp in the flames."

Ket sighs. "Jester is right," he says. "It's too dangerous to backtrack. I know you may want to retrieve your guardian's body, give him a proper burial—but it's not practical."

Tears build in her eyes. She lowers her head, defeated.

"Breaking my heart," Jester says, his words dripping with sarcasm, and Ket thinks if it wouldn't make matters worse, he'd backhand Jester right across his scarred cheek.

He's able to stay his hand, but he's not able to stop his anger from lashing out. He seizes the man by his frilly collar. "Have some fucking compassion," he growls.

Jester's perma-smile only makes Ket's blood pump harder. Because Ket notices the twinkle in his eyes—if his lips weren't stitched that way, into a perfect smile, he'd still be smiling. Because Jester thinks this is comical.

"Calm down, sir," the clown says, putting up his hands in a defenseless, surrendering pose. "I meant nothing by it. The girl has my empathy."

Ket lets go, giving him a forceful shove while doing so, just to drive home the fact he's unhappy with the man's lack of concern.

"We should leave," Jester announces. "At once. Chances are

that werewolf will head home, lick his wounds, and then get back on the hunt. He seems to have a lot to lose and allowing us to live is too detrimental to his survival—so he thinks. I don't know if we can escape his nose, but we should do our best to distance ourselves."

Ket agrees, even though he knows nothing of werewolves and their tracking abilities. All he knows is he stabbed the thing in the throat, and not much could survive that. However, it's turning out he doesn't know much about a lot.

———

BY SUNRISE they make it out of the forest and back to a beaten path wide enough to fit a single carriage. Ket's relieved, but exhausted—last night's confrontation with the werewolf and some troublesome dreams that followed have left him drained. Jester looks beyond fatigued, and has dragged himself much of the way. Ralyanna yawns every ten minutes or so, her eyes are also heavy with the lure of sweet dreams. Walking like this isn't sustainable for much longer—Ket knows they'll need proper food and rest, and clean water to drink, and soon.

"What's the plan?" Ket asks Jester.

"We're doing the plan," Jester says, waving to the road in front of them. "We take this road north until we find another bigger road. Or shelter."

As dawn cracks the horizon and purple light bleeds over the edge of the faraway mountain range, Ket squints, shading his eyes with his hand to see better. A few times he's stumbled, his legs too tired and zapped of the strength required for the weight he's carrying. Eventually he will break and have no choice but to crash, hopefully not in a patch of poisonous shrubbery.

Ralyanna looks sick. Not health-sick, like having the spring flu, but heartsick. Unbelievably sad. A depression demon sitting on her shoulders. She's clearly grieving something awful, and no matter what words of encouragement or support Ket can think of, nothing feels right. Perhaps it's because he's known the girl less than a day and it's not his right to say anything. Who is he to comfort her? But still—he finds the fatherly instinct to soothe and console difficult to ignore.

Hours later, Ket cannot disregard what his body is telling him and continue with the journey. He stumbles sideways and has to use a nearby pine tree to keep himself upright. Jester keeps walking and doesn't notice Ket's stoppage until Ralyanna sees him first and points it out. Jester breathes, clearly frustrated by the situation—but what does he expect? Ket has spent two whole years wasting away beneath the King of Owlton's palace. He rarely got to exercise and stretch his limbs, and his recent activities have taken a toll on his atrophied muscles.

"I need sleep," Ket tells them, finding a seat on the ground.

"Well, you won't get any here," Jester says plainly, projecting a hint of disgust. "Smell that wind? Rain's coming."

He does smell the airy wetness on the breeze, now that it's mentioned.

Ralyanna kneels beside him. She takes Ket's hands into her own and offers him a weak, pained smile. "You can go a little farther, yes?"

There's something in her eyes he notices, something that wasn't there earlier, and probably because he didn't look. Not like this. Not this close. It's a familiar something, but nothing he can adequately explain or articulate. But it reminds him of home, the most recent one—the farm.

"I don't think I can," he admits, feeling the thorns of shame burn roses into his cheeks.

"Yes, you can. Your body is strong. Your mind has convinced you it is not."

A spark of energy flows through him, and although he's nowhere near revitalized, he does feel capable enough to get to his feet, and attempt to travel a little farther. With her help, he rises.

"Come on, soldier," Jester says, winking at him. "You're tougher than that."

"I'm not a soldier," Ket responds sharply.

"No? I always pegged you as a Rovanian knight. Am I wrong?"

Not too far off, but yes, Jester is wrong. "I was no knight."

"Hmm. Curious. The mysterious Legend of Ket Norlath continues."

"I wasn't lying back in Hornrake, inside the king's court—I am not proud of my past."

"Embarrassed by it?"

"I'd rather forget it."

Jester's eyes slim to near slits. "You can try to forget the past all you want, friend—but the past will never forget you. It will always be there to remind you of what you've done. Unless you're fortunate enough to experience some bad case of amnesia; though these days I'm sure you can find a healer to make a pill for that. Or a witch…" His eyes roam the area, settle on Ralyanna.

"I'm not a witch."

"Oh no?" Jester puts his hands on his hips, pouts his lower lip as far as the seamed flesh allows. "That potion you gave Ket worked all sorts of wonders. Grand wonders. Wonders that would suggest something less than natural was used as the main ingredient."

"I know my chemistry."

"Are you some sort of botanical wizard then?"

"Something of the sort."

Jester's eyes glow like shiny tokens—whatever knowledge he hides behind them excites him. "You told Ket you used phrivian leaves in your potion, yes?"

The girl nods.

"We both know that is a fictional leaf, dear. So stop pretending to hide your witchery here with us. We are allies. And we are not Highbeard cunts looking for witches to burn. We won't turn you over to King Ragland's army, nor will we march you to the gates of the Silver Towers and throw you to their league of witchburners." Jester's eyes smile once again. "I promise."

"Phrivian leaves are real, fool."

"I'm no more a fool than you are not a witch, understand?" The girl's comment seems to sting him directly in the heart. Just as quickly as his temper flared, it's gone. "Phrivian leaves are fiction. Just admit it."

"Have you ever been to Glane?"

Jester huffs like this is also an insult. "Of course—do you mistake me for someone who is not well-traveled in the Five Realms?"

"Then you've visited the swamps of Glormoria? You've swam the shallow depths of their stinky, foul bottoms, dodging gators and harobins?"

"Haro-what?"

"Exactly. You've never been to Glormoria, and you've never seen the bottom of a swamp. Where Phrivian plants grow like mold at the mucky base."

Jester crinkles his nose as if he can smell those swamplands. Then he turns and faces Ket. "She has an attitude and I don't like her. About that orphanage..."

"I'm not going to any goddamn orphanage," she says, nearly spitting. Her contempt is palpable, throwing her response like a knife.

"Ralyanna," Ket says, looking at her with soft, pleading eyes. "It's for the best..."

"NO." She shakes her head furiously. "I will not be subjected to another orphanage, those places are...I'd rather spend an eternity in Arkos's Fire Realm than spend another minute inside one of those places."

"I'm sorry," Ket says, unable to offer her anything except a general apology. "You can't come with us. It's too dangerous."

"Why?"

"Because...people will try to kill us."

"People have been trying to kill me my entire life. Some slowly. Some not so slowly..."

"Not like this."

"You don't know me. What I've been through."

She's right about that. And Ket doesn't have a response, not one that will work in his favor. The silence stretches between them.

"You're right," Ket mumbles, "I know nothing about your life. But when I tell you where we're going is dangerous and the chances of us coming back alive are—"

"He means to say we're on a death march to the northern city, to see the boy in the Silver Towers," Jester says plainly, putting it all out there. He gives a dramatic wipe of his brow as if uttering this secret has taxed him greatly. "Whew! What a weight off my shoulders. See how good unburdening secrets can be, Ket Norlath?"

Ket ignores him.

"You're going to Rovan? To the Silver Towers?" The girl shakes her head as if she can't comprehend why anyone would want to go there.

"We were sent by King Ragland himself, on a mission to retrieve something very precious to him," Ket says.

"Some*one*," Jester corrects.

Ket glares at him, then concentrates back on Ralyanna, her confused stare. "Someone," he admits.

"You know King Ragland? Personally?" This news seems to steal her breath away.

"Not really. Only met him once. The conditions were less than ideal."

"What he means to say is that we were both imprisoned for heinous crimes and instead of sentencing us to hang, our punishment is to do the big king a favor. Not that impressive."

"You were imprisoned?" she asks, astonished. "You're criminals?"

Ket lowers his gaze to the dirt, unable to meet her eyes, which are undoubtedly judging him.

"For what?" she blurts out.

"I tried to kill the king," Jester proudly announces.

She ignores him, maybe thinking he's just being Jester, an exaggerator of truths, a liar of lies. Her eyes focus on Ket. "And you?" she asks him, lifting his chin with her thumb and forefinger.

"My wife was accused of being something she wasn't. Ragland's gang of watchmen stormed our farm, murdered her and abducted my children. They threw me in a dungeon beneath the palace. Are you satisfied now, young missy?"

She swallows, her eyes filling with sympathetic tears. "That's...really sad. What was she accused of?"

When Ket doesn't answer, Jester is all too eager to fill in for him. He bounces on his heels while saying, "Witchcraft, as it so happens."

"She was a witch?" There's a dash of hope in the girl's voice that Ket doesn't like. As if she wants the accusation to be true.

"Allegedly." Even as he tells the lie, his memory serves up a vision of soldiers dying by her hand, even though she did not lay a finger on them. He's back at the farm, watching that guard's eyes explode from their sockets as Jennah utters words that sound completely fabricated, phrases from no language known in the most secluded regions of Endlia. An ancient, ugly, dead language that no mortal should remember.

Lost languages from the god times.

"Do you think she was? A witch?"

Lazily, Ket shrugs. "If she had been, I never saw any evidence."

"Isn't my traveling companion so much fun?" Jester says, barking a few laughs. "Just full of zest and life he is."

"Shut up," Ralyanna says, turning to him. "You leave him alone."

"Or what? Will you hex me? Turn me into a black cat? Oh! Please don't turn me into a pigeon. I'm allergic to their droppings. Want to hear how I found that out?"

She's obviously had enough of his jesting, his needling disguised as innocent banter, and storms over to him. Whatever

Jester sees in her causes him to back up a few steps, and the confident twinkle in his eyes dies off at once.

"All right, girl," he says, making an X with his arms. "I'm only kidding."

"Ralyanna!" Ket calls to her. "Leave him be. He's a miserable assassin who is not very good at what he does, and he hates himself. Hates himself so much he disguises his self-loathing with sarcastic quips and boorish jests, and wishes he were someone else, *anyone* else but this pathetic excuse for a man."

Jester brushes off the insults with a sniffling snort. "Well, well. Maybe you were the northern king's personal head doctor, huh? You don't know me either, pal. I am as much of a mystery to you as you are to me. And—for the record—I happen to be a *great* assassin. I'm willing to demonstrate if there are any doubts."

"Please. Even in my weakened state, I could crush you."

"Is that a challenge? Because if it is, I accept." Jester draws the black blade that pierced the werewolf's hide.

Ket slowly unsheathes his sword.

"Enough!" Ralyanna shouts. "You two are children! Stupid children! How the hell have you survived together for this long?"

Ket looks at her, then back to Jester. Feeling his neck begin to cool, he puts his sword back in its scabbard. "She's right. Bickering will get us nowhere."

"Fine," Jester says, returning Ket's blade to where it came from. "But do know I can slay you with relative ease."

Ket plays the role of the bigger person and ignores his bold claim. "I feel a little better. I can probably make it a few more miles."

"Good," says Ralyanna, clearly relieved that their squabble has ended, and they can move on from this. "And I'm coming with you," she adds with a confidence that strikes him. "All the way to the Rovan Territories."

"Impossible," he tells her, shaking his head as she struts past him, down the path. "It's much too dangerous. I will not have your death on my hands."

"I'm coming with you and there's nothing you two can do about it."

"I won't stand for it," Jester says, folding his arms.

"You will stand for it because you need me."

"Why *the fuck* would we need a little girl to accompany us to almost certain death?"

Jester's question doesn't seem to faze her, and neither does his crass language. Ket suspects she's heard much worse. "Because… I'm not a little girl. And because you're right…I'm a witch."

AS THEY TRAVEL, Ralyanna explains her life story, condensing sixteen years down to sixteen minutes: Born motherless and fatherless, she spent her entire life being paraded between adoption homes and orphanages, yet never spent more than two winters in any one place. Tales of abuse that make Ket's skin burn red with anger. Stories of affectionate caregivers who either couldn't afford to feed an extra mouth or who perished in some untimely fashion: disease, murder, or suicide, due to the stresses of daily living. Some of her guardians discovered the truth about her *abilities*: she can sometimes move objects with her mind, or mysteriously start fires, or occasionally fall into a trance and speak ancient languages that have died out long before the seven gods walked the soil in human skins; languages she's never studied. Some of her guardians didn't even wait to hand her back to the closest orphanage—they would just leave her in the street with nothing but the clothes on her back, hungry and alone.

Those had been harsh times. But things got better when she met Borgadine. Their introduction was merely accidental, but Ra uses a different word for their first encounter. She pronounces it, but Ket doesn't recognize the term. He understands the context, though. To him, it sounds like she said "loaf of bread" but condensed into one word.

"*Louvabred*," she repeats.

"What's that mean?" Ket asks, as they walk across an empty field, a seemingly unclaimed stretch of verdant green. The sun shines bright and hot, making Ket sweat through his rags.

"Destiny." She lowers her gaze to the knee-high grass that surrounds them, green like a turtle's shell. "Meeting him was fate."

Thirteen years old and homeless, she had wandered the dirty rat-infested streets of Lockseed, a southern city in Springgaarden, on the day her life changed. She had been alone, and scared, and hungry, closer to death than life those days. Men would pass her on the streets and offer her coin in exchange for "favors", though she had never brought herself to explore those options, no matter how hard her stomach rumbled, grumbled, and begged for even the smallest morsel of food. She fled those brutes, hid from their offers. Sometimes they chased after her, but not often.

On a night much like any other—her days of poverty blending into one another—a tall man on horseback rode past her, stopped, then turned his mare around, and offered her something no street girl could refuse: enough coin to feed her for weeks, with boastful promises of future income. All she had to do was some obscene thing. She still remembers the sour, sick feeling that twisted her guts while he smiled, already anticipating, already imagining her, imagining doing it.

Maybe it was her hunger or her frustration boiling over, beyond aggravated by not being able to walk down the street without some pig of a man telling her how good she would look bouncing on their lap; her tolerance had peaked, and there was nowhere else to direct her contempt except externally—so she told the fucker to eat his mare's shit straight from the old gal's ass, and when he was finished licking up the remains, he'd have a nice clean hole to put himself into.

The man's face reddened like a sunset. He yelled at her. Called her a "cunt." A "worthless harlot." How dare she say a thing like that to him, a *man*, even though his proposition was much worse than any insult she could have given. Way worse. *So* much fucking worse.

He took after her on horseback, chased her down an alley that turned out to have no exit. He laughed when he dismounted the mare, realizing she was cornered. His teeth were too white for the darkness, shining with malicious intent. His grin sickened her, and his eyes reflected his hatred—maybe for all women in general.

She felt impossibly small in that moment, as he approached, working his knuckles with his fingers like he was preparing for a fight. At twice her size, he could have outwrestled her even if she had three or four sisters on her side. His eyes were the worst though. Blank. Emotionless. Black. She could tell he was not only enjoying this, but it wouldn't be the first time he'd terrorized a teenage girl before, a drifter.

Abused them.

She closed her eyes, wishing she could do the thing she'd done before—with her mind. Move things. Set fire to objects while possessing no active flame. Control someone's mind, make them do something or agree to something they ordinarily wouldn't have. It had only happened a few times in her life, only when she needed it.

But it wasn't happening now, no matter how hard she tried.

"Got something to say now, cunt?" he asked, his voice thick with a growl.

She clammed up, spoke not a single syllable. Talking would only give him a reason to go worse on her—she had learned that. Learned it well.

She pictured the man's body on fire, his arms waving around wildly, a drastic attempt to fan out the flames, and—

"Good evening!" a voice boomed from behind the horse, spooking her enough to cause the old gal to whinny and dance.

"Who—what?" Ra's pursuer spun so fast toward the newcomer she thought he was going to dizzy himself. *"Who the fuck are you?"*

"I'm the girl's companion," the man said. When he stepped from

the shadows and into view, she saw the newcomer was wearing a straw hat, gray tufts of curly hair poking out beneath the brim, and he was chewing on a dandelion stem. His clothing didn't scream *rich folk*, but she could tell he was not poor either—his clothes were relatively clean, free from blemishes and stains and the usual wear and tear of frequent traveling. *"She's my grand-daughter. Come now, Ralyanna. It's supper time."*

She remembers standing there, frozen, not sure what to do, at a crossroads, and felt her next decision would change the course of her life, drastically—and she had been right.

"You're not this girl's fucking grandfather," the bad man snapped, hefting an accusatory finger at the newcomer's nose. *"You just want to fuck for yourself, is that it? Well, come on, old man. Fight you for her cunt."*

The newcomer did not flinch. He stood statue-still and glared at the man, tilted his head to the side as if he didn't understand the nature of the monster before him. *"You, sir, are a nasty piece of gutter float. I truly pity you."*

"Fuck you, you—" Whatever insult he was going to hurl next was never uttered because the newcomer put a fist to his lips, opened his palm, splaying his fingers wide, and then blew on a small mound of white dust that had appeared there. A swirling cloud stole the bad man's voice, and his hands went to his throat as his eyes went so white and empty and devoid of life that it frightened Ra, shook her all up.

While the man coughed and choked and sank to his knees, terrified out of any rational thought, the newcomer extended his hand to her. *"Come, Ralyanna. I got you."*

And so he did.

———

SHE HADN'T BEEN Ralyanna on the day she met Borgadine, but in the days after, that became what he called her—what everyone called her from that day forward. She liked that name; it was much better than some of the previous names her foster homes had given her. So many names that she had forgotten most of them. Sometimes she hears a name mentioned in public and she remembers: *Oh yeah, I was a Charlise once. A Deborah. A Lily. A Primrose.*

But she's Ralyanna now—Ra for short. And she likes them, both iterations.

Over the next few weeks after *The Alley*, she traveled with Borgadine, learning his trade, coasting from town to town, city to city, setting up their wagon shop and selling rare herbs and spices and various potions. It was good, honest work. And no one bothered her anymore, now that she was in his company. For the first time in what felt like forever, she felt safe. Secure. Like nothing or no one could harm her. He treated her with respect and fed her, never once insulted her or scolded her, even when she was still learning his trade, everything she could about botany, and still made some mistakes. He never once raised his voice while in her presence. Never laid a finger on her. When she took baths in lakes and rivers and streams, he did not look at her, ogle her like some of her previous foster fathers. He made sure to be absent during these times, but still close enough in case of emergency, if she called to him.

He was the first "parent" she ever truly had.

She learned so much from his teachings. Borgadine taught her everything from mixing simple solutions to treat a common headache, to more complex concoctions, like the mixture that aided Jester's infected and nearly fatal injuries. She mastered most of it, and was convinced there was still more to learn. But she had a wealth of knowledge.

Over the three years she spent by his side, Borgadine's health quickly declined. He was no longer the sprite, sturdy man who could charge down an alleyway and challenge a potential rapist to a duel. Every day it seemed the man took on some new illness or ache or enfeebling discomfort. It became harder for him to work long hours, foraging for supplies and stocking the wagon with ingredients, and near the end, closer to that fateful afternoon at Riverspell, he was barely able to walk or lift much, which left Ralyanna in charge of running things. But she picked it up, and the business never skipped a single beat. He had told her (on more than a few occasions) that he was comfortable with her running the operation once his life was over. She had always tried to convince him that they were both going to live long, fruitful lives, that his condition would get better, and that they would search every nook and cranny the Endlands offered to find a cure for whatever nameless disease was chewing him apart from the inside out, but he just laughed, called her a "silly girl" for such wishful thinking, but doing so in the most fatherly, endearing way possible.

Even though he was convinced Ra could take over the business just fine, and make a good living selling their potions and herbal treatments, he told her he was worried about other aspects of her future—mainly, the powers she was exhibiting. In the first weeks of knowing her, she had exhibited a few peculiar habits, some of them scaring Highbeard's Holy Ghost right out of him. How things sometimes smelled like fabric burning when she got upset, or how she inadvertently moved an object across the wagon whenever she began to daydream. The occasional trances. The muttering of ancient languages while some milky veil clouded over her eyes.

One time, two bandits came to rob the wagon, and she snapped one of their necks just by closing her eyes and screaming at the top of her lungs. She passed out after that event and, later, had no recollection of the act. He had informed her, and she remembers crying for hours, wishing it wasn't true, that she hadn't murdered someone. But Borgadine was no liar, and so, she concluded that something was wrong with her, although, deep down, she already knew that. When she thought back to all those mysterious accidents that previous adoptive parents had accused her of—broken dishes, dead chickens in the pens, irrigation issues —it all suddenly began to make perfect sense.

I'm a witch, she remembers saying to Borgadine. He didn't agree with her self-diagnosis, opting to label her mysterious symptoms as *blessings* instead. Borgadine was never one to discuss or lecture about the gods and their societal role, and Ra never once caught him praying to one or another, but his assessment of the situation leaned *religious* and, in turn, sparked her curiosity about which god he had surrendered his soul to. But she never asked. Never wanted to know. Because in her experience, the people who worshipped fiercely were some of the worst humans she had come across.

I can help you, he told her one day, no less than twelve months ago, shortly after the run-in with the bandits. After her first murder.

I don't think you can, she whispered. She meant it too.

She felt hopeless. Alone. *Cursed.* That maybe she was better suited for death, so that she would no longer burden anyone.

He had gripped her hand—one of the few times he had touched her during their years of companionship. Squeezed. Closed his eyes and kissed her forehead. *I will help you,* he told her, with a confidence she could not doubt.

————

"SOUNDS LIKE A GREAT GUY," Ket says. They pass a sign crafted from hemlock, pointing toward a Crossroad's town called Grumalt, a place Ket has never heard of. Likely because the names of Crossland towns and cities change so often, whenever some new baron is assigned to his new piece of the territorial pie.

"He was," she says, eyes glassy with Borgadine's memory. Ket can see with crystal clarity that the man meant everything to her. He's ashamed for denying her a trip back to Riverspell, to see if she could claim his body and give the man a proper burial. From the sounds of it, he certainly earned one.

"What happened next?" Ket chooses his next words carefully.

"With your abilities, I mean. Did he help? Did he understand… uh…what you are? How you came to possess your powers?"

"If he knew, he didn't tell me. He did help, though. In some ways. He taught me how to control it—sometimes. Most of the time, as long as I keep my emotions even, don't allow the fire to burn in my cheeks, I can prevent certain…accidents."

"Oh goody," Jester chimes in, turning his chin to his shoulder. He's walking in front of them but has been eavesdropping the entire time. A windmill on the outskirts of Grumalt looms ahead. "We're traveling with a sixteen-year-old girl who's capable of popping our heads like swollen pimples should we disagree. Lovely. Nothing wrong with that. I'm sure we'll all be just fine."

"You're extra grumpy this morning," she says to him.

"My breakfast was lacking."

"We didn't have breakfast."

"Precisely."

"Just ignore the grouch," Ket tells her.

"Anyway…" she says, lowering her gaze, "I haven't been able to use my abilities for anything *good*, really. Just here and there. I can't control them when I do want to use them—like…Riverspell. I didn't mean to…" She can't finish the sentence, as if doing so will bring back the memories of those dead men. Ket understands. "But I lit a campfire with my thoughts once. About three months ago. Haven't been able to do it since. The power—it comes in spurts."

"How'd you do it?"

"I don't know exactly. I just closed my eyes, concentrated really hard, and imagined the campfire was going. Pictured a strong blaze in my mind. And it lit."

"Are you sure Borgadine didn't light the fire when your eyes were closed?" Ket asks, immediately regretting it. Tarnishing the old man's intentions by labeling him a trickster.

"No," she says, as if his theory is pure chickenshite. "No, gods, no. Why would he do that?"

Ket knows he shouldn't answer, but he's come this far. He

sighs deeply. "To give you the illusion that you were somehow in control of the power—that maybe if you believed the power could be controlled, you could actually control it." He shrugs; the theory sounded better in his head than it did leaving his lips.

"Borgadine wouldn't intentionally mislead me. He wasn't like that."

"Fair enough—it was just a thought."

The gates of Grumalt appear before them, two armored guards blocking their entrance. When the trio meet the guards, they inform them of the cost of entering the town.

"Cost?" Jester says, like he's never heard of such a thing. "Preposterous."

"Toll for entering Grumalt is three gold a head. If you can't pay, then fuck off to the next town. We don't need you."

Three gold is extortion. They have the change and plenty to spare, and Ket doesn't feel like taking a chance on the next town, wherever that is. Who's to say the next town won't charge them six gold a head? Three suddenly seems reasonable, and the hunger pains in his belly are probably to thank for that.

"Three gold it is," Ket says, taking his pouch, digging his fingers inside, and retrieving the fee. He even pays for Ra.

Jester delays in scooping out the required coin but finally succumbs, rolling his eyes and slapping three shiny tokens in the greedy guard's grasp.

The guard glances up from the coin, eyes the strangers through narrow slits. "Owlton coin, eh?"

Ket nods.

Jester says, "It's still accepted in the Crosslands, correct? Thought you greedy pigs take both Owlton and Rovanian currency."

The guard shoots him a challenging gaze. Then he shrugs off the insult and says, "Aye, we accept it. What're you hiding beneath that cloth, stranger?"

"Me?" Jester asks, feigning surprise. As if there's someone else in the group he's asking about. "Let's just say, I don't have a face for theater."

"Off with it," the other guard says, snapping his fingers hurriedly.

When Jester doesn't comply right away, the guard who's pocketing the toll clarifies, "We pride ourselves in keeping Grumalt relatively trouble-free. How do we know you're not a wanted man?"

The other guard marches over to the gate where a stack of books rests. He snatches a book off the stack, returns a second later. Flipping through the pages, he shows them sketches of bandits and thieves, portraits of wanted individuals and those not allowed past the city gates. "Have to see if you look like these fellas."

Ket feels tension in his shoulders, the unease of the moment slicing through him. He wonders if his *own* sketch is somewhere in those pages. The real Ket Norlath. His past self. But then he thinks that's ridiculous. Even if a younger sketch of him exists there, he has changed so much in the last decade. No one knows what he looks like now. Just the name he once bore.

I will not say it.

I will not think it.

"So, off with it," the guard says, wiggling his fingers, rushing Jester.

"Fine," Jester says, much to Ket's relief. The guards are getting pushy, restless. They reek of violence. There's a special glimmer in their eyes, eyes that have watched their hands commit atrocious, savage acts. "Here you go." Jester removes his mouth and neck handkerchief, revealing his clownish figure. He tussles the bells like a woman would bounce her beautiful curls in a mirror. "So, what do you think? Am I pretty enough to start my career as a sculpture model or what?"

The guards share a glance, then straighten up, craning their heads back to Jester. "Fuck happened to you?" one of them asks, his brow creased with distaste. He appears antsy.

"Eh, some evil jokesters had their way with me. Long story. I'll tell you over ales sometime."

Both men shake their heads, looking away. "Get inside. But one hint of trouble from any of ya's and you'll be booted faster than this clown can juggle."

"Fun fact—I can't actually juggle." Jester shrugs, holding up his hands as if to say, *Oh well.* "Isn't that a hoot?"

"Just get inside, fool."

They enter Grumalt, and Ket sniffs the air, scenting myriad smells, apple pies and melted cheeses, aromas that make his belly feel like a landslide. All he wants is a hot meal, a cool ale, and a soft bed to lay for the night.

And he'll have all three.

WITCHES NEED SLEEP TOO

"I find it funny that witchcraft is so commonly associated with the Blackstone Angel, Arkos, and his anti-god following. To me, witchcraft is no different from any other god magic. And I don't care if this opinion contributes to my hanging—it's the truth and everyone else is just too scared to admit it."

— HERROLD THE PHILOSOPHER,
DEFENDING WITCHCRAFT

————

WHEN THE INNKEEPER asks about their business, Ket and Jester improvise a story, posing as traveling blacksmiths escorting a lost orphan to a family in the Western Crosslands. Jester provides the name of the city, obviously more knowledgeable of the realm's geographical layout. Whenever they reach the Rovan Territories, it will be Ket's turn to take the reins of their navigational duties.

The innkeeper must feel generous because he gives them a key to a room and charges them half the cost scribbled on the board behind the bar. "Good men," he utters with a wink, then looks to the girl, Ra, in the corner sitting by herself, and gives the men a nod.

After a short climb up the staircase to the second level, the three find their room and settle in. Ra falls asleep the second her head touches the pillow. Jester and Ket wait until she's snoring before holding their conversation, the one they've put off for far too long already.

While watching the girl snooze, Jester chews the sides of his fingernails, drawing small blots of blood. "She's not going to dream about killing us and unconsciously decapitate us with her witchy mind powers, is she?"

"How the fuck should I know?" Ket is irritated, tired of the journey so far. His body is not holding up like he suspected, no longer the limber young man he used to be. Aches and shooting pains traverse his body as knots of agony attack him in the most unusual places. Muscles he hasn't used in a long, long time are crying out, and he hears them well.

He's exhausted, and knows a long sleep won't heal him quickly enough.

Because she's waiting for you there. In dreams.

"Of the two of us," Jester muses, "you are the most experienced with witches."

Jennah. His wife's image flashes before his eyes. Her smile. Her eyes filled with sunshine and the zest for life. The best thing that ever happened in Ket's life by a moonshot. But those images are quickly replaced by her horrid ending, her body disappearing over the edge of the bluff, a tendril of blood leaking from her body as it plummeted to the wet crags and crashing waves below.

"That's crossing a line," Ket warns him, his ire stoked.

"Oh stop it. You've had two years to get over her death. Don't tell me her demise still pains you the same way it had on that day."

"Have you ever loved someone?" Ket's not even angry anymore—just heavy with grief. "Truly loved someone?"

Jester's eyes slim, like he might have to think about it. "I've loved."

"But, truly?"

"Sure. There was a whore in—"

"If you ever find love, true love, then lose that love…you'll know there's no such thing as 'getting over it.' Grief is the ghost that haunts us always."

Jester allows him a somber moment, then lengthens his limbs and yawns, so wide Ket thinks he might reopen the seams in his face. "Very well, be a Sour Sally." He nods at the sleeping girl. "She's going to give us problems, you know. Either way. Witchy problems or just plain problems. She's extra baggage we didn't account for."

"I'm aware." Ket wonders what she's dreaming of. The way she sleeps so peacefully. Probably nothing.

She's just a kid.

Ah yes, another voice pops up, *a kid who has seen far too much misery at her age. Too much death.*

He hopes she's not dreaming of her previous guardian's demise. Hopes she dreams of happy places, pleasant situations.

"We could leave her behind. Tonight. Seems like a good town. Full of good people. We'd never have to see her again."

Ket fights the urge to agree with him. "You'd feel righteous about that?"

"It's not about feeling righteous, *Ket.*" The way he spits his new name is like razor wire dragging across his eardrum. "It's about saving her skin and ours. I'd feel wonderful about it."

Ket glances at the floor, ashamed he's even entertaining the idea. "She needs help, Tent."

"She's not your daughter. Your sons. Your dead wife. You are not her family, and you hold no obligation to protect her."

Ket snaps his head up at Jester, his brow fixed in a furious wrinkle. "Obviously. Why do you say it like that?"

"I know you're missing your sons," Jester says in a tone meant to deescalate things, "but that girl is no remedy for that heartache."

"That's not why I want to help her."

"Oh no? You're going to sit there and tell me your intentions aren't the least bit self-serving?"

"Yes, I am."

"I call a flaming bag of horseshit on that, friend."

"Call it what you want—this girl is lost and alone, and she's been through a lot. We cannot abandon her. Not when everyone else has."

"You're a much better person than me," Jester says, licking his ugly smile. "I'd have left her already."

"I don't think that's true."

"It's true."

"I think you're softer than you let on."

"You don't know me, not in the slightest."

"No, maybe not. But I know men like you. Outwardly fierce but filled with cowardice on the inside. I bet you tried to take Ragland's throat from the back."

"I didn't actually," Jester says without skipping a beat. "But I wish I had—because he'd be dead and we wouldn't be sitting in another inn, arguing about what clearly needs to be done."

Ket chuckles softly, almost humorlessly. "Coward."

"Fuck you, Soulthief."

Ket's heart sinks. He stiffens in his seat, regards Jester as if he's just insulted his dead wife, tarnished her legacy by spitting on her watery grave. "Wh-what?"

"You want to talk about cowardice and knocking someone down when they are at their most vulnerable—fuck it, let's talk about you. You're not a soldier per se—your sword skills are much too rough, even for someone who hasn't picked up the iron in a while. Unrefined. But you have no problem killing when it is required, and I can see in your eyes that you've watched many men die by your own hand. So, not a knight, not a warrior, not a guardsman. Obviously from Rovan, a close friend of the Silver

Towers, which gets me thinking of the legend from the Last War—the Soulthefters. You've heard of them?"

Ket's mouth tightens. He turns toward the window. In the black-glassed reflection, Jester winks and smiles at him.

"Group of five men led by one dark wizard, if legend serves true. Tasked with the impossible duty of extracting a live soul from the living. Dark, brutal stuff. Now, Rovan claims all five Soulthefters and the dark wizard, only known as Bluebolt, were killed in a siege during the final battle at the Silver Towers, but! Rumors have always circulated that one of these Soulthieves turned on his brethren, murdered the other four and cut the legendary wizard in half, removing his heart, then leaving it for the grand warrior, Ravenborn, to find on his doorstep.

"A good story, is it not?" Jester's eyebrows dance up his forehead.

Ket sighs, winces like the story has sliced the webbing between his fingers. "You're well versed on Rovanian tall tales."

"Are you saying that the Soulthefters is merely just that? A tall tale? That they did not exist?"

Slowly, Ket faces Jester, eyeing him through a narrow gaze. "I'm simply saying do not believe everything whispered in the inns and taverns throughout Endlia."

"Then educate me, dearest *Ket*." Jester leans forward, resting his elbows on the conference table, placing his chin in his palms, flashing that sick, eager smile. "Tell me about the Soulthieves, of their bold and daring practice of doing what no one other human has tried to do in the history of the world—extract a human soul from one's living body. C'mon. Tell me that doesn't get your cartwheels spinning."

Ket considers for a beat, then decides it's not worth his breath. "No. What happened beneath the Silver Towers during the war doesn't matter anymore. It's in the past."

Jester's face crumbles, and his eyes roll in giant circles. "You're such a bore. At least tell me about the worst thing you did to another human down there. Did you pluck someone's limbs off like the wings of a fly? Or did you remove their organs, hoping to find the soul hiding behind the heart? Is it true the experiments took place while the subjects were still alive and screaming?"

Ket tilts his head back, viewing the ceiling. There are colonies of holes in the wooden beams where termites have feasted. Now that he glances around the room, much of the décor is something left to be desired. The whole inn probably needs to be demolished and built from scratch. At a minimum, it could use some renovations, important structural boards and beams replaced. He thinks it may be wise to offer the innkeeper his services for a few days; he could have most of the vital work done in three days and nights, with Jester's help of course. They could always use the coin. The bank in Owlton gave them enough to get started, but that was about it. Their small wealth is dwindling fast.

"We need more money," Ket says, letting go of a hefty sigh.

"I'm less worried about money," Jester replies, lighting another candle after the one in front of him runs out of wax. "And more worried about how we're going to break through the walls of the Silver Towers. Don't imagine you've brought any big ideas with you. The closer we get to the Rovan border, the more dangerous it becomes for us."

"I can handle it."

"Can you?"

"There's a man in Tirko—it's a small providence in the northern—"

"I know Tirko," Jester says, huffing like he's offended. "What do you take me for? A homebody who's never left the green lawns of his Springgaarden estate?"

"Silly me," Ket says, shaking his head. "Forgot I was traveling with Jester the Great Geographer, the human map."

"Well, don't forget it again, partner."

"As I was saying—I know a man in Tirko who can help us."

"What man?"

"A friend, from back in the day."

Jester waves this idea off like it's pure nonsense of the highest order. "A war buddy? From over a decade ago?"

"That's right."

"And you think he'll be loyal to you?"

"I know he will."

"This man have a name?"

"No," Ket says, straight-faced. "His mother and father never bothered to give him one, so everyone just calls him *Man*."

"Are you…are you joking?" Jester lets go of a single laugh. "Ha, I seriously can't tell."

Ket's stony façade begins to crack, a smile leaking across his face.

"You bastard."

"His name isn't important," Ket continues, unable to wash away the smile. "But he will help us. I guarantee it."

"What makes you think after ten-plus years he'll still know you, let alone be willing to risk his neck and help us murder his king."

"One—because he no longer has a king. He defected, 'round the same time I did. And two—bastard owes me a debt."

"What kind of debt?"

"One that can't be forgotten or refused when it comes time to collect."

Jester twists his face in a way that suggests there are better options available. But if there are, they remain unspoken.

"I don't like anything about this, the direction we're heading," Jester finally says after a few moments of nothing.

"You're more than welcome to leave."

"And be hunted down by Ragland's men or worse—Iradon's warden?" Jester crinkles his nose like he's caught wind of a putrid carcass. "No, thank you. We're in this mess together, on the road to certain annihilation."

"Are you always this cheery?"

"You should have known me before I had my surgeries." He

blinks several times and smiles affectionately. "I was a beaming ray of fucking sunshine."

"Get some sleep." Ket climbs out of the chair and heads for the door.

"Where are you going?"

"Out."

"Out is nonspecific."

"It doesn't matter. Can't sleep."

"Why the hell not? You've been going for days."

"Because…" Ket stops at the door. Speaks over his shoulder, "If I sleep too long, I dream."

"And what's wrong with that?"

"I don't like my dreams," he says. "And they do not like me."

———

RA DRIFTS quickly into the land of illusions. The darkness of pure sleep melts away, and bright colors congregate; vibrant greens and blues and whites, which first appear in swirling spirals, all mixed together. But as the colors separate and form solid objects, Ra becomes aware of a beautiful garden beneath a blue-blanket sky, cumulous white shapes lethargically sailing past, cauliflower giants among the azure expanse.

Ra touches the shiny green leaf of a budding flower as she strolls across the greenscape, the bed of this botanical preserve, covered in short, manicured grass. A layer of mist clouds the air over the garden, making everything wet and heavy. Around her, flowers of different colors live their lives, sprouting and seeding and blooming before her eyes, living their life cycles in mere seconds before browning with winter's touch and eventually keeling over, bending toward their dusty demise. Seconds later they revive themselves under some invisible spring sunlight, rise from their deathbeds, and begin the circle of life all over again. They cycle repeatedly without wear, completing their entire seasonal lifespan in seconds.

She makes her way along the path, the only path the dream unravels before her. Staying the course, not deviating a single toe from the chalky dirt line, Ra sticks out her arm to brush back invading branches and the leafy extensions that crowd her vision. When she gets to where the dream wants her to go, the pathway widens, opens to a grassy glade, where a single oak tree sits in the center, the branches naked, save for large, pulsating sacks, which radiate with prismatic light. There are several of these sacks sitting sparsely throughout the tree's network of branches; Ra counts at least a dozen. The prismatic shimmer of their skin captivates her attention, and she finds herself unable to look away from their shiny shells. They continue to pulse like a heart, transferring blood between the four chambers.

"Beautiful, isn't it?" a woman's voice calls to her from nearby.

Startled, Ra gasps, spins, and holds out her arms, ready for a fight.

The woman before her, garbed in a clean, crystalline dress that sparkles with beaded jewels and wearing a silver crown that corrals her braided hive of blond hair, laughs at Ra's defensive stance. "No need for fists here, lovebug."

"Who are you?" Ra asks, her voice thorny and without breath.

"I'm your Fairy Godmother," the beautiful woman says with a wink. Ra squints at her, knowing this cannot be the truth. Or can it? She can't wrap her mind around this piece of information, so she doesn't prod her memory for the answer—though every fiber of her being is telling her to dig deeper into the woman's identity. Alas, her dreamself accepts this knowledge, stores it for later, when her awakeself is ready. "I am here to help you."

"Help me how?"

"Help you in ways, of which you do not yet understand."

"That sounds like a riddle."

"In a way, you are very much a riddle."

"I don't like riddles."

The Fairy Godmother cackles at this, as if Ra not liking riddles is something comical she can relate to. "Yes, well, the apple does not fall far from the tree, I see."

"What does that mean?"

The Fairy Godmother smirks, tilts her head as if Ra knows the answer and she knows Ra is playing dumb.

"Are you referring to my parents?" Ra swallows some lumpy nothing. "Did you know them?"

"Aye," the woman says, flashing a comfortable smile. The woman's gentleness, the calming sound of her voice, soothes Ra to some small degree, though she does not wish to fall under the spell of a potential ruse. She has dreamed many lucid dreams, some much grander and material than the present dream, but this is the first time someone has ever come to visit her behind the walls of sleep. "Aye, I knew them well. Your mother mostly. She was a great and powerful woman."

"Where is she?" Ra's eyes burn with potential tears. *My mother?* she thinks, but does dare not say out loud, the way she sometimes keeps curses silent. *I have a real...mother?* The thought sounds so ludicrous, even unspoken, that she almost laughs. "Where can I find her?" she asks the woman.

"She's no longer with us, I'm afraid. Not in your world, at least. She's in a place, I guess, much like this one. She's been trying to reach you, but her powers have weakened in death."

Ra feels a piece of her crumble from within. "I don't understand...I...don't understand any of this, what you're saying." *Other worlds? Powers?* Surely this is one of those dreams that make little to no sense, the kind she'll forget later, long after she's rubbed sleep from her weary eyes.

"You will understand. One day you will understand everything. And it's my job—as your Fairy Godmother, to make sure you do."

"What am I?"

At this, the woman takes a giant step toward her, opens her arms, and wraps them around Ra's shoulders, pulling her in for an encouraging embrace. Ra hugs her back—hesitant at first—but once she puts her hands on the fabric of the woman's dress, she feels the buzz of some foreign energy; it fills her bones with excitement, a newfound zest for the world around her. A hunger for knowledge. A need to know more. About this place. About this strange woman.

"You are precious," the woman says, nuzzling the top of Ra's head. "And very important in the events to come. The fate of Endlia—the Second Coming of the Gods."

Ra pulls back. "Second Coming…it's real?"

The woman's blue eyes blaze. "Yes, the long-dormant prophecy has been set in motion. The tides in the northlands change, and Salah Rovan begins to engage in something very dangerous, something he does not truly comprehend."

"What?"

"We have no time for that now, not all of it. Your sleep is almost over, and when you wake, you will not recall all of what we've discussed—write down what you remember. But keep it secret! Just between us. For now."

"Don't tell Ket or Jester?"

"Especially not. They are dangerous men."

"Dangerous?" Ra shakes her head, her forehead aching from the confusion that's settled there. "Dangerous how?"

"They have been sent north on a mission decreed by King Ragland. To retrieve a special prize from the Silver Towers."

"I know. The boy. But a boy is not a prize."

"This boy is. He is the most coveted prize in all of Endlia," she states, her tone changing. Becoming darker. Serious. Each sentence ending with a hiss through her teeth. "He's a weapon, Ra. Incredibly volatile. And he can destroy everything. You must go to him. Find him…and…"

The woman stops, and Ra catches something in her eye—secrets, knowledge she's not sure she should share.

"And what?"

"End him."

"*End*…him?"

The Fairy Godmother gives a single, grave nod. She closes her eyes as if she wishes Ra to understand this essential, vital task, and is frustrated she hasn't already agreed to it.

"I can't...I can't do that—I can't kill an innocent boy," she argues.

"Why not? You've killed before. I know you have. I've seen it. And this boy—he is not innocent. He's the single biggest threat to the Five Realms, and he will be responsible for countless deaths if he's allowed to grow up, become a man. You must stop him, Ralyanna. Cut out his heart. In the name of Highbeard's Heaven, you must cut out his heart and torch his body until he's nothing but ash and bone dust."

Disgusted, her eyes are drawn elsewhere. Something moves in one of the tree's sacks. Its shimmering surface reflects the sunlight beaming in through the glass ceiling above.

"What are those?" Ra asks, distracted by the orbs hanging from the branches, how they are beginning to move, the elastic surfaces undulating in small ripples. "What's inside them?"

Fairy Godmother turns her attention to the stretching skin of rotund sacks. "Souls. Waiting to be reborn. Of our kind."

"Our kind?"

The woman touches Ra's face, a gentle sweep of her cheek, as if she's combing away tears that aren't present. "They call us witches, but we are much more than simple conjurers of magic."

"What are we—"

"Sssh," the Fairy Godmother says, snapping her head in the opposite direction. To gaze at somewhere amongst the collection of flowers and bushes that keep dying and coming back to life. "This place is crumbling. The dream is ending. You will go back. Remember! Write down what you've learned. It will help you retain this knowledge."

"But—"

But there is no time to ask questions. As soon as she begins to speak, the arboretum crumbles around them—actually crumbles, like a brittle castle demolished by manmade explosives. Ra covers her head and tucks herself in a ball so the dream cannot topple down on her, pulverize her into the ground. But it does anyway. And that's when she wakes up screaming.

———

KET'S five ales deep when two seedy gentlemen, their clothes marred by mud splotches, their faces long and weary from a hard day's travel, stroll into the pub. One of them wears a bearskin jacket, the other sports a raccoon-tail hat. Average woodsmen, fur peddlers maybe, but Ket senses something off about their appearance the second they step foot inside the place. He's been on edge ever since they escaped Riverspell, always looking over his shoulder, but this isn't his paranoia speaking up, creating delusions— no, these men scream danger.

They sidle up to the bar and order a round from the innkeeper. Ket keeps to himself, tucking into a booth in the corner of the room, partially out of sight. He pulls up his hood. Then he tunes his ears to the conversation the men begin. Banal stuff at first. Raccoon-Tail talks about his wife and kids, how much he doesn't care if he returns from this job. *He deserves a few broken teeth, badmouthing his own family*, Ket thinks. *What I'd give to go back, relive that day.*

Arkos could have my soul just for the opportunity...

He doesn't know what he'd do, given that chance, what alternate choices he'd have made, but believes there would have been something he could have done to change the outcome. Fight back. Stop his wife from taking that arrow to the—

Forcing himself out of the daydream, he returns his attention to their conversation.

"We're close," Bear-Skin says, speaking his s's with a slight hiss, reminding Ket of snake-speak, a rare, dead language that was once spoken in the southernmost regions of Springgaarden, a place he's never been, but read about in school, when he was younger.

"I feel him here," Raccoon-Tail confirms, knocking back whatever is left in his glass. "Hey, keep," he says to the innkeeper, summoning the man over with a firm waggle of his forefinger.

The frumpy man tending the bar waddles over and starts pouring the men another round.

"Looking for someone," Raccoon-Tail says, lowering his voice to a tone intent on trading secrets. "Maybe you can help."

The innkeeper, looking spineless and loose-lipped, nods along as he sets down the two mugs. The men slap down more coin than the drinks are worth.

"He's a very distinct character. Badly disfigured," Bear-Skin tells him.

Ket quickly drains the rest of his ale. He's faced with the urge to walk over to the bounty hunters and crack their skulls together like a couple of cantaloupes—but they haven't been discovered yet. Jester came in, covered up, so it's possible the innkeeper doesn't know about his face, the disfigurements, or the hat stitched to his head. There's a possibility they can get out of this without the night ending in bloody, brutal violence.

Yeah right, Ket thinks, sorely.

"Guard told us he saw a man with bells on his hat—like a fool —and his face cut up to look like a smile," Raccoon-Tail says, his eyes shining with the prospect of getting rich collecting Jester's head in a sack. "You seen a man like that in here?"

The innkeeper frowns, deep in thought, screwing his eyes up at the ceiling, like that's where his memories are stored. "Nope, can't say I seen anyone looking like that come in here." But then his eyes grow big, like he's remembered something significant. "There were two strange fellows that came in a mite earlier."

"Oh, do tell," Raccoon-Tail says, then takes a sip of his ale.

"One bigger than the other. But the smaller of the two had his face hidden behind a cloth. Wore a hood. Couldn't see his face, but he—"

"That's him," Bear-Skin says confidently. The two men

exchange greedy glances, their eyes twinkling, grins spreading. "That's the bastard, I'd bet my bottom coin on it."

"They had a girl with them."

"A whore?"

The innkeeper wrinkles his lips, contemplating. "Nah. She didn't dress like any scuz. If I'd known any better, I'd say the two were fathering her. Just the way they acted and all."

"Interesting."

"Where are they now?" Raccoon-Tail asks.

"Why, upstairs. Sleeping, methinks."

Ket thanks his lucky stars the innkeeper is bad at recognizing faces—the idiot served him a beer no less than twenty minutes ago.

Bear-Skin goes for the knife on his hip.

"Please now. Don't make a scene," the innkeeper pleads.

Bear-Skin hesitates; looks to his partner for approval.

Raccoon-Tail considers, then says, "You've been mighty helpful. Don't want to jam you up none, make a mess of things here. Knowing they're upstairs and likely leaving soon is a big help, and the Warden of Iradon thanks you."

"Warden of..." The innkeeper gasps as if the men had told a joke at the Highbeard's expense. "You mean it?"

"He'll send coin if it turns out you're right," Raccoon-Tail confirms. "We'll be staying close by, waiting for those two to leave. We'll get them on the road, so as not to trouble you."

"I'd appreciate that, mighty fine of ya."

The two hunters drain the rest of their ales, give the innkeeper a two-finger salute, and then make their way to the door.

Ket fights the notion to take the offensive, to trail the men to whatever room they've booked, and butcher them in their sleep. But instead, he remains where he is and mulls his options.

Security is tight here.

Remembering the guards, how many of them held post at the gate, and how hard they were questioned before gaining access inside, he figures there's a heavy authoritative presence in

Grumalt, and causing any type of violent scene (even one involving self-defense) would delay their journey north. He can't afford to spend a week in another prison cell, waiting for the town's judiciary council to determine his innocence.

Less attention is better. Quieter is safer.

Knowing the men are out there observing the inn, he won't sleep tonight.

Not a wink.

Which is fine.

It gives him plenty of time to plot their demise.

DARKO

CHAPTER TWELVE

"Wizards are nothing but trouble—the world should rejoice in their extinction."

– SOURCE UNKNOWN

———

DARKO RAVENBORN TAKES the steps slowly, reluctance making each footfall sound louder than it should. Once he reaches the bottom and peers into the dark chamber, the smell hits him. He turns his nose, but the longer he lingers, the quicker the stench fades—or the quicker he becomes accustomed to it. Lighting his lantern, he makes his way to the center of the chamber, directing the lantern's glow onto the walls where several apparatuses are stationed. He pauses on one of them, which looks like a giant bear trap, used for catching whole human bodies and not just snagging the foot of some lumbering woods beast. He winces at the memory of the device, having seen it in action.

But that was over a decade ago…no, almost a decade and a half since that device was used.

Why do you keep coming down here, old man? He asks himself. *What good is it to relive your past failures?*

He doesn't know the answer but supposes he might find one down here, one day. Because this is where it all went wrong. This is where his life changed forever, went spiraling down into the pits of utter despair. He lost so much that day. His sons were taken from him, butchered in this cold chamber. Their murders led to his wife's madness, inspiring her to carve deep furrows into her wrists.

If he squints through the dark, he can see their ghosts. His sons lying on the dirt floor, their heads separated from their corpses, severed by an Owlton battle ax. His wife, sitting on what was once an altar, the veins in her wrist open and bleeding, mouthing the words, *We've lost so much, Darko. I don't want to lose anymore.*

She didn't realize there was still so much more to lose.

But that's in the past. And Darko supposes he comes down here because this is where he failed. And the only way to ensure one doesn't fail again is to learn from the past. Educate oneself by basking in one's flaws, embrace one's imperfections. *Where did he go wrong? Was he too trusting? Of his kin? Was he too lenient? Not time-sensitive enough?* That's what the emperor would have him believe. Harsher treatment for his underlings would mean tasks would be completed on time. Perhaps, that's why he's not progressed the boy as quickly as expected. He's too kind to him. Too understanding. Maybe he needs to be pushed harder, challenged.

Yes, Darko thinks, *I can do that. I can be harsh. Cruel even.*

Before Darko Ravenborn makes his exit, he looks down at the ground, the cement block that was the centerpiece for the experiments that took place here. He can still see the dark stain of the murdered wizard, Bluebolt, where the old man's head was bashed open. The stain was never removed, no matter how many times he sent maids down here to soap and scrub.

Maybe wizard blood is different, he thinks, which brings a dose of humor to his dark surroundings. Because he knows—like many others know—that wizards bled the same as men, because wizards were men, nothing more. Nothing special. They weren't witches or warlocks, they had no power. Just ideas, and the brass balls to experiment.

Such as extracting a soul from a human body.

He remembers Bluebolt's speech to the emperor all those years ago; how he convinced the emperor that he could locate the human soul inside a living body, and how he planned to uproot it. Inside every living body, the self-proclaimed wizard had said, is a sack that harbors the soul. We just have to find it.

And that was it—all it took to convince the emperor that souls were harvestable, and that Bluebolt could build him an indestructible army of ghosts to combat his enemies. It was so ludicrous that Ravenborn expected Salah to hang the man for being completely insane—but he bought it. Hook, line, and lead sinker. The wizard claimed his evidence had been rooted in "scientific research", and that, Ravenborn admits, did sound intriguing. Salah's determination (and stinky desperation) won out, and the emperor agreed the wizard's plan sounded like the best ever concocted.

Darko Ravenborn puts the lantern on the altar, tugs down his pants, and pisses on the wizard's bloodstain. Once his bladder is empty, he pulls his pants back up and grabs the lantern. There's a lot of blame to go around for what happened, but it started with that wizard and his belief in the unnatural, his dark desire to play god.

No one is a god.

No one.

If anyone is close, it's the boy.

"And it's my job to make him one," Ravenborn says out loud, hoping the trapped ghost of Bluebolt—if the coward is down here, lingering—can hear him.

He spits in the piss puddle before making his way out, inspired to avoid the same mistakes.

However, now, there are a lot fewer people around that he loves. He has almost nothing to lose. Except himself. And to a man who's seen the world, experienced a little bit of everything, that's next to nothing at all.

A CHANGE OF PLANS

CHAPTER THIRTEEN

"While his worshippers are few, Braxial, the owl-headed deity, has clusters of followers that have made camps across the Crosslands. Sometimes, when not warring with the South, the North King would send troops to these encampments and attempt to convert these followers. By any means necessary."

– MENYARD MINOTOA, *THE GOD SYSTEM*

———

JESTER WAKES, groggily, his left arm asleep and tingling. Ket's right where Jester remembers last seeing him, sitting in a chair near the window, peering out into the streets below, watching them closely. Daylight floods the room, needling deep behind his eye sockets. He covers his vision with his forearm and rolls over, surrendering to the fluffy, cotton blankets.

"More sleep," Jester begs to no one in particular.

"Your appearance has stirred local interest," Ket says calmly. He continues eyeing the main road below, not bothering to face the sleepy jester.

Jester rises like a reanimated corpse after a necromancer's call, suddenly very alert. "What do you mean?"

"Two men. Came into the inn last night. From Iradon. Looking for someone who meets your description."

Jester throws the sheets off his body and marches over to the closed door, where his tunic hangs from a hook. "Why didn't you dispatch them like the others? You fool! You let them live?"

The outburst catches Ket's gaze. "I didn't want to cause a scene. There were too many witnesses, unlike the situation in the alleyway."

"Well, now what?"

"They're watching this inn. Two men, maybe more. With sharp blades."

"Knowing the Prince Bastard of Iradon…definitely more."

The door opens, and Jester nearly messes the britches he's just yanked up around his waist. Juggling three plates of scrambled eggs and sausage and three sets of shiny silverware, Ra steps into the room.

"They were serving breakfast downstairs," she says with a big, childish smile. Like this is her birthday morn and she's woken up to a tower of gifts.

"Where'd you get the coin for that, young missy?" Jester asks, perturbed. Even though his belly is grumbling something fierce and the food entices him, he eyes the purse on the table, wondering how much this has set them back.

"It was on the house, if you must know," she says, snappy. "Honestly, Jester, not every situation is a bad one. Thank the gods for this gift."

"I will thank them for nothing, thank *you*."

"Calm down, Jester," Ket says, never raising his voice.

"Calm down?" Jester grips the ears of his hat in frustration, the bells carrying a brief, melody-free tune. "Calm down? You're not the one being hunted down like a mangy, diseased dog!"

Ra rotates toward Ket, her brow raised, awaiting an explanation.

"Jester has friends outside," Ket tells her.

She nods, understanding.

"Friends!?" Jester barks a derisive laugh. "Ha! No, Jester has *no* friends. No friends anywhere. If he did have friends, he would not be here, stuck with you lot."

"And he's woken up on the thorny side of the bed," Ket adds. "Did you sleep on a pricker bush last night?"

Jester snarls, then equips himself with the short black sword, examining the sharpness of the edge—good enough to slit some throats.

"Jester, you leave first," Ket says.

"What?!"

"Trust me."

"Trust you?" Jester rests his fists on his hips and leans forward. "I *don't* trust you. Yesterday you could barely walk—now, today, what? You're suddenly rejuvenated? You're not thinking clearly!"

"I've rested my eyes enough. Doesn't take long to rejuvenate these bones."

Jester's tongue creeps up the fused skin of his smile, his stomach swirling with nerves. "Go first, then what?"

"Lead them out of town. They won't jump you inside the gate —too risky, and I sense these men don't want to draw too much attention to themselves."

"So, let them jump me outside the gates? That's your brilliant plan?" Jester claps his hands sardonically. "Bravo, gent. Brav-fucking-o! You should be Owlton's next war general with those great ideas! Wait till we return and I tell King Ragland of your grand combat schemes and strategies!"

"Drop the sarcasm." Ket rises to his feet. He strides across the room, stopping at the table, and snuffs out the candle with his fingertips. Then he takes a fork and begins shoveling the scrambled eggs into his mouth. "You take them far out. Let them chase you. We will not be far behind," he says, around his breakfast.

"I hate this plan." Jester grits his teeth, like the words coming out are slicing the inside of his mouth. "Hate it!"

"Do you have a better idea?"

"Yes! I have tens of better ideas! How's this? We leave

together! What a concept! Strength in numbers! Ever hear of that, O mighty war general of small battles?"

"We have numbers, but if those two men see us leaving together, chances are they will back off and send for more men. Perhaps send an owl to the next city, where more of your nemesis's loyalists sit and wait. We can't chance that. We have to let them think you're alone. That you've wandered off on your own, left us behind. Then surprise them."

"Then *kill* them," Jester corrects, growling. "Gut them like fish, leave them for the—"

"We need to keep one of them alive."

Of all the things Ket's told him, this appears to be the most dissatisfactory. "Are you fucking mad? We will absolutely not let them live."

"Relax. I just need to interrogate one of them. Leave him alive long enough to answer some questions."

"What questions?" Jester pounds the wall closest to him with a clenched fist, hard enough to rattle the décor and empty wine glasses on the table in front of him. He's surprised his fist didn't go through the plaster. "These men are after me and they will not stop until they bring my corpse back to Iradon."

"And I want to know why," Ket snaps. This time he keeps moving forward until his chin is nearly resting against Jester's stitched forehead. "How many men are coming after us, and how long this will go on for? Because if I'm to travel with you all the way to the Silver Towers, then I need to know everything. And something tells me I won't get the truth from you."

Jester grins, like always, but also different this time—he senses he's slipped under Ket's skin like a flensing knife, and it fills Jester's heart with instant satisfaction. "You could always rip out my soul—maybe that will coerce me to confess."

"I'd rather not. It would complicate our task at hand."

"Fair enough. You want the truth—here it is. The Warden of Iradon and I used to be great friends. Well, maybe more like business partners. We had a falling out sometime after I completed my end of our arrangement—he didn't claim the surrounding lands all by himself, you see, and let's just say there were several bodies in his path that needed to be unobstructed."

"You killed people for him, got it."

"It's what Jester does best." He waves his hands in the air like he's showing off a valuable prize offered up at some town raffle. "Years later, we soured on each other. Promises and payments weren't kept by him, and as you can imagine, that upset me to some great degree. So, I plotted against him. Rather than just simply murdering him in his sleep—which wouldn't have been difficult—I thought it would be more fun and more challenging to spark a war between Ragland's regime and the good warden himself. How pleasant it would be to watch Owlton armies roll over Iradon like a tidal wave over some underdeveloped fishing port."

"But...you tried to kill him—Ragland, I mean."

"Oh, honey—if I wanted the fat king dead, the bastard would be floating down some river right now, fire arrows falling all around him in the grandest celebration of life only a king can earn." Jester's face suddenly changes, and he chews his tongue, which tastes like burnt ash. "I wanted to attempt the assassination but leave a calling card—lead all evidence back to Iradon. Which I did. Sort of. But I also got caught." He shrugs it off. "You know the rest."

"So, the warden wants revenge on you. For nearly toppling his little estate."

"Did I mention I also porked his wife? Thrice. It was wonderful. I think I even knocked her up—my bastard son is probably a seedling in her belly as we speak."

Thin creases form across Ket's forehead. He chews on some sausage, then looks to Ra, who's taking all of this in with wide, innocent eyes. "You will lead them out. We will follow."

Jester's lips writhe in protest, then relax. "Fine. But if I die...I will come back as a mad cackling wraith and haunt the both of you as long as you live."

———

JESTER DOES what's asked of him, heads out of the inn alone and travels down the single-carriage road, dusty and cloudy, toward the gates of Grumalt. Passes shoppes and stationed wagons set up as selling spaces, huts and brick homes tucked behind them in seemingly endless rows—the village. The knowledge of being followed rests heavily on his shoulders, weighs him down, makes him not so eager to stroll past the gates, for beyond them is not safe, and no one will save him—certainly not Ket and Ralyanna—if his pursuers should take off on horseback and ride him down. But Ket promises the men did not arrive on horses, nor a wagon of any type.

Jester doesn't buy his lies, but he doesn't have a lot of say in the matter. He supposes he could split from Ket and Ra, go his own way, draw the men off into the mountains, sneak up on them in the trees, and bash their heads against some crags, but then there is Ragland to consider, the unfinished business he left behind in Owlton—Jester, *Tent,* is not one to let things go, especially something as embarrassing as not killing a king while he had the bastard right in his grasp—so, no, he won't let that stand, not ever. Running from Ragland's kingdom is not high on his to-do list, and he knows that living his life in the shadows is not how he plans on spending the rest of his days.

How do you wish to spend them? a phantom voice speaks to him, a voice he almost recognizes; maybe a past lover. Someone who loved him. Maybe the last lover he'd bedded.

The Warden's wife. Esrelia. The Lady of Iradon.

He informs the voice that he intends to march back into Horn-rake, with or without the northern king's head on a stick. That's what.

But other than that, he's got nothing. No clue how to spend his remaining days, however many he has left. Killing's lost its flavor after chewing it for so long. It'd be nice to do something different. Maybe become a fisherman. Or a sailor, exploring the open seas.

Maybe a deer hunter, a butcher, providing some small village with choice meats. Maybe he could start over in Springgaarden, change his face, and join their royal army. Wouldn't that be fun? Springgaarden always manages to avoid these conflicts that break out in the Five Realms, so it may prove a peaceful and relaxing line of work. Or maybe he'll just spend his remaining years palling around with Ket Norlath. Ket is interesting, despite their differences and minor tiffs. The girl is even more curious. In all his travels and adventures, he's never met a witch before. Not a real one. A few Arkos worshippers who touted themselves as such, but never the real thing.

So much power available at her fingertips, he muses.

Jester has, of course, heard the old stories, the ones from times long since passed, about witches and warlocks being descendants from the old gods, the Seven, from when they walked the earth as human beings and copulated with members of humanity, thus spawning little half-breeds. Those demigods traveled Endlia for centuries, possessing otherworldly powers, some of them almighty, some of them hardly effectual.

Through the years, the bloodlines became diluted, and the demigods lost their abilities a little more with each generation. Soon after, Endlia believed no more half-breeds remained, but—like all things god-related—there were prophecies and rumors and speculations about the return of the old power—the thunder and lightning of the gods bottled inside the bodies of the living. Some believed those lucky few were born with godlike abilities but grew up blind to their power, their potential never manifesting or, if those powers had, they never pieced the puzzle together, and just considered them odd occurrences and nothing more. Like a milk jug moving across the room on its own, or a candle being snuffed out sans the assistance of fingers or a breath or a wild wind. Strange coincidences, nothing more.

Jester had always been a skeptic. Of everything. Gods and witches. Monsters too. But he's traveled Endlia enough over the last decade to recognize the truth, and now he's a believer.

About half a mile from Grumalt, he checks over his shoulder and sees two men strolling the path. Ahead of him, approaching from the opposite direction, two horses tow a carriage through the mire, the driver whipping them, *hawing* the beautiful creatures to move faster. Probably a noble cart carrying fortune-laden individuals, judging from the lavish silk-threaded curtains that conceal the cargo. Rich scum who probably deserve to be robbed and have their wagon tipped over in the muck. When the driver sees Jester and the two men walking his way, he unsheathes a longsword, allowing the sun to catch its clean sharpness just right, radiating a silver glow.

"Keep it moving, wanderer," the carriage master practically spits at him as Jester passes with his hands raised.

Showing his palms to the carriage master, he watches the wagon cruise by, and the driver continues to hold out his warning for the next travelers to see. The driver gives them the same message and is just as acerbic. Jester's pursuers grumble something contentious in return but keep walking.

No sight of Ket behind them. The men quicken their pace, closing the gap between them by a few yards.

Shit! Where are you, you wild northerner motherfu—

"Ohhhhhhh, Tent!" calls out one of the pursuers, using a folksy, sing-song bravado, like he's a child singing some passed-down nursery rhyme. "Don't drag this out, make this any harder than it has to be."

Jester stops, turns around on his heels. Unsheathes the stubby black blade. His enemies have already drawn their longswords, both of which glimmer in the sunlight filtering in through the branches overhead. One of them cuts the air with a ferocious swipe, narrowly missing Jester's throat.

"You found me!" Jester says, lacing his voice with as much jubilant gusto he can muster. Like it's a show, a performance. Like his only mission in life is to entertain. He twirls his arms through the air like celebratory ribbons for children. *Should have been a real Jester,* he thinks, eyeing the empty road behind them, no Ket

Norlath in sight. And just then it hits him; the bastard set him up, sent him out here to *die.*

He doubled-crossed me.

It can't be true, can it?

There's no other way to read it.

I must have become a burden to him. Or he thought I'd double-cross him first! For the right price, that might have been true.

Bastard, he thinks. *Oh, you dirty rat bastard.*

"What's the matter, Tent?" one of them says. Jester recognizes the face beneath the patchy beard. *Alvin Deerhood.* "Looks like ye seen a ghost!" A delighted chuckle erupts from his sweet-toothed smile.

The other swordsman—though not much of one from what Jester remembers—is Yeldeen Torso. Both low-ranking hoods the warden hires for odd, dirty jobs. Both quite expendable. The bastard hasn't sent him admirable, worthy adversaries, deserving of the black blade. No—instead, he sent these two gutter slobs.

"Gentlemen," he says, pulling down his mask and showing off his permanent smile. They don't exactly shriek and cower at the sight, but the image changes their expressions, taking them by surprise. Jester pushes back his hood to give them the full picture. "It's been a long time since our paths have crossed."

"Not that long," Deerhood says, bunching up his brow. "What in Arkos's Darkhell happened to you?"

"Oh, this?" He combs his fingers through the floppy cloth extensions of his hat. "Just a little cosmetic adjustment—nothing I couldn't handle."

"That's what you get for trying to kill a king," Torso says, pointing at him with his sword. "Where's your companions? Heard you got a little 'hore with you. I knew you liked them young, Tent, but not that young, ya dirty bastard, you."

Jester bites his tongue hard enough to taste copper.

Deerhood clears his throat. "Ahem. The Father of Pale Flesh wants you back in Iradon, alive."

"Father of what-the-fuck?" Jester's eyes slim to near slits. "Are you not working for our buddy the Warden of Iradon now? What kind of gross mistake have I made?"

"He goes by 'the Father of Pale Flesh', now," Torso says, serious. Jester laughs. Hard.

"You won't think it's so funny, Tent, when he strips the skin off your back."

"I'm sorry," Jester says, bending forward and slapping his knee. "That is just too humorous. Surely he doesn't call himself—"

"Enough," Deerhood interrupts, rolling his eyes all the way up. "You can laugh it up later. We need to get you back, now. No time to waste. We've wasted enough following you out here."

"What if I refuse?" A valid question, one Jester doesn't wait for them to answer. "What if I tell you I'd rather die here than be dragged back to the feet of that motherless bastard. Hmm? What will you do then?"

Deerhood shrugs as if Jester's cooperation isn't vital to his plans. "Then we disarm you, knock you out, drag your unconscious body all the way back. We've got a wagon waiting for us two towns over. Alliances in Grumalt can help us get you there. You needn't worry about it."

"What I *would* worry about," Torso says, standing tall and powerful, looking down the length of his weapon, "is that we are not required to bring you back in any certain condition. Which means, if we cut off an arm or leg, as long as you survive, the Father of Pale Flesh will still pay out your bounty."

"I figured that's what you meant," Jester says, yawning. "Gentlemen. Gentlemen! You bore me! Are we not going to duel? Or is barking threats back and forth until one of us forgets what we're doing here, all you've come for?"

"You read my mind perfectly," Torso says, and then he lunges forward, sword out, ready to strike.

———

KET AND RA race through the woods, sprinting as fast as they can, ducking branches and hopping over downed timbers, vines and leaping foliage cutting across their impromptu path, threatening to stall them. Ket lags behind the girl, his strength still not fully restored. Still, he moves swiftly for a man running on a cat nap and lacking proper nutrition.

"Up ahead," he says, directing the course. "Through those trees."

Those trees are two towering oaks, their trunks wider than the room they spent the night. Perfect for hollowing out and making a one-room home inside, perfect for folks who like living small. Ket darts toward the spot, gaining his second wind. He'll need a third wind for what's waiting for him, he's sure of it.

If I'm not too late, he thinks, hating how he told Jester he planned on attacking their quarry from behind, knowing his ideas included no such thing. Lying to him. No, getting ahead of the two hunters is key. His proposed ambush won't work without that basic element of surprise. He just hopes Jester can hold them off until they get there.

When they reach the oaks, Ra slows down and allows Ket to take the lead. Ket crouches, then walks hunched down, toward the clearing where he can see the main road leaving Grumalt. Risking being seen, he pokes his head out from behind the oak, and about fifty yards down the line he sees Jester walking the path, his head down, muttering to himself and pantomiming as if he's having a conversation with someone, trying to emphasize his point by waving his arms around a bunch. Not far behind, the two hunters trail him, heckling him. Where Ket and Ra are crouched, a carriage with a grumpy driver seated behind two horses cruises past. The rest of the road is clear; no witnesses, no one to scream or sound alarms when swords begin to clash. They're far enough from Grumalt's well-barricaded entrance.

A perfect killing ground.

Jester spins, begins jawing with the two men. Ket can't make out what's being shouted between them, but he gets the gist.

Jester is being Jester, mouthing off and probably pissing off the two killers in ways only Jester can.

Then, blades are drawn, and the time to move has arrived.

Ket nods in Jester's direction, then takes off, keeping to the woods, using the small incline to shield himself from the men's line of sight. He hears Ra's soft footfalls on the leaf-carpeted ground behind him. Once he's caught up and parallel to the arguing voices, he spins to Ra, tells her to "stay put", which doesn't go over very well, then draws his sword.

She looks like she might betray his command, but to his surprise she remains standing behind a cluster of white pines.

Ket jogs up the incline holding his silver sword in both hands and emerges from between two bushes. The second he steps foot on the road, Jester takes a swipe at one of the hunter's swords—Bear-Skin's. Even though Jester wields the black blade—a formidable weapon in close combat—he can't get close enough to use it. The killers' longswords easily fend off any jab and stab. Jester blocks what he can, but Ket sees the events play out before he witnesses them—sooner or later, one of them will pierce Jester right through the heart with a stretching, forceful stab. Jester can only dance around them for so long before his luck and skill run out.

Ket rushes forward, his feet landing softly on the packed earth. He approaches Bear-Skin from behind and slashes at the back of his leg. The blow glances off his hamstring, tearing through his trousers and hitting the padding beneath, something that shields the blade from slicing through flesh and muscle, packing wrapped in mail. The strength of the blow takes the man to one knee. Bear-Skin rotates, waiting for Ket to follow this attack. Ket surprises him by planting his boot in the center of his chest, knocking him back, laying him flat on his spine. A small tan cloud kicks up from the road, enshrouding the four men.

Raccoon-Tail snaps his head in Ket's direction. "What—hey! This does not concern you, wanderer!"

"Actually," Ket says, stepping forward, angling his sword for the perfect strike, "it concerns me a great deal." Ket lunges and swings for Raccoon-Tail's head, but the man is spry and dodges the slice, ducking under the silver blur of Ket's sword. In hindsight, Ket wishes he could have that maneuver back; he would have gone for the stomach or legs. Swords aimed at the head are too easy to anticipate, if you're paying close enough attention, and Raccoon-Tail's eyes are firmly set on him.

The two trade offensive attacks, each getting their swords level enough to block the other's incoming assaults. This is the intimacy of combat, where Ket feels out his opponent. He's not the best swordsman, and it's been some time since he's wielded one against a worthy opponent (knocking sticks around with the boys in the barn doesn't quite count). He thinks he can gain an edge on Raccoon-Tail if he keeps him where he is, in front of him, squared up, and just continues to land strikes, keeping the bastard on his heels. Eventually one will get through. Ket may not have the skills or his old strength, but he still has his head. Calculated strikes and well-formed footwork go a long way, and this strategy may just win the day.

He glances over at Jester, who's putting his black blade in the neck of the kneeling Bear-Skin. Bear-Skin howls like a banshee's warning, but once Jester works the blade in deep enough, the voice just cuts out, a gargling whimper replacing the man's final cry. With all his might, Jester finishes tearing through the man's throat, opening him up like a river suddenly undammed.

Ket looks away, concentrates on Raccoon-Tail. He can tell the man is suddenly nervous—it's two-on-one now, and now that the odds have shifted, Ket can see something change behind the hunter's eyes, that he's contemplating laying down his sword and breaking for the trees. If he does take off, Ket's sure he'll get pretty far before they catch up. Even after a good night's rest Jester appears weary-eyed, and Ket—unable to manage more than fifteen minutes of shut-eye at a clip—still feels that lingering bone-deep ache in his thighs, hips, and back. Yes, the man will get far. Maybe back to wherever he was sent from. This Iradon.

Ket eyes him. "Lay down your sword, drop to your knees, and put your hands behind your head."

Raccoon-Tail's raccoon tail flops back and forth. "I'd rather dine on your silver blade than surrender to you." He speaks to Ket, but his eyes are locked on Jester and the grisly murder taking place a stone's toss away.

Jester stands, his chest splashed with dripping scarlet, and has himself a great, belly-shaking laugh. "You really are pathetic, Deerhood. If only your *Father* could see you now."

Jester takes one step toward him, holding up the black blade, slick with Bear-Skin's red.

"Jester," Ket says, his voice calm but warning. "Keep him alive. Only need to disarm him."

"Oh, Ket. You know I can't let my assassins live."

"He's not—" Ket goes to refute Jester's claim but before he can talk sense into him, Jester is sprinting toward his enemy, his tongue flapping through his smile as he arcs his arm back, preparing to lodge the black blade in the enemy's throat.

Raccoon-Tail—Deerhood, Ket surmises—is positioned to slice him up.

"STOP!" Ket shouts at Jester, but it's too late.

***

FROM THE BUSHES, Ra peeks through the leaves and branches and watches the violence unfold, doing her best to follow Ket's command and stay out of sight. But…

But she can't. Can she? Just sit idly by while Ket risks his life to defend Jester. Sure, they're capable, but the two men probably haven't spent the last week journeying across Endlia on foot, scraping for meals and getting way-not-enough rest. They probably rode on horseback, gorged magnificently, and slept like swaddled babes.

She closes her eyes, trying to remember the spells Borgadine taught her, as he read them from the big black book with the gold trim, the one that had no official title, at least on the cover. The one that's currently missing. Well, not *missing*, missing. She knows where it is. It's back in Riverspell, among the wreckage of the overturned wagon, probably buried beneath smashed phials of pixie dust and broken jars of grimroot extract. Or worse—one of those mountain Wilders stumbled across it, scooped it up, and transported it back to their caves, where it will never find another witch's eye again. Either way, the words inscribed in his book are far, far away. Not *his* book, but the book he possessed for a "long, long time." His words. All she has left of it is what she can recall, which isn't much. She can remember snippets of certain spells, but the memories of the directions that accompany these words are murky at best. How she must wiggle her fingers or wave her hand in certain ways (*to manipulate the magic that surrounds you*) gets lost on her, every time she goes to cast.

She closes her eyes, trying to remember something, anything from that book, but just as she thinks she can see the words as they were written on the page, everything goes blank, like someone blowing out the last candle in the middle of the night.

You don't need the words, she hears Borgadine tell her, his voice bleeding through the darkness of her blank thoughts. *Or the fancy hand movements. The spells are in you. The magic is all around you. In your blood. You are the spell, you are the power. The words just give you the courage.*

It sounded like horseshit at the time, but then she thinks back to Riverspell, just before she blacked out—she didn't have the black book before her when she took down that rider. All she had was her fury, her mind, and her imagination—and in that moment, all three came together and she performed the unthinkable.

But not for the first time.

Just concentrate.

Look…

And picture your power.

Ra steps out from the bushes, onto the edge of the road. Jester has slain one of the men and is jawing with the other. Ket is trying to talk him down from committing another atrocious murder, but Jester isn't listening. The lone assassin looks like he wants to run. But he won't have the chance because Jester launches himself, sailing through the air like a cat leaping from hay bale to hay bale, his arm cocked back and his blade angled down, aimed at the man's shoulder.

Ra reaches out, placing her palm flat and thrusting it against the wind. There is resistance, as if something invisible, something malleable, was waiting for her. Waiting to be molded. As her fingers sink in, the feeling so natural, like a spring waterfall spilling over her, she pictures her intent—to stop Jester from carrying out his dark dream. To stop him by any means, but not hurt him. Too much. An old guardian from her home-hopping days once told her, *Pain is the ultimate motivator.*

Jester sails toward the man, then hits something, like a wall, but a wall that's simply not there. *Invisible.* Like a sparrow hitting a glass window because its vision and comprehension cannot process the manmade obstruction. It's like that, only Jester doesn't break his neck or get knocked out cold. The unseen barrier she threw in front of him only takes him to the ground. The man she protected from receiving Jester's black blade in the neck, backs up, staggering, looking this way and that, trying to make sense out of what just happened.

His eyes follow the evidence to Ra, who's still holding her hand out.

"High-highbeard's-g-g-ghost!" he finally whimpers, quivering, every inch of him shaking like a sick dog. When Ra starts forward, lowering her hand, he yelps like a child about to receive his father's discipline paddle. *"She's-she-she's-a-a-wi-witch!"*

While his widened eyes are solely concentrated on Ra, Ket steps forward and delivers a hand chop to his throat, the edge of his hand smashing against the man's larynx, silencing him for what should be a good long while. She hopes he will be incapacitated until everything settles down—when Jester is calm again, and the man is done raving about witches. When it's time to interrogate him, when Ket will force him to talk.

Jester should have stuck to the script, kept his promise to keep one of them alive, but she suspects Jester is someone who enjoys marching to the beat of his own drum, regardless of what's best for the group. An attitude that will likely get one of them killed, she thinks, maybe all of them, if he doesn't quickly change his ways.

Jester pops to his feet, which surprises her considering how hard he smashed into her—what was it? There's no name for what she created there, but *wind shield* seems appropriate enough.

"That was very stupid, girly," he says, sneering. "This man wouldn't think twice about gutting a little girl while she sleeps."

"Enough, Jester," Ket warns him with a steely, side-eyed glance. "Besides—he doesn't look all that dangerous." Ket bends down and binds the man's hands together behind his back with his own belt. The man looks frightened, defeated, and still unable to speak. His wheezing breaths are his only reply.

"Stupid," Jester reiterates, spitting on his fingers, then holding them up for Ra to see. Slimy scarlet dribbles down the length of his palm. "Thank you for my latest injury."

"Sorry," Ra says nonchalantly, not really meaning it and making sure he knows his small injury is near the bottom of her current concerns. "You didn't stick to the plan."

"The *plan* was also stupid." Jester's eyes go wild with frustration and anger. "And speaking of *plans,* what the fuck took you so long? I was beginning to think you double-crossed me. Wasn't the plan to sneak up on them from behind? I would have wished to know if the plan was to flank them!"

"Jester, I suggest you take a walk," Ket says, finishing the knot and hauling the hunter back to his feet. "Burn off some of that anger. Unless you want to stay and listen to what this man is going to tell me."

"I already told you," Jester snaps, "he knows nothing more than what I've already told you."

"I'll be the judge of that," Ket says, a growl merging with his words.

Jester takes a beat, then shakes his head. He slaps the air furiously, then spins around to walk a few paces in the opposite direction.

"How do you feel?" Ket asks Ra.

She feels fine and tells him so. "What will you do with him?"

Ket inspects the man. The hunter hangs his head, maybe because he's hurting, but also maybe because he's embarrassed about how things panned out. "I'll wait until his throat recovers. Then interrogate him."

"And after?"

Ket flashes her a menacing look that almost causes her to retreat a step. His eyes cast a dark and mysterious aura, and for the first time since she's been in the man's presence, she's not sure what to make of him. Of his intentions.

A sick sensation worms its shameful way through her core.

"That depends."

"On what?" she asks, timidly.

"What he tells me."

A NEW PATH

CHAPTER FOURTEEN

"Historically, very few wars have taken place in Endlia that can't be traced back to this simple theological question: which god do you believe in, and do you believe in 'our' version of them?"

– MENYARD MINOTOA, *THE GOD SYSTEM*

———

THE FEISTY FIRE crackles and snaps, a knot of wood splitting in its roast, as the flames push swells of heat into Ket's cheeks. Its ruddy glow peels back only a few layers of shadows past their immediate huddled shapes. The three of them and their unwilling companion have retreated farther into the woods, and are now trying to beat back the cold of night. Their captive, the man Jester calls Deerhood, sits on a felled tree trunk, his hands tied behind him, his mouth stuffed with a balled strip from Ket's torn shirt. Ket was gracious enough to let the man walk a few miles without it, but he ruined his freedom by screaming at the top of his lungs for help, for anyone passing the main road from Grumalt to hear, and Ket couldn't risk drawing any unnecessary attention. Here, in the woods and far from any traveled path, no one will hear the man scream, no matter how loudly he tests his vocal cords.

Ket removes the makeshift gag. "Now that you have your voice back," he says with no sympathy for what he's done, "why don't you tell me a little about your friend here."

Deerhood eyes Jester, who regards the situation with mild interest.

"Don't be shy now," Ket encourages. "Now's a chance to air your grievances. Why does your lord want Jester so badly? You're not the first wave of hunters to follow us, so the price on his head must be quite the purse. I find it difficult to believe that revenge is his sole motivation."

Deerhood's eyes glimmer for a second before he turns his head to Jester, an ugly smile cracking his face in half. "He doesn't know, does he?" He hoots when Jester's stand-still expression and unusual silence become the answer he's looking for. "Oh, High-beard's giant cock and balls, he really doesn't know?"

Ra blushes at the man's vulgar expression.

The tip of Ket's blade lifts Deerhood's chin, arresting his smile. "Refrain from using coarse language in the presence of the young lady. Understand?" Ket glares at him, hard, and the hunter curls his lips, liking that he's found a way beneath Ket's skin, but not liking it enough to test him further.

"She doesn't look like a young lady to me," Deerhood says, his brow arching. His eyes roam her body, and Ket can see the long gander is filling his head with impure thoughts. Ket resists the urge to backhand the bastard across his cheek. "She looks like a woman. Full-grown." The man's practically drooling.

"If you don't start looking at her with respect," Ket says, "I will grant her permission to turn you into a toad. Then I'll squash you under my boot."

"She can...she can do that?" Deerhood's eyes flare, wonder and fear sparking in equal measure.

"Want to find out?"

Deerhood shakes his head.

"Good. Now. Tell me. Jester. What's your lord's true business with him?"

"Jester…" Deerhood begins, a twinkle in his eye. "Morlo Robyn Tent."

"What?" Ket furrows his brow. "What are you saying?"

"That's his name. You call him Jester, but his real name is Morlo Robyn Tent. He's thirty-six years old. And he's about the biggest double-crossing-scum-sucking-rodent-rat-faced-fuck-bag you'll ever meet." Deerhood squints over at Ra. "Apologies, milady."

"Tent…" Ket says, nodding, remembering that the first wave of bounty hunters called him by that name. "What did he do?"

"This scum-fucker here," Deerhood says, grinding his teeth, "stole something. Something very important. Before he marched south to Owlton's capital and tried to start a war with the king."

"Stole something?" Ket studies Jester, who's actively avoiding his gaze and continuing to direct his sights into the flickering flames. "He must have left that part out when he advised me of his situation."

"How convenient," Deerhood says, mocking. "Our dear friend Morlo here lifted a very precious item from the Father's private collection of ancient artifacts."

"Lies," Jester says, yawning while speaking the word. "I took nothing from that man. Except maybe his dignity."

"You're really going to sit there and claim you had nothing to do with the missing Mind Stone? After all this time? Come now, Tent—no one believes your story, and furthermore, the Father is so convinced that you're responsible that he's *tripled* your bounty."

"Flattering," Jester says, yawning, feeding another handful of twigs to the hungry flames. "But he's after the wrong person."

"No? Then why did you march to Hornrake and attempt to kill the king, leaving nothing at the scene of the crime except the Father's colors? You planted yourself because you meant to start a war between them, erode that alliance that's stood for the better part of thirty years, and use it to ensure that Iradon never comes looking for you."

"It's a grand story, one I'm sure our friend the Warden—I'm sorry, *Father*—has convinced a great many people of…but it's not true. I have not taken his precious Mind Stone, nor do I have the item in my possession. You're welcome to search me."

Everyone studies him for a beat, but no one takes the bait.

"As for the attempted assassination," Jester continues, "well, your good Father owes me quite a bit of coin for taking out his laundry. He simply could not pay up. I couldn't exactly break his legs, so I figured I'd call on King Ragland to settle the score for me." Jester yawns again as if relaying this story is a strenuous bore. "It all ended up being much more hassle than I anticipated. Ten years ago, when I was in my prime, well—we probably wouldn't be here right now, and I would be watching Hornrake and Iradon armies march out to meet each other on the Hot Plains."

"You're so full of shit, Tent," Deerhood says, shaking his head incredulously. "You know damn well you plotted to take the Mind Stone—"

"What is the Mind Stone?" Ket interjects, leaning forward and trying to swim through the bullshit both men are spewing.

Deerhood rolls his eyes in an *oh c'mon* sort of way. "You never heard of the Mind Stone?"

"If I had, then I wouldn't have asked you about it."

Deerhood snorts, relaxing his shoulders; the way his arms are pinned back is clearly beginning to bother him. "The Mind Stone is an ancient artifact said to be imbued by the touch of Ciminen."

"Ciminen…" Ket says, liking the way the name sounds on his tongue. It's been some time since he's heard her name mentioned. "The Goddess?"

"The one and only," Deerhood confirms smugly. "Ciminen's powers were said to be great—it's no secret she's the second-most-worshipped deity behind Highbeard. Her powers were of the mind…and it is said that the Mind Stone was carved by her hand. The exact purpose of the Mind Stone was never clear, but if you believe the stories passed down from the First Dawn, then special hands can wield it and it gives the wielder the ability to control the minds of their subjects."

Ket huffs, a sort of laugh that seems to annoy Deerhood.

"What's that?" Deerhood says, his questioning eyes narrowing to thin lines. "You don't believe in the mysticism of the old tales?"

"I believe in many things—most of which I can see. Old stories filtered through generations and generations of lying mouths—not so much."

"Indeed—but there is a grain of truth to every fable, no?"

Ket doesn't see any reason to answer that.

"There is truth," Deerhood continues, "whether you believe it exists or not. Which parts are real…one day all of us will know."

"So, your Warden," Ket addresses Deerhood, but his eyes can't help but wander over to Jester, "he collects these artifacts?"

"He has a collection like no other. I'm talking about the Scepter of Dunaria, the Sword of Helaton—he has priceless artifacts that few men have ever laid eyes on. No one is permitted into his chamber unattended by him and at least a dozen of his men, all armed and ready to kill if given the word. Few are privileged to set their eyes on those wonders, and noblemen from all over the Endlands have paid top coin to witness the spectacles."

"So, how did you steal the Mind Stone?" Ket asks Jester.

Jester titters, mostly to himself. "You don't actually believe this rubbish, do you?"

"I have great difficulty believing anyone."

"But you believe him?"

Ket's stare sharpens on their prisoner. "I don't know."

"I can help," Ra says, speaking up for the first time all night. There's a scratch in her voice, and she clears it away with a forceful *ahem.* "I can…sometimes, that is…I can…"

"Spit it out, girly," Jester says, flaring his nostrils, his patience apparently withering.

"Borgadine taught me a spell," she says, then gulps as if she's unsure whether she should speak these things aloud, "to read people's minds. Their thoughts."

"Who needs a Mind Stone, huh?" Jester says, winking at Deerhood.

"Horseshit," Deerhood spits. "I don't want this freak doing anything…anything…anything *witchy* to me."

"You're in no position to demand anything," Ket tells him, and it shuts the man's mouth. Ket is thankful for the reprieve, though he doesn't expect it to last. He twists to face Ra. "What does it entail?"

"Um…silence. Concentration. I remember some words from the book…I think it may be enough to enter—"

"*Some* of the words?!" Deerhood shouts. "No, no, no, I will not allow this cuntling to perform any half-assed magic—"

Ket cracks him across the face with the back of his closed fist. The impact is enough to dislodge him from the downed tree. Bloody drool leaks from his mouth, and Deerhood spits a glob into the shadows below.

"Speak another word," Ket warns him, "and I will remove one of your ribs. It's a painful, violent procedure I prefer not to perform, but…I will if you disobey my wishes one more time. Or disrespect Ralyanna again."

The man's face contorts into a mask of silent rage. His cheeks burn hotter than the campfire before him.

"Now…" Ket says, spinning back to Ra. "As you were saying…"

"Yes," she whispers, quiet as a mouse. Her confidence isn't inspiring, but Ket really wants to know what secrets the man is keeping. Also—the girl's powers themselves are somewhat alluring. Curiosity overcomes his logic. "The spell…I can perform it."

"And what will it do to him?" Ket points to his temple. "His mind. Will it hurt him?"

"No. I don't think so."

"Scramble him up? Make him…*disturbed?*"

"There's no reason to believe it would."

"You've done this before?"

She hesitates, glances around the faces staring at her, waiting for her to expel the truth. "Well…no…not really. Not like this."

Jester can't help but chuckle.

Deerhood looks like he wants to protest again as he feels around his midsection, his ribs, wondering if it's worth losing one over an attempt to dissuade Ket from going through with this.

Ket hangs his head. "Damn it."

"I've done it once. On Borgadine. And it was fine."

"I won't risk this man's mind based on one controlled experiment," Ket says, sending another twig to its fiery demise.

"Oh, thank Highbeard's magnificent cock." Deerhood shudders, beads of sweat dribbling down his forehead. He closes his eyes and mutters a prayer under his breath.

"Coward," Jester says, then turns around and begins to trek toward the edge of darkness, where the light from the flames falls short.

"Where are you going?" Ket calls out to him.

Jester waves, says, "Going for a midnight stroll. Then maybe I'll be tired enough to sleep."

Jester's outline fades into the dark.

"You have to protect me from him," Deerhood pleads, not long after Jester disappears. "He'll try to kill me if you fall asleep."

Ket knows that's true. He nods, agreeing with the man's concern. "I'll stay up the night. You can sleep fine. Tomorrow you will march back to Iradon and tell your boss to stop sending men after us. Or by the Highbeard's good graces, I will slaughter every single one of the Jester's pursuers. Understood?"

The stillness in the man's stare suggests he understands wholly. "Why do you care so much? About Tent? Wouldn't it be easier to see the man to his death? What advantage does he gain you? In life? On your journey?"

Many times since their journey began, Ket's asked himself those very same questions. "He has his thorny side, but he has his uses."

"Like what?"

"He's a survivor. Like me. And survivors…we stick together."

———

THE NEXT MORNING while Jester still sleeps, Ket takes Deerhood back to the main road and releases him, issuing one final warning before undoing the ties around his wrists, sending him back into the wild. Deerhood shoots Ket one final look of disapproval, one last flare of the nostrils, then starts his run back to Grumalt. It's a coin flip whether the man will do what Ket has instructed: return to Iradon and convince his lord to stop sending more men. But Ket knows the reality is more likely the man will return to Grumalt, gather a dozen or so men for his cause—in the name of hunting a witchling—and offer them top coin to ride out after them, fully armed and prepared to maim, burn, or slaughter.

Because Jester is lying, he thinks. *He's stolen something important and this Warden will stop at nothing to gain it back.*

That's why Ket has decided the three need to alter their path, take the woods west and get off Iradon's trail.

When he returns to camp, he rouses Ra and Jester and begins to pack up their belongings.

Jester rises with a yawn and bone-tugging stretch. Ra just holds her sleepy head in her palms, not eager to face the grueling hike ahead. Ket is packed and ready to move out before the two can climb to their feet.

"What's the big rush?" Jester asks, rubbing his eyes.

"The rush is your friend will be back soon with six times the manpower." Ket points with his chin toward the new direction. "Which is why we need to be gone. I'll cover our tracks and lay a false trail."

"You can…do that?"

Ket nods, smirking. "It's worked before." *A long time ago,* he almost adds.

A few minutes later the three are off, their camp dismantled, and Ket pushes them west through the forest, some paths manmade, more not, to keep any pursuers off their heels, should they follow. Veering from the obvious routes just long enough would cast doubts in the minds of even the most seasoned trackers. Ket assumes there will be at least one decent tracker among their pursuers, so he pushes them off the path as often as possible, making sure their footprints are hidden in the leaf-laden dirt, tampering with their tracks where he can, and making false prints that lead nowhere. At the very least he hopes to buy them time, or that they'll get far enough north that any pursuers will abandon their mission.

With the scheme laid, Ket leads them farther north through more patches of sparse woodland, places that look familiar. He realizes he must have tracked this way when he escaped the Rovan Territories, over a decade ago. Memories rise of him running through these woods, hounds chasing him, their barking and howling slicing through the trees; him unable to shake their tail, unable to cover up his scent, no matter how much mud he bathed in, no matter how many rivers he dove in to cleanse the sweat and stink from his pores. Those were hard, bloody days, ones he hasn't thought about in years.

That's in the past, he grimaces, finally reaching a road well-traveled and wide enough for two wagons to pass each other. *It's in the past and now you're headed back there.*

To die all over again.

Ket killed himself off years ago, at least in the eyes of Rovan, the Silver Towers, his father, his brothers, his fellow Soulthieves, and everyone else who knew his true name. He doesn't expect his return will be well received, and fully anticipates dying at the hands of this empire, built on greed's fortune, and the lust for blood and violence and endless wars where no one really wins, and everybody loses. With each stumbling step toward the northern border, he can almost feel Ravenborn's fingers tightening around his throat. The thought of climbing the Silver Towers brings a bitter, coppery taste to his mouth.

He's been biting his tongue.

"Are you…?" Ra asks, noticing his painful wince.

"I'm fine."

"You don't look fine."

"Trust me," he tells her, not realizing how aloof he's sounding. "I'm fine."

"I see," she resigns.

"How much longer until we catch a rest?" Jester asks, breathing heavier than he has all trip. "I'm in need of new winds."

Ket turns to see the man completely fatigued, sweat streaming from his crown of stitched flesh.

They push through the next few days, only stopping every two hours or so. The rests are brief by Ket's design. He wishes the breaks were longer, but this section of road doesn't provide much cover, and besides, he saw a road marker a few miles back that suggested a village up ahead, though he's seen no evidence of civilization. Which he finds strange. Typically, trails this wide are clean and well-traveled; it's not unusual to see dozens of travelers out and about, heading to jobs or visiting neighboring towns and cities.

"Do you know where we are?" Ket speaks into the silence.

"Middle of the Crosslands," Jester says with a shrug. "Maybe."

"I don't recognize this road from my travels with Borgadine," Ra says, almost disappointed, like it's a road she *should* know, and know well.

"Saw a sign for a village about three miles back," Ket tells them, hoping he didn't imagine it. No one else confirms noticing it, which bothers him even more. "We'll stop there, see if we can find a spot to rest and eat, get our bearings. Ask for directions."

"I'm starving," Jester says. He touches the delicate spot on his forehead where the fabric and skin are fused together. "Might need some ointment for this hazard—it's itching like a bitch."

"Why don't you just remove it?" the girl asks.

Jester glances at her like she's just uttered the magic words of a wicked spell. "Oh, it's that easy, yeah? Just have my scalp removed? *Again.* You know any surgeons willing to participate in that operation?"

The girl shies away from opening her mouth again.

"Besides? What am I to do? Wear another man's scalp in its place? No thank you. At least this hat is mine, belongs to me. I own it." Jester toys with the dangling bells, an act of fondness. "No, this is me now. The new me. Morlo Robyn Tent died in Hornrake—and the Jester was born."

Ket's not looking at the man, but he can hear the smile in his voice.

"We'll get you ointment," Ket says confidently. "Unless you know any healing spells?" he asks Ra.

Ra shakes her head, almost as if she'd be too embarrassed to know any. "We never practiced healing spells. Just medicines. I could try…"

"I will not be a test subject for this lass's spooky charms!" Jester calls out.

"Relax," Ket warns him. "She won't turn you into a goose. Isn't that right?" Sensing her edgy, guilt-ridden anxiety climbing, he winks at her.

She smirks, then looks down at her feet.

They travel three more miles before the road brings them to a vast opening, populated by fifty cabins, a small abandoned village that gives Ket a bad case of the ghostly chills the second he strays from the path and approaches the first cabin.

"What happened here?" Ra asks. She ducks under a laundry line near the edge of the first cabin's property. Clothes lie strewn across the overgrown grass, which is mostly overrun with weeds and wildflowers.

Ket peeks through a dirt-frosted window. "Empty. No one here."

"Townsfolk were raided or threatened and ran off," Jester says, surveying the entire length of the village. "Simple as that."

"What scared them, I wonder."

"You got me." Jester shrugs, then adds, "But whatever or whoever it was, they're clearly gone."

There's a chill in the air, a soft wind swirling around Ket's feet, penetrating the leather of his boots and coiling up his calves. An instant unease stops his heart for a beat. Gooseflesh spreads across his body, icing his bones. A static charge buzzes in the spaces around them, pulling at the hairs on Ket's arms and neck. The fragile, translucent outline of an old woman holding a broom pauses outside one of the cabins. One moment there, gone the next, her image flickering like a struggling flame. Then back again. Her broom sweeps back and forth in furious strokes, the rhythm aligning with the beat of Ket's pounding heart. She refuses to quit, just like her entire essence is refusing to…what? Move on?

Ket's mouth is a pocket of desert. He hears Jester drawing lungfuls of air, oblivious. Ra has sat down, her face tilted back, her tiny pores drinking the shimmering sparkles of sunlight. Exhausted. Peaceful. And so unaware.

The old woman lifts her head, her vacuous eyes all white, yet, somehow still focused, their line-of-sight meeting as a word springs into Ket's skull.

Drifter.

Spirits that haven't left the Endlands for the afterlife that awaits them. Souls of the dead, trapped in a mimicry of the lives they've led. It's unclear if she can see him, something alive, something living on the periphery of her experience. But then she opens her mouth. Tries to speak. A greeting? A warm welcome to her humble home? Ket knows this is false the second he thinks it. The way she opens her mouth…the way her lips stretch, elastic and wide…the way she tenses…

A warning. She's warning us.

Ket shudders.

And then she's gone. Just like that. Like pinching out a candle flame.

"What is it?" Jester inquires, frowning, his face asking the same question. Ket shakes his head, clearing away the image of the woman, what her presence might portend. "Nothing," he says. Jester frowns but shakes his head, too tired to inquire further.

Ra lets herself fall onto her back, smiling, sighing at the break.

"We rest. Here." Ket's jaw tightens, his eyes flitting to the space in front of the cabin. Where there is nothing to see. He sits beside her, his gaze unflinching, as the cabins seem to stare back at him.

"Just not for long."

DESPITE HIS UNEASE, they decide to spend the night in one of the empty cabins, sleeping close to one another, each of them promising not to drift too far off into the dreamlands, in case whatever drove these people from their homes (or killed them) comes back. Ket commits to sleeping with one ear open, tethering himself to reality with the power of only his mind, a feat he's gotten quite good at since leaving that Hornrake prison and journeying across Owlton, deep into the Crosslands. It's a necessary survival tactic, he thinks, to sleep but remain half-awake in case some bandit runs across you and wants to slit your throat while you're unconscious. But the quality of his sleep suffers, and even though he's not fond of dreaming in the first place, he always finds himself tired, dragging his rear come the following morning.

It's late—a few hours past midnight—when his eyes and brain combine to sabotage his plan, and he drifts off, away from waking, and enters the land of dreams, no longer chained to reality.

He walks across the farmland he once owned, the barns and house at the center of the property on fire, the flames eating through the structures' walls, belching black smoke into the air, as tall as mountain giants. Ket stumbles toward the destruction, unable to veer from the path set out before him. Flames heat his face, crawl across his skin, almost a caress. Screaming filters in from somewhere, but he can't tune his ear to the source: an unfamiliar wail, so it can't possibly be coming from the boys or Jennah. Can it?

No, there are too many screams, more than three, possibly more than a dozen voices, the chorus of cries piping in from several directions, impossible to determine one particular source. As they continue, they become less human. More animal. Shrill and constant.

In the distance between the two burning structures—the house and the west barn—he spots Jennah, standing in a white dress, the same dress she wore the day they wed. A wreathed crown sits atop her head, decorated with purple-budded thistles and yellow dandelions with green nettle. Her eyes have frosted over, a spooky white film, her pupils and irises erased during the throes of some malignant trance. Some *spell.*

She's casting something, and he remembers this is not the first time he's been here; he's dreamed this before.

Jennah waves her arms in the air, her fingers gracefully dancing through the smoke-clouded atmosphere. Her lips move but release no sounds. Intermittent seizures rack her body, like there's something beneath her skin that wants to inhabit her, wants to pull her this way and that. But she resists, continues to project her magic, introducing the dream realm to her godlike touch. He can't tell what she's doing, what kind of spell she's placing on the environment (or on him?) but she's taking her time getting started.

Their sons behind her. Sitting quietly on the ground, looking up as if they can see Highbeard's Heaven, their eyes also veiled in a milky white film, mumbling a series of unheard whispers.

Ket's heart nearly breaks at the sight of them.

He wants to run to them, his family, and collect them in his arms, hold them tight and never let go—remain in this dreamworld forever. But it's not the kind of dream he can control. He's twenty yards away, and the dream will not let him take a single step toward his family. An invisible wall in front of him, behind him, to his sides; he's encased in the dream's unfathomable grip.

Jennah's head tilts, her eyes projecting halos of white light at him. Her lips are moving too fast for him to make out the words, but she begins to speak, slowly and calculatedly, in a way he can understand. *"Climb the Silver Towers, Find the Boy, Bring Me His Head, or All that You Love Will be Devoured."*

While listening to the recited poem, his dreamself shivers.

She waves her arms again, casting more magic at the sky. The wind blows, fanning the smoke and sending great swirls of floating ash from the burning buildings away from her. The boys continue to glance at the spiraling clouds above, indistinguishable from any form the clouds in Ket's reality have ever held.

Ket tries to speak and ask his wife questions, but his lips are sealed, held together by the glue of the dream. Instead, her voice rings her message as if stuck in a loop, her demand his entire reason for existing:

Climb the Silver Towers, Find the Boy, Bring Me His Head, or All that You Love Will be Devoured.

SILVER SECRETS

CHAPTER FIFTEEN

"Some of the most impressive structures in all of Endlia are the Silver Towers of the Rovan Territories—they stand tall, and those who have witnessed their marvelous architecture will tell you their spires can tear apart the passing clouds."

– PENNY BOOTS KERWAGEN, *WORLD'S BEST ARCHITECTURE*

———

THE BOY SITS ALONE in the northern tower, leafing through his studies: the chapter of the book he's supposed to be reading for an exam, later—but concentrating has never been more diffi-cult. Not that *The God System* by Menyard Minotoa isn't somewhat interesting—it is, in its own way—but he has so many other thoughts on his mind, particularly about Ravenborn and his lessons, his own abilities, powers he's yet to see sprout from his fingertips. He dreams about the day his supposed abilities work in full; when he can shoot fire from his palms or cast magical spells on the guardsmen—mind control charms to make them do whatever he wants. Will he use his power for good, or will he give in to his mischievous side? He knows what Fen would choose, if he were here to give advice.

Make the guards act like chickens! would probably be Fen's recommendation. *Make them cluck and flap their arms like wings!*

The boy giggles, his star-shaped eyes and childish mind drifting further and further away from his studies. After reading about early iterations of a particular southern Springgaarden Highbeard cult, he finds himself spaced out, unable to read another word about gods and cults and religious mysticism. He casts the book aside, then hops off the bed and heads to the lone window of his chamber. Looks out. Peers across the sunlit sky, then down at the Rovan kingdom, the droves of people clogging the streets, going about their typical day.

From here they look like ants scurrying to and from their homey hills. He supposes they're not much different from those tiny insects; driven by the basics, living to survive. To eat. To multiply. To provide for the rest of their hive. Repeat and repeat, until the cycle of life loops closed, and the spiritual passage to the Further Lands commences. That place between worlds where the soul goes once it leaves the body.

The soul.

The boy wonders if ants have souls too, or just people.

A knock at the door derails his thoughts. He faces the partially open doorway, as Ravenborn's face slides through the gap between the door and the frame. The general is especially cheery this morn, sporting a wide grin, like someone's just recited the best joke in Rovan history to him. The boy wonders if Ravenborn got *laid* last night, then wonders if he's using that term correctly. Fen's explained it to him before, has used the term in that very context, but the boy is still hazy on what it truly means. He almost asks Ravenborn if he was *laid*, then decides against it. Repeating what Fen says usually gets him in trouble, and he's had a good start to the morning so far—why spoil it?

"Morning, boy," Ravenborn says, practically dancing into the center of the room. Whatever's gotten into him, it's weird.

The boy keeps a wide berth, sticking to the wall near the window. He can't rule out a ruse. "You're early."

"Yes, we have a lot to accomplish today. It's going to be a big one."

"A big what?"

Ravenborn almost loses his response in a roar of laughter. "A big day. For you. For me. Today is going to be different."

The boy isn't following. "What are we doing?"

"We're going on a trip."

"Where?"

"Not far. Outside the kingdom walls. But not far."

The boy's only been outside the kingdom walls a handful of times. Mostly for hunting trips. He doubts that's what's in store for today, considering how jovial Ravenborn is acting.

Maybe he's still drunk from the night before, chirps Fen's phantom voice. The boy almost chuckles out loud but manages to maintain a straight face in the presence of his elder.

"Where?" the boy asks, wanting—no, *needing*—to know exactly where Ravenborn plans to take him.

"Do not worry, pipsqueak," Ravenborn says, planting himself on the edge of the boy's bed. "We're going to see an old friend. Maybe he will inspire you, help you progress with your lessons."

"Are we going to see a wizard?"

Ravenborn throws back his head and cackles at the ceiling, at the mural of Highbeard's heavens, painted so vividly, gifted by Rovan's most talented artist—Bendra Pyles. As he looks down from the illustrated golden gates and the tropical plains beyond, shaded over with brushed wispy white clouds, he wipes a spot of drool from the edge of his lips. "No, we are not going to see a wizard. We both know wizards are a thing of the past."

"But some—"

"Let's put magical tales of wizards and witches and warlocks on the shelf for now." His mood shifts, his smile shrinking like an exhausted earthworm. "There is only one known magical being left in this world, and that title belongs to you, boy with the star-shaped eyes."

"But why me?"

Ravenborn's smile reappears, if only for a moment. "That, my young friend, is why we're leaving today. It's what we will find out."

———

THE GROUP RIDES out farther than the boy's ever been in his thirteen years, past the forests he's been through on hunting expeditions. Past streams and rivers he's crossed before. Through green valleys and brown fields, places that have previously been labeled "forbidden lands", unless accompanied by Ravenborn's watch. The boy nestles in the center of a company, seated atop a strong horse named *Sky*—*a* black gelding, the only horse the boy has ever mounted.

The farther they ride, the more anxious the boy grows, and he can sense Sky's uneasiness. The company stops once, only to relieve themselves and snack on strips of boar jerky. Ravenborn announces they will keep riding, straight through until they reach their destination, and the men seem to have no problem with this command, not a grumble among them. The boy has doubts, all of which he stores silently to himself, not daring to speak a syllable of his concern.

We're way out here so they can kill me…

I've failed to produce…

Like a lame hen…

They have no further need for me.

He convinces himself these are dumb, childish thoughts, and if Emperor Salah or Ravenborn were to sentence him to death, they wouldn't have gone through the trouble of organizing this party and marching out this far away from the Silver Towers just to hang, burn, or lop off his head. No, they would make a spectacle of that, right in the center of Rovan, probably charge admission to the show. *Who wants to witness the untimely demise of the prophetic one!*

It's more likely Ravenborn told him the truth earlier that morn; they are meeting someone who can help progress his abilities. Draw that special godlike sorcery right out of him, the way botanists extract medicine from certain greens.

To make me the man I'm destined to become.

Hours pass, which feel like days on Sky's saddle, Ravenborn leading the troop down a path that intersects with a dense forest, heavily stocked with lush green trees and swaying willows. Glowing particles float through the air, small flecks of light one of the men identify as "pixie spit", a spore shed annually from a certain species of willow. It's interesting because the boy has never heard of such a thing, not even during his studies. They really do look like pixies, some thimble-sized faeries, dancing with the winds.

The boy reaches out to touch one of the spores, but a rider close to him slaps down his hand. Rubbing his aching knuckles, the boy turns and glances at the rider, his eyes demanding an explanation.

"Beautiful to look at," the man says, nodding at the floaters. "But deadly allergic to some folk. Problem is, you won't know you're allergic—only the people who find your corpse can make that diagnosis."

It's enough of a warning to stop him from trying to touch one again. Gripping the saddle horn, the boy does not move until a few miles later, when the trail leads them to a small house built in the center of the woods.

Surrounded by green bushes, the house boasts a colorful flowerbed of the richest and brightest petals Endlia has to offer; marvelous buds of purple and gold and ruby reds. The house itself is painted banana yellow, its shutters a melting-sun orange. Shoots of roof straw caps off the home, looking dry, as if it's never seen a drop of rain.

Stopping at the hip-high white-picket fence, the company

dismounts, every single rider leaving their saddles. The boy hops off Sky and waits for direction. As one of the men strides over to the gate and drops the latch, Ravenborn approaches the boy and kneels before him.

"You will enter that house," Ravenborn says, nodding over his shoulder. "And speak to the man inside. He will give you counsel."

The boy's skin ripples with gooseflesh. Freezing in place, something tugs at his chest. Like there's a loop around his heart and some invisible puppeteer is giving it a proper yank. He does not want to enter the house. In fact, he wants to hop back on Sky, ride off in the opposite direction, and never look back at this field again. Even though this house and the surrounding beauty have been ripped straight from the pages of his favorite fairy tales, he's certain what waits inside is anything but a happy ending.

Ravenborn's finest stand evenly spaced apart, forming a wall behind him. *As if they're expecting me to run.* Their eyes are dodgy, more than usual when interacting with *The Boy*, and some of them have gone as pale as milk-froth. Dread is a familiar companion, and it wraps its arms around the boy's shoulders, stirring a sour feeling in his gut. The cottage stands before him, looking at him through soulless, darkened panes of glass.

He spins to Ravenborn with soft, cherubic eyes. They water to the brim, and he does nothing to dam the tears rolling down his cheeks. His sadness only seems to stoke Ravenborn's smoldering anger. "Go," his mentor says, past gritted teeth.

The boy knows there's no getting out of this, and if it comes down to it, Ravenborn will pick him up by his neck and drag him into the house kicking and screaming.

"Fear nothing. You are safe. And my men will be outside." Ravenborn stands and then steps out of his way. "Go. He's waiting for you."

The boy approaches the gate, passes through, and takes the cobblestone walk all the way to the front door, painted a dark midnight blue. He feels every one of the watch's eyes on him.

And the house—the house watches too.

Maybe from the windows, which themselves look like the leering eyes of some fairytale monster, pretending to be a friendly, a protective respite for a fable's young protagonist.

He bows his head, not wanting to enter this place.

I don't want to know about my powers…

I don't want to know anything.

I just want to be left alone.

But he will never be alone. He cannot change who he is, any more than he can change the shape of his eyes.

He lifts his hand to knock, but the door is already open, just a crack, inviting him inside. Taking one last glance over his shoulder, wishing to see Ravenborn change his mind, wave him back over to the horses, he hears someone scuffling inside.

A voice, raspy and roughened by time, bites through his hesitation. "Come, boy. Nothing to fear in here. And you can't stand there forever."

Ravenborn doesn't call him back. His gaze holds him, and the more the boy tries to delay the inevitable, the redder Ravenborn's face shines.

The boy closes his eyes, succumbing to his fate. Faces the door. Pushes it open, letting the bold, bookish stink of inked papers and binding glue waft toward him. Stepping inside, his eyes are drawn to the most immediate conclusion; the inside of this home is not as pleasant as the exterior suggested. While his first glance presented him with a cheery and vibrant abode, the inside is darkened by shadows, the décor dull and lacking. *Disorganized* is the first word that comes to mind. Pots and pans are stacked on the kitchen counter. Spoiled food—a hint of fish—sits in waste bags on the floor, flies buzzing near the opening, from where a foul stench escapes. Behind the initial library scent lies the accumulative odor of dust. He takes a few steps forward, bypassing the path into the kitchen and entering the open living area, which is mostly populated by mountains of books, most of which look well-loved. There's also a couch.

And a man reclined on that couch, an empty chair across from him.

"Come closer," the voice says from the shadows.

The boy shuffles a few steps forward.

"Closer," the gruff voice beckons. "Come now. Don't be shy. We don't have long. Time is not our ally."

The boy still can't see the man's face; shadows occupy that side of the room, obscuring almost everything. He spots the man's legs in the hazy light coming in from the window across from him. The man sits, tapping his foot against the floor, his patience thinning with each aggravating second.

"Good," the man says, though he doesn't sound satisfied. "Just there. Stop. Let me look upon you, yes."

He has never felt more uncomfortable in his life, and this includes those awkward, awestruck stares he's received from classmates, back when he was permitted to attend public classrooms. If he wasn't so petrified of Ravenborn's infamous methods of punishment, he might consider running.

"You've grown since the last time I saw you," the man says, wheezing laughter escaping the bowels of his throat.

"...Saw me?" The boy sounds like a mouse, even to his own ears. Pathetic, he knows. He wishes his spine were stronger, wishes he had not an ounce of fear in his bones. Then again, he wishes for a lot of things. Things he'll never have. "Do I...sir, I mean, do I know you?"

A tiny ball of fire appears in the corner of the shadowed room, no bigger than the boy's thumbnail, and seconds later, plumes of smoke bloom into the light. The man puffs on a pipe, the same kind he's seen Ravenborn toke on from time to time, after a hard day of lessons.

"You do not, for the last time I saw you, you were just a wee thing."

The boy squints at him, as if doing so will peel back the layers of shadows and reveal his mystery host.

"When?" he asks, timidly.

"Well, on the day of your birth, of course." The man leans forward, leaving obscurity behind.

The boy does not recognize him, but also...*he does.* There's something oddly familiar about his face, the drooping beard, unmaintained and wild and stained with dried red cooking sauce, and the sunken eyes that rest below bushy, wiry eyebrows.

He kind of looks like the boy's own reflection, only...aged. By decades.

"Welcome home, son," the man says.

———

THE BOY DOES NOT SPEAK for what feels like several eons. He tries to. A few times. But all the words he wants to say bottle in his throat.

"It's fine, son," the man says, his forehead smoothing over, as relief absorbs his wrinkles. "It's a lot to process, this."

The boy opens his mouth, his lips quivering, and it's not even cold in there. Heat blazes from the hearth against the far wall. "You're...you're my father?" Even as he speaks the words, they don't seem true. Impossible. Like these were words plucked from a pleasant dream, one that occurred many, many nights ago, and by some miracle he still remembers hearing them.

Surreal.

The man bows his head. "Aye, I'm your father." He places a hand over his heart. "My name is Jerrin. Jerrin Pierce. And I was there the night your mother gave birth." His eyes grow soft and wet, and the boy thinks his father might begin weeping. In truth, the boy feels as though he might weep too, but he's still so uncertain that any of this is true. The dreamlike quality of the moment keeps his emotions grounded. For now. "And that was the last time I saw you."

Glancing around the place, the boy searches for proof of this far-fetched story. "I was told my father was a fisherman."

The man laughs, but it sounds like a crackling firework going off in the center of his chest, something Fen might steal from the market and shoot off in the maid's chamber when he's feeling extra delinquent. "Yes, yes. I *was* a fisherman. Once. Until you came along. Everything changed after that. My life...altered. Forever. In many ways."

This isn't a trick... His heart flutters like a butterfly flying away, carrying the weight of his mounting anxiety. *This...could actually be real? Not one of Ravenborn's cunning ruses? Not just another ploy to coax my powers?* This man sitting here before him might truly be his father.

The wonder and unconditional affection he immediately felt toward the man shifts, and a burning anger ignites within him. "Why did you leave me? Huh? Why did you abandon me? WHY DID YOU LET THEM TAKE ME?"

The man doesn't flinch during his outburst. As if the words mean nothing to him. "I'm sure you have many questions, but know that we have little time, and what I need to tell you is very important. For us both."

The boy's chest heaves as he continues to see red.

"Please sit," his father commands, motioning to the lone chair across from him.

The boy denies his request.

"Please," Jerrin says again, with more bite.

The boy finally does as he's asked, but he's slow to sit. Anger —it seems—will earn him no answers and only waste their time. He's learned a lot in his thirteen years, but if there's one valuable pointer he's certain to always abide by, it's that sometimes saying nothing and listening is better than saying too much and hearing nothing at all.

"Thank you," Jerrin says, closing his eyes, gathering his breath. "Your mother and I—I hope you will understand—had no choice in the matter."

"Where is she?"

"Dead. Died in labor."

"I…" An invisible fist punches him in the gut, hard enough to knock his heart out of rhythm for a few beats. "I…I killed her?"

Jerrin wags his forefinger. "No. You must never think that. Her death was not your fault, not even slightly. If anything, you can blame the gods—if you feel the need to distribute blame." He casts his eyes on the front windows, the soldiers outside stationary, keeping watch. "The Highbeard priest that watched over your delivery…had no choice in the matter either. He sent word to the Rovans, and in return, the Rovans sent their men to collect you. I put up no fight. If I had…you and I would not be meeting here and now."

"Why *aren't* you dead?"

"I've asked myself that many times, in the years since." He goes quiet for a moment, but then comes back, shaking his whole body like a wet dog, snapping out of the reverie that derailed his thoughts. "At first I thought the Rovans were going to leave me for dead. Kill me off, dispose of any paternal evidence, sever the link between myself and you. But they kept me around over the years. Brought me here. To live out the rest of my days, under Ravenborn's watchful eye."

"You've been here the entire time?"

"Close to you, yes. But not close enough. Ravenborn has kept me updated on your progress. I've shared information with him."

"What information?"

"Family secrets."

The boy's eyes crave more answers, but for some reason his father does not venture more, unprovoked. "What secrets? Come on, father. You cannot hide things from me. I demand to know all."

"I'm sorry," Jerrin says, shaking his head, a feeble smile working its way onto his face. "I have to remember you're still a boy. These are…heavy burdens to carry. The knowledge of our past. Who we are…the truth can weigh you down. Break you. For example…" He points to his face, the gray in his beard, the wiry white strands that salt his hair. "I am not as old as I appear. Time and knowledge have been unforgiving."

"I am old enough to know these things," the boy yells, somewhat surprised by his own confidence. "I demand to know!"

Jerrin winks at him. "I'm sure you think that. When I was your age, I also believed I was ready to know everything. I hungered for truths that were hidden from me. But…some things…we're never old enough to learn."

The boy can't hide his annoyance. "Please, father. Tell me. Tell me what I need to know."

"Well, first, you are the last of us—the Pierce line ends with you. My brothers are all dead, gone before they could reproduce—and you were my and Merrygo's only child."

"Merrygo…"

"Your mother's name. She was a beautiful woman. I wish you could have seen her."

"Do you have a portrait?"

Jerrin chuckles at this. "No, no. A fisherman's life never afforded such luxuries."

"What else? What else do I need to know about us?"

The question freezes Jerrin. Like a stag caught in the eye of a hunter's bow. He swallows—perhaps whatever truth lingered on the tip of his tongue—and then clears his throat. "Your grandfather used to tell me and my brothers stories. We always thought they were tall tales, gross exaggerations of the truth, and in some cases, outright fiction. Stories of our ancestors being direct descendants of the one true god himself—the *Highbeard*."

Jerrin pauses, allowing that information to sink in. The boy blinks, the knowledge not fazing him.

"I suppose you already know that, though?" Jerrin asks.

Unimpressed, the boy points to the stars he has for eyes. "I've been told the basics, the prophecy surrounding my…condition."

"It was foretold that one day a descendant of the Highbeard would be born with star-shaped eyes—"

"Which, in turn, would signal the second coming of the gods," the boy finishes for him. "To prevent Arkos's Darkhell from rising."

Jerrin nods. Shrugs. "So it has begun."

"Is it true?"

Jerrin dips his head again. "Aye, it is true. You are living proof of the prophecy at work."

"I do have powers then?"

Jerrin regards his son with some concern. "Ravenborn has informed me of your struggles, your lackluster progression."

"Do you have powers? Maybe you can…"

Jerrin vibrates with a hideous laugh. "I have no powers, my son. If I did…" He glances up at the ceiling, then over to the hearth, then around the collections of books in the small library. "…I would certainly not be locked away in here. I would have Highbearded my way out of this prison a long time ago."

"Doesn't look like much of a prison," the boy says, admiring the library, its wealth of knowledge and stories.

"Not all prisons are dark and dank, hidden beneath the keep of some evil overlord." A cunning smile cuts across Jerrin's face. "Sometimes they are chambers at the top of the Silver Towers, others are quaint homes in the centers of unremarkable, unnamed forests.

"Now, about your lessons with Ravenborn…"

A fiery sting burns the boy's cheeks. "I have no power. It's all a lie."

Pouting his lips, mocking his son, Jerrin says, "Do you really believe that? Do you think the prophecy is a fallacy? That you just so happen to have matching eyes with the boy from some story that people have dedicated their entire existence to worship?"

The boy shrugs. To be honest, he does not know. There are times he feels a power coursing through him, a special current flowing through his veins that most may not feel. Sometimes he feels one with the wind, the earth, the sky, like he's a part of the lands, not just a movable piece on a *Knights & Dragons* board. But sometimes he feels nothing. Hopeless. A barren wasteland of a human being. Nothing more than ordinary, save for the shape of his irises.

He tells his father this, exactly how he feels.

"Maybe I am what the people whisper about, behind closed doors," the boy admits. "What people in Rovan chatter about in the streets. What the maids gossip about behind my back, when they think I'm not listening."

"And what's that?"

"A phony. A lie. A political pawn used by the so-called emperor to inspire hope, that the second coming is upon us, and I will champion a new age where the common man will live like a king. No more poverty. Illnesses gone. War will no longer claim the lives of young, capable men, because we will all be united under the Salamandian's banner."

At the last mention, Jerrin rolls his eyes. "As long as proud men exist, there will be war." He waves off his son's entire claim, shifting in his seat to find a more comfortable position. "I can tell you this, my boy. As long as I have been alive, I've always held doubts about the gods. Stories of witches and warlocks and wizards, tales of the unnatural of any kind always greased my ears with disbelief. But...the day I saw you...the day I held you in my arms, however brief, I knew...it was all true. All of it. You are special. You are godlike. And the second coming of the gods is upon us."

A chill flushes the boy's veins, turning his heart into a block of ice.

"What do they call you?" Jerrin asks.

"Call me?" The boy shrugs. "My name?"

Jerrin nods.

"Mostly they just call me *The Boy*." He shrugs like he doesn't care, even though he does and can't hide how much it bothers him, not having a proper name. "Ravenborn does anyway. His guards, when they *do* address me. Mostly I am 'Boy.' But Fen calls me—"

Jerrin stops him with a wave. "It doesn't matter. Whatever

they call you, it is not your true name. Not the name your mother and I planned for you."

The boy's heart skips at the prospect. "What did you name me?"

"You want to know?"

He nods, trying not to seem too eager.

"You were named after your grandfather...my father." Jerrin smiles pleasantly, like the mention of his father draws from a pool of welcoming memories. "His name was Thomassen. But mostly everyone called him *Thom*."

Thom. He plays the name over and over in his thoughts, repeating it like it's a tough word to pronounce, commit to memory. But it's simple. One syllable. Not pronounced Tom like some may mistake it for—but spoken like the word *tome*. Like a long book. Which suits Thom just fine. He likes long, immersive books. Long books are long journeys you can live inside.

"Thom," he tests the name out loud. It feels heavy on his tongue, like saying it too much will tire him out. "Thom," he says again, more confident.

"Thom," Jerrin repeats. "You do look like a Thom. And...you remind me of him. Your expressions. Your face in general is very much your grandfather's face. A little bit of your mother too, but you're definitely a Pierce."

The boy smiles at this, so elated that he doesn't feel the flood of tears pushing through his eyes until it's too late, until they are already spilling down his cheeks.

"Names have power," Jerrin continues. "Now that you know who you are, where you come from...I think that will inspire you to do great things."

"Great things?"

Jerrin shrugs, leaving the meaning open for interpretation. "That part is up to you. What you do with your powers."

"What can I do?"

Again, his father hefts his shoulders. "I suppose whatever you want. You just have to unlock yourself. The mind is a powerful weapon. People think wars are won and lost on the battlefields, that the winners are stronger and fiercer than their adversaries… but that is not true." He gathers a breath. "Wars are won here." He taps the center of his forehead. "All wars. Not just the kind fought on battlefields."

"Unlock myself…" Thom shakes his head. "But I don't understand how…"

Jerrin smiles. "That's the fun part. Figuring it out. But know this—you are powerful. And you are the most important person in our world. And you will be there to guide all humankind when the second coming comes…when the gods of Endlia have returned."

"What if…what if I don't want to."

"Sometimes…we don't have a choice. Just like your mother and I did not have a choice when you were born. When you were…when we had to give you up."

Thom imagines he wants to add, *When you were stolen from us.*

"I hate Ravenborn."

"He can be a grouchy fucker, yeah?" Jerrin laughs, and so does Thom, more so because his father uttered a curse word he finds funny. "He's not a good man. Remember that. He's loyal to his king, his country. Will do anything to protect and serve him. To garner his king's love and admiration. Did you know he murdered his own son?"

Thom's heart stops on a beat, is slow to resume its rhythm. "What?"

"Maybe that's a secret between us, for now. But maybe you use that secret later when it benefits you. If it does in any way."

"I don't understand."

"Maybe you will. One day." Jerrin pushes himself to his feet and peers out the window on his left. A cluster of guards are marching up the walkway, toward the house. "Looks like our time has expired."

"No! I want more time. I want to…I want to know all about you." A familiar sting needles the edges of his eyes. "And mom."

"We'll have more time. Later. Sometime soon." He winks, and in that moment, Thom believes the next words out of the man's mouth will be a lie. "I promise."

A knock on the door, three fast raps. The guards call his father's name, then open the door without permission. Three of the company crowd the foyer. They inform the father-son duo that their meeting time has come to an end, and that Ravenborn has requested Thom ride back to the Silver Towers.

They do not call him *Thom* though. It's just *you* or *boy*.

"My name is *Thom* now," the boy tells them.

The men look on, frozen, as if responding will earn them an admittance to their own hangings.

"Say it," the boy says to them. "Call me by my true name, then ask me to return to the Silver Towers."

The guards—utterly baffled—look to each other, searching, perhaps, for an answer to their unspoken questions.

Not a request, Thom almost says out loud. *A command.*

He already feels different. There's a new energy flowing through him, a static buzz that charges through the marrow of his bones, like when he sometimes touches a door handle that gives him a small shock. Though, this is more concentrated and actually *flowing* inside him. Like waves. Cresting bursts of energy he thinks he may be able to manipulate with the right amount of concentration, focus.

The men do not speak, defying his order, but maybe not on purpose.

"I will not ask again," the boy says, shooting them a look that backs the three men into the open doorway. They look at him differently. Terrified. Wide-eyed and open-mouthed. One of them backs out, marching hastily back down the walkway to where Ravenborn is waiting on their arrival, his arms open in the form of a silent question.

"Gods!" the other guard says, then drops to his knees like someone's slugged him with a whole quiver of arrows. He bows his head with the utmost reverence, a bend of his body held only for the most religious kind of respect. He presses his lips to the floorboards, kissing the ground where the boy traveled, holding that position until the boy verbally releases him.

The last guard stumbles backward, as if Thom has turned the bones in his legs to jelly. Thom loses sight of him, mostly because he's too shocked by how the kneeling man is reacting.

He's never garnered this kind of respect. Not inside the Silver Towers.

It feels good. Better than good. For once he feels important. More than just a prophecy, some words written long ago that may or may not prove true. And he's so tangled in these thoughts he doesn't even question *why* they are acting like this.

He rotates back to Jerrin, his father. And when his father's face begins to change, morph into something that almost sickens Thom to his core, he begins to realize that something is very wrong.

"W-what is-s it?" Thom asks, unable to smooth the waver in his words.

"It's your eyes," Jerrin says, swallowing, as if trying to keep himself from throwing up. "The stars are on fire."

SLAUGHTER FOR SINNERS

CHAPTER SIXTEEN

"In tumultuous times, religions will buckle and go to war with each other. We have peace now, but we are creatures of habit, doomed to repeat the sins of the past. At some point a king will weaponize the words of their chosen deity, and that's when Arkos's true Darkhell will begin."

– VICENZO WORLAGGI, *DANGEROUS GODS: A PAMPHLET*

―――

THIS TIME *he's in a tower, looking out across Endlia, seeing everything from the Black Isle (miles and miles off the coast of northern Rovan) to the sunny beaches of Southernmost Springgaarden. Jennah sits across from him, with her back against the tower chamber wall, and he stands near the ledge, peering out, shielding his eyes from the cloudless sky's sunbaked shimmer. He's not sure what he's doing there other than contemplating the majestic lands, the towering cities, the dense forests, and the stretching fields of this great continent. But he feels like he owns a particular piece of power. Almost like a god himself.*

Is this how Highbeard feels? Sitting on his throne in the White Heavens?

"It's yours, you know?" Jennah says, and he turns to see her radiant smile, red lips, and snow-white teeth. "It's all yours."

"No," he says, after considering her statement. "No, this land belongs to no one."

"I believe the gods will beg to differ." She winks not once, but twice. "Once they set their feet back on man's soil."

"Are they really coming?"

She nods without hesitation. "Oh yes. They are coming. And you can be there, to stop them."

He laughs at this, and even though he cannot control the actions of this dream, he agrees with this version of himself, would have laughed exactly the same way. "I am just a man."

"Not just any man," she says, shaking her head, losing some of the charm from that smile. "No, I felt it when I first met you. It was why I was drawn to you. Keten Norlath. The last living Soulthefter."

"Drawn to me?"

"Like a pirate to buried treasure."

"Why? I'm not special...I'm not what you think I am."

Jennah's lips curl, so much so that the elastic movement of her face frightens him. "You can doubt yourself, but you cannot doubt the truth. The truth doesn't care what you believe in."

He pounds his fist against the interior wall of this tower chamber. "You speak in riddles, dream-witch. I will not have it."

"You will have it," she says with a sharp tongue. "Dreams do not provide answers; dreams grant access to the correct questions so you may discover those answers for yourself. That is their power."

"I wish to dream a normal dream for once," Ket admits, sliding down the wall.

"I wish you had opened yourself up to me," Jennah says, twirling her long, strawberry-shaded hair with her fingers. "We could have helped each other. But—we continued to live our lives, hide our pasts, protect our secrets."

"What were you?"

She smiles like this is something he should already know. "Keten... this is how you would like to waste this dream? By asking me questions to which you already know the answers. I was a witch—a good witch, at that."

"You served the dark one, Arkos."

"I served things you will never comprehend, not here, not in this place. Remember: there are no real answers here. Only questions. But you can find all the answers you want. You must go back."

"Go back where?" Ket leans forward, jaw clenched. "Go back where?"

Her eyes narrow, the knowledge behind them great and powerful. "You must see him again. Face him. Once and for all."

Ket shakes his head. "No…no, I can't."

"You will have to. If you are to save Clive and Bentley, then you must face him again. And this time, you cannot run."

"That is not my mission. My mission is to—"

"I know what your mission is!" Jennah snaps, and her face changes. Not just her expression, but the shape of her entire head. It morphs, like her skin is made of jelly, starting to lose its battle against gravity. "Remember: I am in your dreams, I see inside your head, your thoughts —I am like…another part of you. A limb you can extend when you need to fight."

"What am I fighting against? Huh? Tell me that."

Another all-knowing smile, and if this version of Jennah is truly a part of him, it's the part that hates himself. "You're fighting yourself, Ket. Who you were. Who you are. What you will become. All of the versions of yourself clashing to fulfill one single purpose."

"I hate your riddles," he sighs.

A titter escapes Jenna's smirk. "We can get through it together. Like old times. We can figure out this mystery as one."

"If I see him. That's what you're saying?"

"He's an important piece to this, I think. You will have to confront him before it's all over."

She inches her way across the tower floor, over to where he's sitting. Softly places her palms against his cheeks, as if he's a dog she's not sure will bite. Jennah directs her cool gaze at her husband's eyes. There's love there, an abundance. He feels her warmth and affection, even inside the *walls this dream has built. His heart swells with the notion that one day, when the last grain of sand has fallen to the bottom of life's hourglass, when the days become endless and there is no more night to speak of, he will see her again. The* real *Jennah Norlath, not the apparitions his dreaming brain has constructed.*

She kisses his lips, and he tastes her favorite wild berries. Just like he used to.

"Protect them," she says to him. "Protect not just our children, but all the children of Endlia. The special ones, the ones like her." She looks to the edge of the tower, and he follows her eyes, sees the back of a familiar figure standing on the edge, contemplating a fall toward the streets below. Ralyanna. "Dark days come to our lands, and the land needs a true hero. Someone to slay the gods, once and for all."

"That is of no concern to me."

Her eyebrows wrinkle. "It will be."

The tower trembles, a sign of the dream dispersing.

She kisses him one last time before—

———

A LONGSWORD POKES him in the chest, whisking him away from the dream.

Confusion crowds his thoughts, his mind still coping with the transition between the dreamworld and the material realm. When things clear, when he has most of his bearings and the shadowy shapes crammed into his line of sight define themselves, he realizes he's in trouble.

They're all in trouble.

Ralyanna sits in the corner of the room. Two men wearing Rovan colors hold swords to her chest, their tips resting against her shoulder blades. She looks worried. *Too* worried. The girl who, yesterday, looked more mature than the average sixteen-year-old now looks like she's about six and has just been told the boogeyman under the bed is a real monster. She's been crying too. Her face is a glossy trough of fresh tears.

Jester is gone. Nowhere to be found amongst the crowd. Which means he either abandoned his post and fled, or they've already dragged him from the cabin, probably to his execution.

Ket counts eleven men. All of them armed and their swords drawn, and he's fetched himself a personal audience of four. The quartet of blades aimed at his throat do not relent when he opens his mouth to say, "Good morning," to whoever's in charge, which isn't immediately clear—mostly because the dreamworld still has a piece of his mind. He still feels…*floaty* is the best word he can use to describe his current state.

"Who are you?" one of the men says, stepping forward. A tall muscular man, built like a well-crafted wagon. Long, black hair falls around his shoulders, shooting out from under his Rovanian helm. The top of the helm is embellished by a figurine of the Great Salamandian, of Rovanian legend and lore. He's the only one with the additional ornament, making him the leader of this troop. He's young—Ket can tell by the lack of gray whiskers in his neatly-trimmed beard—and probably not old enough to have served in the Last War.

"My name is Ket Norlath," Ket tells him, opting to use his new name, not daring to speak his past name aloud, in front of this company. He's lucky the men do not recognize him. But they all look young, were probably children when Ket fled the north. That other name, though. That, they would recognize. "My niece and I are weary travelers, and we were looking for a place to rest."

The leader glances over at Ra, then returns his cold-fire gaze to Ket. "Travelers from where?"

"We're Crossland folk. We have no base."

"Without home?"

"Aye. We are peddlers of healing potions and natural remedies."

The leader eyes him with some concern. And doubt. "Where are your wares? We notice no inventory in this godless town, no wagon carrying the items you claim to sell."

Ket sighs heavily, knowing it will take a grand lie to bypass the roadblock. He puts on his best acting face, feigning a sorrow so deep it makes his eyes water. He's thinking of Jennah, of course. Clive. Bentley. "Yes. We were robbed the day before last. A crew of bandits tipped our wagon in the middle of the forest. They stole everything, left us with only the clothes on our backs."

Disbelief forms a smile on the leader's face. "In which forest were you attacked? Fangborn or Yesepi? Choose carefully, weary traveler. I shall know if you're lying."

Ket swallows. He doesn't have the faintest knowledge of the geography out here, let alone names of forests that have always looked the same to him. He figures he has a fifty-fifty chance of getting it right, and opens his mouth to choose one of them. But Ralyanna rushes to speak first.

"It's a trick," she says confidently, still looking upset, her eyes filling with tears. "Fangborn is a forest in Springgaarden, and Yesepi isn't a forest—it's a desert way out east, somewhere in the Crosslands. 'No man has ever returned from the Yesepi.' " She says this last part as if it's a recited line from a book or manual— or maybe it was some wisdom Borgadine had bestowed.

The leader listens to her words, absorbs them, but he doesn't address her and continues to fix his hard glare on Ket. "Very good, *niece*. It was a trick. And you passed. Only forest around here is a nameless one, about three miles south of here. We don't patrol the area much—not much activity, and our focus is aligned elsewhere." He steps forward. "Tell me, Mr. Norlath—where does your worship lie? Which deity do you serve? Emperor Salah would like to know."

Ket's taken off guard by that last statement. "Emperor...Salah?"

Amused laughter makes its rounds amongst the men. Ket certainly doesn't find humor in it. The way the question was asked made it seem like there is a right and wrong answer. Obviously he knows the *wrong* one, but no person who wishes to live a long, fruitful life would admit to bending the knee before a Blackstone Angel statue. *Arkos* is the only answer that will bring him trouble. As for the other six gods to choose from…well, when Ket left these lands over a decade ago, the Rovanian people were free to worship whom they pleased, though Highbeard worshippers enjoyed certain privileges—better access to churches, education, and household tax rebates just to name a few—while other religious folks were treated more like second-class citizens. Still…you were free to worship who you pleased…

It's been almost fifteen years, Ket reminds himself. *A lot has changed. Things are different. Darker. And I do not recognize the realm I left behind.*

He figures it wholly possible Salah has outlawed freedom of religious choice.

"We are Highbeard's people," he says, lowering his head respectfully.

"Is that so?" the leader says, allowing his blade to dip some, but not instructing the others to do the same. "Then perhaps you wouldn't mind reciting the Beard's Six Laws of Inner Amity." The man arches his brow, waiting for Ket to expel the correct answers.

Ket shifts uncomfortably. It's been a long time since he's heard the Six Laws, even longer since they've rolled off his tongue. Jennah handled most of the boys' religious studies, and even then, the two weren't big on installing worship in the Norlath house-hold. He bows, praying his memory remains on his side. "Law One: Thou Shall Not Murder, unless it's required to protect your land, your family, or your god."

The leader nods, his smile faltering. He was clearly expecting Ket to botch the first Law.

Ket continues, reciting the Six Laws, but not without stumbling through them. A few times he stops to pause, collecting his thoughts and drawing the answers from the depths of his memory, which is still foggy because of that goddamn dream. He gets through them, and after proving he—at the very least—knows the Six Laws, he waits for the leader to announce his next request. Or tell his men to sheath their swords.

Instead, the leader just stares, like he's waiting for Ket to break down, reveal all that's true and expose his lies.

Ket glares back at him, equally intense.

"Very good," the leader finally says. "At least I know you're not completely full of horse dung. *Men.*"

His inflection is the command the men were waiting for; they drop their swords at their hips, and Ket feels the enormous pressure of almost being fatally skewered leap off him.

"You're free to go," the leader says. "But be wary of more bandits in these parts—the next ones you run into might not let you escape with your lives."

He nods to the door, and the troops begin to file out. Ket stands up and follows them to the threshold. Outside the cabin, Ket is greeted by at least sixty men on horseback. It's a wonder he didn't hear them coming from a mile out, that the stampede did not rouse him from his dream.

The dream....

It took me too far under this time. Maybe it's because I'm closer to them. To Rovan.

My people.

That place.

Him.

Prisoners, common folk wearing dirty, torn garments, are bound to the men's horses, thick rope tied around their wrists and hitched to the backs of saddles. Open, bleeding wounds mar their arms and defeated faces. Small lacerations, caused by some affray.

"Who are these men?" Ket asks the leader, who, in turn, just grins proudly.

"They are what happens when you cannot recite the Six Laws," the leader responds, not even trying to hide the glee in his voice. "We found them trying to erect a Blackstone Angel statue some miles back."

One of the beaten men opens his mouth in protest, but before he can eke out a single syllable, one of the men on horseback applies a whip to his back, erasing a strip of flesh in a single crack.

The man yelps, drops to his knees, and begins to shudder and weep loudly.

The leader doesn't flinch, his grin remaining sturdy.

"What will happen to them?" Ket asks, though he knows he shouldn't. He should take this as a firm warning, confirmation that the world has indeed changed since he's been gone, and move on with his journey north. To count his blessings. But…Ket —the old Ket, the man he was before—always was curious.

"They will be tried for witchcraft. Then either hung, burned, or thrown into the viper pits at Delmarr, where an audience will bet on who will survive the longest. My money is not on that man," the leader says, nodding at the whipped man, whose tears have still not let up.

"Me neither," Ket says, flashing a phony smile, and when the leader looks at him, he smiles too. "Have there been many Arkos witches in these lands of late?"

At this, the leader's eyes slim.

"Ashamed to admit we haven't kept up on current affairs," Ket tells him. "We've spent most of our recent days in the south. Business in Springgaarden has been good to us."

"Does Springgaarden not have messengers to relay the news of the north?"

"No reliable tongues, I assure you."

The leader chuckles, nods like *Oh, yeah, that will happen,* as if he knows the troubles of messengers and misinformation, and how easily rumors can spread throughout the Five Realms. Like fires with no water, just left to burn. "Yes, yes, of course. We've seen an uptick in activity over the last ten years or so—since the Last War. It's like Arkos is out there somewhere…like he's come back, gathering up his minions. If we don't hunt down every last Blackstone witch and warlock, they will rise up. Burn down our churches. Rape and impregnate our women with their demon seed. It will mean the Darkhell, I'm afraid."

Ket nods as if he understands without question.

"It's all about that boy…" the leader adds with a certain

amount of distaste. "Some think he's the savior, supposed to welcome back the old gods to defeat Arkos—but I've always wondered...maybe he's a product of the Blackstone Angel himself."

Ket lets those words simmer, not wanting to debate the man's suggestion. Mostly out of fear that he could end up like one of the roped men.

"But!" The man holds up a finger, pointing it toward Highbeard's throne. "I guess, as good Rovanian soldiers, we have to trust in Emperor Salah's visions."

"Visions?"

"Oh yes—Emperor Salah is now guided by his visions. Ever since the boy was brought to him thirteen years ago, he began having clear visions that influence how he governs the north. It's been quite the transcendent experience. You would think Owlton and Springgaarden would recognize this, admit that the Rovan Territories are the true holy land, band together and form one nation under the Salamandian, but no. Their stubbornness to concede has been a thorn in our side since...well, forever. But that thorn grows almost too painful to bear, and the Emperor...well, Salah has plans."

Ket nods, understanding.

"I was in Springgaarden during the Last War," Ket lies. "I didn't fight..."

"Lucky you. I was just a boy. But I remember my father coming home from battle. The stories he told...it inspired me."

Ket winces, diverting his thoughts away from the past—he's spent too much time there already. "I appreciate your kindness regarding our situation here. It's been a trying couple of days. I was wondering...have you seen the third member of our party?"

"Third member?" the leader asks, confused. "I thought it was just you and your niece?"

"I apologize—I forgot to mention there was a third member of our company, an assistant. He's a strange-looking fellow. Wears a jester hat, the kind with bells. Face is severely disfigured from an…an accident. With a knife. You would remember his face if you saw him."

For a second the leader gazes upon Ket's face like he's crazy, as if he's just described a character from an old fable. Surely not a real person.

Slowly, the leader shakes his head. "I have seen no such person."

"Thank you. He wandered off during the night and has not returned. I'm beginning to suspect the worst."

The leader nods. "Maybe some Arkos worshippers got him. Or worse—a monster. A wolf man or a troll beast. Dangerous times out there. Even the friendliest territories harbor a monster or two. Another consequence of the Arkos effect. You should be mindful during your travels. I recommend sleeping with one eye open and…no dreams."

The last part makes Ket's skin crawl. It's like the man knew how deeply he had dreamt. Maybe even knows the nature of that dream.

"Will do," Ket says, sounding thankful. "I think—given light to the situation in the north—I may travel to the Silver Towers and pay my respects to Emperor Salah."

The leader's eyes go dark. "I would recommend staying clear of the Silver Towers, friend."

Ket tilts his head, not understanding. He thought announcing his intent to pay respects to the king, showering him with praise, would be a pleasant way to end their conversation. "And why is that?"

The man looks over his shoulder, making sure none of his soldiers are eavesdropping. Then, he leans into Ket's ear. "Because…the good king fears a new war is coming…" He tilts back his head and sniffs the air. "And I, for one, can smell blood on the wind."

———

AFTER THE TROOP leaves the abandoned village, Ra and Ket take their time collecting their things and eating breakfast, and then get back on the road. Less than five miles into their walk, they come across a clearing, empty save for a few sturdy oaks. Hanging from the branches are the familiar men and women who were last seen in the troop's company. The detained accused of Arkos witchery, who were being escorted back to the Silver Towers for trial.

"Some trial," Ket says to Ra, who cannot look directly at the swaying bodies. Their throats were slashed before they were hanged, bright red gashes like lipstick smiles across their necks. *Probably best*, Ket thinks, knowing that Rovanian trials include being tortured for weeks on end, until it becomes too much and the captives have no choice but to admit their guilt.

Ra strays from the path, her back facing the corpses.

"What is it?" Ket asks, watching the girl continue to shuffle off course, trekking through a field of dandelion willows. "Ra?"

She sprints, racing away from him.

He chases after her, jogging at first, but then realizing she really wants to get away. Leave this place. Or him.

He follows her past the field, toward another wide stretch of towering, sturdy oaks and pines, a shrouded area where the entries are blocked by fallen timbers. She tries to squeeze through the downed tree trunks, but has trouble finding access to the other side—so, she begins to climb. Ket catches up.

"What are you doing?" he asks, not quite out of breath, but not *not* out of breath either.

She doesn't stop her pursuit of finding a way over.

"Ra?" he snaps. *"Ralyanna!"*

Finally, she halts. Cranes her head back to him. She's a good ten feet in the air and was just about to raise her leg over the top timber.

"What's gotten into you?"

Her eyes are wet, her lips trembling softly as she projects her broken gaze at him. "They killed them. They killed them all!"

"Yes, I figured they might do just that. Rovan has never been one for fair trials—even back before the world turned over."

This comforts her not at all.

"Come down, Ra. You'll hurt yourself."

"I can't go with you. To that place." She shakes her head, shedding beads of tears. "That place is death."

"Yes, and we will find much of it along the way, for sure. I don't blame you, not a single morsel." He sighs, runs his hand through his tangled mess of long hair. "It was me who wanted to spare you from those sights, remember? And it was you who insisted on coming with us."

"Jester's gone!"

"Yes, it seems he either abandoned us or perhaps he's marching back to Iradon to settle his score there." Ket considers this a moment longer. "But, knowing Jester, he's probably swimming to the Black Isle by now."

"We should leave," Ra shouts down from her throne of timbers. "Something bad is waiting for us in Rovan—I can feel it. Like a filth. Covering me. We'll…we'll all die there!"

Ket nods, his intuition sensing something similar. "What awaits us in Rovan is absolute hell, in every sense of the word. I warned you the journey wouldn't be easy and that you'd witness many atrocities before our journey ends. Where we need to go, no flowers grow. There are no springs or gardens in the north, the soil is too dead to grant life. The skies are always gray and dark. The sun barely visits Northern Rovan. But…it's also a place, that for us, the stars still burn bright. A promise of a better tomorrow. Ra, what we're doing is important. But I understand if you want to leave—I truly do." He swallows. "However, the time to find you shelter elsewhere has passed. We will be crossing into Rovan in the coming days, and I'm not confident you'll be safe if I drop you off at some Rovan orphanage. And it's too late to travel back."

"I will go on my own then. Back south. The way we came."

"Too dangerous by yourself. You've seen the roads—bandits,

raiders, religious zealots. Literal monsters. You won't last a few days by yourself. Maybe if this were Springgaarden…"

Ra hangs her head, the tears still flowing. "I won't do it…*she* can't make me."

She?

Ket crosses his arms. "I don't know what you mean."

"The woman…" Ra sniffles, then wipes her nose on her sleeve. "In my dreams…"

Ket's first instinct is to recall his own dreams, but it's impossible to believe that Ra is dreaming of the same woman. No, there's no way—she cannot be dreaming of Jennah. Still, it's a curious coincidence. One that gobbles up his other thoughts and musings.

"What about her?" he asks, hoping she comes down from the timbers, before she falls and breaks her neck. Her vulnerable position makes him nervous.

"The Fairy Godmother," she says in the same voice one of his sons would describe dreaming of the boogeyman. "She tells me I'm special. That I have a purpose. That something is waiting for me in the Silver Towers…that there are others like me, waiting to be reborn."

Ket tries to understand, can't, and then holds out a hand and says, "Whoa, whoa. Back up. The Fairy Godmother?"

She gauges his reaction, then her face begins to sour. "You don't believe me. You think I'm crazy."

"I never said that, I merely want to underst—"

"Borgadine believed me," she says, hurling this information at him like an insult. "He never looked at me the way you're looking at me now."

"I'm sorry, Ra," he says, meaning it. "I don't mean to pass judgment. I'm just trying to understand. Dreams—where I come from—can be very powerful tools. They can be used to discover truths about ourselves and the world we live in. Helps us explore mysteries and explain anomalies. And I do believe you. If you say you've dreamed of this…Fairy Godmother?"

She nods.

"Then it must be true," he concludes. Ket extends his arm, reaching for her with his grasping fingers. "Why don't you come down from there and tell me more about your dreams. We can figure this out together." Then he adds, as if this is a secret he would have preferred to keep from her, "I dream too."

"You do?"

Nodding, he says, "Yes. Of Jennah, mostly. My wife. She comes to me, brings me riddles to solve. Some of which seem impossible to understand, but that is the trick when it comes to dreams."

"I know of dreamroots that help make dreams more vivid," she says, no longer crying and almost...excited? Like the prospect of enhancing one's sleep visions has revitalized her. "They are rare but can be found throughout the Five Realms—*if* you know where to look. They grow under a certain type of rock, found—"

"I know all about dreamroots," Ket tells her. "Trust me. I know them well, and where to find them. But they are a dangerous, mind-altering substance, and if used incorrectly, can have long-lasting side effects. Have you ever seen someone go Dream Crazy?"

Her eyes close halfway, and she shakes her head.

"I don't recommend ever subjecting yourself to the sight. When taken inappropriately, the dreamer can no longer determine the difference between reality and the dream, and often, the new reality takes over while they are awake—and, often, their visions slip into the nightmare lands, if you catch my meaning."

Her horrified eyes suggest she catches it just fine.

"Come down," he repeats.

She's hesitant at first, but then she crouches and begins to descend the stack of timbers. When her feet are back on the muddy terrain, she looks up and faces Ket, shame blossoming on her cheeks. "I'm sorry. I'm just...scared. The Fairy Godmother... she won't leave me alone. I dreamt about her all night, before those men came."

"Does she threaten you?"

"Not directly. But it's...inferred."

"What does she want from you?" The girl dodges his eyes. "Is she direct in her plans for you?"

"Yes."

"And?"

The girl struggles with speaking the truth. Whatever it is, it's shaken her to the core.

"She wants me to kill him," Ra finally blurts out.

"Who?"

"The boy."

"I see. You know...sometimes dreams hold significance, but sometimes...sometimes, Ra, they are just dreams."

"Not these. They don't feel like regular dreams. They're so...so real."

"They can sometimes feel like that when you're stressed or grieving, going through—"

"She's a real person," Ra says, cutting him off. "I can sense her, even when I'm awake sometimes. She wants me to kill the boy, cut out his heart. She demands it of me, and I can't help but think if I do not, she will kill me."

"Your dreams can't kill you."

Now her eyes find his and latch on. Her cold stare penetrates him, piercing his empathy. "What if this one can?"

"I've seen many men die," he tells her, striking his best confident smile, "and not once have I seen someone die from their dreams."

"There's a first time for everything. I bet you hadn't seen a girl break a man's neck from thirty feet away until Riverspell?"

His confident smile shrinks some. "I have seen some things like that, yes."

"Right." Her gaze darts. "Your wife."

"Let's not speak anymore of this now. But let me make a promise to you." Ket drops to one knee so that she's taller than him and has to look down to meet his eyes. "I will do everything I can to protect you. You have my word. I didn't..." He stops himself, not sure if now's a good time to mention it. "I didn't tell you this earlier—and I should have, forgive me. But when I removed you from Riverspell, I found something."

"You did?" Her eyes light up like she's just stood and witnessed the marvelous beauty of the Crystal Mountains.

Ket nods. He sifts through his pocket and produces a necklace made of some brownish vine, a silver pendant hanging from it.

She takes it from his fingers, gently, her eyes captivated by its metallic shine. Like it's taken control of her mind, a hypnotist's charm.

"I'm sorry I didn't give it to you earlier. I thought...I thought giving it to you might make things worse, for your grieving. So, I waited and waited, then I...sort of forgot about it. That's terrible, and I'm—"

"It's fine," she says, and her forgiveness drives cold needles into his nerves. "I thought I'd lost it. Borgadine—he made this for me. He would give it to me during my lessons. Said it would help with my abilities. But he...uh...never fully explained what that meant. What it does. Just that it would help." She shrugs, the mystery lost on her. "He kept his secrets, thinking he'd live forever, I suppose."

"I'm sorry he's gone. But he clearly loved you. That piece..." Ket nods to the pendant, the silver circle with a silver bird—a soaring eagle—in the center. "It was crafted with the care of someone with love in their heart."

"You can tell?"

"Aye. It was something I would have crafted for my own sons. Or my wife."

She looks down at the pendant, blinking away more tears. "Why an eagle, you think?"

"Eagles are fierce creatures. Fearless. Maybe that's why he chose it for you."

"But I'm not fearless. I'm terrified."

"Eagles aren't born fearless, Ra. They need to experience fear before they can learn to conquer it—just like anything in life. In the army, they taught us, *know thy enemy.* You can't defeat what you cannot understand."

She nods, brushing away the falling tears with the back of her hand. "Thank you. I shall cherish this. Keep it close to my heart."

"I think that's a fine idea." He glances back over his shoulder. In the distance, looms the hanging tree. Black vultures have begun to feast on the dying flesh, circling in small droves, bloodying their beaks on the recently expired flesh. Their gleeful squawks echo across the fields. "We should probably head back to the road. We'll have to sneak our way into the Silver Towers. To do so, I have to visit an old friend. Are you ready?"

"What about Jester?"

"What about him?"

The girl looks up from the medallion, sadness still flooding the rims of her eyes, reflecting the morning sunlight. "Won't we look for him?"

"Something tells me Jester doesn't want to be found. Like I said, probably the reason for his disappearance altogether."

"What if he's in trouble?"

"I suspect he's more likely *causing* trouble, than *in* trouble." He can see she doesn't like this answer. "Jester made his choice. I have a feeling we won't be seeing him again. At least...not anytime soon.

"Now come. Before those vultures mistake us for the dead or dying."

As they walk on, Ket takes one last glance at the hanged, and the lingering spirits—their souls—standing still, beneath the dead's dangling feet. The souls watch, and Ket feels their collective stare follow them out of their haunted palace of trees and ferns.

THE SILVER COURT
CHAPTER SEVENTEEN

"Highbeard smiles upon the north; don't you forget it, and may the Endlands remember this fact when our complete history is told."

— KING ARON ROVAN, YEAR 661

———

EMPEROR SALAH ROVAN enters the council chamber, and everyone stands and bows, reverently. The meeting consists of sixteen members, two from each of the eight noble houses. Emperor Salah invites them to sit before he and the queen reach their silver thrones at the head of the table. He's in no mood for gestures of forced reverence. Today is all about business, and there's too much to discuss to waste time with false admiration.

"Where's Ravenborn?" Salah asks, scanning their faces.

No one answers.

"Fuck it," Salah says, rubbing his forehead near the crown, doing his best to quell his rage before it boils over. Seemingly sensing the heat emanating from him like a dragon's belch, Queen Ameera holds his hand. "We assemble without him. Who's first?"

The man on Salah's right clears his throat, puts his hand to his own throat like he's adjusting his voice. His name is Clayton Boarhest, one of the richest noblemen in the Rovan Territories. His keep is located closest to the Silver Towers. "Your majesty, I was hoping we could come to terms on the luxury tax proposal. Myself and my fellow constituents find the new figure…less than reasonable."

No one in the room speaks in support of Clayton's claim. His wife, Ralene Boarhest, squeezes his fingers, prompting him to continue.

Salah nods, knowing this was coming. "I appreciate your interest in wanting to protect your own pockets, Clayton—all of you, really. But we are on the brink of another war and need those funds to secure weapons, and build our army. Wars are not cheap, as you know. And I will not have what happened a dozen years ago, happen again. Nor will I let expendable money prevent our expansion into the Crosslands deter us from our main goal—uniting the entire Five Realms under the Salaman-dian flag."

"It's an admirable, ambitious goal, Your Majesty," says Kreed Philips, the man sitting across from Clayton. Third or fourth richest in Upper Rovan, maybe in all of the Five Realms, not born or married into royalty. He's more reasonable than Clayton, more precise with his words, and Salah finds him an easier, more pleasant conversationalist. "And we are in full support of your efforts."

Uneasy nods and downcast eyes suggest that may not be the case, but Salah doesn't care. He has these noble families by the proverbial gonads. *Watch them pack up and leave Rovan, make a new home in the Crosslands or farther south. See if they flourish like they have behind my walls. My protection!* Salah almost smiles listening to Kreed's proposal. "And while we support your efforts and wish to procure more land for the Rovan flag and wish to see the bastard king in the south come to his senses, we would like to allocate our taxes for other purposes."

"Such as?" Salah finds this charade amusing. No matter what

answer Kreed gives him, he will likely shoot it down and take great pleasure in doing so.

"We wish to build an underground shelter, but bigger, like a small town," Kreed says with a minor gulp in his throat, as if he instantly regrets the words he's just spoken. But the man doesn't break eye contact with his emperor. He keeps his cool gaze fixed on Salah, awaiting a response.

Salah's jaw feels fixed, wired shut. This is not the proposal he was expecting. He came in here fully expecting a pitch about allocating funds for recreational affairs—more bars, brothels, gambling arenas—or something to keep the kids occupied after their schooling sessions. Sporting fields or obstacle courses.

Certainly not a...

"An underground shelter? A town?" Salah asks, as if the concept is so foreign to him that he can't visualize it. Then he laughs. Throws his head back and roars at the vaulted ceiling of their meeting chamber. He's—apparently—the only one who finds this hilarious. Not even Queen Ameera, his loving and devoted wife, accompanies him in his hysterical outburst. "Have you lost your minds? What good will an underground town serve us?"

"Well, I'm glad you asked that, Your Majesty," Kreed continues, scratching his white mustache. Suddenly, Kreed is no longer Salah's favorite. "Perkins has a well-planned, thoroughly thought-out proposal for you."

Perkins, the timidest noble among the parties, pushes a stack of bound parchment into the center of the table. He returns to his seated position, eyes bouncing about the room, unable to look the emperor directly in his eyes. As if doing so might burn his own.

Coward, Salah thinks, grinding his teeth. He doesn't reach for the proposal, and no one assists with passing the thick text down the line. *Because it's meant to be read later. Because it's much too long to read right now.*

"In a clamshell," Kreed explains, working the air around him nervously with his hands, "this paperwork is an outline of materials, estimated man labor, and the projected cost to the city. We feel it's necessary—for the sake of our people living inside the city—to have a safe place to fall back on in the coming years."

"A safe place?" Salah feels himself vibrating with anger. Underneath the table, Ameera pinches his knee. It does nothing to bring him down from his mountain of outrage. "A safe place? Perhaps you want to rethink your strategy here, Nobleman Kreed."

"I mean absolutely no disrespect, Your Majesty."

"And yet you infer my city is not safe. That I have not put effort after effort into protecting the people who look up to me. Who go to work. Who participate in a meaningful and productive society, who contribute great and wondrous things, who further our cause. Have I not protected them?"

"You have, Your—"

"Then why do you sit here with that *smug* look on your face and insult my efforts in making the Silver Towers the greatest version of it that's ever existed? I have done more for this city than my father, his father, and all the Rovan leaders throughout our history, going back to the days when Highbeard himself sat in the Silver Towers."

"There is no mistaking that, Your Majesty," Kreed says, cowering a little, sweat beading near his retreating hairline. "I meant absolutely no insult. We just believe—all of us—that dark times are coming, and it would be better if there was a safer place to go, should the city fall under siege by sinister forces."

Salah can hardly believe it. "Dark times," he says, calmer than he has been all morning. "Dark times are coming, my friends. Indeed, the old prophecies are coming true. The boy is progressing with his training, and the lands have fallen into the start of chaos, haven't they?"

"Yes, Your Majesty," Kreed says, hopeful now. Like he's turned a corner in convincing the emperor. "That's all we're saying. Dark times are upon us, and the safety of our people is paramount. No cost is too high to save lives. If we allocate our taxes and build an underground city, utilizing the cave space near the shores and under Rovan, then we will put a lot of people's minds at rest. And if the dark times never get that dark, well, then we have breathing room. It's no secret that the streets have gotten overcrowded with peasants. Families are having four, five times the amount of offspring than in decades past, our census shows. We will need to expand somewhere, and—"

"Precisely why we continue with our expansion into the Crosslands. Which is going well by the way, if you haven't noticed. The barons in the north are just about ready to swear their lands over to us. My talks with the Crosslands' king have progressed."

"We have noticed," Clayton speaks, giving Kreed a breather. "And we thank you for your leadership. But for many families, being close to the Silver Towers is important. The underground city...it can be magnificent. It will draw people from all over. Think of the taxes you'll pull in then."

"It will practically pay for itself," Kreed adds, "in twenty years' time."

"Twenty years," Salah says, snide laughter bubbling up his throat. "Kings are lucky to *live* that long." Salah shakes his head, tired of this conversation. "I've heard enough. We will not be expanding underground, thank you very much. And because I'm feeling generous today, I will strike this conversation from the records."

He waits for someone to object, anyone, and for a second he thinks Kreed will. The man has a look in his eye, one that signifies determination and a cunning strength, not to be misjudged or taken lightly. But...that anticipated objection that assuredly will start with the word *but!* never comes. Everyone falls into an awkward spell of silence.

Then the chamber door opens, relieving them of the uncomfortable aftermath. Ravenborn steps into the room, looking far happier than any present soul, almost beaming with positivity.

His face quickly sours when the mood emanating from the discussion table washes over him.

"What'd I miss?" Ravenborn asks, bending a single brow.

"Nothing," Salah speaks. "The Nobles were just telling me how much they love the new tax plan I've set forth. Isn't that right?"

No one speaks a word otherwise. Everyone either lowers their head or nods somberly.

"Excellent," Ravenborn says, and Salah isn't sure how genuine this response is. Although the proposed tax plan won't hit his pocket the same way it will the wealthy families of Rovan, it's not exactly a cheap expense for his right-hand man either. "I've come bearing good news."

"Please tell us."

"Our boy is starting to flourish." Ravenborn flashes a smile meant for a dentist's chair. He strolls over and sits down in his assigned seat, next to the King, opposite Queen Ameera. Throwing one leg over the other, he says, "Last week I took the boy to see his father."

"His father?" Salah asks, confused. "I thought his father passed away, years ago. In some fishing port in western Glane."

"Negative. Those were rumors. Fact is, many years ago, when the boy was four or five, we discovered Jerrin Pierce snooping around the Silver Towers. Actually caught him trying to break in, free his son from what he perceived as 'slavery'."

"Why was I not made aware of this?" Salah asks, concerned, and he's not sure why. It's not as if some lone fisherman from Glane could cause him any significant trouble—however, when it comes to news regarding the boy, his lineage, Salah believes any and all information should be reported. And accurately.

"I'm sure it was reported to you," Ravenborn says, and the confidence in his voice gives Salah pause, like maybe Ravenborn *did* tell him, and he simply forgot. Emperors have much to remember and it's impossible to recall every single detail of everything that's ever happened, both inside the Silver Towers and out.

Besides, Salah's mind is not what it once was. Forgetting things is not uncommon. "But if I remember correctly, you and the Queen were vacationing on the eastern shores that summer when it happened, and when you came back you were not your typical self."

Ah, yes. That could explain it. He'd eaten an exotic fish on that trip, one that left him poisoned and nearly dead. Needless to say, he survived, and that cook had cooked his last meal in the Rovan Territories. *And anywhere else,* Salah thinks, amusing himself. "Yes, now I remember. Continue, please."

"Instead of throwing Jerrin Pierce in the dungeons or having him executed, I decided to relocate him outside the kingdom's walls, to a nice slice of land deep in the southern forests, where no one would ever find him. We struck a deal with him—to stay out of his son's life, and every week someone would ride out to the cottage and provide him with updates on his son's health, activities, accomplishments, and general information regarding his life. In return, we'd keep the man nearby, in case one day, he would be needed. I had a feeling he would come of good use, and when the boy's powers did not manifest in ways the prophecies suggested, well...I knew the time had come. The boy needed to meet his father, his kin. I didn't know what to expect exactly but figured meeting someone who shared the same blood would...*stoke* his abilities." Ravenborn pauses to take a breath, then nods at his own accomplishments, appeased by his efforts regarding the boy. "And I was right."

"What did the father say to him?" Queen Ameera asks, clearly invested in the boy's story. She's always been the sensitive type, a sucker for family dramas. "What did he say to spark the boy's abilities? What caused him to flourish so suddenly?"

"All good questions, my queen," Ravenborn says, twiddling his fingers now. "But I do not know, and I did not ask. That was a private conversation. It needed to be, I think, for the plan to work. Whatever the case is, in the past two weeks, the boy's powers have manifested in ways I didn't think were possible."

"Such as?" Salah asks, sitting up in his seat, nearly drooling over the anticipated answer.

"The ability to fling heavy objects across the room, at targets. Mind control—I witnessed him entering a guard's mind, taking over his body, and marching the man down a flight of steps. He did fall down the second half of those steps, but still—with the correct training and proper environment, I think we can utilize the boy's skills to swing our quest in the south in our favor—once and for all."

Salah can't stop his grin from spreading. "Will he be ready for the impending war?"

"I can't promise that."

"Will he be ready?"

Salah knows that Ravenborn knows that this isn't a question as much as a demand.

Ravenborn shakes his head. "My men estimate that the south has already started moving armies in place. It's my estimate we have a month before they attempt a siege. I have garrisons in place all throughout the northern Crosslands—"

"Southern Rovan, you mean," the emperor corrects.

"Yes, Your Majesty, of course. However you see it. We have garrisons stationed there, and I have thousand-men troops in parts of the Silver City—we are prepared for any attack they throw at us, but..."

"But?"

Ravenborn swallows. "To prepare a thirteen-year-old boy for war...without knowing the extent of his abilities...it could take years, Your Majesty. Hell, it took a decade to get where we are today."

"You don't have a decade," Salah says, but not angrily. Maybe bitterly, but not angrily. "You have two fortnights. I want him battle-ready. I want him to control more than just small, inanimate objects found in a bedchamber. Or weak-minded guards. He's supposed to have the power of the Highbeard. Control weather.

Build fortresses with a nod of his chin. Clear trees from entire forests with a wink. Turn water into wine."

"Impossible," Ravenborn admits, not afraid to challenge the crown.

"You must make it possible then." Salah winks at him. "We will speak no more of this. Don't let your past failures in dealing with young men haunt you, Ravenborn. You can do this."

At this, Ravenborn's eyes go cold. "You speak of my son."

"I speak of your past failures." Salah snaps his fingers, finished with the conversation. "Is there anything else on the docket this morning? I'm feeling like I already need a nap."

PART THREE

ORPHANS OF FATE

"A God must be loved. And sometimes feared. But loved above all else."

— THE WORD ACCORDING TO THE HIGHBEARD

———

THOMASSEN PIERCE WAKES UP, sits, stretches his arms, and yawns into the harsh morning light beaming through the open window next to his bed. Though groggy and sleepy-eyed, he's more awake now than he's ever felt in his thirteen-year lifespan. It's a new day, and the past couple of weeks have been rife with fresh starts that have seen new accomplishments, posed new challenges, and the process of developing his strange new abilities has never been more exciting or rewarding.

Thom can't get dressed quickly enough. He throws on his tunic, rushes to the door, opens it, and finds the same two guards stationed outside his bed chamber from the night before.

"Gentlemen," he says, prickly. "Did you sleep standing up?"

The guards maintain their statuesque positions, not even flicking their eyes in the boy's direction.

"Be that way," he says, then saunters off down the hall.

"Where are you going?" one of them calls, and it takes Thom by such surprise that his heart flurries in his chest.

Thom spins back, feeling a mischievous grin leak across his face, curling smugly at the corners. "I'm off to visit Fen."

"You have lessons with Ravenborn in one hour," the guard says sternly, taking zero gruff.

"Then I shall return by the time that grumpy oaf sets foot in the Silver Towers." Proud of this statement, he turns to leave. But the footfalls behind him hinder his momentum.

"We cannot let you leave our sights," one of them says, and he's not sure which because he doesn't turn around this time. "Ravenborn has us under strict orders to keep you here until—"

He doesn't wait for the guard to finish. Thom takes off, sprinting down the long hall as fast as his legs can carry him. The guards shout, commanding him to return at once, but their voices are soon lost behind him, and the air whooshes past his ears as he runs faster than he's ever run before. He takes the hallway to his left, darts down a seemingly infinite stretch of red velvet carpet, and then finds an accessway out onto the keep's curtain wall. From there he takes the curtain all the way to the end, finds a ladder to the bottom floor, where he ducks into the courtyard and shields himself in the bushes, watching above for the guards to catch up, peer down at him from the base of the left tower.

Sure enough, right on cue, he spots their two heads peeking over the edge of the curtain, looking down and scanning the courtyard for any signs of their missing boy.

Thom stays behind the bushes, staring up at them. Waiting for them to pass.

"Fuck!" one of them shouts, and his cuss word echoes down, bouncing off the well-manicured hedges. A few seconds later, their heads retract, their presence gone, and Thom can breathe again.

Thank fuck for that, he thinks, then wonders if he could have used mind control on them—what Ravenborn calls *Takeover.*

Maybe he could have confused the two, planted alternative commands in their heads, and maybe they wouldn't have followed Thom at all. Or maybe he could have instructed them to battle. Draw their swords and duel until one bled. Probably too extreme, and would likely piss off Ravenborn to no end. Thom remains under strict orders to avoid using his abilities outside their training exercises, not until he's fine-tuned his skills and can control them.

Fuck Ravenborn's strict rules, he thinks. Now he wants to use his abilities out of spite.

Thom meanders from the courtyard and into the kitchen area, dodging the cooks and servers as they make morning breakfast for every mouth in the Silver Towers. The kitchen area is pandemonium, which makes sneaking through that much easier. Everyone's too concentrated on their tasks to notice a young boy darting past them, keeping to the less-traveled paths around the butcher stations, sinks, and pantry cabinets.

Once he's out of the kitchen, he takes the fastest route to the maid's chambers—where Fen is already waiting for him, keeping a lookout left and right, his brown eyes flicking this way and that, making sure no guards are coming.

"You're late!"

"Hold your horses," Thom says, briskly approaching his friend. "I had to lose the guards. They actually chased me today."

Fen's face turns a shade paler. "Ravenborn is really keeping you under his eye, no?"

"Fuck Ravenborn. *He* needs to be taught a lesson."

"Oh?" Fen doesn't seem to like the look in his best friend's eye. Which is unusual considering Fen's troublemaking history. But for some reason the boy fears Ravenborn. Thom can see the weight in his cheeks jiggle at the mere mention of Rovan's general. "What lesson is that?"

Thom winks. "That he can't control me."

"Oh brother. What are you up to now?"

"Follow me." With that, Thom takes off, down the pathway leading to the shoppes behind the Rovan castle's walls.

"Where are we going?" Fen calls to him, quiet though, not quite a whisper, but loud enough so Thom can hear.

Thom shushes him, then speaks in a much softer tone, "We're going to get some coats. It's cold outside of the Silver Towers this time of year."

———

FEN ISN'T sure about his best friend's plan, doesn't really know what the plan *is*, because Thom won't tell him, not the whole thing. *Going beyond the walls* is all he's disclosed, and Fen has a bad, sinking feeling that has hollowed out his stomach.

After they raid the lost articles room behind the shoppes and appropriated two fine coats (that are much too big for their bodies), they hustle outside the castle walls and stroll down the main street of the Silver City. With their hoods pulled up over their heads, the boys weave their way through the pedestrian traffic and avoid getting trampled by passing wagons. People shout over each other, bargaining over wares, holding conversations about the political climate of Rovan and the newly proposed religious sanctions prohibiting the worship of certain gods. On the way out of the city, they pass a Ciminen temple and a group of Highbeard Priests making their monthly pilgrimage around the perimeter, holding up signs that read, HE SAVED US, and HE WILL SAVE US AGAIN. The boys pay them no mind; their mission is focused and clear—get to the gates undetected before Ravenborn discovers they left with no intention to return—at least for some unspecified amount of time.

"Hold up." Fen stops Thom once they near the gate, pulling on his cloak.

"What is it?" Thom asks, and Fen's never seen the boy so determined. So intensely focused on something. The intensity in Thom's eyes scares him on some primal level.

"You haven't told me where we're going," Fen says, scrunching his face like he's holding a full bladder.

"It was supposed to be a surprise."

"Dangerous fucking surprise," Fen blurts out, nodding to the gates and the guards blocking their way out. They check the paperwork of every single person coming and going, making sure they have the proper credentials. It's a bit chaotic this close to the border, and Fen thinks that's exactly what Thom was hoping for—a little chaos.

"We're going to see my father," Thom says, a drop of sadness accompanying those words. Like something's wrong with his old man.

"Jerrin?" Thom told Fen all about his excursion, how Ravenborn had taken him to see the man, what he had told him, and how—since his return from those fairy-tale forests—improvement in his abilities has increased tenfold. "What? Why?"

"Because I want to save him."

"Save him?"

Thom nods. "Ravenborn is keeping him there...like a prisoner. He's not happy. I could see it in his eyes during our visit. He wants to be free. And I can free him."

The look in Thom's eyes takes a dangerous turn. This is evolving into something more than just some simple misadventure around the castle, a couple of children playing make-believe or being rascals or getting into harmless hijinks.

This is...well, *treacherous* is the word that comes to Fen's mind.

"We...can't," Fen says, his face shrinking. He takes a step back—the closer to the Silver Towers, the better he already feels.

Thom grabs his arm. "Come with me."

Now Fen's really scared—the starry shapes of Thom's eyes begin to glow, a soft moonlight ambiance that lights up the rest of his peculiar pupils.

Fen gulps. "Thom...you're...you're *different*."

"I know what I'm doing," Thom promises him. "I remember the way. We can sneak past the guards—there's a fault in the fence they do not know about. It's how immigrants sneak into the Silver City. I've seen it. In my dreams. A woman…she showed it to me. I know it's there. Will you come with me?"

"A woman…from your dreams?" Fen shakes his head, hardly believing any of this, hardly believing he's come this far. "What are you talking about?"

Thom leans into his ear. "Fen…Fenir…*come with me.*"

That whisper takes hold of him. And there's no other option than going forward. Following the boy to the hole in the fence, crossing the threshold and entering the wilderness of the northern territories—it's all he can think about. He becomes obsessed with it. Turning around is unthinkable.

The idea of embarking on dangerous adventures consumes him.

And he thinks he'll follow Thom anywhere. To the end of the world, to the edge of it, hold his hand and gaze into Arkos's Dark-hell. Highbeard's Heavens, he'll even jump into that nether-world's pitch-black mouth if Thom wishes it. All he needs to do is say the words. Command it.

Because he'll do anything to hear the boy's angelic whispers one more time.

VISITORS
CHAPTER NINETEEN

"All traitors to the northern crown will perish by fire and flame. If you wish to betray us, I will personally see to it that your ashes are pissed on by every member of the Rovanian army, and our Highbeard priests will curse your remains."

———

MASON FRIKES LAYS the molten steel on the workbench and strikes the metal with untamed fury, taking all the frustration he's accumulated over the last two weeks, and channeling it into every forceful hammer blow. Sparks scatter around him in his work area. He hits the steel again, flattening the hot metal beneath his hammer. He smacks it once more. Then again for good measure. But it's not good enough, so the metal takes another pounding. It's after eight strikes that he forgets he's supposed to be counting, but it doesn't matter—not long after, the sword has gained the length and shape of a reasonably sharp blade. He holds the glowing weapon to his eyes, inspecting the craftsmanship, quite proud of the work he's put forth.

Kelanda rushes into his workshop, out of breath like she's been chased by wolves. Her wide-eyed stare shouts *emergency*.

"What is it?" Mason asks, feeling his own breath escape him. If Kelanda is spooked—then surely it's something.

Her stone mouth finally moves. "We have visitors."

His heart knocks against his chest. "Are you sure?"

"They tipped the owls," she confirms.

The owls. He trained them—Olivia and Jackson—last year to report any movement on the perimeter of the property, no matter how small. He had to correct this behavior when they began hooting (reporting) every single field rat and abandoned fawn that strayed past the perimeter, even when the latter somehow got through the bear traps without triggering the poison-tipped arrows. Now, they only report biped creatures. Which, thankfully, hasn't happened often. He can count on one hand the number of times they've reported movement inside the property's demarcation.

Mason drops the unfinished blade on the bench and wipes his greasy hands on the cotton rag resting on the worktable. "Elgar's crew?"

She shrugs, has no idea. The owls—unfortunately—cannot distinguish threats from non-threats.

"Get your bow," he says to her. She takes off running, disappearing into the shadows of the late night to retrieve her weapon of choice.

He grabs a new sword off the display—there're a hundred to choose from, lining the wall, but he goes to the one he made for himself and no one else. The one with the all-black hilt, a glittering silver jewel in the center where his dominant hand goes, the stone in the shape of a human eye.

Anastasia, he's named her. All great swordsmiths name their swords. It's Rovan tradition.

After grabbing *Anastasia*, Mason ducks out of the converted barn-turned-workshop, crouching as he hustles back to the main house, the moonless shadows keeping him concealed against whatever—or whoever—has dared cross the compound's threshold. Creeping through the back door and into the kitchen, he sees Kelanda marching down the stairs, her quiver strapped to her back, bow in hand, an arrow already loaded onto the string.

She's quick. That's part of the reason why he married her. Because she's the perfect match for him. Someone willing to engage in this life of partial solitude, tucked away from the Silver City's watchful, overbearing eyes. Making weapons for the most villainous scum in all the Five Realms. Ready to grab a bow and fight for their freedom at a moment's notice.

Highbeard's Ghost, he loves her.

He gestures with his hand, speaking the silent language they've created for times like this, established back when they first set up operations on the outskirts of southern Rovan. They've made a lot of dangerous enemies since then. Dangerous allies too, which oftentimes was way worse than the enemies; at least with enemies, you knew where you stood. Having dangerous allies was sometimes complicated.

How many? he signs.

She holds up two fingers.

Where?

She points in the direction of the front door.

Before he can ask anything else, two resounding knocks hit the oaken barrier, heavy fists that create an echo effect down the bare hall.

Interesting, Mason muses. If Elgar was planning to storm the compound, he certainly wouldn't come knocking. No clever assassin would. *So, who are these late-night visitors? Wanderers looking for food and shelter?* Wanderers don't usually come out this way, this far from any main road or obscure path. No, whoever is on the other side of that door came here with a purpose. An intent.

Mason looks to Kelanda as if she might venture a guess—but she only shrugs.

"Who's there?" Mason calls out, observing the back door, just in case the knock at the front is a diversion.

"An old friend," the voice calls back, and at first Mason doesn't recognize the tone, timbre, or inflection of that voice. No friend, old or new, he's aware of.

Definitely a diversion, he thinks, then points to his eyes before directing those two fingers at the back door, making Kelanda aware of the impending ruse.

"You don't sound friendly to me!" Mason shouts back, now spying on the windows. Everything outside the main house feels eerily still and silent. Like any good waiting surprise.

"You can put *Anastasia* down," the man says, lightheartedly. "And tell Kelanda to lower her bow—I'm willing to bet my last coin she has it trained on my throat."

Mason glances back at Kelanda, who's indeed ready to let one fly at the unseen intruder, should the bastard attempt to kick down the door.

But how did he know about *Anastasia*? Only a handful of people know the name of his oldest sword—and most of those men are dead, lost in battle well over a decade ago.

Has it been that long?

Sometimes it feels longer.

"Identify yourself at once!" Mason shouts louder this time, just as he starts to rise, lengthening his posture. "Or Highbeard help you, I will cut your throat slowly. And it will give me great satisfaction to do so! Trespasser! Devil!"

"You will do no such thing, Mason." A soft chuckle. The visitor not taking Mason seriously only boils the blood beneath his skin. "We both know you're a big softy on the inside, despite your growl. Isn't that why you left Rovan's military? Company nineteen?"

Company Nineteen.

Dead, most of those men. Maybe all of them. All but...

It hits him. Mason's face melts, all the anger and fear and

anxiety he was feeling suddenly evaporating like warm sweat meeting cool air.

"No…" Everything feels weightless. His fingers go numb with a tingling sensation, pins pressing into his fingertips, and *Anastasia* falls, clatters on the floor near his feet.

"Mason?" Kelanda asks, astonished, watching him drift toward the door, her voice like a specter, floating across a grim and starlit graveyard on the Night of the Hallowed Moon. *"Mason!?* Speak to me. Who is—"

But Mason doesn't answer, tunes her voice completely out. The only thing he can hear is the beating of his own heart and the death cries of thousands and thousands of men as they died on a Crosslands' battlefield, *Anastasia* relieving them of their earthly duties, one by fucking one.

"Is it…" Mason rips the door open, sees the ghost of dreadful pasts just standing there, a young girl he does not know waiting obediently at his side. "The Last Soulth—"

"It's Keten now," the ghost says. "Ket Norlath."

———

THE GIRL EATS GREEDILY, stuffing her mouth full of blackberry muffins, shoving them in as fast as she can swallow. It's a remarkable sight, even for someone like Mason, who's prided himself on his eating habits and has the belly to prove it. He looks to Ket, who eats with a more measured, paced approach. His old friend, partner in battle, bites into his sliced bread, then takes a spoonful of soup and swallows it down like medicine.

"Don't like Kelanda's cooking, eh?" Mason asks him with a chuckle.

"What kind of soup is this?" Ket inquires, pointing to the concoction containing potatoes, lamb, and a wild vegetable native to these parts called *stickle*. The latter has a peculiar taste, especially to the unsuspecting tongue, but the way the combined ingredients complement the meat broth is unparalleled.

"We don't name it, but it's good."

Ket glances over at Kelanda, who seems to be waiting for the verdict of this last-second, thrown-together dinner. "It's very good," he lies, and Mason laughs, seeing no reason to call out his fib.

His interests deviate from simple banter about food to more pressing, interesting matters. "I thought you were dead—er, what are you calling yourself now? Ket, is it?"

"Ket. That's my name. I no longer go by any others. I'm proud to say, the past me is dead."

"Not all the way dead, though," Mason says with a wink, "otherwise your arse wouldn't be back in the north, heading toward—oh, well, I suppose I know where you're going now, don't I?"

Ket gently rests his fork on the edge of his plate. "That's why I'm here, Mason. I need a favor…"

"Of course you do. You haven't come to catch up on old times —I know as well as you the memories we'd both love to forget."

"I have to…I must…get back inside the Silver Towers." Ket admits this in the same tone he would a shameful secret.

Mason shakes his head. "My, my. Never thought that would be the reason to visit ol' Mason Frikes. How'd you find me out here? What brought you to this compound?"

"You did," Ket answers. "You brought me here during the wars, said if you were to ever leave the Silver City, you'd stake a claim out here, rebuild your life. Don't you remember?"

Mason doesn't, but many bottles of ale have been consumed since then, so it's likely he's forgotten certain conversations of trivial nature.

"I figured this was as good a place to start looking for Mason Frikes."

Mason nods, the answer satisfying enough. "All right. You're here now. And you're not here for a sword or a bomb or a shield, some mail either—you want…what? An escort?" At this, Mason lets go of a long series of grumbling laughs. "I'm not in the escort business, old friend. As you can probably see." He gestures to the seemingly endless rows of swords, some of them battle-ready, some of them misshapen and bent, needing some extra love and care before being shipped off for sale.

"I wouldn't be going back if it wasn't the most important thing in the world."

"Oh, sure. Sure. What is it? You're going to be the one to save the Five Realms, is that it? Kill Salah and restore balance to Rovan, free the people of religious oppression and the shackles that keep them rooted in poverty and filth? 'Cut the head off the snake and the body will die' type hero-shit?" Mason's smile widens. "Is that it?"

"Something like that."

"You won't get within a thousand feet of that place," Mason tells him, now opting for a more serious tone. "Garrisons in the Silver City are a few thousand strong, not to mention the guards that watch the towers like hunting hawks, and Highbeard-only-knows what other dark artsy tools they have hiding beneath those gray clouds—let's keep it at, *there are many obstacles.*"

"That's why I've come to you. You knew that city like your own reflection, all the tunnels and passageways, routes no one else knew. Look, I just need to get inside the castle walls. Ra and I will handle the rest."

Ra. He looks to the girl, who only shows the faintest grin. Like she's perhaps as mad as her—what? Father? Uncle? Too young to be his lover, unless he's—

Mason shakes his head, keeping those dark troubled thoughts at bay.

"Who is she?" he asks, pointing at Ra. An accusatory finger. Not even Mason himself knows what he means by it.

"I saved her from an attack in Riverspell. Wilders killed her grandfather."

"You've adopted her?"

Ket glances over at Ra, Ra back at him. Mason can see the chemistry between them, bright as an afternoon on the Nutley shores. Perhaps they've been through a lot together and have shared many adventures. Bonded through their struggle. Forged an unlikely alliance out of the oppressive hate this world has stored up, then cast down upon the inhabitants of their fractured society.

But Mason doesn't want to hear about their adventures. In total honesty, he wants this ghost out of his home, and he can take his ghost-girl with him.

"You could say that, yes," Ket confirms.

"I'm happy for you, *Ket*. Truly am. But I'm afraid you've come looking for help in the wrong place."

Ket leans forward, his eyes begging. "Please…Mason. During the Battle of End-La, I escaped from the Silver Towers. *Escaped.*"

"Everyone knows the tale, *Ket*," he says, not meaning to sound like he's spitting the words out. "You left the kingdom, the army, in complete and total disarray. You betrayed the Rovan Territories. Killed your brothers in arms."

He expects Ket to hang his head but he doesn't. Instead, he raises his chin and sharpens his gaze. There's no remorse in that look.

"I left and made a home down in the southern reaches of Owlton, where no one from the north would dare look for me."

"Ravenborn spread rumors of your death," Mason says, recalling the upheaval it caused within the kingdom. "Said he watched you die with his own eyes. I always thought it was funny that no body was recovered."

Ket grimaces, and his eyes fill with small pools of tears. "I escaped. I had my reasons. I saw things no man should see."

"We all did. That was war."

"Not like me, Mason." Weeping a little, he wags his head slowly. *"Not like me."*

Mason studies his teary eyes, understanding his agony. It was true; Ket, though not *Ket* back then, had endured many hardships, had witnessed innumerable atrocities, most of which would drive even the most hardened, sense-numb warrior to the brink of madness. *Soulthefters*...the rumors of the experiments that took place in the dungeons beneath the Silver Towers—it was the stuff of nightmares. "Aye. So, what is it you want then? What brings you back there? Revenge? Are you that simple and stupid? Tell me it's not about revenge, *Keten Norlath.*"

"It's not about revenge," he confirms. Then he explains everything; his past, his life in Owlton, how a once feared and revered warrior and torturer and eventual student of the dark arts converted himself into a simple farmer, had a wife and two lovely children who were eventually taken from him, one murdered and two stolen because of wrongs in *Jennah's* past.

"A witch," Mason says curiously, after learning of Jennah's long fall on the black rocks. "Fifteen years ago I wouldn't have believed witches still existed...but nowadays...with rumors of prophecies and dark times ahead...the Darkhell falling around us all..." He shakes his head and snorts out a laugh. "Yes, witches have become quite the fear of all five crowns nowadays. They're experiencing a revival. Just yesterday I noticed a wanted poster for a coven not half a day west of here. They're to be hung without trial, these blasphemers."

"Darkhell?" Ra asks, speaking up for what seems like the first time all night.

Folding her arms, Kelanda clears her throat. "It's what Arkos worshippers call the end of days, when the gods return to walk amongst us again, forge their armies and fight for dominion over the lands of Endlia. It all started with the boy's birth—I'm sure by now you've heard of it. Thirteen years ago, shortly after the last war petered out and both sides agreed to retreat, the Boy with the Star-Shaped Eyes was born. Since then...the Five Realms has become a scary, haunted place."

"Monsters," Mason says, "rising from the ground. Emerging from caves. Witches, gathering in blackwood forests. Wilder people storming peaceful villages..." Ra shrinks away at this, the memory slicing her across her soul, but Mason continues. "The moons are changing. People dream darker these days. A grave and terrible future awaits us all."

"But…" Kelanda says, almost smirking, "it's been great for business."

"Oh, aye," Mason agrees, his eyes brightening. "We've quadrupled our profits on swords and shields alone. People are preparing for the end, and we have just what they need."

"The Boy," Ket says, "is why I need to reach the Silver Towers."

"You don't say," Mason says, mildly stunned. He sits back in his seat, hands behind his head. "What business do you have with him? Other than you know…trying to do what others have already tried? To assassinate him in some feeble attempt to stop the Darkhell from happening."

"Ragland wants him," Ket says.

Mason pauses. Then he looks to Kelanda, who looks back at him—then the two burst into a fit of laughter, the belly-holding, knee-slapping kind that takes several moments to stifle.

"That's a funny one, *Ket*," Mason says, holding his gut as if trying to keep what's inside from coming out. "You're making deals with kings and trying to instigate wars with rival countries —not simply just a sorcerer-turned-farmer anymore, are you?"

Ket sniffles at this, clearly not amused. Then he pounds the table, making the silverware and ceramic plates jump and jangle. "I was never a Sorcerer," he snaps.

Mason shows his palms, surrendering the notion.

"I'm doing what's necessary to save my sons. That's all. I care not about prophecies and unwinnable wars."

"You should care, because when those two idiots—Ragland and Salah—burn down the Five Realms, it will be easy pickings for whatever maniacal force decides it wants to swoop in and take over."

"You believe in this stuff?" Ket asks, almost indignantly. "You believe in this…Darkhell? The gods returning…"

"I've seen things that make me believe, yes," Mason admits. "I believe you have too. I don't know exactly what went on in that dungeon, what *Soulthefting* was all about, but I imagine you saw some things that challenged your concepts of reality. There's enough evidence out there. I don't know why your king in the south—"

"Not my king," Ket says, gritting his teeth.

Mason pauses but doesn't correct himself. "I don't know why he's so hellbent on fighting another unwinnable war. He should talk peace with Salah, unite the Five Realms, and prepare for the real war."

Everyone waits for Mason to clue them in on what that is, but he allows them to figure it out on their own.

It's Ra who sniffs out the answer first. "Against the gods?"

"Why not?" Mason muses aloud. "You don't think everyone in the Five Realms banding together stands a better chance against these unearthly creatures?"

Ket shakes his head, lips tight like he's holding in a scream. "If everything foretold is true, there are seven gods—and possibly a few that haven't been recorded in the annals of history—and they are immortal creatures with immense power. They could blink and destroy us."

Mason shrugs, not caring. "Then why haven't they? If they're so powerful, why don't they climb down from their celestial thrones and seize us? Wipe us all out? And why did they leave Endlia in the first place?"

"I don't think anyone has the answers to those questions, Mason," Ket says. "If they did, we likely wouldn't be sitting here, holding this discussion."

"True, true. But I think," Mason says, holding up a solitary finger, "that it's all horse hokey. One hundred percent, grade-A bull manure, shoveled to the moons. I think—the gods have no more power than your late wife."

"Watch it now," Ket says, a low growl in his throat.

"No disrespect meant. Just mean to say—I don't think the gods offer any true power."

Ket side-eyes him, then stiffens in his chair. "Likely won't be around long enough to see it, either way."

"Not if you're heading to the Silver Towers, thinking you can somehow thwart the greatest empire the world has ever known."

"'Greatest empire?'" Ket nearly cracks a smile. Mason can see the faintest trace of one.

"I jest, of course—but your outcome is likely the same, no matter what you think of Salah and his armies. You're one man." He addresses Ra with a curt glance. "And one young lady. You do not stand a chance."

"Just give me *a* chance. Get me inside."

There's no wavering in his voice. Mason flicks his eyes to Kelanda, who hasn't moved from her position, leaning against the cabinets, arms folded across her midriff.

"What are you paying?" Kelanda asks him.

Ket hesitates, breathes in a deep sigh, like the answer might not go over smoothly. Mason thinks he'll say something along the lines of, *Old friends don't take money, do they? Old friends provide favors, right?*

But Ket surprises him when he reaches into his bag and pulls out a small purse, and drops it on the table, the clinking and clattering of coins a soft violin to his ears. The purse is the size of a small house cat, and Mason leans forward, his eyes not moving from the burlap sack tied at the top with a fraying length of string.

He's self-aware of his own greed and does nothing to hide it.

"Every coin I have," says Ket, turning to address Kelanda. "Every single one."

Kelanda doesn't seem impressed. "There's a catch."

"It's in Owlton currency," Ket admits.

"Of course it is." Kelanda rotates, facing her partner. "Exchanging might be tough."

"Not that tough. We know people." Mason reaches for the bag. Once it's in front of his unwavering eyes, he's untying the knot around the bag's mouth. Inside, a gold mound of Owlton coins gleams up at him. "My-my. That is a chunk of coin."

"It's all yours," Ket says. "As long as you get me inside the Silver Towers."

Mason licks his lips. "Well, I *am* easily persuaded by coin."

"You always were."

"Mason," Kelanda says, stepping toward the table. "Maybe we should think it over, yeah? A night or two to talk it over."

Pondering this, Mason squints, although he already knows what he's going to say. "Not sure there's much to think about."

"It's been years since you've gone to the Silver City. *Years.* Routes change, paths alter, and besides, if it's true—the talk of a new war—then the Towers will be on high alert. There's no way you can pass through the gates undetected. Or under them. Or around them."

"I have my ways, darling." Mason turns on his sweet, charming voice. The one that sometimes coaxes her into making love late in the evening, even when she claims she's too tired. "You don't trust me?"

Kelanda gulps. "I think your eyes are bigger than your head."

"I dunno. I have a pretty fat head."

"He just needs to get us inside the gates," Ket reiterates. "That's all. I will handle the rest of the way."

Mason glances up at his partner, shrugging in a *what could possibly go wrong?* sort of way. "See? Just needs to get inside the gates. No problem at all!"

"How do you plan to do that? What if Owlton storms the Silver City before you can reach it?" Tapping her foot, Kelanda waits for a response.

"You worry too much."

"These are things you need to consider. The Five Realms is on the brink of crumbling, and you want to leave your work behind, and what—go off and play war like old times?"

Mason grunts at this, heat burning the flesh around his collar. "You know nothing of the old times. What we saw then."

"You don't need to do this," Kelanda says, pointing at the bag of money. "The jobs you have lined up for Elgar are worth five times what's in that purse."

"Yes, and they will be waiting for me once I return. Why can't I have both jobs?"

Ket sighs, gets up from the table, as if excusing himself from a conversation he shouldn't be hearing. "I think I better—"

"Is Elgar the type of man you want to keep waiting?" Kelanda asks.

"No, but—"

"Don't do this, Mason. It's an unnecessary risk."

Watching her eyes grow glassy, the desperation choking her tone, Mason calms down. He can't be mad at her, upset because she wants the best for them—for *him*. She's only saying what he needs to hear—because she's right. He doesn't need this job. Elgar's order of swords and shields and bows is enough money to get them through a whole year, possibly two.

"Kelanda, baby," he says, avoiding her harsh gaze. "Wi—I mean, *Ket* and me. We go way back. We were good friends, and we've been through a lot together. Most men like us—we do not win. We do not come out on top. We do not get to lead normal lives." He finds Ket's eyes. "This man saved my life once. More than once, and probably in ways we can't rightly calculate, even if we were to break down every event, fight, battle." Now he faces Kelanda. "His sons need him. If this gives him a chance at getting them back..." Mason eyes the purse. Then he does the unthinkable—pushes the bag back across the table. "Then money isn't the reason."

Ket swallows, his eyes misting. "Thank you, Mason Frikes."

Kelanda slumps her shoulders, knowing she's lost this battle. "Aye," she simply says, her voice soft as cotton. "I will lay out your equipment and armor. I suspect you will leave tonight."

He shakes his head. "Tomorrow will suffice. We will rest and go over the plan."

"Do you have a plan?" Ra asks, resting her elbows on the table.

"My dear lady," Mason says, feigning offense, "of course I have a plan. Mason Frikes *always* has a plan. First, we will all need new attire."

"Attire?" Ra shakes her head, not understanding. "What's wrong with our clothes?"

"Well, they're beyond dirty for starters. And besides…they're not simply going to let us walk through the front gate like that, without papers."

Ket's eyes narrowed with concern. "Through the front gate? I was hoping for a far less blatant risk."

"Oh, this will mitigate risk aplenty. I promise." Mason winks at him. "We are going to need to make a stop on the way. A secretive place, where I know some of Rovan's finest guards will be stationed, watching over it.

"A little cottage in the woods. Very quaint. You'll like it. I promise."

UNDER THE RAVEN'S EYE

CHAPTER TWENTY

"To reap a human soul from a living body is perhaps the darkest, most unimaginable crime against the gods I can think of. Of course, I accept the task at hand. I am happy to provide this service for you, true Emperor of the Five Realms."

– THE WIZARD, BLUEBOLT, DURING A
PUBLIC MEETING WITH KING SALAH
ROVAN

———

WHEN RAVENBORN LEFT the council meeting, he marched straight to the boy's chamber, ready and eager to start the day—he had many plans for the boy's next lesson. Of all the talents the boy was beginning to possess, his mind control had improved the most dramatically. He thought he should hone that skill some more, allow the boy to work on his abilities, using the guards as—for the lack of a better term—"target practice." Get inside their heads, poke through their thoughts, channel their minds and kindle emotions and feelings. *Fears.* He'd start there, utilizing the tricks of conquering one's ability to conceptualize and produce meaningful ideas. Then he'd switch to harder tasks, such as controlling actions via the cerebral output.

Yes, it's all coming together. Not as fast as Emperor Salah would like, but the Silver Towers were not built in a single day, nor were they erected over a single year. Ravenborn is in it for the long haul.

For the first time since he's left the council—those noble men and women who believe that because they have a mountain of riches most people can only dream of, that they should run a city —Ravenborn feels great, uplifted by his own thoughts. It's surprising how taking the boy under his black feathers has improved his mood of late. He used to hate waking in the morn, with the day's first thought of the boy and knowing he has to help bring his power to light. Now, it's one of the few pleasures he has waiting for him after breakfast and coffee.

He turns down the hall that leads to the boy's chambers and instantly knows something is off; that uneasy feeling increases exponentially within a few darkening seconds. First, the guards are not stationed outside the room, which normally wouldn't concern him, as a changing of guards could be taking place, but the odds of him catching the change at this precise moment are highly unlikely—besides, the shift change doesn't happen until later, around lunchtime, and judging by the fullness of his own belly, they're not quite there yet.

The boy's door hanging open is the biggest sign that something is wrong. The two things together send up all sorts of confusing, mixed signals, all of which point to *Fuck, we're in trouble here.*

He picks up his pace, jogging toward the open doorway, but stops when he glances down at the floor and sees a small bloody trail leading inside. Slowly, he draws the Ravenblade, the long black sword forged with obsidian steel, one of only a few in existence. He edges closer to the opening and peeks inside.

There, he sees the body of a guard on the ground, a thick red gash in the man's throat, a scarlet puddle fanned out beneath his head. His lifeless gaze is directed at Ravenborn, and for a split second he thinks the man is still alive, pleading for him to reverse this. But he's dead, deader than dead, and has been for at least a short while. Ravenborn looks for evidence of a struggle, finds none, and then traces the man's arm down to his hand, which holds a bloodied knife. The very knife used to cut his own throat.

"He took his own life," a timid, weak voice says from behind Ravenborn, the second he pieces this whole scenario together.

Ravenborn turns, sees the fallen guard's partner standing there, head hung in shame and despair. The man bites back a few sniffles.

"What the fuck happened?" Ravenborn's fury starts a firestorm in the center of his chest, heating the rest of his body.

The guard has trouble keeping focused, doesn't dare set his eyes on his superior. "The boy…"

"Where is he?"

"I don't know, my lord. He escaped. Just took off running. He was so fast…" The man swallows something large, maybe his tongue. "Tapper here…was so beside himself…he said suicide was far better than anything you had in store for him."

"Highbeard's Balls," Ravenborn mutters, trying not to break a tooth from gritting them too hard. "Where did the boy escape to? Do you have any idea?"

"No, my lord. He ran off—we think—with that maid-whore's son. Fenir Spolstra is his name."

Ravenborn nods, upper lip quivering. "I know of him."

"My lord, I can't begin to tell you how sorry I am. But the boy—he tricked us! It wasn't our fault, you see."

Ravenborn half-believes him. He hadn't thought the boy's skills would have evolved so much yet, but then again…

Maybe he's been holding them back, Ravenborn muses. *Wouldn't that be something?*

"We'll discuss this later," Ravenborn says. "Have some men clean up this ungodly mess, then gather a small troop and have them meet us at the gates in fifteen minutes."

"Do you know where he is? Where he might be?" The guard seems ignited by the hope, as if the boy is his own kin and finding him is paramount.

Because it is. Even if the boy is found safe and alive, not a hair on his head out of place, the potential punishment for losing sight of him could be monumental.

Could mean *death*.

"Yes," Ravenborn says, doom settling in around him, like the bottom of the world will drop out beneath him at any moment. "Yes, I believe I do." He passes the guard, but not without stopping, putting a hand on his shoulder, gripping him to the bone, squeezing as hard as his strength will allow. "Fifteen minutes. The gates. Or so Highbeard help you, I will find your soul and rip it apart."

NOT-SO-LONELY ROADS

CHAPTER TWENTY-ONE

"If roads could talk and trees could whisper, the world would have enough stories to last several lifetimes."

– OLD ROVANIAN PROVERB

———

THOM AND FEN make it past the streams with no problem, not a single traveler taking an interest in their situation. *Why aren't you in school? Why are you so far from the Silver City without an adult?* Just some of the questions they expected, but have gone unasked so far. They scurried past everyone on the road, kept their heads down, shielded behind the hooded fabric of their new favorite robes, making them look like dwarven Highbeard monks. A pretty good disguise, and Thom's glad Fen had the fore-sense to think of it. Two boys traveling down the Silver Path would have drawn unwanted attention, but these appearances haven't attracted a single wayward glance. Plus, it will keep them from trouble should they run into King Salah's religious watch, those packs of enforcers known to execute men on the spot without trial, just for simply misremembering Highbeard's Six Laws of Inner Peace.

Scary times.

That's what Fen says.

And by Fen, Thom really means, *That's what Fen's mother says,* because Fen—like most kids—gets his expressions and knowledgeable quips from his parents.

Not that Thom would know about the parent thing.

Maybe he will someday. Maybe starting today, he will know what it's like to have a parent, an *actual* parent, not some forced adoptive guardian who acts more like a slave master than a beacon of guidance.

"How much farther?" Fen asks, sucking wind as they crest a small hill, the way up made treacherous by muddy grounds, and rocks the size of human skulls.

They face more trees, but there's a manmade path that intersects, which will lead them straight to Jerrin's, if Thom's memory serves him correctly—and he's confident this is the way.

"I don't know. An hour?"

"Another hour?" Fen frowns.

They've been through two hours of this already.

The journey, Thom reminds him again, was much shorter last time because he was on horseback, and he doesn't rightly remember how long it took. But they weren't galloping, just walking most of the way, so it has to be similar, time-wise.

Fen looks at him like he's taken a piss in his beef stew.

"Come on, Fen," Thom says, rolling his eyes. "Don't be like that." He claps his friend on the shoulder. "I thought you were the adventurous one."

"Inside the safety of the Silver Towers, yeah. Playing tricks on guards and maids is fun, mate, but this—Thom, we could get in serious trouble out here."

Thom flashes a too-proud grin. "Relax. You have me to protect you."

"Oh, is that right? Are you going to mind spell a bunch of thieving raiders who want to gut us, is that it?"

"Maybe?" Thom winks at him. "Won't know unless we try."

Thom moves down the path, but he only manages about ten steps before he realizes he's going it alone.

He turns back, faces Fen. "What is it?"

"We should turn back. Now. Ravenborn…"

Thom clicks his tongue, tired of hearing the man's name. "What about him?"

"He might get pissed at me. Might think this is *my* idea."

"I'll tell him it wasn't."

"Even so—what if he punishes me just to spite you?"

Thom hadn't thought of that.

"What if he punishes my mother to spite us both?"

Thom certainly hadn't thought of *that*.

"I want to go back," Fen says, stomping his foot on the soggy earth.

Thom approaches his friend, his own mind whispering to him, telling him that he can influence his friend to keep pushing ahead, with promises of a new adventure. After all, that's how he got him to come on this trip in the first place. A little *mind push* was all Fen needed.

"I know it's scary," Thom says, looking at the trees, the walls of the forest that stand in rows that seem to go on forever. "I'm scared too. But just *relax*," he says, using the voice, the one that sometimes gets people to do what he wants.

"I want to go home," Fen says.

The *push* doesn't work. He tries again. "Come on, Fen. Don't you want to see other places besides the same ol' chambers and hallways—something new? Something nice? Somewhere not covered up under gray skies? Don't you want to…*explore?*"

Fen blinks. Then shakes his head. "We could die out here."

Highbeard's Balls, Thom thinks. *Why isn't this working?*

Just as he thought he was beginning to really understand his skills, the one thing that makes him special, truly a talent of the gods, here he is failing spectacularly. He can't even influence a scared kid to put one foot in front of the other. Not like he did with those guards, during his sessions with Ravenborn. Or back when he convinced Fen this was a good idea in the first place. This is more like the time he tried to plant thoughts of suicide in that one guard's head, just to see what would happen. *Slit your throat,* he'd whispered to him. But it didn't work. The guard didn't do it. And right now, Fen won't take so much as another step.

He settles on a different approach.

"Fen, what do you think Ravenborn will do to you if you abandon me?" Thom asks, glaring at his friend as if they weren't friends at all.

"Wh-what?"

"Ravenborn…when he finds out you left me in the woods, strayed from the Silver Path, leaving me all by my lonesome… don't you think he'll be much angrier about that than leaving the Towers in the first place?"

Fen blinks as if he hasn't considered this. "I…I haven't thought about it."

"He'll be angry, Fen. Very, very angry. And he'll hurt you. And he'll hurt your mother too—he'll kill her. He'll take his Raven-blade and lop off her head. Put it on a spike in the center of the city square. Would you like that?"

Fen looks like he wants to cry. His eyes become red and puffy, and his shoulders slump, defeated. Slowly, he shakes his head.

"Good," Thom says. "Then walk with me. We're almost there."

With that, Thom turns from his friend; smiles when he hears Fen's footfalls getting sucked by the muddy terrain, finally understanding what true power is all about. *Knowing what somebody loves the most and threatening to take it away from them.*

———

AN HOUR LATER, they're back on a main path which Thom recognizes—it's the one that leads them directly to Jerrin's house. Thom takes the lead, sensing Fen's reluctance with every step— though his friend hates every second of this adventure, he doesn't say another word about heading back to the towers. Thom tries to strike up a conversation, something banal and redundant, but Fen ignores him.

"Come on, Fen," Thom says, still grinning, enjoying this new dynamic between them. The control he feels—it's sweet. *This must be what a king feels like, to have people obey simply by uttering a few nasty words.* "You have to talk to me. I'm your friend."

"We don't feel like friends," Fen says, his voice small, fingers of fear curling around his vocal cords. "Friends don't threaten each other."

"Who's threatening whom?" Thom stops, spins around, pointing a finger at Fen. His cheeks heat up, partly from anger, but a blush of embarrassment is also blossoming. "I never once threatened you."

"You said Ravenborn might kill my mother."

"Well..." Thom shrugs. "He might. You know what he's capable of. He killed his own son, for Highbeard's sake. I'm just being honest about our situation here. We decided to leave, go on this adventure...and we have to see it through. My father—my true father—he can help us, Fen."

"You've changed," Fen says, narrowing his gaze, as if looking at his old friend through a new lens. "It's like...I don't even recognize you anymore."

Thom's heart dances strangely. "I'm still me, Fen. Just a better version of me. I see things differently now."

Dark clouds converge overhead. The wind picks up, blowing harshly through the trees, whispering amongst the branches.

"Thom..." Fen says, stepping back.

"*What?*"

"Your eyes..." Fen trips over his heels and stumbles to the ground. Scampering away like a crab on the shore, Fen whimpers softly—like a baby unsure of what to expect of the future. "They're...changing..."

A surge of anger fires through him, and Thom can't stop it. He wants to, wishes for this hatred to halt and bleed away. But he can't. The fiery sensation runs through his veins, causing his heart to pound faster, like a blacksmith hammering the heaviest steel. He feels something exploding behind his eyes, like everything behind them is expanding, gaining mass, a star ready to explode into a burst of space dust, and he wishes he had a mirror to check them. It feels like his whole head might explode. "What's wrong with me?"

He closes his eyes, trying to imagine something pleasant, something that will calm him. He thinks of his room, looking out across the Silver City, watching the people below scurry through the streets, heading to work or off to see loved ones, the business-as-usual hustle that almost makes him feel like he's a part of it, just by watching. It stabilizes him. Keeps him grounded. Makes him feel more...

Human.

What am I? It is probably the scariest thought he's ever had.

He lets go of the anger, casts it aside, and his own fears and worries replace what was once an untamed fury. His heart rate slows to a reasonable pace.

The roiling dark clouds above disperse, allowing sunlight to beam through the blue gaps. Stormy gales wither to a soft breeze. Busy leaves hush their secrets. Thom drops to his knees, covering his face, embarrassed by what he's become.

Fen inches closer to him. The rustling of leaves gets closer and closer. Then he feels his friend's arms around him.

"Do you think..." Fen says but can't finish because the words catch in his throat. He gulps, then speaks: "Do you think Jerrin can help you?"

"I honestly don't know."

Fen picks him up from the ground, then lifts his friend's chin so they can stare each other in the eyes. "Your eyes..." Fen smiles. "They're normal again. Well, normal for *you.*"

"I don't know what happened. I got so angry...I felt..."

What? What did I feel?

It was almost indescribable. The best he can come up with is, "It felt like I was going to explode."

"That's...scary."

"I don't want to feel it again."

Fen gulps. "I'll continue with you. To Jerrin's. Maybe he can fix you."

Thom nods. "All right."

Wagon wheels squeak in the near distance, and the clopping of hooves rises. The boys turn to a wagon rolling north, up the path —heading in the direction of the Silver Towers.

"What do we do?" Thom asks.

Fen hikes his hood up over his head. "We just pass them like the others. It'll be fine."

"What if they're not friendly?" Thom's the scared one now.

"Then maybe you can scare the shit out of them," Fen suggests with a shrug. "Like you just did me."

Thom doesn't like the idea but has no time to ponder a different plan—the wagon is approaching them quickly, and the driver already has them in his sights.

"Whoa, whoa!" the driver says, pulling back on the reins, whistling to the two geldings towing the wagon cart. "My, my, what do we have here? Hello there, fellow travelers!"

"Just ignore him and keep walking," Fen says, muttering under his breath.

Thom follows his friend. They scurry past the horses hoping to dodge a second greeting.

"Now, now!" the driver says. "I says hello, and it's polite to respond and says hello back, fellow travelers. Perhaps we can trade? Barter for a bit? Doesn't look like you have anything to offer us, but..." A quiet snicker, one that unsettles Thom from the bones on out. "Well, maybe you do!"

Thom peeks up at the wagon, sees another body pulling himself out of the cart. The second man jumps to the ground and lands with a hard thud on sturdy knees. They're not old—older than Thom and Fen, but only by a decade, maybe more. They don't look great healthwise, though. The road appears to have been hard on them. One of them, the second man, is missing half an ear, probably the result of losing a knife fight. The driver wears an eyepatch, and half the teeth in his smile have been replaced with silver caps.

Eyepatch stands, stretches his bones. "Where you going in such a hurry?"

"Keep walking," Fen says. "They won't chase us."

Thom isn't so sure of that, but he does what his friend says, keeps walking and picks up the pace.

When he glances back over his shoulder, he sees Fen is wrong—dead wrong. The two men are following them. And they are not taking their time either. Half-Ear is already jogging toward them. There's a limp to his gait, but he moves with the quickness of any determined, injured animal.

"Run!" Fen says, and takes off, leaving Thom in his dust.

Thom bolts forward, kicking his legs and motoring himself as fast as he can. But Half-Ear is far faster, and the goon runs him down in under a minute, grabbing him by the scruff of his hood and throwing him to the ground with force. Thom lands lip first in the dirt, eating some grit. When he looks up, he can't find Fen anywhere.

"Don't worry about your friend," Half-Ear says, his tone somewhat pleasant, as if what's happening here is a good, natural thing to occur. "We'll find him."

Thom shuts his eyes, hoping to Highbeard they do not see who he is—*what* he is. Nothing good will come of them discovering his identity.

"Where'd the other little bastard go?" Eyepatch says, sounding pissed.

"Off ahead, darted into the woods," his partner replies, gripping Thom's neck and hoisting the boy to his feet.

"Eh, I'll get him." Opening his eyes, Thom watches Eyepatch hustle after Fen. Thom hopes Fen is still running, not wasting a precious second even thinking about turning around to save him.

Because Thom can save himself.

Can't I?

"Come 'ere, you," Half-Ear grumbles, dragging Thom back to the wagon cart. From the piles of baled hay, a figure rises, yawning and stretching. Thom thinks it's a man, but he can't be too certain, because, like Thom, the figure is wearing a hood. No facial hair. But that's not the only noticeable feature that separates this figure from most of the other men in the Five Realms—it's the scars on his face, the ones running up his cheeks, nearly touching the bottoms of his ears. It looks like a…

Highbeard's balls, Thom thinks, finding the man hard to look at.

"Hey, you," Half-Ear calls to the disfigured man. "Come down here and help Kerwin find that other boy. Bastard couldn't have gotten far."

The man in the cart throws back his hood, and Thom is doubly surprised to see a jester's cap sewn to his scalp. The wounds look old, fully healed, and his hat is now a permanent fixture atop his head. Well, not permanent—surely someone could supply a pair of scissors, cut the threads and release his head from this bizarre, everyday accessory.

"Didja hear me?" the bandit shouts to the court jester, who is cleaning wax out his ear with his forefinger. "You hitching a free ride to the Silver City, you best pull your weight around here. Collect the bastard children—we know slavers in eastern Glane who'd take them off our hands for a hundred coins each."

"Hundred coins?" the jester says perkily. "That's quite the purse." His eyes travel from whatever they were focused on in the wagon, all the way over to meet Thom's. Thom can tell immediately this man is different from the other two. The other two had a desperate way about them, like the mischief and thieving they partake in cannot be helped. Their criminal enterprise is based on survival. But this man—this Jester—is a different story. There's a sparkle in his eyes, one that suggests his mischief and thieving (*murdering,* the boy considers) is done for an entirely different reason.

Because he enjoys it.

Thom can't say why or how he knows this but understands it to be true. He tries to turn away from the man's gaze, those cold eyes that hold no empathy—just two, soulless orbs that float in the white spaces like dead faraway planets.

The Jester.

Just reciting the name he's given the man draws a cold tingle down the boy's spine.

"Now, now," Jester says, rising from the back of the wagon. "What delights do we have here?"

"Are you listening, beggar?" Half-Ear asks, clearly rubbed the wrong way by Jester's carefree approach to the situation. "Get yer grits moving. We need to—"

"Do you know who you have in your possession?" Jester hops off the wagon, lands on his feet, and then strolls over to Thom and Half-Ear. He's cracking his knuckles, a bone-popping snap accompanying each step.

"What?" Half-Ear shakes his head, stunned by Jester's insubordination. "Perhaps you didn't hear me. I said get—"

"No, I heard you just fine. If you quit yapping your goddamn flapper, you'd understand what priceless equipment we've just come into possession of."

Half-Ear glances down at the boy, the top of his head, and then looks up at Jester, blinking stupidly. "What?"

"The Boy."

"The boy?"

"No, *The Boy.*"

Frustrated, Half-Ear stamps the earth with his foot. "What in Arkos's Darkhell are you talking about, beggar?"

Jester's grin deepens. "Have you looked at his eyes? I'm going to guess you have not."

Half-Ear spins Thom around, forcing him to face forward. Thom clenches his eyes shut, refusing to open them. "Open your eyes, boy, or I'll slice you open and play a long game of Toss the Sausage with your belly parts."

Thom reluctantly opens his eyes.

"Highbeard's Swinging Dick," Half-Ear says, his eyes lighting up as if he's just located the endless riches beneath a high lord of Silver City's keep. "It's…it's *him*."

"Yes, it is," Jester says, advancing. "Just so happens, my business in the Silver City pertains to this exact young man. Isn't that a coincidence? Some may call it fate. Perhaps the Highbeard is on old Jester's side after all."

Half-Ear cackles madly, unable to look away from the boy's star-shaped eyes. He dances in place, stomping his feet in the dirt. "We're going to be rich!! The Silver Towers will pay a fortune for his return!! He'll—"

Half-Ear stops talking, and Thom glances up, seeing something change in the bandit's eyes. He can't tell what it is at first, but once the man's grasp slips and Thom distances himself, he finally sees the knife protruding from his neck, squirts of syrupy red gushing out of the sizable wound, now revealed. Half-Ear makes a choking sound, as his hands gravitate toward the stuck knife.

"Sorry it had to end this way, friend," Jester says, dancing out from behind him. He was so quick in his execution that Thom did not see him move. "But I have alternate plans that will not benefit you."

Half-Ear collapses on his side, writhing on the ground as he struggles to free his neck from the inserted metal. His fingers slip on the blood-slicked hilt, working lazily to regain a grip. Jester skips around his flailing body, kneels, and curls his fingers around the knife. With a quick jerk, he removes the blade. A gout of red follows in its wake. Half-Ear's hands plug the wound, but blood wells up through spaces between his fingers. Jester tilts his head, confused. Then he brings the knife down on his stomach, not once but half a dozen times. Scarlet puddles bloom on the man's garments, and Jester watches—his eyes smiling—as the man's kicking legs slow to a stop. His skyward stare becomes frozen, endless.

"Now," Jester says, standing, sighing as if the world's most inconvenient obstacle has been removed. "I am very pleased to meet you...*Boy*." Jester tilts his head to the side. "Does thou have a name?"

Thom gulps, wondering if he should open his mouth or opt for silence. In the end he decides that making this comfortable killing machine of a man angry is no way to proceed. "Thom."

"Thom! I like it. Now, Thom. I have a very special mission for you. You will accompany me on my journey south, all the way back to Owlton! Isn't that exciting?"

Thom blinks several times. "What?"

"Yes. The king in the south has summoned for you, and has employed me to be your guide. Has a great, important message for you, one I think you'll be very happy to hear."

Thom glances over his shoulder, toward the woods Fen escaped into.

"Are you worried about your friend?" Jester claps the boy on the shoulder, and Thom nearly jumps out of his skin. "Don't worry about him—we can find him. And he can come with us."

"No," Thom says, an instinctive response. "No, I can't go."

"And why the bloody hell not?"

"Because..." Thom has trouble locating an answer. Nothing's keeping him tethered to the Silver Towers—in fact, a part of him wants to leave the Silver City and never return. But... "Because I can't leave my father."

"That is a conundrum for sure," Jester says, wearing his best *serious* face. "Family is important—but, see, the thing is...you don't have a choice." He bends down, grips the knife in Half-Ear's stomach, then yanks it free, putting his foot on the dead man's leg for leverage. A small red geyser erupts from the man's intestines, now slightly hanging out, but the spray quickly peters out and pools around the slitted opening. "You're coming with me to Owlton, to see King Ragland. He's eagerly awaiting your arrival."

"I'm dangerous."

"*That* I don't doubt. But..." Jester leans his shoulder toward the downed fella. "I'm equally dangerous. I don't know what powers you might have, but if you look at me funny in any way or chant some Highbeard mumbo-jumbo—I'll have you bleeding out like a boar on New Year's roast."

Thom believes him, wishes he could channel that rage again. It felt so good being able to collect that energy, feeling it build inside until it was too much, until it felt like he was going to burst. But now it feels like there's nothing there.

He's powerless.

"My father...he's not far. Please...find my friend...save him... and let me see my father." He lowers his head, unsure of the words standing on the precipice of his tongue. "Then I will go with you, willingly."

Jester chews the inside of his cheek. Rolling his eyes, he mutters, "Fine. But we must hurry. Something tells me we don't have much time. You're too important to go missing for long."

NO CLEAR SIGN

CHAPTER TWENTY-TWO

"It's safe to say the people of Endlia both fear and welcome the return of the old gods, and wish to see the prophecy fulfilled. The prospect of an end to war is almost worth the potential of Arkos's Darkhell taking over."

– MENYARD MINOTOA, *THE GOD SYSTEM*

———

RAVENBORN LEAVES the Silver City with twenty of his best men, riding into the forests at a speed most would consider highly dangerous, but he doesn't care. The only thing that matters is retrieving the boy, getting to him before someone else does. The *wrong* someone, though anyone who discovers the boy outside the Silver City is bound to be the wrong someone.

Stupid, he thinks, chastising himself for not foreseeing these events. The boy's powers were coming along nicely, and at a surprising pace, and he was bound to go exploring sooner or later, test his powers out in the wild. Plus…the introduction to the boy's father was a risk. A necessary risk, but he should have known the boy would want to see him again. Unsupervised.

No, it's that wimp, Fen's fault, he thinks, pushing his horse into the deep shadows of the Tall Woods. *Always convincing Thom to act out, explore places he shouldn't! I'll hang him and his mother for this. Actually—fuck it—I'll decapitate them both. The whore first, so the kid can watch.*

They ride for two hours straight, only stopping once, for the horses to catch their wind. The men seem just as tired, as this particular troop is part of a garrison that never leaves the city, and are not accustomed to field missions. It's too late to trade them in for a more capable crew, so Ravenborn gives them the standard speech—shape up quickly or be left behind. And if you're left behind, you're no longer welcome back behind the gates of the Silver City.

The men nod gravely at the warning and whisper their promises to keep up with their leader. Minutes later, Ravenborn is pushing them deeper into the woods, taking the Lonely Road out to where Jerrin Pierce has been stashed.

On the way, Ravenborn can't help but think of the emperor's last words to him:*"Don't let your past failures in dealing with young men haunt you, Ravenborn."*

Even though the events of that infamous story are years in the past, and he's had over a decade to forget his middle son's death—he's still far from *over it.* Every day he wakes up wondering what he could have done differently to stop him, to prevent the young man from cursing his family's name, throwing away everything he had, and betraying his country. For what? He still doesn't understand why William Ravenborn did what he'd done on that day, but the look in his son's eyes when he drew his blade against his own father, his own flesh and blood—well, that memory has haunted many of Ravenborn's dreams.

"Darko," one of his men says, snapping Ravenborn out of his distant reverie.

Hearing his true name, Ravenborn glances up ahead, realizing he's fallen behind and is no longer leading the troop. "Yes?"

"Ahead," the soldier says, one of his captains, one of the few who can call him *Darko* and get away with it.

He follows the captain's finger to an overturned wagon lying in the middle of the road, its contents strewn about the forest. The horses that were carrying this wagon are nowhere to be found, though one of the troops suggests they had run off *that way* as he points in some nondescript direction. Ravenborn doesn't give two bear shits about the horses—he only wants information about the boy.

"Any sign of the children?" Ravenborn asks, dismounting his horse and hustling over to the overturned wagon.

The captain shakes his head, continuing to examine the scene with interest. "No, but there are a bunch of footprints leading from the struggle."

"Struggle?"

The captain steps aside, and Ravenborn sees. A man, dressed like a common traveler, perhaps a peddler of small wares, lies dead in the road, a knife wound in his neck, his stomach mutilated.

"Blood's fairly fresh," the captain proceeds. "Can't be more than an hour since his demise."

Ravenborn nods, then calls to the scout who is bending over the tracks in the mud. "Anything useful?"

"Two sets of two," the scout says, rising to his feet. "Two of them are small—probably children, definitely smaller than the other sets."

Ravenborn nods again, feeling hope flutter in his chest. "Good. Let's mount up and follow them. Can you get a good direction?"

The scout bites his lip. "Yes, but they go off the road just up yonder." He points toward the edge of the road where the mud meets the leafy treeline.

"Do your best," Ravenborn says. "If they are still alive, I know where they're headed, and if we don't find them in the woods, we head to the boy's father's home."

The men mount their horses and scatter into the woods.

Ravenborn hangs back, watching them get to work, scouring the woods for the missing boys.

He glances down at the cut man's throat once last time, thinking of his son again, William Ravenborn, and wishing he could go back in time, to face that moment all over again.

Oh, what might have been different.

WISPS OF A DREAM

CHAPTER TWENTY-THREE

"Dreams can be interpreted as messages from the gods."

– PENYA CURTIS, *DREAMING OF THE ENDLANDS*

———

SETTLING HERSELF TO SLEEP, Ralyanna's final cohesive thought is a plea to the gods that they leave her dreams alone. But —as gods often do—they ignore her request, and she returns to that familiar garden. Where the woman is waiting.

The Fairy Godmother stands in her chamber, surrounded by drooping plant life, her exotic flowers displaying colorful petals. In the center of the chamber sits a circular gold-plated dais; upon it, a spinning gyroscope. Ra carefully walks around the gyroscope, captivated by its fluid, hypnotic movement. The tree that grew sacks full of fresh souls is no longer present, perhaps reserved for a different dream.

Or maybe they've been born already, she thinks, approaching the Fairy Godmother, unsure of how this dream is supposed to play out.

The Fairy Godmother turns from the glass window that overlooks a dark and empty abyss. Her lips curl at the ends, and her eyes shimmer with a hopeful kind of anticipation, like she's awaiting good news.

"My dearest sweet pea," she says, her voice sticky-sweet with affection. "You've come back to visit."

Not by choice, Ra thinks, questioning the woman's claim. Ra guesses she's been summoned to this green palace, this dream.

Summoned by whom?

The grim thought plagues her.

"I…I don't know what I'm doing here," she says sheepishly. "I don't know what is expected of me."

The Fairy Godmother considers this, then straightens the lacy cuffs on her lavish robe. They dangle from her wrists like old, broken spiderwebs. "You're close to him."

"Close…"

"The Boy…" Her eyes shine with a special kind of malice. Ra wishes to look away from them, but the dream keeps her focused. "You must kill him. Cut out his heart."

"I don't think I can."

"You've thought about it. My offer—what killing the Boy will do. You can save the Five Realms, Ralyanna. You can restore peace to the entire world. Why do you reject such an opportunity?"

Ra shakes her head, her lips quivering. "It…it feels wrong."

The Fairy Godmother lowers the crown of her head, glowering. "Sometimes, my dear, the things that are the hardest to do can feel wrong, even if they produce the best outcomes."

"I don't know this boy. He hasn't done anything, except exist. Right?"

"But it's what he *will* do. That's the problem. He will destroy everything. The lands will scorch. The oceans will rise. The sky will crash down on the Endlands, leaving our majestic plains and forests and mountains nothing but barren wastelands of perpetual death and decay."

"But how do you know?" Ra's on the verge of weeping now. Because she feels there's no avoiding what's to come, the confrontation with the prophetic boy. And because she fears she's not in total control of the power inside her. "How can you see the future?"

The Fairy Godmother passes the gyroscope, putting her hand inches from its spinning spires, hovering over the wind its motion produces. "The Gyroscope of Ages shows me all things, past, present, and future."

"What if it's wrong?" Ra gulps, sensing she's entering forbidden territory, that going against the woman's claims might prove detrimental to her own future. "What if the Gyroscope of Ages lies?"

Shadows crawl over the room like roaming storm clouds, and the darkness outside the glass-wall window begins to seep in. The plants begin to curl, their leaves browning more and more with each terrible second, like some malignant disease has infected them at the root. Flower petals lose their color, wither and arch from their stems, the pistils that bloomed them.

Ra's aggravated something here. Provoked the Fairy Godmother or the dream itself. Either way, Ra blinks several times, hoping this will wake her up. Transport her back to the real world, where it's safe—relatively speaking.

"I want to go home," Ra says in a whisper.

"You have no home, child," the woman says as her face begins to warp, no longer maintaining the appearance of a benevolent queen. Her skin is rough, stippled, and marred by deep trenches of scars. Warts, wet with a buttery discharge, dot the woman's face, as her skin begins to melt and run like creamed ice drink. "I am your home now. You will do as I say or suffer the consequences. You may be able to outrun your task of killing the Boy, but you will never outrun me, or your dreams, and I will always be with you."

"I'll kill myself," Ra tells her. "I'll kill myself and be rid of you and your task."

"Oh, child," the Fairy Godmother says, her face a mask of what looks like runny goose eggs. Ra can see bone beneath the canvas of translucent flesh, the woman's skull. Spiders and worms and ticks crawl through the gaps between her teeth, her nostrils and cavernous eye sockets. "You will never be rid of me. What do you think death is? Death, my darling, is nothing but a long dream. Only you can choose how pleasant or unpleasant your dreams will become."

Ra doesn't believe her, but there's a small part that wonders. *What if she's right? What if I can never escape her?*

She swallows, begging for the dream to end.

She can't take much more. Physically, her body begins to hurt, pulsating with an all-encompassing pain that needles her every nerve, that stabs through the center of her.

"Our time is coming to an end," says the skeletal figure of the witch before her. "You will do what is right, I know it. Ralyanna, you must kill the Boy with the Star-Shaped Eyes. You must cut out his heart, and you must eat it."

"Eat it?" This is getting worse and worse.

"Eat the Boy's heart. Cook it or devour it raw; it matters not." Those black eyes that produce fat, juicy spiders, stare down at her. She's unable to dodge its black gaze. The skeleton's amiable, motherly voice begins to change, warp into something much more menacing—a demonic tone that reverberates like the growling thunder. "You will eat this boy's heart, and you will bring this world back from devastation. The Gyroscope does not lie. I have seen it! *I HAVE SEEN IT!*"

Two skeletal hands shoot out and grip Ra's shoulders. The girl screams, perhaps louder than she's ever screamed before, and when she blinks, she's—

———

KET HAS HER, is shaking her awake, but Ra still screams and doesn't want to stop, if for nothing else than to make sure she's far away from the dream's reach.

Safe again.

Ket shouts at her, telling her she's fine.

She doesn't believe him. As the foggy dream shrinks from her, turns to nothing but wispy smoke that quickly clears away, she sees two more faces peering at her through the shadows of night. A lantern clicks on, and in the grainy light she sees their two hospitable hosts hanging near the open doorway, rubbing sleep from their eyes.

"What happened?" Mason asks. Kelanda has a knife in her hand, though the way she's holding it, angled down, makes Ra wonder if the woman realizes there's no real threat here.

"Just a nightmare," Ket answers for her.

"Figured," Mason says with a yawn. "Bad place to be for nightmares."

Ra, trembling, finds this statement quite odd. And somewhat unnerving. "What do you mean?"

Mason and his partner exchange glances. Then, Mason sets the lantern on the bureau closest to the door. "Old Rovan stories—these parts in the wilderness, far from the Silver City, can sometimes have strange effects on the mind. The closer you are to the fabled Rainbow Springs."

"Rainbow Springs?" Ra's curiosity piques.

Ket clicks his tongue. "Mason, now is not the time for old legends and fables."

Mason combs back his bed hair with both hands. "Well, since we won't be sleeping anymore tonight, I'd say it's the best time to discuss old legends and fables."

"I'll make four teas," Kelanda says, rolling her eyes as she exits the doorway.

Mason takes the seat in the corner of the room next to a writing desk, throwing one knee over the other, leaning back and joining his hands together on his belly. "The Rainbow Springs is located somewhere in Rovan—or it's possibly in Glane, or perhaps the Crosslands." He says this with a wry smile, and Ra arches her brow, waiting for some clarification. "Fact is," he continues, "no one knows where the Rainbow Springs are actually located, because few have claimed to find the place, and whenever explorers set out to the coordinates provided by the original storyteller, they find nothing."

Ra shakes her head, more confused than ever. "I don't get it."

"He's messing you with you, Ra," Ket says grumpily, as if he's exhausted by not just Mason's story, but the night itself. "No such place exists. Old Rovan tales make for good story fodder, and Mason likes to spin his yarns."

Mason holds up a *that's-not-exactly-true* forefinger. "This is not *some* tale. Rainbow Springs is a real place. But no one can find it because it *moves*."

Ket laughs through his nose. "Now I've heard everything."

"It's true! C'mon, *Ket*. Don't tell me after everything you experienced inside the Silver Towers, that you do not believe in things considered unnatural—in legends and supernatural tales of the olden times?"

Ket's boyish smile falls off, slowly dies. "I believe only what my eyes show me. I have seen many things unnatural, and of course I believe—but what you speak of is fairy tales, stories best kept in fiction."

Mason paws the empty air. "Come off it, man. You of all people should know some things exist that go beyond rational explanation, that defy and challenge all logic."

"It's too late for this debate, Mason," Ket says, yawning, stretching his neck. "Or too early."

Kelanda strolls through the door, puts down a tray with four steaming mugs of tea on the furniture next to the lantern. She distributes the mugs to each of them. Ra blows on her tea before sipping, but Ket dives right in, putting the hot drink to his lips and taking it down in gulps. She wonders how he hasn't burned his throat.

"Let's chat about where you're taking us this morn," Ket says, placing his empty mug on the bedsheet beside him.

Mason leans forward as if he's about to tell another story of fairy-tale places. "We're going to pay a visit to Jerrin Pierce," he says as if the name should mean something to them.

Ra looks to Ket, hoping he'll clarify. But he looks just as lost as her.

"Jerrin Pierce?" Ket shrugs. "That a name I should know? Because it means nothing to me."

"Highbeard's cunt, you really haven't been keeping up with the times, have you?"

Ket smirks humorlessly.

"Anyway," Mason says, leaning back now. "Jerrin Pierce is the Boy's father."

Ket lifts his brow, intrigued. "The Boy? The Boy we're looking for?"

"Indeed. The high-ranking officials of the Silver Towers are keeping him stashed away in some cottage in the middle of Nowhere, Rovan, and the area is heavily patrolled by Rovan troops. We'll head there, take out a few of the guards—covertly, I may add—and steal their effects—their wardrobe mainly. That way we can pass through the gates of the Silver City without anyone lifting an eyebrow at us."

Ket nods, taking in the proposed plan. "How *heavily patrolled* is *heavily patrolled*?"

Mason kicks some numbers around his thoughts. "Eh, twenty tops."

"Twenty? Well, it's best we stick to being sneaky." Ket spins, facing Ra. "Probably best you stay behind too."

"No!" Ra shouts—an instinctive response, but even after she speaks out, she knows she doesn't want to be left behind. "No, please—don't leave me alone."

Ket points his chin at Kelanda. "Kelanda can watch you, and we'll return before you know it."

Mason grimaces like he doesn't want to refute his friend's claims but has no choice in the matter. "Actually...it's a few hours ride from here, even on horseback, and I only know the proximity of the place—no exact location. It's probably best if the girl comes, that way we can make for the Silver Towers promptly after."

Ket freezes for a beat but then nods along with the new plan. "Hmm," he grunts, looking down at his feet. "Let's get going as soon as possible then. And, Ra?"

Ra stares the man directly in the eyes, the eyes of her new protector—the only one in the entire universe she trusts. "Yes?"

"If things go badly," he says almost somberly, like he expects things to happen that way, "I want you to listen to what I say— you understand?"

She swallows what feels like a few broken teeth. "Yes."

"Good," he says with finality. "Then let's get ready to ride out."

She sips her tea, then winces as the liquid burns her tongue, still too hot to consume all at once. Ket is already asking Kelanda for a second cup.

And then the three adults leave the room, leaving her to get dressed. As she does, all she can hear is the phantom woman from her dreams whispering in her ear: *Kill him. Eat his heart. KILL HIM. EAT HIS HEART.*

RUN FEN RUN

CHAPTER TWENTY-FOUR

"Wanted: ALIVE. Morlo Robyn Tent. Reward: 20,000 in Rovan gold. The Pale Father of Iradon wishes to bring justice to this man's crimes against the Five Realms."

– OFFICIAL STATEMENT POSTED ON
VARIOUS BULLETIN BOARDS
THROUGHOUT THE CROSSLANDS

———

AS THE TREE branches whip his face and dice up his cheeks, Fen urges himself to run faster, knowing the villainous bastards behind him will not give up, or succumb to tired legs and gasping lungs. He glances over his shoulder every few seconds, hoping to not see the shapes materialize in the mist developing around him, shrouding the trees and branches in its soft, milky haze.

You can do this, he coaches himself, ducking under some foliage, wild branches of unrooted witch elm. *Just a little farther, get back to the road that leads back to the Silver City. Run all the way there! Don't look back! Just—*

Something wallops him in the face. He doesn't see what. There's just impact—a hard, crunching smack that he thinks will leave his face permanently flattened, his nose smooshed into the center of his brain, effectively killing him. The lights of the world go dim, and for a second he thinks he *is* dead. This is it, this is the end, and there's no coming back under blue skies.

He finds himself on his back, lying awkwardly across some knee-high bushes and fallen branches, a bed of crispy autumn leaves. The world moves sideways; to the left at first, but then slides right, his vision doing its best to piece the two ghosting images of the forest together, his senses trying to catch back up to the world around him. Black stars pop in and out of view.

"Hello there," a voice says, a shadow edging its way into his sight. When the world sharpens its focus, Fen sees the voice belongs to the bandit wearing an eyepatch. The man smiles, flashing blackened nuggets of decaying ivory. His voice sounds as if he's constantly speaking with his lips around a sandwich. "Where you running to?" A short giggle, one that supplies Fen's veins with running ice.

"Doh-don't hurt me," he begs, putting up a hand, like that'll stop the guy from bashing his brains in.

"*Don't hurt me,*" Eyepatch mocks, doing a pretty good job of mimicking the boy's frightened tone. "I'm not gonna hurt you, boy—you're far too valuable to damage. Merchandise that will make us a whole six months' salary!"

Fen doesn't know anything about what Eyepatch just said but knows it has to do with coin, and when it comes to coin, adults get all crazy, so it's no wonder the man has gone insane. "I can give you coins if you want it! A thousand coins!"

"Oh, kenya?" Eyepatch feigns interest. "How's a simple boy like you got scratch like that, huh?"

Fen points in the direction he thinks home is. "I live in the Silver Towers—my mother is a maid to the emperor himself!"

Eyepatch goes quiet, like Fen's just unlocked some great secret of the universe for him, but the quietude is short-lived. Eyepatch throws back his head and howls with laughter, rather wolf-like.

"That's a good one!" the man shouts, reaching down and grabbing Fen by his throat. "Most entertaining!"

Fen resists at first, but the man socks him in the gut, releasing all the air from Fen's lungs. After that, the boy has no choice but to go along with whatever Eyepatch has cooked up for him. After he pulls the boy to his feet, Eyepatch marches Fen back to the main road, probably to where they have Thom hidden, where they have probably already butchered him.

Probably.

Fen begins to cry, but the tears do not affect his captor—not even a little bit. In fact, it only delights the man even more, enhances his smile.

"You know," Eyepatch says proudly, like he's done a good day's work here, "when I was your age, just a boy, my mother would not let me leave her sight, not even for a second. That old bitch had her eyes on me every goddamn moment, and I couldn't so much as—"

A heavy *thwack* interrupts him. The man stops—not just talking but walking too. It takes Fen a second to glance up, to see what caused him to abruptly halt in his tracks. When he does, he sees something sticking out the back of his head, a small dribble of blood leaking down the man's forehead, worming its red stream between his eyes, crawling along the contours of his nose. Slowly, Eyepatch turns around to see what struck him, and when he does, Fen sees a hatchet embedded at the top of his skull. It's a marvel he's still standing.

"Who-who," he says, sounding like an owl. "Who-what?" His brain trips over these few simple words, the hatchet clearly stealing away basic thought patterns.

From behind a tree steps a man garbed in a jester's outfit—complete with a stemmed hat, bells at the bottoms of each ear, jingling as he strides toward them. The Jester unsheathes a knife, smiling as he advances, and when he's close enough, Fen can see the smile painted on his lips is not painted—it's a red, raw scar that's been carved into his cheeks.

Jester sticks the knife in Eyepatch's belly, and Eyepatch doesn't react, doesn't fight it, and probably can't find the strength seeing as though he's got an axe in his head. Jester works the knife through the man's guts, cutting, slicing, severing everything he can in a few short moments. He does so with precision and passion, like a proud and prize-winning butcher tending to a cow carcass. There's a delayed reaction from Eyepatch—he just watches with mild disinterest. But then he realizes what's becoming of him, as a moment of clarity bursts in his eyes, and maybe he feels the pain too, that spreading agony that runs throughout every limb, every extension of him, and he screams, hollering up at the tops of the trees, begging for help, imploring Highbeard to come down from his golden throne and save his soul.

Not the first time someone's asked that of Endlia's most popular deity and it certainly won't be the last. The desperate prayer goes unanswered, like all of them.

When Eyepatch's dead body crashes to the ground, Jester stands over him, shrugging like the world has lost no major component, nothing more significant than a fallen leaf.

Then, Jester eyes Fen.

Fen shakes—this is not the first time he's seen a dead body, but it is the first time he's witnessed a man's grisly murder.

"You can come out, little one," Jester says, grinning that menacing grin. Fen isn't sure what he means—Fen is right in front of him, cowering like a frightened squirrel that's been chased into a corner by a pack of troublesome boys. But Jester's eyes leave Fen, roam across the trees and settle on one in particular.

From behind the stunted witch elm, a head pokes out, one Fen recognizes.

It's Thom, and he's been crying, his face glistening with two fresh tracks of tears.

Jester returns his hideous smile back to Fen. "We found your friend."

A PAST TO KILL

CHAPTER TWENTY-FIVE

"The Silver Towers experimented with many *supernatural* strategies, including a method of torture known as *Soulthefting*—a procedure where a human soul was stripped from a dying body. Salah Rovan has refuted these accusations publicly, but numerous sources who served in Rovan during the Last War attest those rumors to be true. It's unclear whether the experiments were successful."

– JOKIC HARROWING, *WHAT WENT WRONG IN THE LAST WAR*

———

KET IS off his horse the moment Mason comes back for them. Ra follows his lead, dismounting her ride, allowing Ket to help her off, giving his hand for balance. Mason strolls up the path, adjusting his brown leather wrist cuffs.

"I count fifteen men," says the renegade weapon runner.

Kelanda is plucking her bowstring, testing the resistance. "Are they separated enough to take them out one by one?"

Mason bites his lip and shakes his head. "They're all within short range of each other, pacing their zones, utilizing perfect distance—Ravenborn has these men well-trained."

Ket's ears twitch when he hears that name—like it's the first time he's heard it spoken out loud in so long. "Yes...he was always good at training them."

Mason approaches Ket, looking grim. "I thought this was going to be easier, old friend." He pats Ket on the shoulder. "Looks like we might have to make a mess of things here."

"Fifteen men isn't many," Kelanda says, removing an arrow from her quiver and loading it onto her bow. "I can cull half of them before they know what's hit them."

"She's right." Mason paces around their small campsite. "They're not heavily armored—she can take out most of them on this side of the cottage while we flank the other side, hit them when they have their backs turned."

"What about me?" Ralyanna asks.

Everyone turns to the girl, but no one speaks. They wait for Ket to answer.

"You will stay here," Ket finally answers, his voice calm, using his best soothing tone.

Ra shoots to her feet. "No, I'm coming with you. I want to help. I want to fight!"

Ket almost laughs. "You don't know the first thing about fighting, Ra. You will stay behind and wait until all is clear. That's an order."

"Not fair," Ra says, and tears begin to brim in her eyes. "I can help you—you know I can."

"I don't know that."

"You watched me. I killed that man, I—"

"That was an accident. You don't know how to control what's inside of you—whatever *it* is."

"Borgadine—"

"Borgadine is dead," Ket snaps, silencing Ra. Her face changes, pales some. It's like she's found out about his death all over again. "I'm sorry, Ra. I didn't mean to—"

She storms off. Disappears through the drooping foliage that covers a path, not truly meant for travel.

"Ra!" he calls to her, but his voice does nothing to bring her back. He stands up and begins to charge after her—the last thing they need is her getting lost in the woods.

Kelanda puts a hand across his chest to stop him. "Maybe I should go. She doesn't know me well, and maybe I can get through to her better—girl to girl."

Ket considers it. He doesn't know this woman very well, other than she's confident in her ability to sail some arrows, but there's a benevolence in her eyes, a motherly spirit that roams her irises, projecting a sense of warmth and compassion—two things Ket Norlath never had, but once grew to learn. Things he's had to forget since the death of his wife and the entrapment of his two sons.

He nods, stepping back.

She pushes ahead, following Ra's trail through the trees.

Ket returns to his log, sits down, grabs himself a pinch of jerky and chews on it.

"Women, right?" Mason says, his gut shaking with a laugh. "What would we do without them?"

Ket glances up, not too happy with his choice of words. It calls back too many memories of Jennah, those harsh days after her death—granted, those days were spent in a dank, disgusting dungeon, where rats were his best company. But still—he imagines his grieving process wouldn't have been much different had he been allowed to breathe fresh, Endlian air.

"Sorry," Mason says, hanging his head, realizing he's touched a sore subject. "Your wife—didn't mean anything by it."

"It's fine." Ket lowers his gaze to the dirt. "It's funny how much you can miss a person—how lost you can be without them."

"Aye," Mason says in agreement, but Ket wonders if he really understands. "I never lost a wife," he admits, "but I've lost people. Lots I've cared about. Brothers. Like you did. Our unit was tightly knit back in the early days of war, wasn't it?"

Ket nods. "Yes, we were very close. More bonded than brothers."

"Even if what we were doing was wrong, all that killing and bloodshed…whatever you were subjected to, down in that chamber…it doesn't change us, how we got through it. How we relied on one another to help us past it."

Ket nods, distant, the memories of those days spent during the war calling to him. He knows if he goes to them, finds himself back in that place, he'll have to take the good with the bad. "I have good memories of them, but I do my best to forget…not because of our brothers, but because the bad memories hurt too much. They're like a slow poison, sickening me to my core. Jennah used to help. Her being there just washed all those old thoughts away, like they never happened, like they were part of a dream I almost don't remember. When she died…" He feels himself breaking from within, unraveling at his core. Sadness creeps into his throat, constricting his voice. "It was like the two people I had been merged together, and those bad memories came back."

"That's why you want to go back there," Mason says, understanding, nodding along with Ket's realization. "Not just to get your sons back."

"To kill my past, once and for all."

Mason breathes a deep sigh, as if the task has been put on his shoulders. Like it's his burden to carry. "You might run into Ravenborn before this whole thing plays out."

Ket's cheeks tighten, his jaw flexing. "I'm counting on it."

"I hope I'm not there to see it," Mason admits, then strides across the small opening in the path, taps his friend on the shoulder, as if this lets him know everything will turn out the way he wants. "I think we've wasted enough time here. We should get going."

"Let's wait for Kelanda to return," Ket says, not budging. "I think Ralyanna needs all the time we can afford."

A PAST TO KILL II

CHAPTER TWENTY-SIX

"Witches get stitches."

– BANCROFT MERO, FAMED WITCH
HUNTER FROM THE 4TH AGE

———

RALYANNA COMES TO A STREAM, stops, looks at the waterfall dumping white water from a twenty-foot drop, and wonders if she would be better off just diving in, headfirst, bashing her skull on the wet rocks below. Killing herself would solve a lot of her problems—all of them, actually. But every time she closes her eyes and thinks she'd be better off dead, she spots Borgadine's face, a fuzzy outline of the man she once knew, in her inner darkness. In that image he's smiling. His lips whisper phrases she cannot hear, but she knows they are words of encouragement. Words of motivation. He's telling her to keep going, keep pushing, don't stop, that she can—

What?

Save the world?

No, she can't do that. She doesn't know how. And there's no one here to teach her, to sharpen her skills, not like Borgadine could have. Because he knew more than what was happening inside of her—he knew *her*. Understood her. In a way no other human being truly had, in all her life.

Hopelessness settles into her core as she peers down over the edge of the waterfall, the ambient noise of the rushing water filling the air, silencing all the other sounds of the forest.

"I know what you're thinking, girl," a voice says from behind her, and she whips around to find Kelanda standing near the path, her bow still in her hands. "But killing yourself isn't the way out."

"How do you know? It all stops when you die, right? Everything goes black. No more pain, no more suffering."

"Maybe," Kelanda says with a frown and a shrug. "Maybe that's how it ends for us. Maybe all the old-time religious tales of an afterlife are made up to give us something hopeful to look forward to. Or maybe there is a place after Endlia, after all of this," she holds her hands up as if the lands fit within her palms, "and perhaps it's a good place and perhaps it's a bad place. Maybe if you jump, you land in the bad place."

"I don't know if I believe in the gods anymore," Ra says, almost breathless. "I don't know what I am," she cries, breaking down, her chest shuddering as the grief and sadness overwhelm her and drive her to her knees.

Kelanda walks over, kneels next to her. Puts a hand on her back while Ra sobs, her whole body shaking.

The woman leans in, whispers in her ear, "No one knows what they are," she says, "until they've lived and discovered their souls for themselves."

It sounds simple, but also…*right*.

No one knows what they are until they've lived. And she hasn't lived, not really, not nearly long enough. Borgadine always preached her important years were still ahead of her, that she would discover more about herself in them than she had in the sixteen previous. If he were alive today, would he relay the same message as Kelanda had? She thinks he would.

Knows it.

Through a teary blear, she faces Kelanda, the woman's spreading smile.

"You're a strong young woman," Kelanda says, rubbing Ra's back for comfort. It's working. Ra feels a sense of friendship, a smidge of motherly attention. She no longer sees jumping as a viable solution to her problem. "You are intelligent," Kelanda continues. "And you have something special inside you that the world needs right now."

"My power," she says, wiping the tears away.

"Something more than just moving things with your mind. The most important thing of all, something the world needs more of these days." Kelanda places her palm against Ra's chest. "Hope."

Ra hugs her. Seconds later, as if the woman is surprised and doesn't know how to respond, Kelanda slowly places her arms around Ra, squeezes her close.

Ra cries some more, soaking the woman's chest.

Kelanda doesn't stop her or tell her to toughen up. Nor does she say that their time is short and they need to move out. Kelanda just holds her until the well of her eyes dries up, and no more tears remain.

Until hope swallows up the sadness.

———

BY THE TIME Ra and Kelanda return to the circle, Ket and Mason have broken down the campsite and are ready to move out. They go over the plan again—it's simple really: Ket and Mason go first, make a wide berth around the cottage and get into position on the east side of the valley, while Kelanda finds a concealed spot that overlooks the whole western edge. She will hit her targets, and while the eastern guards focus their attention on whatever is attacking the men on the west side, Ket and Mason will charge them from behind, lay waste to as many as they can before they figure out they're being flanked.

Simple.

"What will I do?" Ra asks, her starry gaze hopeful.

Ket sighs, gives her those *come-on-now* eyes.

"What?" she asks, not understanding. She assumes Ket would have determined a role for her in the time she was gone.

"Ra," he says, like he's disappointed he has to tell her this again.

"No, I'm coming with—"

"It's too dangerous."

"She can come with me," Kelanda says, interrupting. "I will be keeping a distance from the guards, and I will keep her back even farther from the action. And I will protect her with my life if it comes to it—which it won't."

Ra swallows, hoping Ket will go along with the plan. It's better than her staying here, by herself, which seems almost just as dangerous as going to the cottage.

Ket thinks it over for a beat, then says, "Fine. But if things go bad," he says to Ra, "you run. As fast as you can in any direction —just don't look back. Understood?"

She nods, quickly.

"Good," Ket says, then spins toward Mason. "Are you ready?"

"Been ready," Mason says, jerking his head in the direction they are set to travel. "Shall we?"

Ket follows Mason through the trees and disappears. As he goes, Ra can't help but think it's the last time she'll ever see him.

———

"IT'S TIME TO MOVE," Kelanda says, fifteen minutes after the men leave. "They should be in position now."

Ra's heart drums against her chest. Her nerves fire off throughout her entire body. Every limb tingles with an achy numbness.

She closes her eyes. Breathes. Imagines Borgadine is with her, by her side, holding her hand through whatever comes next.

She's not ready for this.

I can't do this. I can't go, she tells herself, and then, in the blackness of her thoughts, a face emerges—it's her Fairy Godmother from her dreams, those smiling lips that cut through the swollen dark, separate, and display teeth whiter than waterfall foam. *You can do this. Kill the boy. Cut out his heart. Eat his soul.*

Absorb him.

She shakes her head, opens her eyes, ridding herself of this woman and her pestering demands.

"Are you coming?" Kelanda asks, gripping Ra's shoulder. "Don't blink out on me."

She means, *Don't be such a tit and find your courage, girl.* But she's much too polite to speak the truth. Ra wonders if Kelanda has any children—or *had* any at some point. Maybe a little sister? The woman would have made the best sister or mother, either way. Because Ra feels safe, empowered, and ready to charge behind Kelanda, into whatever battle they may face up ahead.

"Yes," Ra says. "Let's go."

Ra ignores the haunting vision of that woman's face, and follows Kelanda down the path, pushing through the foliage, keeping her vision trained ahead, careful not to step on a branch or visible tree root, while also being sure not to make too much noise. Kelanda warned her about what *could be* lurking in these woods.

Dark things. Worse things than men with swords and arrows.

Monsters.

They continue for about ten minutes until they come to the clearing that Mason scouted out an hour earlier. Kelanda raises her hand, halting Ra in her tracks. She creeps her way to the edge of the overlook and peers down at whatever is below—what Ra assumes is the target, the cottage holding a very prominent prisoner of Rovan.

The boy's father.

Ra wonders if she's supposed to eat his heart too or just the boy's. Then she shakes her head, ridding herself of those disgusting demands.

Just the boy's, a small voice whispers, echoing through the chambers of her darkest fears. *It will be delicious, I promise.*

The thought nauseates her, and she doesn't even want to contemplate the image of her sitting at a feast of hearts, digging into the organs with a sharp knife and ready fork.

Kelanda shakes off Ra's thoughts, summoning her to the edge of the overlook by wiggling her fingers. Ra creeps forward just as Kelanda had, gets close enough to the edge to peer over. Looking down, she takes in the expansive clearing in the middle of the woods, the small cottage surrounded by fruit trees and flowers she's never seen before, only read about in books, eye-popping colors that she never knew existed in real life. Marveling over the sights, she completely ignores the Rovan guards stationed around the cottage, and those hiding in the trees and bushes near the perimeter of the clearing.

"This is going to be tricky," Kelanda says, grabbing an arrow from her quiver and gently placing the poison-tipped projectile on the bow's shelf. "Don't touch the arrows. They've been dipped in blood rot. One prick will kill you faster than a guillotine drop." She raises the bow to her eye but doesn't notch the string. She waits.

For the signal.

It comes within minutes, a bright light flashing across the way —Ket and Mason using a pocket mirror and the sun to let them know they are ready for action.

"Here we go," Kelanda says, then holds her breath. Pulls back the string. Looses the first arrow.

The arrow is gone before Ra can blink. She tries to follow the arrow's path, but can't, only knows it landed when she sees the guard closest to them drop his shield and apply both hands to his bleeding throat. The guard sinks to his knees, tugging at the arrow, doing his best to free himself of the immense pain that must be firing through him. He falls into a pad of lilies and wildflowers, and Ra can't see if he removed the arrow before the fast-acting poison coursed through his bloodstream, effectively ending his life.

"One down," Kelanda says, already loading another arrow. They'll have to shoot quickly, now that the first has fallen.

Before she can fire the next shot, Ra sees movement from the north side of the property. A company of three heading toward the cottage. Two hooded—dwarves, maybe?—individuals being pushed along the path by a taller person, one that nearly causes Ra to shout.

She stands up, and momentum nearly carries her over the edge of the lookout.

Kelanda curses, drops her bow, and grabs fistfuls of Ra's clothing to pull her back. "What the hell's gotten into you, girl?"

"Him," she says, pointing at the three newcomers.

Following her finger, Kelanda mutters, "Shit. Unexpected company."

"That's Jester," she says, her trembling finger following the man walking behind the dwarves. "I know him. He was with Ket and me, traveling north. Then he left us."

"Well," Kelanda says, "what the fuck is he doing here?"

Ra doesn't have the slightest clue, but figures they won't have to wait long to find out. Rovan's finest are starting to notice their new arrivals.

A PERFECT DAY FOR MURDER

CHAPTER TWENTY-SEVEN

"Rule #1 for being the perfect court jester is simple, as it is in any art—always give the people what they want, no matter the personal cost."

– ADRIAN KEYMEISTER, *RULING THE KINGDOM WITH LAUGHTER: A GUIDE FOR JESTERS*

JESTER DIDN'T HAVE a plan when the cottage first peeked into view, through the army of trees standing guard at the bend in the path. He doesn't have one now as he pushes the boys forward, muttering obscenities in their innocent ears.

Innocent, he thinks. *Yeah, right.*

There are no innocent eyes and ears in these lands, not as far as he's concerned. By the time he was the boys' age, he had already seen his own mother murdered right before his eyes—savagely stabbed to death by a caravan of murderers who plagued the villages he grew up near, a quarter century ago. His father already left them before that, to join some civil war between neighboring Owlton cities, a war he had no business going off to.

His old man never returned from that war, and no one from the army ever reported his death.

He probably just left, Jester always assumed. *Just left us and never looked back.* There probably wasn't even a civil war either; when he was old enough, he went to a historical society in Braag, researched this alleged battle, and was shocked when he found nothing recorded in the history books dealing with Owlton affairs.

But the older he gets, the less he blames his old man for abandoning his family. Living in poverty in some Owlton village, barely scraping by for meals, working hard and gaining nothing for it; it all takes a toll on a person. And Jester doesn't blame him for wanting to start his life over somewhere new, with two fewer mouths to feed.

Thinking about his father gets him thinking back to the boy's father, and wondering why he's agreed to take this side trip in the first place—it seems like suicide.

The boy needs his father…

You heard his story…

He needs him.

Yes, before agreeing to come out here, he sat the boy—Thom, he had introduced himself as—down, along with the boy's friend, Fen, and listened to his tales. Thom kept it brief, for which Jester was thankful, but the part of the tale that intrigued Jester the most was the boy meeting his birth father and the exponential increase of his powers thereafter.

More than intriguing.

It seemed like a pretty obvious correlation. And Jester knows if he is to deliver the boy to the Warden of Iradon in return for his freedom—his true freedom—and to clear his name from stealing the Mind Stone, then he'll need both the boy and the old man.

Jester thinks the Warden will be pleased with his offer.

More than pleased.

The sackless brute might even throw in some extra coin in the deal.

Gold coin.

"Keep walking," Jester urges the two boys.

The friend, Fen, the wider of the two, glances back. "But... there are guards..."

"And I already told you—I will handle them. Properly."

As the cottage comes closer, he sees how many of Rovan's best have been stationed here, counts about twelve that he can see, and figures there are about another dozen he can't. The odds aren't great, but today is the perfect day for a mass murder—the sun is shining down through the trees and there is a crisp autumn chill in the air, the kind that dances icily down your spine when the wind hits right.

Passing by a rose bush, Jester spots two of the guards noticing him, their backs going rigid, their hands going to their sword hilts. Jester stops, grabs the two boys by the shoulders, and holds them close.

"Halt!" commands one of the guards—he's the first to draw his weapon.

"Gentlemen!" Jester announces, making a spectacle of things. Because there's no other way for a Jester to make an entrance. "I am honored to be in your presence! Such fine company from the looks of you!"

This confuses them. Six of the guards have clustered near the gate that opens to the cottage's front yard. They exchange glances, all of them returning their stares to Jester the moment they've decided that *this is not normal.*

One of them, a gruff-looking fellow with a dangling auburn beard, expands his eyes, like he's just witnessed the second coming of Highbeard—and in a way, Jester thinks maybe he has.

"Highbeard's balls!" the guard shouts, pointing at the boy, clearly recognizing his face, what he can see in the shadow of his hood. "It's HIM!"

One by one, like they've all been infected by the same enlightening truth, their eyes light up. As if realizing what they must do, they draw their blades, pointing their tips at Jester's heart.

"Now, gentlemen," Jester says with a proud grin. "I was

hoping to resolve this matter peacefully, without the need for violence." He speaks this last part with a giggle in his throat.

When the guards advance on him, he bends down and whispers in the boys' ears, "This is the part where you two run inside, and don't come out until the screams die."

KILLING FIELD

CHAPTER TWENTY-EIGHT

"Love nature, all of it. The trees we climb, the waters we swim, the air we breathe. Let it fill our senses in abundance. Humankind is nothing without an environment to prosper."

– THE WORD ACCORDING TO CIMINEN

———

"SHIT," Ket mutters, watching the three unexpected wanderers shuffle down the path, enter the valley, and step onto the playing field. *Killing field,* Ket silently reminds himself. That's exactly what this area will become. Unless there's a new development over the next couple of minutes, these guards will fall to Kelanda's bow.

But she hasn't fired once since the arrival of these three travelers, two of whom he doesn't recognize—but one face is familiar. One face he'll never forget.

"Who the hell are these bunch?" Mason asks, his hand remaining still on the hilt of his sword. "Ket?"

"One of them I know—he was the one I told you about, traveled with us from Hornrake. I was imprisoned with him in Ragland's dungeon."

"The Jester?"

Ket nods. Then he eyes the two smaller figures, which from his vantage point, look like children.

Slowly, he realizes who at least one of them is, and Ket's heart plummets.

"Oh no…" he says, standing up.

"What are you doing?" Mason grabs him, pulling him back down to a squat. "You'll give up our position!" he yells in a hoarse whisper.

"It's him, Mason," Ket says, not taking his eyes off the boy. "It's the Boy. The prophecy…he's here."

"Horseshit," Mason grumbles. "You think Ravenborn would let that creature stray from the Silver Towers, eh? They have that boy chained to the Tower walls, I'll bet my last coin on it."

Ket doesn't have the heart to tell him he'd lose his last coin, because he can tell one of the boys that Jester is shoving along is indeed the boy they are looking for.

Jester found him first. How?

Ket guesses it doesn't matter how, that the simple explanation *"Jester is just superior at finding things"* is as good as he'll receive.

"It's him," Ket says, based on nothing but a quick glance at the boy's face. "I know it is."

"Suppose it is," Mason says, yielding to the argument with a sigh. "What does that do for our plan now?"

"Well," says Ket, not needing to give it much thought, "it means we don't have to march into the Rovan capital and storm the Silver Towers."

"Well…*good*. But…do we just take him here?"

"We already have him. Jester is with us."

"Is he now?" Raising his brow, Mason glances over at Ket. "Because if he's with us, why isn't he *with* us?"

"We're all going to the same place—back to Hornrake, to Ragland, to hand the boy over in exchange for our freedoms."

Right? doubts a little voice in the back of his head. *Are you sure about that?* another asks, and this voice he recognizes—it's Jennah, his voice of reason. Of superior intelligence. And right now she's asking the questions he needs to hear. Needs to answer. "Shit," he says, realizing she may be right. As well as Mason.

"I believe your friend has an ulterior motive," Mason says, nodding at the field of view below them. "Otherwise—he wouldn't be here, would he?"

"Shit," Ket says again, like it's the only word he now knows. Things have just gotten a whole lot messier.

This *Killing Field* has just gotten a whole lot bloodier.

"We stick to the plan," Ket says, nodding ahead. "Signal Kelanda and tell her to keep firing. They haven't caught onto that first death yet."

"Preoccupied by the new distraction, just like us."

"That's right. Let's use that to our advantage. Have her cull the herd."

Mason swallows, then uses the mirror and positions the small reflective oval in front of the beams of sunlight that slant through the gaps in the hanging vegetation. He flashes the signal. Seconds later, another arrow flies, taking down its target.

Mason gives Ket the thumbs up. "We're back in business."

Ket nods, watches another guard take an arrow in the back, tumble down the lush, grass-covered hill near the outskirts of the valley.

Watches the green stain red.

RUN

CHAPTER TWENTY-NINE

"Anyone who runs from battle is a coward, and I shall personally see to it that they earn a blade across their neck."

———

THOM SPRINTS TOWARD THE FENCE, sensing his friend's presence behind him. He doesn't bother using the gate; instead, he grips two pickets, plants his feet, and launches himself in the air, vaulting the barrier in one single, athletic leap. He sneaks a glance over his shoulder, sees Fen struggling, though he doesn't require a sturdy arm to help him over—fear is a potent motivator. Once the boys are past the fence, Jester strikes first, swinging his sword at one of the guards. The guard parries the attack and catches Jester in the face with an elbow. The guards quickly surround Jester on three sides, circling him like desert hyenas targeting wounded prey. A few others have strayed from their posts to come see what the fuss is all about.

Thom doesn't wait for the guards to take down Jester—he knows it's coming, and he doesn't need to witness the man's murder, even though he terrifies Thom the same way the boogeyman under the bed does most children. Jester is a killer, plain and simple—Thom saw that firsthand when he dispatched the two bandits—and Thom feels no safer in his presence than he would marching up the mountains and running into a swarm of Wilder men.

Once Fen catches up, Thom sprints for his father's front door. Without knocking, he barges inside and shuts the door quickly behind them after Fen crosses the threshold. He seals out the noise, the clash of metal-on-metal, and keeps his shoulder pressed against the door as if someone from the outside intends on battering their way through.

"What is the meaning of this?" Jerrin says from his seat in the living room. The hearth next to him is lit, kicking out embers that swirl and dance in the air before disappearing.

"Father!" Thom says, ripping himself away from the door and hustling into the next room. "We're being attacked!"

Jerrin doesn't seem to understand. Confusion pushes his brow up near his receding hairline. "What are you doing here, Thom?"

"I've come to rescue you," the boy says, as if the answer is obvious. "From captivity."

Jerrin's confusion smooths out, and a smile (that isn't much of a smile at all) overtakes his lips. "Thom…that is…very thoughtful of you. But you cannot rescue me."

"We can!" Thom rushes over to him, grabs his hands, and tries to yank him to his feet. "Let's go!"

Jerrin remains glued to his seat. Thom tries harder to remove him, but the old man keeps his bottom stationed where it is.

"Father?" Thom's eyes demand an explanation, something to make sense of this. Surely the man should be on board with his scheme, even though it's been placed on him so suddenly. *Why won't you let me help you?* he thinks. "The guards—they are distracted. There's a man outside—"

"Ravenborn will not allow me to leave," Jerrin says, his voice trembling, like when someone musters a ton of courage to speak truths people do not like to hear.

And Thom does not like this truth. "Ravenborn isn't here!" he practically shouts, not caring if he sounds disobedient. "We can leave before he even knows what happened!"

Eyes falling on the stack of books near his feet, Jerrin shakes his head. "No, son. Ravenborn is most definitely here—maybe not inside the valley, but he's close. I can feel him." Now his eyes shift back to Thom. "I bet if you search hard enough, you'll sense him too."

Thom swallows. His father is right. Of course he is. It doesn't take someone with special abilities to know that Ravenborn is not far behind. That he's racing toward this valley at speeds that threaten his own safety. Even if they leave now, Ravenborn will eventually catch them.

Running is useless.

"I don't want to go back," Thom says. "He can't make me."

"Son..."

"He can't!"

"Son, please..."

"I HATE HIM."

A book flies off the shelf, goes straight through a window on the opposite wall.

Fen ducks, even though the book is already past him and never even came within striking distance. Jerrin doesn't flinch, not even after peering at the damage, the shattered window glass. Instead, he sighs, like it's more annoying than surprising.

"Son," Jerrin starts again, pressing his fingers against his temples. "This is the way it is. The way it must be."

Tears building in his eyes, Thom begins to lose control of his emotions. Everything inside his body feels like it's melting down, a molten river of liquefied vital organs. "Why won't you fight?"

Jerrin peers up at him, looking as if he wants to shed a tear or two. "It's not that simple, boy. For years I've thought about fighting back. For years...that's all I wanted to do. But you see—if

I had done that, then I would have never gotten to see you. Looked upon your face. Saw that you have your mother's hair. Her lips." He smiles warmly. "Her sweetness. And her instincts to fight, apparently."

Thom wipes his nose on his sleeve. "And what do I have of yours?"

Jerrin offers a faint laugh, but Thom doesn't find much humor in the situation, or the proposed question. "Well, you have my elbows."

"Elbows?" It sounds funny, and he wants to laugh, but his anger and determination won't let him. He holds it in, growing angrier with his father and his refusal to leave this prison, disguised as a suitable home. "Father, I don't—"

"And you may not have the *shape* of my eyes, but you do have my eyes." There's a twinkle in his gaze, and Thom gets the distinct sense he's looking into a mirror, though the reflection is showing him something different from what it should be. "It was passed down through me, Thom. And I gave it to you."

"What was?"

" 'What was?' " he repeats with a chuckle. "What do you think? Our family's disease, that haunts us like ghosts. We are descendants of the old gods. Which one, we do not rightly know." He shakes his head. "For whatever reason, you were chosen. Born with the mark of the stars, and you must carry out your duty as you get older."

"Why? Why do I have to? Why can't they just leave me alone?"

Jerrin shakes his head. "Because..." He glances to the broken window as if that's evidence enough. "That's why. You're too powerful, son. This is only a fraction of what you will be capable of when you get older, near your eighteenth birthday. You will be the most powerful of all of them."

"All of them?" Thom doesn't understand, isn't sure he wants to.

"The others like you."

"Others like me?"

"You're rare, one of a kind—but there will be others like you, other children born around your time who have incredible powers and abilities—and they will want to harm you."

"Why? Why would they want to harm me? What have I done to them?"

Jerrin sighs as if he's out of breath. Or simply tired of telling stories. But Thom's stare begs for more. "You haven't done anything to them, yet. But there will come a time when you have a choice to make—either restore the Five Realms or destroy it forever. Sides will be chosen. Wars will be fought. The End of Everything will be a nasty business."

"I don't want that, I don't want any of that."

Jerrin nods like he understands. "I know. I don't want that for you either. But sometimes, son, we do not get to choose what the fates have in store for us. We do not get to cut our own path. We must walk the one destined for us, and we can only stray so far before we loop back around, before the path finds us again— which is why I cannot run away with you." He glances up at the door, eyeing the oaken barrier like it's a thing that's caused him great anguish. "And it is why I cannot let you leave."

"Father?"

"Thom," Fen says, backing away. Thom doesn't notice the hearth growing darker, the flames dying some. But Fen seems to notice—it's all he can look at. "Thom, I think we should be going."

Jerrin leans forward in his chair, raises his hand, his fist uncurling, fingers splayed like he's reaching to grab a doorknob. His face changes. Thom steps back, not liking the way his flesh morphs, the way it mutates into something hideous—like a monster, only worse. Because it is his father's face, only it's not.

It's godlike.

"Father?" Thom says, his voice small because it feels like a belt has been tied around his throat, making it hard to breathe, to speak. "Father...what..."

Something pulls on his shoulder and Thom yelps. He spins, sees Fen pulling on him, tugging him toward the door.

A bookcase separates from the wall and falls forward like a soldier taking an arrow in the back, nearly crushing both boys, misses them by a few steps. The boys jump back and press themselves against the far wall.

"I've tried to keep this from you," Jerrin says, his flesh sagging now, nearly falling off his face. Like he's been wearing a mask the whole time, and the glue holding it over his true form is melting, liquefying. His eyes become black beads made from the same dark as outer space, nothing there to confirm his humanity—he's mostly monster now, one that will haunt Thom's dreams for years to come. *Decades.*

My entire life, he thinks, now realizing his father may be dangerous—might hurt him. Even if he doesn't want to.

Whatever is inside him might want to.

"Thom!" Fen shouts, yanking on his clothing, trying to tear his friend away from imminent disaster.

"I went a long time before revealing this to your mother…" Jerrin says, falling out of his chair, landing on his knees, as if he's suddenly come down with the urge to pray and worship. He even clasps his hands together. "But the power of Arkos is too strong. Sometimes I can't help it…it…it changes me…" The facial skin around his eyes and mouth has thinned out, becoming translucent like a shedding snake. Thom can see Jerrin's muscle and bone beneath his almost transparent flesh. Jerrin applies his hands to the human mask and rakes away fingers full of dead, dying skin. Blood drips from the fresh trenches he's carved into his face by simply exfoliating. No matter how gentle Jerrin is with his removal, the skin falls, and so do droplets of fresh scarlet. "*It makes me a monster…*"

His voice changes, growing hoarse and gruff. Like the monster he claims to be.

Will this happen to me? Thom wonders to himself. *Will I become…that?*

He doesn't know what *that* is, but his father mentioned Arkos, and well—he has a pretty good idea.

He's a demon...

From Arkos's Darkhell...

"Thom," Fen says, grabbing the boy by the waist now, dragging him toward the door.

"*I wish I could have helped you!*" Jerrin says, crawling now—not toward them, but toward the hearth, which has been renewed, has come alive with furious bursts of hot flames and ash. Jerrin nears the hearth, the orange fire burning bright in his black eyes. "*I wish I had more time to tell you the truth...about me, about us...about everything.*"

Thom shakes his head, wishing he understood more, wishing he could leave this place with more answers than questions.

Before he can profess his hunger for this knowledge, Jerrin cranes his head toward the boy and whispers, "*You must destroy them all. Before they destroy you. That is what must happen.*"

Before Thom can open his mouth and request clarification, Jerrin dives headfirst into the hearth, screaming the second the flames welcome him inside. The fire dances hungrily as the orange spreads over his face, down his back, igniting his clothes in a glorious, sunny glow. Despite his agonizing screams, Jerrin keeps his face positioned inside the flames, allowing the fire to melt away his flesh, transforming his skin into a canvas of black char.

Thom cries out and lunges forward, wishing to remove his father from this self-inflicted tragedy, but Fen stops him, wrestles him to the ground.

"NO!" Thom shouts, reaching for him, for Jerrin's boot, which isn't that far out of reach—but Fen stops that too.

Within seconds the fire has spread across him, and Jerrin has stopped screaming, lying still as the flames die down. Some of the flames have jumped from his body to the window drapes, and fallen embers have scattered across the floor, sparking up the bear rug near the chair, both exploding with hellfire.

It won't be long before everything burns. Before the two boys are one with the flame.

Fen grips Thom, who feels lifeless, empty and floating. He hoists his best friend to his feet, tries to usher Thom toward the door, screaming in his ear, relaying the message over and over; they need to get out of there or they will suffer the same fate, go up like tinder, their little boy bones burning like papyrus.

But Thom hardly hears him, his message.

Everything is still and silent in Thom's world.

Nothing gets through.

Then he blinks, realizes the whole living room is decorated in flames—even the ceiling—and he begins to cough. The thick smoke fills up the room while working its way into his lungs.

He lets Fen drag him to the door, the heat on his face threatening to transform his skin to a burnt brisket. He stumbles, backwards, the door flinging open, and his legs twist him around, sending him pirouetting through the mayhem that overloads his senses.

Men scream; some roaring like the lions in fables, some wailing like sick babies. Metal clashes together. Arrows whistle through the air before punching into their targets. Blood soaks the lawn, speckling the shrubbery and flower gardens. The stench of a thousand coppers assaults his nasal passages.

The fire may be behind him, but hell is still waiting.

THE BATTLE
CHAPTER THIRTY

"The only wars that should be fought, should be in my defense. Anyone who initiates war for any other reason should perish a thousand times over in the flame-world of Arkos's Darkhell."

– THE WORD ACCORDING TO THE HIGHBEARD

———

DARKO RAVENBORN'S heart stammers in his chest as he enters the valley and comes speeding down the hill on the back of his mare, his crew in tow, riding as if their very lives depend on it. It's not any one particular thing that kicks his heart into this strange arrhythmia, but a collection of the sights before him. The first thing he notices is that the small troop stationed here have banded together on Jerrin's front lawn, and all of them have their swords drawn, actively positioned for a fight. It seems they're only fighting one person, a traveler wearing a jester's hat, who's also brandished a weapon—something cheap and dull from his perspective—but also forged in some black element, much like his own weapon. In any case, his guards have taken turns swiping at the jester, and in a few seconds, the peculiar-looking bandit will be surrounded, have nowhere to escape, and Ravenborn's men will shove their swords into him, taking him down.

But before they can, the second thing wrong with this picture enters Ravenborn's view—it's the cottage itself.

It's been swallowed by hellfire.

The second his eyes fall upon the roiling back smoke shooting out from the windows, the hot glow within, his nose locates the ashy scents of everything inside burning to a crisp.

He wonders if Jerrin is still inside.

Then a worse thought slugs him like a drumstick hitting a village warning bell—*what if the Boy is? What if he's burning to death right now?*

Horror seizes control of his body, and sweat begins to dampen his raven-feathered tunic.

He points to the fire, commands two of his closest soldiers to inspect the cottage, drag out any survivors (or corpses), and then clear everyone out of the way.

That's when more trouble arises, in the form of an arrow landing squarely in the chest of the soldier to his left, knocking him clean off his horse. The man falls, dead before the hard ground breaks his neck. Ravenborn scans the trees, the endless groves that cover the hills surrounding this valley, wondering where the attack has come from, and who's doing the attacking.

Nothing adds up.

Nothing makes sense.

And Ravenborn feels both hopeless and helpless as his horse takes him forward, toward the burning cottage, great roils of black smoke unfurling into the sky above.

As his men surround the Jester, they are taken out, one by one. Arrows strike them in their chests, their necks, some of them taking shafts through their legs. Screams rip across the valley. Ravenborn still can't locate the archer, but he's stopped trying. He's worried about the fire, the Boy; his safety is his chief concern. This jester and his friends, whatever they're planning, is ancillary.

They want the Boy, a voice speaks up, echoing deep from within his mind's catacombs. *They've come to steal him away from you. These are Southern men.*

From Owlton.

That's Emperor Salah's voice, his grating tone. It's easier to ignore when the man isn't in his face, spouting commands, sending him on arduous tasks, and floating wild conspiracy theories that make little-to-no sense. The man's been so paranoid over the last several years—his trail of insanity stretching far enough back, expressing his concerns almost daily—that it's not hard for Ravenborn to dismiss his voice.

But this phantom voice of the king speaks the truth—or, at least, Ravenborn is starting to believe it. Maybe these *are* men from Owlton. Maybe King Ragland *is* reigniting the old war, and this is his first attack in over a decade.

The walls of the temporary peace have come crashing down; this is it.

War again.

This is how it starts, and maybe in ten or twenty years they will trace the new war's last battle back to a single moment—this one. When Owlton grew balls and sent spies into the Silver City, child abductors, to steal away Salah's most prized possession: the Boy with the Star-Shaped Eyes.

The jester runs his sword through a guard's abdomen, lops off the head of another a second later. As he gets closer, Ravenborn witnesses his mad smile crawling across the jester's face, from the sheer delight he's having while slaying these men. And when Ravenborn gets even closer, he can see the smile is not natural—his lips have been elongated in the form of two thick keloid scars.

Ravenborn dismounts his mare and draws his sword. Another arrow speeds out of the misty hills, and sails into a guard, facing Jester. The guard spins 180 degrees in the air before crashing to the ground. He squirms in a flower bed, writhing, trying to pull the arrow free, but Jester ends his struggles by stabbing the man in the throat, severing his connection to the material realm.

It infuriates Ravenborn. He advances on Jester, his sword

arcing back in a furious swing. Jester adjusts, blocking the attack. He crouches, a defensive stance that's ready for another wild hack, but Ravenborn doesn't grant his invitation. Instead, he hangs back, holding his sword across his chest, playing defense too, inviting Jester to take a swing, attempting to lure him onto the offense, into an off-balanced position, so Ravenborn can strike, and strike true. But Jester doesn't fall for the setup, and the two begin to circle each other, their speed no faster than a dry slug.

"I love your feathers," Jester says, smiling with his eyes.

"Who are you?" Ravenborn strikes, a weak attack that doesn't leave his body exposed for a counter. Jester nonchalantly blocks, parrying Ravenborn's sword with ease.

"That is a long story, friend," Jester says. "Perhaps we should discuss it over tea. An ale? I could go for either right now."

"Who sent you?" Ravenborn barks, his patience thinning. Not that he had much to start with.

"That's even a longer story—most of which will probably bore you to tears."

One of the guards tries to take the Jester from behind, but the man is good, senses the attack coming, and dips out of the way. The guard lunges past him, off-balance, and Jester drives his sword through the man's back, then retracts his blade. He kicks the dying man forward into a spreading puddle of his own leaky red.

Jester whirls back to face Ravenborn. "As we were saying? Oh, yes—very boring tale. I suppose you're here to recover the boy?"

"Yes," Ravenborn grunts. "Where is he?"

"Well, I saw him go in there…" Jester nods to the cottage, the blazing inferno.

The Boy.

It can't be.

"That's right," Jester says, a smile in his voice. "I bet he's awfully crispy by now."

"You lie!" Ravenborn shouts, then spins on his adversary, swinging for his head.

Jester leans back, dodging the blade, the tip missing his neck by mere inches. "Look at this honest smile. Trust me when I say I'm crying on the inside."

"Tell me where he is, and I shall spare your life!"

Another arrow whistles past Ravenborn's ear, and he wonders if it had been aimed at his head.

"Let me live?" Jester cackles with amusement. "That's a riot. If you're lucky, I'll let *you* live. And you don't look that lucky."

"Call off your archers in the trees," Ravenborn demands.

Jester's smile changes, still there, but less now. "*My* archers? You're sorely mistaken and have misinterpreted the scenario, Mr. Blackfeathers."

"My name is Darko Ravenborn," he says, furious. Tired of the game, this Jester's flippant responses and carefree regard. "I am the first general of Emperor Salah's army, the lord of death, the North-born raven—cousin of the king, and proud to serve the Rovan Territories."

"That's..." Jester says, breathing out a long sigh, "quite a mouthful. You should really look into shortening all of that, for the sake of brevity."

Darko's thoughts go white with fury. He can't think of anything else but what this man's head will look like on a pike in Silver City Square. He rushes forward, attacking with only basic instinct motoring his functions—his need to kill. To slaughter.

"Ravenborn!" a voice calls out behind him.

Everything stops.

Everything.

A few swords fall to the earth. He hears some of his men—the ones still left—gasp, as if a worse horror has fallen upon them. But they aren't reacting to it, just stopping and standing and looking at whoever has come to introduce themselves.

That voice, though.

No.

Ravenborn blinks, unable to believe what his ears tell him. *It can't be...*

"Lay down your sword," the man says.

Ravenborn does no such thing, but he turns to the voice, expecting to hear another whistling arrow, the final arrow he'll ever hear—but the arrows have stopped. Perhaps…this man was the archer all along.

It can't be…

But it is. He turns and sees him, the face from his past, coming toward him, walking with his chest forward, sword drawn and ready to take on metal and bone. His hair is longer. A beard covers his once-youthful face. There are more lines in his forehead, around his eyes. He looks bigger and bulkier, like he's been keeping in shape. Keeping strong.

Ravenborn can barely coax his voice into action. But he manages two words: "Hello…son."

HELLO FATHER
CHAPTER THIRTY-ONE

"To thieve a human soul is the most dangerous risk another human can attempt. To be human and strive to be godlike is invariably foolhardy."

– ANSON WELLES, *POWERS OF THE GODS*

———

KET HAS PREPARED for this moment ever since he left Rovan at the end of the Last War. What he'd say when he got here. What he'd do. But it all went out the window when faced with the actual moment, when the man who helped deliver him into this world is standing in front of him again, looking thirteen-plus years older than the last time they saw each other.

He's wearing the same confused expression—right where they left off. Two men, eyeing each other down, neither knowing what to say, or how to officially end things. Last time, they parted without surrendering to their violent tendencies.

But this time a fight is inevitable.

Last time he let me go. Last time I was his son.

Now I'm Ket. A stranger to him.

No, not a stranger—a defector, a traitor, a rebel against the

Rovan Empire. Worse than a stranger, much worse. An enemy of the territories.

"Hello, father," Ket says to Ravenborn. "It's been a long time."

Ravenborn's mouth drops open. A few of the soldiers look to their leader for counsel, but Ravenborn is too stunned to give even the simplest command.

Finally, a guard speaks. "I thought your son was dead," the man says, loud enough for anyone standing nearby to hear.

"So did I," Ravenborn replies, finally able to find his voice. "Imagine my surprise at this moment. William..."

"Tell your men to lay down their swords," Ket says, "or I'll have my archer end them all."

"Do not lay down your swords," Ravenborn snaps, half-turning to his second in charge. "He's bluffing."

Ket, confused, points to the fallen men, evidence to the contrary. "You wish to see your whole troop massacred, that's on you. I assumed you'd have gotten smarter over the last thirteen years—not more foolish."

"It's good to see you, son," Ravenborn says, ignoring the insult. "Why don't *you* lay down your swords—all of your men— and have your archer come down from his elevated position, so the lot of us can hold palaver. Get to the bottom of what to do next." His eyes flick behind Ket, to where he knows Mason has the two kids by the neck, holding them in place—they're scared, covered in ashy soot, and trembling, but more importantly, they're not going anywhere. "And have that buffoon release those children into my custody."

"I'm afraid that can't happen," Ket replies. "The kids—I'm taking them. Actually, you can have the chubby one. I just need the Boy."

Ravenborn's men stand upright at this announcement, positioning their swords at a suitable angle for slicing.

"Hold," the Rovan general says, raising a fist. Ket can sense the impending violence in the air, the way one can scent fresh rain on a wild breeze. "William...whatever you're doing...whatever you're involved in…we can fix it. We can make things right again. Just like the old days. Your brothers…they miss you."

Ket doesn't respond. He holds firm to his position, about fifteen feet away from his father, looking in the direction of where Kelanda and Ra remain well hidden; although he can't see them, he knows they're there, waiting for his command.

"Come home, son," he says. "I will speak with Salah. He will pardon you for your transgressions against the Territories, and he will—"

"Fuck that," one of Ravenborn's men spits, his face flush with anger. His eyes hunger for Ket's blood, and Ket suspects he knows why—the man wants to make a statement, here and now. Wants to be the brave Rovan warrior who brings home the head of the most infamous, traitorous filth the North has ever known. Boost his name and create a legacy that will never be forgotten in the Silver Halls. "I will not have you bring this traitor back to the Silver Towers and spout lies to the Emperor! We know the truth now, *General*. He betrayed us during the Last War, and you let him go. Didn't you? You let him go and then lied to us, everyone, including the Emperor himself, telling us that the Soulthefter had died in battle."

"Soulthefter…" Jester says, gripping his chin. "I must say, I saw this news coming."

Ket, and everyone else, ignore him.

"I will not let that happen, General," the man says defiantly, pointing the tip of his sword at Ravenborn's chest. "I will not have you make a mockery of our people. Of our lands. And of our Emperor."

Ravenborn smirks, like he's amused by the threat of mutiny. "Lay down your sword, Gobbles."

Gobbles does no such thing.

"*Now!*" Ravenborn spits with tremendous fury, his eyes shadowing over. "Before I cut you down here, right in front of everyone."

Gobbles runs his tongue through his thickening smile. "No,

Ravenborn. You will not." The other men turn their swords on their general. The red swelling in the general's face fades some, is replaced by a quick flash of worry that he quickly masks with more rage. He puffs his chest. "Your time in the Silver City is over. We are tired of your follies, tired of the Emperor always backing you through thick and thin—he doesn't know how to shed dead-weight, doesn't realize *you* are the one dragging the realm down. If it weren't for you, your carelessness…your loyalty to your fami-ly…" Gobbles turns an eye on Ket. "Loyalty to traitors…if it weren't for you, we would have won the Last War. Not been forced to retreat and give up our expansion into the Crosslands."

"You pathetic welp," Ravenborn snaps. "I will murder you for your—"

"Silence!" Gobbles shouts back. "No more talking, Darko. That's all you do—talk, talk, talk. Well, no one is listening to you anymore. You've had your time. It ends, now."

"You'll kill me, is that it?" Ravenborn looks around at his remaining men, watching their line of sight shift as they avoid direct eye contact with the man they are keen on initiating a mutiny against. "You'll return to the Silver City with tales of my demise? Tell Salah I was cut down in battle?"

"Yes," Gobbles says, seemingly delighted by the plan. "Yes, exactly."

"My sons—my other sons. They will succeed me."

"We will handle them. It's time your family's run in the Silver City came to an end."

Ravenborn's eyes dart between the men before him, as if he's predicting where the first attack will come from. Although scared and tentative, the men stretch their arms, loosening their joints, preparing to carry out Gobbles's plan, whether fully on board or not. Ravenborn grips his sword with both hands and bends his knees, taking a defensive stance.

Ket feels sorry for him. Wishes he could help. Wishes he could provide his father with the same opportunity that he was given all those years back—a way out. Another chance at a new life. But he doesn't see one.

"Father," Ket says, raising his hand, bringing his fingers together. "I truly am sorry. For everything." He snaps his fingers.

An arrow zips from the trees, hits a soldier dead in the ribs, finding the weakness between the armor plates and punching the wind right out of him. Wheezing, the soldier falls to the ground, dropping his sword and clamping both hands around the shaft, tugging and pulling to no avail. Blood spurts out of him, staining the nearby flowers.

Gobbles screams, hoists his sword in the air, then leads the charge at Ravenborn. Ket's father lifts his sword and shuffles his feet, his quick footwork already in action. Defeating a dozen trained soldiers seems unlikely, but Ket's underestimated his father before.

He readies his nerves and raises his blade, then looks back to Mason one last time. "Keep the boys safe," he says, and Mason nods, tightening his grip around the kids' shoulders.

A blink later, Ket charges into the fray, slicing his way through, cutting his way back to freedom, keeping his own boys' lives in his thoughts as he commits to the bloody brawl, the sickening violence, crossing lines he swore he never would again.

RA MEETS THE BOY (CUT OUT HIS HEART)

CHAPTER THIRTY-TWO

"If I were to come across one of these prophesied children, I'd smother them in their cribs. No human being should be imbued with godlike powers. It's nonsense. And our kingdom won't stand for it."

– KING ELVIS BARTHOLOMEW RAGLAND,
THE 6TH KING OF OWLTON

"SHIT," Kelanda says, watching the men charge at Ravenborn, wildly swinging their swords, trying to cut the man in half with unskilled attempts.

"What is it?" Ra asks. She's about fifteen feet back from the leafy window overlooking the valley, the vantage point Kelanda chose to loose her arrows upon the guardsmen. Her fingernails have been gnawed bloody.

"Things are getting heated down there. Ket has engaged."

"Engaged?"

Kelanda summons her over, nodding to the action taking place below them.

Ra hustles to the edge, has herself a peek through the foliage. "Oh no…"

She watches Ket cut through a man, ripping open his victim's stomach with his blade, spilling his insides across the green grass. Once the man has fallen dead, Ket turns his attention to the next; this time, he chops down, cleaving off a man's arm at the shoulder. Worse than the violent images imprinting on her is the look in Ket's eyes, the smoothness of his motions. How easy and graceful it all looks. Like it's automatic, built into his behavior. Normalized.

Ra shakes her head, looks away.

"I have to help them," Kelanda says, nodding back to the fray. "There's too many Rovan soldiers, and Mason has his hands full with those kids."

"Kids?" Ra was so focused on Ket's disturbing acts of violence that she hadn't noticed Mason and the two boys.

Kelanda points, and Ra sees them.

"I have to help," Kelanda says. "Meaning I have to go down there."

Ra nods. "I'm coming with you."

Kelanda shakes her head. "No, I promised Ket I'd keep you safe."

"Leaving me alone is not keeping me safe. I'm coming with—"

"It's safer up here than it is down there," Kelanda says, her no-nonsense tone making Ra feel guilty for even speaking up. "You know how to shoot a bow?"

Ra shakes her head.

"Dammit." Kelanda hands her the bow, unshoulders her quiver, and hands that over too. "You understand the premise. You've seen me do it."

"I've never shot an arrow before."

"You'll learn quickly. Just do what I did. Practice on that tree while I'm gone." She nods somewhere behind Ra, but to which tree she's referring, Ra doesn't know. There are too many trees to choose from.

"Be safe," Kelanda says, pulling out two daggers that were strapped to her thighs. Ra hadn't realized they were there, hidden beneath the hem of her cloak. "I'll be back to get you before you know it."

With that, she's off, sliding down the hill, toward the valley, charging into battle to help her friends.

Ra watches, anxiety mounting in her chest. It's only a few minutes later before she decides she can't stay here. The woods behind her creak, whisper to her. Tell her there's something back there, hiding amongst the shadows, waiting to pop out any second now, something big with a wide and cavernous maw, a monstrous creature from her nightmares, come to gobble her up.

She can't stay.

Can't.

She grabs the bow and quiver, though she has no idea what she'll do with them, and exits the woods, following Kelanda's path. When she reaches the aperture overlooking the valley, she sees the fight below has intensified. Clouds of dirt, kicked up during the scuffle, shroud the battle in a brown fog. She can't tell who's winning or losing, can't make out Ket behind the dirty veil. For all she knows, he's been killed already.

No, Ket can't die.

He CAN'T.

He promised to protect me. To look after me. He PROMISED.

She wonders what Borgadine would tell her, if he were here, alive. He would have probably told her to be smart, to hang back and listen to her elders—but she's already established that staying put is off the table. Her eyes roam the valley and find the house that's roasting inside the conflagration, huge tongues of flames lapping at the sky. The structure has mostly collapsed in on itself, reduced to a heap of smoking char. Beyond the burning house she sees three figures; Mason and the two boys. It looks like the boys are struggling to break free of Mason's hold, and it looks like Mason is having a tough time keeping them clustered.

Kill him, a voice says, a whisper in her ear. She turns to the voice, but no one is there—just the trees drenched in shadows, a slight breeze swimming through the branches. *Rip out his heart. Eat it. Bite into it like the Forbidden Apple, sink your teeth into his life. Consume the Boy, his Power.*

She puts her hands over her ears, but it does nothing to drive out the phantom voice.

The voice is in her.

It *is* her. What she's becoming.

"Stop," she whispers back to it, thinking of other things, hoping to distract herself, hoping that doing so will drive out the mysterious speaker.

The voice doesn't let up, but gets quieter. So, she decides to picture Borgadine's face, the smile he wore whenever she did something he was proud of, whenever she used her ability in a way that pleased him—moving an object ever-so-slightly with her mind or accessing someone else's thoughts, gaining insight into something she had no business knowing. Little things that happened during their travels. Victories that amused him.

Before she knows it, she's walking across the valley toward the boy. She doesn't know how this will play out, but she thinks this feels right, like it's supposed to happen. Her meeting him. *Borgadine would want this.* For the two of them to meet. And the Fairy Godmother? Ra doesn't trust her, not one bit, and maybe she wants him dead for a different reason, a sinister cause. Maybe she can talk to the boy—maybe he dreams too?

Maybe they can solve this puzzle together.

Lots of maybes. No answers. No reason for her to put her faith in anything she's thought of over the last few minutes.

Maybe she should wait for Ket?

But he could be dead. He was outnumbered from the start. There's no way he could take on those men and kill them all. Not even with Kelanda and her twin daggers coming to the rescue.

She's close to them now. The boy. His friend. Mason struggling to contain them.

"Stop struggling, you shits!" Mason shouts.

She doesn't know why, but she walks up to them and tells Mason, "Let them go."

All three of them freeze, gazing at her like some uninvited guest. She stands before them, breathing heavily, and the boy's eyes, their star-shaped pattern, trap her attention and refuse to let go. His hypnotic eyes lure her into a sleepy state, as if the cosmic colors within hold access to some other world, and the longer she stares, the more lost within them she becomes.

Kill him.

Now's your chance.

Reach into his chest and pluck out his—

"Who are you?" the boy asks, swallowing, like he's afraid— like he's more afraid of Ralyanna than he is of Mason, or any adult holding sharp weapons.

"My name is..." she starts, then almost uses one of her old names, a name from way back, before Borgadine gave her her current alias. "My name is Ralyanna," she finishes. "But everyone calls me *Ra.*"

"Ra," the boy repeats, seemingly fond of how easily it rolls off his tongue.

"Ralyanna," Mason says, gripping the boys closer now, tucking them against his hips, one on each. "Ra, what are you doing here? Where's Kelanda?"

In response she turns toward the inferno, the blaze that's starting to die down on its own, having no more structure to feed from.

"No," Mason gasps, his grasp on the boys forgotten. The pudgy boy seizes the opportunity, cranks back his arm, and drives his elbow into Mason's groin. Mason doubles over, his face scrunching up, wrinkling like someone's driven a stake into him and not a bony elbow.

She can't sympathize, but it looks really painful. He stumbles forward, lands on his knees, and begins coughing.

"Run!" the pudgy one says, pushing the boy away from Mason's weakening grip. The two boys separate themselves as

Mason reaches out, one last feeble attempt to corral them—which fails, of course, and the two boys begin to sprint away, in the opposite direction of the fire.

"Kelanda…" Mason says, forgetting all about the boys. He gathers himself to his feet, then starts to limp toward the smoke and dust clouds beginning to overtake the entire valley—or most of it. He hobbles toward the fight.

Ra turns her back on him, concentrating on the boys. "Hey, wait up!" she shouts.

But the boys do not listen. They run toward freedom, and Ra runs after them. They have a good head start, but the boys are slower, especially the pudgy one. She catches up to him, grips him by the back of his tunic and yanks him back. He makes a stran-gled, choked yelp—*ycck!* The noise draws the boy's attention, and the kid stops in his tracks, spins back toward his friend.

"Let him go!" he cries out, panic seizing his face.

"No," Ra says, tucking her forearm under his neck, holding him in a way he can't wrench free. She saw Borgadine perform this maneuver on a thief he caught in their wagon one midnight. Made the man swear he wouldn't return before letting him go.

"I'll hurt you," the boy says. "I can do that. I don't even have to be close to you to hurt you."

"I know," she says, and the boy's face does a funny thing. His lips move but no sound comes out, his brow creasing with utter confusion. "You're like me," she clarifies. "I can hurt people too."

Slowly, he makes his way back to her, eyeing her with suspi-cion. "Your eyes…they're normal." As if this makes things clearer for him, he adds, "You're not like me then."

"My eyes might be normal, but I can do things."

"Prove it."

She tenses. "I…I can't control it. Not all the time. I was hoping…was hoping you could help me."

The boy shakes his head slowly. "Why would I help you? Your friends are trying to kill me!"

"They're not trying to kill you." She swallows something hard, and maybe that's because it sounds like she's lying. Maybe she *is* lying. "Ket wants to rescue you from Rovan. Bring you south. Please..."

"Bring me south?" The boy doesn't understand, continues to stand there, one foot ready to race in the opposite direction.

"Thom, toast this bitch!" the pudgy boy chokes out, despite the pressure she has applied to his throat. "Set her on fire! Kill her!"

She tightens the pressure, making sure he can't speak again. "I don't want to hurt him. Thom?"

"Let him go then," Thom says. "You're hurting him—he's turning purple."

She glances down, sees the kid's flesh has darkened several shades. Then she lets go.

The kid lurches forward, falling to his knees, coughing several times and grabbing his throat as if that's going to open the airways leading to his lungs.

"I don't want to hurt you," she says again, addressing no particular boy. "I just...thought we could be friends."

Kill him. CUT OUT HIS HEART.

"Why would I be friends with you?" Thom says, flaring his nostrils. "Your friends attacked us."

"You were running away...weren't you?" she says, not exactly sure how she knows this—she's been trying to access his mind, and even though she's had a hard time entering his thoughts, she catches flashes of what *she thinks* he's thinking. "From the Silver Towers. From that man back there. He's...he's bad to you, isn't he?"

Thom ruffles his brows. "No..."

Ra knows he's lying. "There's no sense in selling me lies, Thom. I can see into your heart. I can tell when you're telling me the truth or not."

"You're a witch then!" he says, then moves his hand toward her, like he means to strangle her.

"Thom, no—well, maybe. I don't know what I am. But if you

have…*abilities*. If you can do things, see things, *know* things that no one else knows, then…maybe you're like me. Or rather—I'm like you."

He considers this, pausing, but keeping his hand directed at her. "You're a witch…Rovan burns witches. Hangs them sky-high. Drowns them in the Black Sea."

"As do most who do not understand what we are. But they haven't burned, hanged, or drowned you."

"I am different. I am the prophecy."

"Yes. The one who was born, destined to restore balance to the Five Realms, bring back the gods of old—I've heard the tale. Borgadine told it to me, many times. He believed you were real."

"I am real," he says, like he's insulted that someone would suggest his existence may have been a fabrication. "And who's Borgadine? Is he back there? Fighting Ravenborn?"

"No," Ra says, shaking her head. "No, Borgadine was my…" She gulps. "He was my father."

"Where is he now? Your father?"

"He died," she admits, an unexpected tear rolling down her cheek.

Thom lowers his hand, lets it fall to his side. "My father died too. He was…"

Fen gets up, brushes the dirt off his knees. "He was in that cottage."

Ra turns on cue to watch the dying inferno reduce the cottage to rubble. Then she spins back, facing the boys. "I'm so sorry."

Thom doesn't say anything. He glances down at the dirt, pensively.

"I'll be honest with you…my friend, Ket—he's the one fighting your…*Ravenborn* was it?"

Thom nods.

"Ket's two sons are being held captive by King Ragland."

Fen perks up. "In Owlton?"

"Yes. Ket was sent to—" She thinks carefully about which

word to use. "—rescue you from captivity, bring you to Owlton, where you belong."

Thom looks confused, then quickly shakes his head. "I don't belong anywhere. I'm a...a freak."

"That's not true," Ra says adamantly.

"All the kids in school call him a freak," Fen says. "Behind his back."

"To my face," Thom corrects. "I couldn't even go to school because it got so bad—*too distracting*, Ravenborn said. I wish I had my powers then. I could have shown them. Shown them how much of a *freak* I am."

Ra nods, understanding what it's like to play the role of the outcast, never fitting in anywhere. "We're not so different, you and I. If you come to Owlton...I dunno, maybe things will be different."

He looks to Fen, like his opinion matters almost as much as his own.

"Don't look at me," Fen tells him.

"Can Fen come with me?" Thom asks.

"Me?" Fen scoffs. "I can't go to Owlton. My mother..."

"You hate your mother."

"Hate is not the word I'd use, more like...she annoys me sometimes."

"Fen can't come," Ra says, not that they wouldn't take the boy if it was necessary—but they don't need Fen. They need Thom. And only Thom. And honestly, if Fen comes along, she can't guarantee his safety when they get back to Owlton. She can't even guarantee her own. "I'm sorry," she says to him, "but you can't."

Fen's face sours, as if he was expecting an invite.

"If you run," Ra continues, "those men will hunt you down. And they will find you. And they will bring you back to the Silver Towers, put you right back in your cage."

Thom stands tall. "What if Owlton is just a different tower, same cage?"

"It won't be," she says, hating the lie as it rolls off her tongue with ease. "Ket will see to it. So will I."

"Promise?"

"I promise." She swallows, her throat on fire from the lies she's told today. More lies today than she's ever told in her life.

Thom squints, like he's double-checking her for the truth, then glances over to Fen, who shrugs, unable to come up with a better solution for their dilemma. Then he eyes Ralyanna again. "If you give me your word, I will come. You have to protect me. From Ravenborn."

"Right now they're fighting," Ra says, turning her shoulder to the squabble, still unable to see through the dust clouds that have fallen over the entire valley. In the distance, over the crackling fire, she hears metal clashing, men fighting and dying.

She hopes they're not too late.

"We can save Ket and his friends," Ra says. "But they will need our help."

The boy thinks, wasting several precious seconds, seconds Ket probably doesn't have. Ra waits, patiently, hoping she's done enough to convince him to cross over, align his future with theirs.

Finally, the boy cracks his knuckles. "Fine," he says, breathing out a long, exaggerated sigh, as if a huge task has just been removed from his plate. "I'm in."

NO PAST, NO FUTURE

CHAPTER THIRTY-THREE

"William Ravenborn was found dead this morning in a Silver Towers basement chamber. The cause of death is presently unknown, but the other members of his unit were also discovered dead, along with the wizard known as Bluebolt. Foul play is currently suspected. We will update Rovan when we have more · information."

———

JESTER PLUNGES a dagger into a Rovan soldier's throat, the motion graceful and practiced, a maneuver the man's pulled off a hundred times or more. Jester's satisfaction with his efforts is disturbing—Ket's never understood men who revel in the blood-soaked glory. He's known his fair share of fierce warriors who enjoyed the battlefield, got off on standing atop piles of the slain, laughed at the way the dead twitch just before they die. Those men have hearts of ice, not a loving bone in their bodies. But

Jester...he's different. He's like them...but also...not. There's a goodness Ket detects; somewhere in Jester's core is a garden where love blooms. But right now, it's overshadowed by his addiction to killing.

Ket turns away, takes on another charging soldier. This one falls easily, after Ket drives his sword into the delicate space beneath his ribcage. He pushes the standing corpse aside, not avoiding the arterial spray shooting in his direction, and tries peering through the hazy dust that's crowding the battlefield. Another Rovan soldier goes flying past him, crashing into the white gate surrounding the burnt cottage. Ket looks to his right, sees Kelanda turning her daggers on another approaching figure, who appears only as a silhouette in the dusky atmosphere.

There are way more of them than we expected, he muses. Ket's not sure if Mason's initial estimates were off, or if Ravenborn brought more to the party than he originally counted, or if a nearby garrison came to assist, but they are outnumbered, and even though they are thinning the herd, he's not sure how long they can keep this up.

Ravenborn is still trading blows with Gobbles—the two men have dropped their swords and are now punching each other, each looking to deliver the knockout strike. Ket sees a few shadows pacing the area as they watch the fight drag on, each eye lacking patience and craving to see the blood of the raven. He knows what this means for his father, even if he defeats Gobbles— Darko Ravenborn will not return to the Silver Towers alive. These men plan to slaughter him.

The mutiny is full-on.

But Ket intends to give his father a chance—like the old man once gave him.

Ket charges the outer circle, brings down his sword on one soldier's back, and cuts him to the ground. Some might have called it a coward's move, but when the numbers are stacked against you, there's no time to fight fair, and he feels no shame regarding the stealthy assassination.

His kill is quickly noticed. The shadows rotate toward him, their swords drawn high, ready to swing at their new nemesis. Ket takes on the two swordsmen nearest him, blocking their attempts with relative ease. He slashes at the soldier rounding his right—too quick for the man to react—and catches him at the elbow, shearing off his dominant appendage. The man's forearm sails into the dust storm. Ket doesn't see where it lands because he's too busy fixating on the gouts of blood spraying forth. The gore sickens him, weakening him from the inside out, like a rotting apple—if someone were to bite into him, they'd get a mouth full of worms.

The man screams and falls on all threes, and crawls in the direction his arm flew, to search the ground for it. The other soldier doesn't bat an eye, impervious to the violence. Ket fixes on him.

"You can spare yourself a similar fate," Ket warns him, not wanting to amputate another limb today—or ever again. "Walk away."

"Traitor!" the soldier shouts, lunging forward. He takes a big hacking swing at Ket's head, which Ket smoothly ducks. He's surprised how much athleticism his body has retained, how easily the battlefield moves come back to him. *Like riding a horse; your body and mind never forget how to use the reins, just like they never forget how to swing a sword.*

Ket stabs the man in the thigh, feels the bone split when he twists the blade, hears the whip-crack of the soldier's leg breaking over the cries and calls of battle. A jagged white extension punches through the man's muscle, flesh, and outerwear, and he falls onto his back, screaming up at the sky, begging for a god to help him. Deaf gods, who do not listen to the prayers of their people, and who care not about the victims of violence.

Ket ends his suffering, stabbing him in the throat, turning away as the blood pools around his tainted silver sword; he considers this a benevolent act, more so than any god has done for a fallen soldier throughout the history of time.

Then he's spinning to catch Ravenborn and Gobbles finish their fight. He watches his father land an elbow against Gobbles's nose, smashing it with a hard crunch. Gobbles stumbles back a few feet, dazed by the impact. Ket thinks this is it, Ravenborn's chance to end this—pick up his sword and kill the man where he stands.

But Ravenborn doesn't. Instead, he marches forward, his bloody fists close to his ears, ready to finish their fight the old-fashioned way—by beating the man to death.

It's a poor decision, Ket thinks, especially considering his surroundings, the numerous opponents, the jackals licking their lips, already tasting victory. He doesn't step in to help him—not yet. But when Gobbles stumbles, falls on his ass, and the spectating soldiers step forward to pick up where their new leader left off—well, Ket sees no choice.

He leaps in front of them, sticking out his sword, challenging whoever will take him on first. A soldier on his right obliges, takes two steps forward and tries to chop off Ket's head in a single swipe, but misses by a whole sword's length. Not even close. Ket almost laughs at the attempt—would have if he wasn't so zeroed in on the next attack, which comes from his left. This soldier garbed entirely in Rovan green sends his sword forward in a quick jab, so quick it catches Ket by surprise. Ket's knee takes the worst of it, and the metal slices through his flesh, bounces off his bone. The force sends him to the ground, but his adrenaline kicks in, helping him to jump back up like it never happened.

The soldier seizes the opportunity—the second Ket was on one knee—to barrel ahead, bringing his sword over his head, ready to deliver a death blow. Ket tucks and rolls out of the way, and the blade comes down on the grass, gets stuck in the dirt. As the soldier lifts with his legs, Ket dives ahead, stabbing the soldier in the ribs, not deep enough to kill him. The soldier knocks the blade away with his gloved hand, removes the sword from the ground, and spins on Ket.

But Ket is ready for him and slashes at him twice. One blow is defended but the other sneaks through, catching the soldier in his armored leg. The force is enough to drop him to one knee, and Ket doesn't squander the chance to finish the fight—he takes the loyal Rovan's head clean off at the neck, sending his decapitated head spinning into the brown shroud.

Weakened from the attack, Ket uses his sword as a walking stick to steady himself. He doesn't see any more men—the other soldiers have been dispatched by Ravenborn, and their corpses lie in the garden, their faces obscured by streaks of blood and gore. He wonders if he'll eventually see their ghosts gathered on the battlefield, mourning over the lives they did not get to finish living.

Ravenborn, breathing heavily, clambers to his feet.

"Father…" Ket says, watching his old man continue keeping his back to him. "I never got the chance to thank you."

Ravenborn doesn't respond. "You ruined life for me that day. You betrayed the Emperor, killed your Soulthiever brethren, not to mention—cut off the head of the most legendary wizard that ever graced Rovan with their allegiance." At this, Darko Ravenborn snarls, turns his head just slightly. "Bluebolt."

"I'm sorry," he says. "But I was never for the war—you knew that. And I certainly wasn't for what you signed me up for in that dungeon. I told you not to make me…"

"We were so close. We would have had our army of souls, we would have *won* that war."

"They were foolish experiments and nothing more—don't you get that? The King—"

"Emperor," his father corrects, flaring his nostrils like an aggravated bull.

"King," Ket reiterates, refusing to address Salah Rovan as the one true ruler over the entire Endlands. "Don't you see what he is? He's a dreamer—he wants ghosts to win him wars, boys with no combat skills to destroy entire armies. He's mad."

Darko Ravenborn turns around at that. Prominent scars brand his face, thick white lines running vertically down his cheeks, his chin, ensuring no hair will ever grow there again. "You were supposed to be loyal to me. To your mother. Your brothers." He snarls. "Two of them died because of you and your antics. Their blood is on your hands."

Ket hangs his head, the news hitting him harder than he had expected. Ket's family life had always been complicated, but he certainly wished no single member of his bloodline ill will. "That's horrible. I'm…how?"

"Your brother—Moses—died in the war. But Brolyn and Belgar, your twin brothers, they died after you left Bluebolt's chamber. You left a trail for Owlton soldiers to follow inside the tower walls. They were slaughtered, unsuspectingly. And your mother…" Ravenborn's face seems to ache with a knowing sadness. "…she died shortly after."

Ket's eyes beg for a reason.

"She killed herself," his father clarifies. "She slit her wrists atop the north tower. When we found her, it was too late."

"Father, I'm—"

"Save your apologies for someone who cares." Ravenborn grits his teeth. "I certainly don't. As far as I'm concerned, you also died in the war. That's what I told everyone, that's what everyone believes. You are a dead man."

"And yet here I am—breathing. Alive."

Ravenborn nods like this is information he wishes to alter. "Yes, you do." He raises his sword, smells the blood on the black blade. "Allowing you to live is one thing…but allowing you to betray the Rovan Territories, commit an act of treason against the Silver City, *steal* personal belongings from the Emperor himself— that is entirely another thing."

"A human being—an innocent child—is no personal belonging."

"That child is far from innocent. He has the power to destroy us all."

"I sincerely doubt it."

Ravenborn bends his knees, ready to engage.

"Father…" Ket says, shaking his head, almost amused. "You're weak. You cannot fight me."

"You're injured. You cannot fight me."

"Here we are again." Ket nods to some nondescript location beyond the veil of frail brown light. "Let's go our separate ways. And this time—I promise—you will never see me again."

Ravenborn doesn't budge. "No, son. I'm afraid this is not like the last time. See, that child means something to me. He didn't at first—at first, he was a chore. An impossible task given to me by my Emperor, and it drove me crazy looking after him, trying to help him exercise his abilities, his extraordinary, albeit dangerous, powers—but…after years and years of bonding with him, I'm proud to say…he's like a son to me."

Ket can't tell for sure, but his father's voice has a ring of insincerity to it. It's like he's trying to convince himself that what he speaks is true.

"A son…" Ravenborn says, tasting the repetition on his tongue, as if needing to sample the flavors between his teeth. "Yes, he's a son—my true son, the son I've never had. He loves me. Unlike you and your brothers."

There's something wrong about the way he's speaking. More akin to a man who's lost his mind on the battlefield rather than a man who's gained fame and fortune for winning wars—or at the very least, *not losing* them.

"You've changed, father. You're not the same man you were."

"And you are a ghost," Ravenborn says, positioning himself in a dueling pose, planting his feet evenly apart, standing his ground. "A ghost that needs to be cleansed from the Raven's House."

Ket grips the hilt of his weapon. "You don't need to do this."

Nothing but anger fills in his father's eyes now, and Ket knows—there's no escaping what's to come.

"I really do."

But before Ravenborn can attack first, a rumbling takes over the valley that's become a bloody battlefield. Hooves, stampeding. The collective cry of charged warriors coming from the north.

A garrison from the Silver City?

Ket's heart sinks. It sounds like a lot of men. Too many soldiers. Much too many for Kelanda, Mason, Jester, and himself to handle.

Ravenborn begins to laugh. But then his face morphs. No trace of humor or gloating remains. Tears stream down his face. Then he charges, swinging his blade at Ket's neck.

THE LAST LESSON

CHAPTER THIRTY-FOUR

"We should only fear the Boy with the Star-Shaped Eyes if he grows up learning to hate. Whoever takes on the responsibility of protecting him must teach him love. Love, above all else. Love over everything."

– HERROLD THE PHILOSOPHER, *THE GOD TEXTS AND OTHER THINGS WE SHOULD FEAR*

———

THOM STANDS, mouth agape, as dozens of soldiers descend the hill leading into the valley, all of them wearing Rovan green, all of them emptying their lungs with claims of victory and calls for blood.

"We have to stop them," Ra says, stepping forward.

"What?" Fen objects. "You can't be…there's too many of them!"

Thom turns to Fen. "Run."

"What—no! I'm *not* leaving you behind."

A cool frost burns his eyes, and Thom knows they're changing again. He spots Fen's terrified stare, which confirms his suspicion

—something in his blood is changing. Becoming something else. Something godlike.

"Go, Fen. Run back to the Silver Towers. Go to your mother. Hold her tight." Then, as if he doesn't quite believe it himself, he squeaks out three words: "I'll be safe."

Fen's face twists with worry and sadness.

"Go," Thom urges one last time. "It's not safe to be around me anymore."

A part of him believes it won't matter; wherever Fen runs to, the chaos will find him.

There's no running from men who want to play gods, and gods who want to play men. The quote jumps into his head, but he's not sure which text it came from or who originally penned it.

Fen spins on his toes and takes off in the opposite direction. He runs steadily for his size, a pace faster than a jog, heading for the woods, where there's cover from the ensuing madness.

Thom glances at Ra. "How do we stop them?"

"I was hoping you had some sort of idea."

"Uh, this was your plan?"

"I know—I'm not good at this part."

Thom cocks an eyebrow. "What part?"

"You know…" She nods to the growing brown haze, made worse by the approaching army.

"Fighting?" Thom holds out his hands. "I've never fought anyone before! Not a real person. Have you?"

"A few times," she says quietly, and Thom thinks there's a story there. If he's lucky, if they both are, he might hear it later.

When it's safe, and we're away from Ravenborn, and the eyes of the Silver Towers.

"Look—can you do anything with your powers?" Ra puts her hands on her hips, waiting for his reply.

"Yeah, I can…sometimes move things. If I concentrate hard enough. Sometimes I can…"

Her brow lifts. "What?"

"Sometimes I can read people's thoughts, and sometimes… plant ideas in their mind."

"Whoa, that's actually pretty neat." She raises her hands to her eyes, surveying them like tablets written in a language she doesn't quite know. "I can move stuff too sometimes. If I use these words that Borgadine taught me—sometimes I can do other things too." She gulps. "Sometimes I hurt people."

"I've never hurt anyone," he sort of lies. He dragged Fen here using good old-fashioned intimidation, and if he ends up not making it back to the Silver Towers alive, then he's responsible all the way.

"It's not fun."

"But your friends…they're in trouble."

"Yes. Yes, we have to go. Save them."

Thom closes his eyes, wishing his powers could transport him to another place or time, where he doesn't have to hurt anyone. Where he can be left alone to read, play kickball, or go on adventures with Fen in safe places.

Not here.

Not on a battlefield.

Not watching men die for senseless causes. Reasons he can't begin to fathom.

"Let's go," he says, opening his eyes to the battlefield, trying to gaze through the murky tufts of brown smoke.

Back where his true father lies in the ashy ruins of his home.

"Take my hand," Ra says, extending hers.

Thom is hesitant at first, as if she's a leper asking to be fed a spoonful of porridge. But he takes her hand, squeezing her soft, delicate skin.

As they walk toward the battle, Thom feels something charge through him—a current that pulses, like having a second heartbeat—and it throbs against his bones. It feels powerful, almighty.

He stands tall.

Godlike.

THE LAST LESSON II
CHAPTER THIRTY-FIVE

"There's no running from men who want to play gods, and gods who want to play men."

– MENYARD MINOTOA, *THE GOD SYSTEM*

———

RA FEELS IT, that kinetic swirl inside her, almost as if it's taking out her organs, reshaping them, and placing them back. Her heart flutters like a mad pigeon when she enters the dusty realm that's swallowed the whole middle of the valley, obscuring the cottage's charred remains and the surrounding greenery—the colorful flowers that make up the garden, what's left of it. Thom's heart is fluttering too; she can feel it in her grip, the fast beating, and can almost hear the *thump-thump* like a haunted echo.

His heart.

Cut it out.

Eat it.

Swallow it down. Every fucking bite.

The Fairy Godmother's request is not far from her thoughts. She does her best to ignore it, keeping her eyes on the task at hand and her mind vacant. When she does find herself gravitating toward her thoughts, she pictures Borgadine, listens to his words of encouragement, if he were still alive and here, right now—*you have this, girl. You can do anything—just set your mind to it. Concentrate on what you want, and then seize it. Witness the outcome in your heart and mind. Then watch it happen.*

It's easy to say, but the *doing* is so much harder. In her mind, she can see the riders falling from their horses, getting trampled beneath galloping hooves, all because of some magic word she shouts and because she *thought* of it—but actually facilitating these thoughts, making them become a reality, is an entirely different skill she has not mastered.

The heat of the charred house presses against her; they are close to the fray now, can see bodies strewn about the grass, some draped over the broken white fence like laundry left to dry. Pools of blood have soaked into the dirt, creating dark puddles she opts to dance around. Dark silhouettes appear in the murk before her, some of them crawling on the ground, some of them holding swords. Some of them dueling.

She spots Ket's outline, knows it's him from the way he swings his weapon, the way he defends himself. He's fighting the one Kelanda called "Ravenborn."

As she gets closer, a giant man—not an actual giant, not like the kind the Wilders employed when they carved up Riverspell— steps in her path, holding his blade upright, close to his body like he means to swing. His face is stretched in a wicked snarl, and Ra puts up two palms, an instinctive gesture that has no malice behind it. At first. But then she gets angry. And then she uses Borgadine's advice—*picture what you want, then see it.*

So she does.

She envisions the man putting that sword through his own leg, then shouts a single word: *"Sprount'morlus!"* It's an old word from a dead language that few people know, and as she utters it, she wonders how Borgadine first learned of it. That book of spells? Where did that mysterious text originate from? Did he always have it? Come into possession of it during his travels?

Who was he? She finds it silly that she's never asked herself this question before, when Borgadine was still alive to answer it. She was so elated to find someone who didn't want to hurt her, who genuinely wanted to guide her along this crazy path called life, that these questions seemed unimportant at the time. But now… *How did he know these things? These OLD things…*

Ancient.

The giant man's scream rips her from her thoughts. She glances down, sees he's jammed the blade through his thigh, the silver coming out the other side slicked with blood and dangling scraps of muscle.

"Shitballs!" Thom shouts from next to her, which gives her nerves a powerful jolt. "You did that? Didn't you? You made him stab himself." He seems confident about that last part.

"I guess I did," she says, almost dreamily.

Thom's smiling, but should he be? She still feels weird about these powers, like maybe she shouldn't trust them. Or herself. Or anything her eyes show her. These seem like dangerous abilities to flaunt, and now she kind of understands where Borgadine was coming from, why he always warned her never to use her abilities unless it was in secret, or there was no other way out of a cornered situation.

Unless it was life or death.

For now, he used to say. *There may come a time when you will need to let the world know who you are.*

What you are.

But isn't that time now?

She thinks so.

"Do it again," Thom says. "Wait, no. Let me try."

Another soldier, not more than thirty feet away, his silhouette facing Ket and Ravenborn, watching the two trade strikes that only connect with opposing steel, catches the boy's eyes. Thom points to the man. Closes his eyes. Imagines.

Ra doesn't say anything when nothing happens. She just lets the moment pass.

"Dammit," Thom says, realizing he's failed. "You do it."

Ra imagines the soldier angling his blade toward his stomach and jumping down on the pointy end. She repeats her process, points, says the word—*words* this time, a whole string of them—that Borgadine committed to her memory, then marvels over how the man touches his ear like someone's been whispering an unwanted secret to him. The soldier takes his sword, throws it in the dirt, the hilt buried, the tip of the blade pointing up, angled at his abdomen—then he simply falls forward. The blade pierces his battle cloak, weak mail, and flesh before disappearing inside him, then reappears a few seconds later out his back. The man works his body down to the hilt, does it without speaking a single word, which disturbs Ra most of all. Like this is routine. A simple task he must complete and make no fuss.

I did that.

Bewitched him, then made him kill himself.

No, I killed him.

Another voice speaks up, the woman from her bad dreams: *No, you didn't. You didn't do a thing except encourage it—and that's not the same as running the blade through him yourself.*

Sure feels like it, but she doesn't challenge the more optimistic viewpoint. Seems useless to argue with the insidious voice.

"Him next," Thom says, pointing to the one called Ravenborn.

Ra steadies her fingers, her mind. Before she can see something horrible happen to the leader of this small army, Kelanda steps onto the path before her.

"Ra!" she shouts. The woman is covered in streaks of blood—not her own from the looks of it; she looks like a stable boy who met a bucket of goat's blood on prank night. "What are you doing here? I told you to—"

"Move aside," Ra says, no longer liking being told what to do. She's had enough of that kind of thing; now it's her turn to decide the actions she takes. All her life—even in her dreams—she's been instructed to do this or that.

Not anymore, she says, concentrating on Ravenborn, picturing what his head would look like separated from his shoulders.

"Ra!" Kelanda shouts, and the images in her mind disperse like pieces of a completed puzzle being tossed against the wall. "It's too dangerous! Go back! Now!"

Ra grits her teeth. "NO!"

Kelanda steps back, her face shriveling up, a mix of confusion and horror taking hold. Ra's not sure why the woman has reacted so strongly to her refusal, but something about the way Ra looks must have spooked her.

"Ra?" says a small voice, and Ra looks to see the boy gawking at her. "Your eyes…"

"What about them?" she asks, but she knows. At least, she knows something is different about them. They burn like the fires of Arkos's Darkhell, a deep pain that flares in the center of her brain, the flames licking every nerve. "What is it?"

"They're…like mine."

"Glowing?" she asks.

The boy nods. "And…they're shaped like mine."

"Stars?"

The boy's still stare confirms this—*Yes. Stars for eyes.*

"Highbeard's cunt," Kelanda swears, backing away, as if Ra is a slow, sweeping landslide heading her way. After a few steps, she spins and disappears into the sepia shroud.

"Ravenborn!" she shouts, hoping to grab the man's attention— she wants him to look at her while she dreams up his demise. "RAVENBORN!"

This time, the man hears her. He blocks one of Ket's attempts, knocking his steel aside, and then spins toward the sound of his name, squinting through the shroud.

Ket misses the opportunity to land a killing blow—he has enough time, but the sound of her voice attracts his wandering eyes too.

"Ralyanna?" he asks, confused. He takes one limping step

toward her, scrunching his eyes. "What—what are you doing here?"

"I've come to help," she says, stepping toward Ravenborn, closing her eyes, envisioning something nasty—his head exploding like when you mix fire water and Springgaarden leafling powder.

"We don't need your help!" Ket says. "More men have arrived —it's too dangerous. You must—"

He ducks as Ravenborn uses the distraction to his advantage, swings his sword at the back of his head. Ket dips out of the way, nearly falling to the ground in the process.

"Hey!" the boy shouts, stepping in front of Ra. "Ravenborn!"

This time, Darko Ravenborn is all ears. He pivots away from Ket, casts his hard gaze on the legendary orphan. "Boy...you're alive."

"I am. And you—lay down your sword!"

Ravenborn sneers. "Shut up, you pathetic pup. You will do as *I say* and you will do it now. Keep walking north. My men will find you and—"

"NO!" Thom's voice thunders, and with his unexpected outburst, a gusty wind blows through the center of the battlefield —there's an icy tinge to the airy current, and Ra's bones fill with dread.

Something bad is upon them.

That charge she felt when she touched the boy's hand—it's back. And it's flowing through everything. The battlefield. The soldiers. Her core. Every nerve is alive and tense. She feels like she might explode.

It's him.

He's doing this.

She's reminded of Riverspell, when she acted on instinct and killed that rider, knocking herself out cold in the process. She wasn't wise then, didn't use her ability in the way Borgadine had taught her, and she paid for it.

Concentrate. See it. Say the words.

This boy's energy feels raw, unrefined. Unpracticed. And he's about to unleash a storm upon them, a godlike surge from which the lands here may never recover—which might kill them all.

Do it now, that woman's voice says, slithering into her ear. *Kill him. End it here. Reach into his chest and tear out his heart!*

She couldn't even if she wanted to.

"I'm sick of you!" the boy shouts, shoving his finger at Ravenborn like he means to poke the man in the chest from several yards away. "You lied to me! About my father! About my family! About me!"

Ravenborn's smile dries up. "It was to protect you, son. I planned on telling you everything when you were old enough to understand."

"You always treated me like a kid!"

"You are a kid!" Ravenborn almost laughs, finding any alternative notion ridiculous. "You are just a boy! An important—"

"SHUT UP!"

Lightning flashes overhead, brightening the fog. Not a second later, a thunderous bang tears through the sky, sounding like a dragon sailing through the clouds just above them. The ground rattles. A few of the shrouded figures trade glances, unsure of what to make of the scene. A few of them have the good sense to retreat. Horses whinny, some of them rearing back like they mean to rid themselves of the human cargo on their backs.

"You are not my father," the boy says, and Ra can see *his* eyes now. The stars, glowing hot like molten coal. "You *killed* my father. You drove him insane!"

Ravenborn shakes his head. "Your father was damaged when we found him. He had delusions—he wanted to harm you, at first. We caught him trying to assassinate you!"

"LIES!"

More thunder, lightning, and the ground quakes like Highbeard himself has descended onto the valley floor.

Ravenborn pleads, holding out his hand for the boy to take it. So he can lead him somewhere, a safer place. But Ra can see through the man—at least, she can see *into* him. It's like she can hear his thoughts, his musings, his dark plans.

Come here, child, she hears him think. *Come back to me and let's end this. You will be my son and do what I command, and together we can take over Rovan, kill the Emperor and unite the Five Realms once and for all.*

A shiver runs down her spine.

"I know I haven't been good to you," Ravenborn tells Thom, taking baby steps toward him. "But I can change. I can be the true father you never had. We can work less, have more fun—we can go fishing, I'll take you on boar hunts. I can take you to see the Crystal Falls and the Eastern Mists."

These sound like pleasant promises, but Ra knows them as lies.

Even so, the boy seems to consider it. His eyes burn out, regressing to the black star-shaped forms they were before he grew agitated. His cheeks tremble, tears glistening on the rims of his eyes. Thom breathes deeply, ignoring the dust cloud and the gritty granules entering his mouth.

"Promise?" he asks, sniffling. He begins to walk toward Ravenborn, who's summoning him with wiggling fingers.

"Oh, I promise," he says. But what he's thinking is an entirely different claim. *I will break you, break your mind, and you will be forever chained to the Silver Towers. You will have no life outside of my dark desires.*

Ra grabs him by the collar, pulls him close. She drapes her arms over his chest, holding him in a bear hug. He doesn't fight it but looks up with confusion.

"He's lying to you," she explains.

"Tell that whore to shut her mouth," Ravenborn snaps, eyeing Ra like he means to drive his sword down the middle of her skull, cleave her body in half.

"I swear—I can hear his thoughts."

"What's he thinking?" Thom says. "Tell me the truth."

What if I can show you? a voice says, and it's not hers, not the

Fairy Godmother's either—it's Borgadine's, and she's reminded of another lesson, one that took considerable strength and only garnered success on only one occasion. Where she was able to transfer her ability to the old man, imbuing him with a touch of her talent; for a brief moment he could see into her mind and diagnose her dreams, back when she used to have terrible night terrors that caused her to wake up screaming in a pool of sweat.

Ra brings her hands to the boy's face and presses her fingers against his temples. She begins to hum a tune, reciting the words she's recalled from those early lessons.

"What are you doing?" Ravenborn asks, a question no one can answer.

More men have gathered around them. Ket rotates in a full circle, mindful of the potential impending attack, keeping his sword upright, ready to defend.

"Keep away from him, whore!" Ravenborn shouts, taking a few steps in her direction. Then he stops, maybe not realizing exactly what's transpiring, but seeing something in her he doesn't like, or doesn't understand—or maybe he understands all too well. "Witch! She's a witch! An Arkos whore!" Ravenborn points to her, calling upon the calvary that's surrounded them. "Kill her! Cut off her head and remove her heart! Kill the—"

Ra tunes out Ravenborn's mad pleas, and whispers in Thom's ear, "Listen to his true thoughts."

She hears them again, his secret plans for dominating the Realms. And she knows they are being transferred into Thom, that he can listen in.

"LIES!" Ravenborn shouts, stomping his feet on the earth. "DO NOT BELIEVE HER L—"

She feels something change inside the boy. Something hot and heavy, something *angry,* that *charge* of powerful energy building and gathering—a storm within, taking over. Ra tries to release her fingers from his temples but finds them stuck there. Wincing, she watches a golden light flood her touch, spreading across the boy's head, his face. The light is hot against her flesh, and the burn travels up her fingers, into her hands, the length of her arms, and doesn't die there. This fiery grip takes hold of her whole body, and it feels like there's an inferno blazing inside her.

She screams. The boy wails, a shrill noise that sounds almost birdlike. The light they've created blinds them, the whole battlefield, erasing the fog and everything inside it.

She's still screaming when everything goes black.

WHITE.

That's all she sees as far as her vision will allow. A dreamy blank landscape.

Highbeard's Heaven?

She supposes she died on the battlefield from the explosion that she helped originate. Not her intention, but one of Borgadine's favorite slices of wisdom was always, "Sometimes the best intentions have the most disastrous consequences."

This qualifies.

She hangs there for several moments, inside the white, wondering if this is how it's going to be, moving forward, if she'll float in this timeless, shapeless vacuum forever. There are worse places to end up, she thinks—like the fabled lands of Arkos's Darkhell. This big empty nothingness could be filled with towering stacks of hellflame, tortured demonic entities, and creatures the size of entire kingdoms rising from a black, toothy abyss.

When it's framed that way, this isn't so bad at all.

"Welcome, child," a serene, velvety voice says from somewhere close to her. It's welcoming, refreshing, especially considering her state of limbo. She's not sure if the speaker is a man or a woman—it's the most androgynous voice she's ever heard. "I've been looking forward to our meeting for quite some time."

She doesn't have a voice, can't respond—if she had a body, maybe she could. But she's nothing, nowhere, just a speck of dust floating in all this white.

"It's normal," the voice says with a chuckle in their throat. "Don't be scared. You don't even need to talk—I can hear every thought inside your head." Another chuckle breaking through a smile. "I know you go by Ralyanna now. That's a lovely name. Did Borgadine ever tell you what that name means?"

No. He did not.

"I'm sure he did—maybe you forgot? It means 'the daughter' in one of the oldest languages known across the Five Realms."

This information causes her eyes to burn—wait, she doesn't have eyes. So how can that be? But she feels something, a small sting. Maybe she does have eyes after all. After all, she sees the white. She is there, floating. She just can't see anything else but the nothingness. But she must have eyes. To see, you need eyes. And she can see.

The white.

"Heartwarming that he chose that name for you. I think he loved you dearly. He had many things to teach you before he died—alas, sometimes the world spins in ways we cannot predict, and his untimely demise was a real shock—even to us. He was…well, he was the last of them."

Them? Who is them, she wonders.

"They," the voice continues, "were a small group of scholars who passed down the knowledge of the gods from generation to generation—they were known as Templesons. Each god had their own close advisors who passed down their ancient arts to them, and even though they could not perform these wondrous spells and godlike enchantments, they knew how to draw the power out of those who had the gift.

"You, Daughter of Borgadine, have a rare gift."

Rare? Not that rare, though, since the boy has the gift. And there is talk of others…

"Others are out there, yes, waiting to be discovered, some of whom hide in the shadows of the Five Realms, hoping they will not be discovered, cowering in fear of being hung as Arkos witches."

There are others like me then. The Fairy Godmother was right.

"This brings me to my next point—we don't have much time here, you and I, and, well, I might as well come out and say it: do not trust her. That woman. The one who is trying to poison your mind."

Her Fairy Godmother?

"That's an…interesting name for her. She is hardly a fairy and has certainly never given birth to anything resembling a human—but godlike…ah…she is very much indeed that. I don't know everything about her and what she wants, but she is certainly creating waves…the less I speak about her the better. Trust me on that. You'll understand in due time. Just know this—if she tries to contact you through your dreams, just ignore her. Pretend you're listening. Pretend you care. But do not allow her to access your thoughts and see inside your head. You must learn how to do this."

How? How do I block something I have no control over? I can't control my dreams, what happens in them.

"I do not possess the power to do this myself, so this is a lesson I cannot bestow upon you. But there is a way. You must learn to block her from finding a way in. She is a true threat to the Five Realms, and she will stop at nothing to use you and the other Godfallen."

Godfallen? She's heard that name before, but it certainly doesn't apply to her. She can't be…

"You are," the voice says, a chuckle capping their sentence yet again. "Ralyanna—you are strong, maybe the strongest of all of them—you will succeed in this, I assure you. Borgadine would be so proud of you. If there is a place beyond the material world, if he's watching down on you from some high heaven, then he is most certainly proud."

If?

"I do not know what lies beyond this world."

Aren't you…aren't you a god?

Another chuckle, this one long and measured. "I wish. What I am is something else entirely. I cannot say what—for I do not truly know. All I do know…is I am connected to you. To all of you. I am a guiding light, and I will be there for you when you need it. Now, I must go—I have answers to seek myself. There is a war coming—and it's not going to be between the north and the south, between Rovan and Owlton.

"It will be between the gods and the living."

Ice pelts her invisible bones.

"Go now. Back to the real world. You have much to do."

In the distance she can almost make out a faint, gray outline, the silhouette of some figure—the source of the voice. She wants to run to it, peer through the whiteness and see who she was speaking to. But there's no movement here. This is a stationary realm, a place she has no control over.

Everything goes gray before it fades to black, until there is no light left in this world, this other side.

———

SHE WAKES UP COUGHING, huge hacking barks that make her sound like she's caught some respiratory illness. Sitting up, she pounds her chest like that's going to knock loose the fluid in her lungs. No, what she needs is time and a few more coughs to clear it up.

Once she can breathe somewhat regularly again, she surveys the surrounding battlefield, which still remains shrouded in the dusty fog—the sunshine brightening the area with a harsh, nearly blinding glow. Ra shields her eyes as she climbs to her feet; a strenuous task, because everything hurts from head to toe.

Standing, she observes the immediate area. Slain soldiers lay in the dirt, lakes and streams of dried blood beneath them. *How long was I out?* Couldn't have been long. Certainly didn't feel long, but she supposes time works differently in the worlds her mind inhabits. An hour in a dream can be several hours of real life.

She steps over the corpses as tears spring forth from her eyes. She can't find Ket or Thom, Kelanda or Mason, or even Jester. No traces of anyone she recognizes in the hazy valley of death.

"Hello?" she says, not liking the softness of her tone, the smallness in her timbre, that *lost-scared-little-girl* voice. She means to sound tough, confident, so if an enemy hears her, they'll know she's not some easy target.

You are an easy target, she says to herself, unable to hide the truth from her own mind. *That's exactly what you are.*

She continues to wander the field of dust, and every ten steps or so she wonders when she will see the end of it. It's lasting a long distance, more than she thinks was present before her and Thom's explosive reaction.

"Anyone there?" she calls into the fog.

No one. Nothing. She's alone. The only survivor of—

"Ra..." says a voice, raspy and quiet. It's coming from some-where close. She searches the fog, running her eyes over more slain troops and fallen horses, paths of scattered limbs. *"Ra...is that you?"*

She follows the voice, hopping over a small pile of three dead men, and finds Ket lying in some shrubbery near the white gate guarding the entrance to the razed cottage. Skipping over to him, thankful he's alive, she rushes to his side and kneels next to him. Helps lift him to a seated position.

"Ket..." she says, scanning his body for injuries—despite a few bleeding cuts on his face and a nasty wound on his knee, he looks intact.

"What...what happened?" He coughs too, clearing a cloud of dust from his lungs.

"Thom...the boy...something happened between us."

He eyes her suspiciously, clearly wanting to know more.

"I let him listen to Ravenborn's thoughts...he got angry...and there was...like an explosion."

"He got...angry?" More coughs. Ket turns his head and spits a wad of lung snot into the bushes.

"Ravenborn...he was planning on using Thom against the Rovan king. As a weapon."

Ket's face morphs into a mask of disbelief. "Are you sure?"

"I heard his thoughts. I saw into his heart's desires."

"Ravenborn was always loyal to the north. My father...he was always one to serve his king, no matter what." He shakes his head as if the past is a thing that no longer matters. "I find it difficult to believe he planned on betraying his so-called emperor. His blood relative."

Ra's heart pounds furiously. "I'm not lying," she says, offended.

Ket waves this away. "I'm not saying you are. Just hard to believe." He bites his tongue, his face pensive, looking like a sculpture of some early-age philosopher. "People can change, though. Time has the unique ability to wear down our minds, break them. Over time we learn things, experience different views, meet new people. We live. I suppose like everyone else in the Five Realms, my father was not immune to living."

She understands this piece of wisdom but might appreciate it more, later. More pressing matters require their attention. "We need to find Thom."

"The boy?"

She nods again.

"Yes, we do. Hopefully whatever happened—" Ket stands, with her assistance, "didn't kill him. He's far too valuable to lose like this."

"Maybe we shouldn't," she suggests, surprising herself.

"Beg your pardon?"

She glances around the area, scoping out the dead, their expressions capturing what they saw in those final moments—the horror of knowing this was it for them, the end of the path.

"What if we don't bring him south, to Owlton." She stares hard at Ket now, not dodging his gaze. "He's just a boy. A scared boy."

"That scared *boy* almost very nearly killed us all."

"Exactly why we shouldn't just hand him over to a king who wants to use him as a weapon."

Ket lowers his head, not in a defeated way—more exhausted than anything. "Ra...my sons." He stares back up at her, his eyes glossy with sadness. "They're without me, their father. I...this is the only chance we have at being together again. A family. *My family.*"

Ra swallows her own sadness. She's wanted a family more

than anything. How can she suggest the man give up his sons for a boy he doesn't know?

She can't.

"I understand," she says, sniffling. "Just promise me something."

"What?"

"You won't let them hurt him."

Ket eyes her, then nods. "I promise." He approaches her, wraps his arms around her, pulls her close. Hugs her. It's the most physical affection she's ever received from another human being—not even Borgadine, despite his love for her, embraced her like this. She hugs him back, the movement so foreign to her that she's not even sure if she's doing it right.

Family, she thinks. *This is what family feels like.*

"But first," Ket says, "we have to find him."

A SHORT GOODBYE

CHAPTER THIRTY-SIX

"All roads come to an end; but some people never learn to veer off and take a new fork, to continue their journey forward. Some are content with wandering back the way they came, wondering where they went wrong, where they got lost."

– HERROLD THE PHILOSOPHER, THE LAST LESSONS OF HERROLD THE PHILOSOPHER: A COLLECTION OF STORIES, POEMS, AND MUSINGS FROM THE GREATEST MIND THAT EVER LIVED

———

KET AND RA find the boy not far from the house, standing up, staring at the ground as if he's mourning over the grave of a lost loved one. A father, a mother—maybe even a sister or brother. But the only thing Ket sees on the ground below him is a long ashy smear, black like char. Like something's—or someone's—been burnt into the ground. He can't make out what or who, but by the time he reaches the boy his eyes are elsewhere—on the boy himself.

"Thom," Ra says softly, careful not to spook him.

The boy doesn't move. He continues staring at the earth like the grass might open up, form a toothy maw and swallow him whole.

She looks to Ket, waiting for him to take the lead. Ket approaches the boy, kneels next to him. Finally, his eyes settle on the ashy imprint. The charred stain is in the shape of a raven taking flight, big black wings extended above its head. Exactly the same emblem on the flag that hung outside of the family keep on the day Ket turned his back on the Silver City.

"He was my father," Ket admits, then feels the boy tense with this knowledge, like Ket might be cut from the same cloth. "He was not a good man," Ket confirms, quickly establishing his position. "I'm sorry if he hurt you."

The boy regards Ket warily, keeping a few feet between them, like maybe Ket is a wolf hiding inside the flesh of a man. Ket doesn't reach out to him or try to influence him in any form. Instead, he nods along like he understands everything that's on the boy's mind.

Ket pushes himself to his feet. "He hurt me too. A long time ago."

The boy gulps. "What did he…do to you?"

Ket sighs. "He loved his king and his country more than his own family. Made my brothers and I do things that were… unspeakable. That no man should ask another to do, let alone their own flesh and blood."

"He made you hurt people."

Ket remembers those chambers, filled with corpses of women and children, survivors from raided villages, people who resisted the Rovan expansion. Their mutilated bodies on slabs of concrete, hanging from ropes chained to the ceilings. The torture devices slicked with blood. His mission, given to him by the king who never saw himself as a king, but the Emperor of Endlia instead; to learn the ancient method of extracting a human soul from a living body.

His stomach turns, creeps into the back of his throat, triggering a gag.

"He made me hurt lots of people. Innocents. Those who deserved nothing but to live their lives free from captivity. Free from the Rovan Empire."

"And you refused his demands?"

"Many times."

"Yet…you complied? At least for a little bit."

"When I was younger. For a little. Because he was my father, and I felt like I had to."

"But then you left."

Ket recalls that day, during a siege from the south—Ragland had sent his army in from the west, through Glane, and attacked the Silver City. A surprise raid, and the garrisons couldn't hold them off initially. They very nearly claimed the Silver Towers. It wasn't until garrisons from the east came back to the city, after word reached them that the Rovan capital was on fire, that they were able to overcome the attack.

On that day, he left. Told his father he was leaving, that he would no longer play the part, the butcher of innocent people. "*I will not commit another act of murder in the name of this witless campaign,*" he remembers saying.

On that day he was willing to kill a member of his own bloodline, if he had to. That day, he was prepared to murder his own father. The day Ravenborn let him go, told the rest of his family, and all those close to them, that he watched their son die in battle. Ket's not sure if the old man offered up a corpse that had been mutilated beyond recognition as evidence—but whatever the case, no one came looking for him.

"I left," he tells the boy. "Went south. Where I thought I could find peace from the nightmare I had lived."

"But now you're back." This sounds like an accusation.

"My boys…my sons…were taken from me." His eyes swell with tears, just the thought of his sons summoning a stinging mist to his vision. "King Edwill Ragland III has offered me an exchange."

"My powers for your two sons," the boy says, nodding. "Ra told me."

"Yes. I don't feel—I don't feel it's right to ask this of you." Ket drops back to one knee, bows his head toward the boy. "If there was some way to free you…some way to get my boys back…"

The boy shakes his head. "I realize now how important I am." He quickly glances at the evidence around them—the bodies, the massacre. The burnt-down cottage. All this chaos, most of which he started, directly or indirectly. "I will never be free from men like Ravenborn. Or from the kings of the Five Realms. They will kick over every rock just to find me. Nowhere is safe."

Ket chews this over. "There must be some way…"

Bells begin to jangle. The outline of a figure appears in the shroud behind the boy, and the first thing Ket recognizes is that silly jester hat.

"Might I make a suggestion?"

The boy spins to him, raises his hand like he plans to obliterate Jester on the spot.

Jester drops his dagger and puts up both hands in surrender. His stitched smile widens at the threat. "Now, now. I am not your enemy."

Ket reaches out, puts his hand on Thom's and lowers his arm. "He won't hurt you."

"He's like them," the boy says, anxiety building in his voice. "A murderer."

"Yes. But he is not like them."

Jester doesn't agree, nor does he argue Ket's claim. "I couldn't help but overhear your dilemma, and thought—why, I think there is a solution that benefits all parties."

Ket and the boy exchange glances.

Ralyanna steps out of the dusk and stands next to Ket, wanting to be included.

Mason and Kelanda become visible in the bright haze, both of them covered in the blood of their enemies. But alive.

"What is it?" Ket asks. "What do you propose?"

Jester doesn't respond straight away; he only smiles.

4 MONTHS LATER

THE RETURN

THE JOURNEY back south was an arduous one, filled with paths and pastures that had mostly gone unexplored—Ket's choice, and similar to the route he'd taken when he left Rovan all those years ago, while the Silver City was under siege. Their route made to ensure they wouldn't be tracked by the soldiers who discovered and investigated the aftermath at Jerrin's cottage. Once they made their way far enough south, there were other dangers to avoid. Mostly people, but creatures too. Jester had been right about that—in the years since leaving Rovan, Ket found the Five Realms a lot stranger, and a whole lot more treacherous. It felt apocalyptic, with the number of monsters and inhuman threats they came across. Nothing they couldn't handle, although there was an incident with a tree troll that nearly cost them their lives (a story for another time, perhaps).

But they made it all the way back to Owlton relatively unharmed, their bond stronger. The Boy, who revealed his name was Thom and insisted they call him such, got along swimmingly with Ralyanna. The two laughed and played games like they were brother and sister, and on those tough days when food was scarce and the environment had teeth, they were able to keep the group's spirits high. Even Jester, typically negative and finding all the wrong with the world, seemed to find their bond warm and cozy. He watched them often, a fond twinkle in his eyes, and Ket wondered if observing them brought back some of Tent's childhood memories. Good ones, perhaps. It certainly sparked memories within Ket, of his two sons running around outside, getting into trouble and creating lasting moments he would cherish, forever. Their laughter and smiles even got Kelanda and Mason talking about kids, saying that maybe when this journey was over, they might settle down somewhere nice, give up their underground blacksmith business, and start a family of their own.

For Ket, the worst part of the journey was also the best part of the journey—seeing everyone happy in those moments. It only reminded him of Jennah, and how he would never gain back complete happiness. Sure, having Bentley and Clive free and clear would be a step in the right direction, would fill his heart considerably, but…

But there would always be a piece of him missing. His heart would remain fractured in that one special spot, the place in his chest Jennah had claimed and would hold forever.

He was reminded of that every time the kids laughed, every time Jester laughed at them laughing, and every time Kelanda and Mason mused about starting a family.

Inside, he cried to himself. Outside, he had to remain strong. Impenetrable. Because he was their leader.

And he was going home.

———

KING EDWILL RAGLAND III stands before them, clapping his hands together enthusiastically, his smile outshining Jester's. He even lets out a bark-like laugh that dies the second it hits the air. Behind him, his queen remains seated on her throne; her eyes have not left Thom, and her radiant expression shines on. She regards him as if she's overseeing her own son's wedding day. Even the throne room guards are wearing happy faces. Ket is waiting for one of them to break out the sitar, invite everyone to a song-a-long, and dance and drink to celebrate the occasion.

This is an important day in Owlton's history.

Ket will celebrate later, once his children are returned in the same condition they were taken.

"I must say…" Ragland says, twisting curls into his beard, "I did not expect you to succeed."

Ket bows his head with respect, though he has none for the king—no king has Ket Norlath's respect, because no king in the Five Realms is worthy. "It was a long journey. The Five Realms are not how I remember them."

Ragland raises his chin in acknowledgment. "Scary times. We're nearing The End, some might say. But I think they might be wrong. The Second Coming of the Gods is not nearly The End for us—but a New Beginning."

"Sounds…hopeful."

"Indeed. You have restored much hope to Owlton." Ragland raises his hand and snaps his fingers. Two guards step out of the antechamber, into the hallway. There's shuffling, chains jingling. "I will uphold my end of our agreement. To both of you." He gives Jester a cursory glance but seems unwilling to behold his scars. "And to you, Mr. Norlath, I return your two sons—just as promised."

Ket spins toward the hall, tears bursting from his eyes, blurring the room. The strength in his knees fails him as Bentley and Clive are escorted into the throne room. They look the same, but older—three years may not seem like a long time, but during those younger years, they are an eternity.

"Sons," he says, falling to his knees, his arms open in a wide embrace. They spot their father, confused at first, but then it clicks in their minds, almost simultaneously. He's not sure how much information Ragland's company has told them—for all he knows, they are seeing a ghost right now.

They sprint over to him, arms open. It's the embrace he's dreamed of since they were separated, full of tears and love and hope. He can't stop crying, no matter how hard he tries to stop, tries to remain tough in front of the king and his royal servants, the guards—that bastard and wife-murdering Sir Henry included. But after about ten seconds he submits to the tears of joy, lets them run freely from his eyes. He shudders with each sob, feels the tickle of his sons' tears against his neck as he squeezes them tighter.

"Lovely reunion," Jester says, clapping his hands together and resting his cheek on them. "Almost brings a tear to my eye."

"Sir Henry," the king speaks up, cutting off Jester before he can fill the room with more sass. "Please escort our jester out of the kingdom—give him a hot meal and a cold drink before his departure. And please be sure to show him what will happen if he's ever seen anywhere near Hornrake's walls in the future."

Jester bows to the king. "Your Grace."

Ket watches him go with Sir Henry, but before he leaves, Jester glances over his shoulder at Ket. Winks.

Ket winks back, then grips his sons tighter and cries some more.

———

TWO DAYS LATER, Ket Norlath returns to the farmlands he once owned with his wife, free and clear, a cozy space in southwestern Owlton where no crime happens, where no god worshippers come to preach and spread lies, and where no monsters roam.

The barn is in decent shape, could use some restorative lumber on the side that faces the ocean. Inside the house, it looks like raiders had their way with some of their belongings—that, or the men who murdered Jennah went through their possessions after they flung her from the bluff. They hadn't owned much, nothing of great value, so he doesn't worry about it. He's expecting to find squatters on the property, but, surprisingly, he finds the rooms unoccupied, along with the barn stalls. The animals had been stolen or escaped—probably taken to slaughter, and used for food. Or they were claimed by a neighbor and now reside on some nearby property. Either way, he'll have to replace them.

If they stay...

The memory of this place, what it was, haunts him. Like Jennah's ghost in his dreamworld. But also—can they really stay? With what's to come? He thinks relocating is their best option, and they will, soon, but not now. The boys...they need to be here. At least for a little while.

The boys view the house from the top of the hill. Ra watches them as Ket goes through the house and barn, deeming it safe for reentry. Once it's safe, he whistles to them from the front door.

Ra leads them down the hill on horses, courtesy of King Edwill Ragland III. Once there, Ket shows them to the barn where they stash their mounts, feed them, and give them water. Then they head inside the house—their once loving home—and Ket finds it even emptier despite three-quarters of their family (and one new, honorary member) returning. The weight of Jennah, a wife and mother, absent, has fallen on them all. Ket squeezes Bentley's shoulder, hugs Clive close, and tells them it's fine, it's time to move on. The next chapter of their life awaits, and even though their mother is gone, the memory of her will live on forever. Inside this home. In every speck of dust. Every meal. Every cup of coffee. In every word spoken between these walls, she will live.

Once they're settled in and have eaten dinner, once the brothers are asleep in their old rooms, Ket travels outside, down the path leading to the bluffs, the moonlight guiding him.

He peers over the edge, listening to the waves crash against the rocks, wondering if she's still down there, or if the tide carried her bones out to sea. He weeps again, his eyes still only partially recovered from the previous waterfalls. As he's there, he senses something behind him—someone.

He knows who it is.

"This is where it happened," Ra says, sidling next to him.

"Yes," he grumbles, more gruffly than he meant to.

"I'm sorry. If you were having a private moment—"

"It's fine," he says quickly. "Actually, I'm glad you're here." He means in the moment, as her arrival stops the tears, but he also means in general. "I think you'll be a great big sister to the boys. They will need it."

"They seem like good kids," she says, looking back at the house, the glow from a few candles lighting up the windows with a peachy aura.

"They're the best. I hope the last three years didn't change them too much." He fights the sting in the corners of his eyes. They did change—he can sense it, see it in their faces—and not for the better. They've lost something. Their innocence perhaps. They're not boys anymore, but young men, forced to grow too fast.

Who knows what horrors they've experienced?

You can help rehabilitate them, says his wife's voice, which comes like an echo across the waves. *They're still your boys. You'll see.*

Our boys, he thinks. *Ours.*

"They'll be fine," Ra says. "Now that they have their father. Sometimes, in this world, all you need is someone who loves you to guide them."

Ket nods. The stinging becomes too much and the waterfall starts again.

Ra wraps her arms around his waist, resting her head against his shoulder. He drapes his arm around her, holds close the daughter he never had.

"You're a part of our family now, Ra," Ket says. "I will do my best to pick up where Borgadine left off."

She sniffles but holds her tears. "Speaking of our family," she says, letting go of him. "Do you think Jester will arrive soon?"

Ket almost laughs. It feels good to *almost laugh.* He can't wait until the sadness erodes, when he can enjoy laughing again. "I have a feeling he will."

THE LAST LAUGH

"To be a jester, you must have an infectious laugh, even on days that don't seem all that funny. That's the true talent of any court-yard jester—spread laughter and cheer, no matter what."

– ADRIAN KEYMEISTER, *RULING THE KINGDOM WITH LAUGHTER: A GUIDE FOR JESTERS*

———

KING EDWILL RAGLAND III has unsettling dreams that night, perhaps the strangest of his adult life. Maybe it's due to the excitement of the big day, a day that will go down in history as the most important event in all of Owlton: an event that changes the tide in the war against the northern enemy, the self-proclaimed Emperor of Endlia. This is the stuff that creates legends. But maybe it's not the excitement that's fueling the strange visions of glowing faeries dancing in the purple waters of bubbling streams, cyclopean giants roaming the Crosslands, stepping over mounds and mounds of dead soldiers wearing Owlton lilac. That strange machine he thinks is a gyroscope spinning out of control, until hot orange sparks come shooting out of its orblike center. Maybe the dreams haven't derived from the excitement at all, but the *fear*. The pressure of what's coming. The tides have turned, sure, but what will the great King Edwill Ragland III do with the Boy that will help him win the war? Convert the other four realms into believers and raise the Sign of the Owl in the yards of these opposing kingdoms?

The future—though bright—is uncertain, and maybe that's why his brain has gotten away from him that night, stuck in this restless void of visions he does not wish to see.

He wakes up in a pool of sweat, every inch of him drenched. His heart stuttering, beating erratically to the point where he thinks this might be it—all of the feasts and glorious cake parties where he's stuffed his face and stomach with decadent sweets have finally caught up to him; have come to exact revenge on the body he's abused with overeating, and tobacco, and a sedentary lifestyle. *Too much time on the throne*, he thinks, *not enough exercise*; maybe the Hornrake doctor men are right; maybe he needs to get up and walk, lose some weight, start eating healthy.

But maybe not, too. Doctors don't know everything. And maybe he feels this way because of the dreams, and nothing more.

Ragland looks over to his queen and finds her half of the bed empty. Not uncommon. Sometimes she can't sleep and goes for strolls through the castle, sits out on the balcony overlooking Hornrake and just watches the moon and the stars, gazing out amongst the vast stretch of night, enjoying the hypnotic ambiance of it all. He doesn't know why, but he feels compelled to join her there. Sleep doesn't seem friendly tonight—*proper* sleep, that is— and he could use a calming conversation with the stars to settle his nerves.

He moves through the castle, a lantern lighting his way, and passes several guards who silently bow their respects as he goes by. Normally, he doesn't like to ignore the people who protect him around the clock, likes to at least acknowledge their presence (it's the least he can do), but he's too tired to even look them in the eye.

Less than ten minutes later, he arrives at the queen's favorite balcony, sees her sitting in her favorite chair, slumped, gazing up at the great black beyond. Pushing through the thin silk drapes and entering the balcony's alcove, he can see all the stars that have come out tonight, each of them burning brightly enough to make the lantern unnecessary. He brings it anyway, sets it aside on the small table used to stand goblets of wine, where he can roll some tobacco. He wishes he brought some. He sits down next to Queen Sharla, arches back, and sighs while taking in the stars. The moon is especially bright and low, flooding the darkest corners of the balcony with pale luminance.

"Beautiful night," he says, inhaling a big lungful of fresh, Hornrake air. The city's never smelled so clean. Sometimes there's a whiff of burning trash or greasy food, but not tonight. Just cool, untainted winds breezing in from afar. "Reminds me of when we were wed. Do you remember that night?"

Sharla doesn't respond, just remains there, stargazing.

He turns to her. Her head is tilted away from him.

"Sharla?" he says, smiling, wondering why she isn't responding. "Hey?"

She's fallen asleep, he says, then has a laugh about it. It's not like her to come out here and pass out, but then again, the day has been exhausting. He supposes it's very possible.

Instead of calling the guards for help, he decides to pick her up and carry her back to bed. An act of romance, something she wouldn't expect—their marriage has been lacking romantic trysts of late. Maybe carrying her to bed will spark some of that youthful fire their marriage once had.

He goes to her, puts his arms under her, and when he does, her head tilts toward him—the scream he lets out echoes across the whole city.

Ragland doesn't know what's worse—the fact her eyes have been removed so cleanly (hardly any blood) or that a wicked smile has been carved into her lips, two huge gashes that run from the corners of her mouth to the bottoms of her ears. The recognizable signature causes him to gasp, lose his breath, and his brain starts running ten thousand miles in different directions all at once.

The next thing he knows, a knife is pressed against his throat, the sharpness breaking his skin.

"Good evening, my king," the proud, sinister voice growls in his ear, low as a whisper. Ragland doesn't dare move, even though he's going to die anyway. "And it is good, isn't it? The best of nights, yes?"

Ragland doesn't reply—he owes this bastard assassin nothing.

"She's lovely, isn't she?" the jester says, forcing him to gaze upon his murdered queen. "She was already dead when I gave her the smile—I want you to know that. I would have kept her alive, but then she would have screamed, like *I screamed* when your men carved me up so funnily, and we couldn't have that, no sir. This was an intimate moment we were to share, and I couldn't have your guards ruining that. Not again."

Ragland's eyes flood with tears. He operates his jaw, trying to work out the sounds. He wants to say something, protest his impending death, but his voice is not cooperating.

"Here's what's going to happen," Jester says, his breath hot in Ragland's ear. "You're going to call for your guards right now— tell them to bring the Boy. Command them."

"No," Ragland whispers in a breath.

"Yes," Jester says confidently, "or I'm going to tie you to a chair, stick a sock in your mouth, and make you watch me cut another smile into your queen's corpse—this one will be in a much naughtier location, I assure you." He giggles into Ragland's ear, the laughter echoing all the way to the center of his brain, living there, and echoing forever. "Now, call them. Bring the Boy. And we can proceed with this evening. I promise you—if you do this, I won't hurt you."

It takes a second for everything to sink in, for his brain to convince himself this isn't just another weird dream. Once he's positive this scene before him is no active nightmare, he does what he's told, calls for the guards and tells them to bring up the Boy from his private chamber, a place where few know the location.

Ten minutes later, they hustle back with the Boy in their possession. Per Jester's request, the guards do not speak to anyone else, and the same unit returns with no additional backup. The guards leave the Boy at the entrance to the balcony and return to their posts.

"Very good," Jester says, letting his knife relax a little.

Ragland stares at the Boy with the Star-Shaped Eyes. He looks sleepy, confused, but even more so—he looks at Ragland with such contempt. Such pure hatred. And deep down, Ragland can see the Boy is enjoying this exchange.

Like they planned it.

Oh, Highbeard's cunt, Ragland silently swears, *how could I have been so stupid?*

"You'll let me go then?" Ragland says around unsteady, air-deprived breaths.

"I'll let you go," Jester says. "To Arkos's Darkhell."

Ragland struggles to break free. "You bastard! You son of a whore!"

"You know," Jester says, and Ragland envisions that rough grin inches from his ear, "you really should smile more."

And then Jester carves a smile into the king's throat, opening a toothless black maw that leaks and leaks and leaks beneath the star-studded twilight.

ACKNOWLEDGMENTS

Every novel is a journey. And a traveler (author) never walks alone. Would like to thank the following people and friends for helping bring this novel to life: Maryanne Chappell for being the first reader and providing invaluable feedback. Austrian Spencer, *Godfallen*'s editor, who whipped this book into shape. Ket's story wouldn't be the same without you. Zach McCain for his incredible cover art. I've been lucky enough to have Zach illustrate a few covers for me and his artwork blows me away every time. David Walters at FanFiAddict.com, who reignited my love for the fantasy genre, and who has always been a huge supporter of my work. And, of course, my wife, Ashley, who continues to spark the light that is my dream, of telling stories.

-TM

ABOUT THE AUTHOR

Tim Meyer dwells in a dark cave near the Jersey Shore. He's the author of more than fifteen novels, including *Malignant Summer*, *The Switch House*, *Dead Daughters*, *Limbs*, and many other titles. When he's not working on the next book, he's usually hanging out with his wife and son, shooting around on the basketball court, playing video games, or messing with a new screenplay. He bleeds coffee and IPAs. *Godfallen* is his first fantasy novel.

You can learn more about his books at timmeyerwrites.com.